Charles's breath was a caress on her neck, his words a heady elixir. And Rose had to admit . . . she liked it.

But this was not the Charles she'd known before—predictable, solid, and safe. As his heavy-lidded gaze drifted over her, her pulse leaped in her throat, confirming her thoughts. There was nothing safe about him.

It was too dark to see his face—to see anything, really—but somehow she felt the intensity of his gaze upon her, heating her skin. The air fairly crackled around them.

It was funny how one little transgression led to another. Her heart pounded in her chest from fear, desire, and delight at her own daring. No one would believe that the always obedient and demure Rose was hiding in the shadows of Lady Yardley's drawing room. With a man. The same virile, breathtakingly handsome man whom she'd once believed she loved.

The man she'd never been quite able to forget . . .

"An incredible romance that made me want to climb right into the book and be a part of it all...Barton is really becoming one of my favorite writers."

—HerdingCats-BurningSoup.com

"Exciting...Fast-paced, sweet romance...Reminds you of *Beauty and the Beast*, except the hero is no beast, but a dark-tempered, handsome, sexy earl. Well done, Anne!"

—MyBookAddictionReviews.com

"A stunning, heartwarming, and unbelievably sweet romance...brilliant characterizations...[an] engaging story with an enchanting set of secondary characters, written in eloquently elegant prose."

—BuriedUnderRomance.com

WHEN SHE WAS WICKED

"Sensual and solid, this debut is a story demanding to be read. The characters are believable and relatable, and Barton smartly blends issues of morality and Regency-era social class with passion and excitement."

—*Publishers Weekly* (starred review)

"Delightfully smart, fun, fast-paced, and just different enough for readers to take note of Barton's charming voice, this novel is filled with wry humor, and compassion intrigues readers. The intrepid heroine, arrogant hero, memorable secondary characters, and the colorful depiction of the era add to the reading enjoyment."

—*RT Book Reviews*

One Wild
Winter's Eve

One Wild Winter's Eve

ANNE BARTON

FOREVER

NEW YORK   BOSTON

Copyright © 2015 by Anne Barton
Excerpt from *When She Was Wicked* copyright © 2013 by Anne Barton

Forever
Hachette Book Group
1290 Avenue of the Americas
New York, NY 10104

www.HachetteBookGroup.com

Printed in the United States of America

First Edition: October 2015
10 9 8 7 6 5 4 3 2 1

OPM

Forever is an imprint of Grand Central Publishing.
The Forever name and logo are trademarks of Hachette Book Group, Inc.

The Hachette Speakers Bureau provides a wide range of authors for speaking events. To find out more, go to www.hachettespeakersbureau.com or call (866) 376-6591.

The publisher is not responsible for websites (or their content) that are not owned by the publisher.

Grammy—
thank you
for violets,
tea parties,
and books.
Always books.

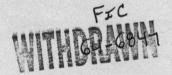

One Wild
Winter's Eve

Prologue

Summer 1815

*E*ven nice, obedient girls needed to escape now and then.

Lady Rose Sherbourne left Huntford Manor shortly after breakfast. A warm breeze whipped tendrils of hair against her cheek, and the heels of her boots sank into the deliciously soft grass, still slick with dew.

Each step across the vast lawn took her farther from the house, its imposing grandeur, and its paralyzing memories.

Better yet, each step took her closer to Charles.

She glanced over her shoulder, assuring herself that no one had seen her slip away. Her visits with the stable master—like so many other things—were best kept secret.

But the truth was, there was nothing improper about her relationship with Charles. Not really.

Perhaps the sight of his tanned forearms, large hands, and easy grin made her breath hitch in her throat. There wasn't a seventeen-year-old girl in all of England who'd be unaffected by his strength and confidence. But her visits with Charles were not about flirtation. They were about preserving her sanity.

Some days, when she could feel it hanging by the very thinnest of threads, she fled to the stables and watched him work. The even strokes of his brush over a horse's coat and the rhythmic flexing of his shoulders as he pitched hay soothed her frayed edges. With him, she could forget who she was and what she'd seen. She could simply bask in the moment, and if she wasn't completely happy, well, she was close.

She sighed. Yes, the very best thing about Charles was the way he made her feel...normal.

As he tended to an injured horse or poured water into the troughs, he'd talk to her, his deep, expressive voice washing over her and healing her soul. While she perched on an upside-down pail, he'd tell funny stories, without seeming to find it odd that their conversation was completely one-sided.

Without minding that she never spoke.

Upon realizing that she was mute, some invariably analyzed her. *When, precisely, had she stopped talking? Could she make any sounds at all? What doctors had she seen and what treatment did they prescribe?* Others took her silence as a personal challenge, saying all manner of outrageous things in order to provoke a response—one that never came.

But Charles didn't treat her as an object of curiosity. He simply accepted her.

In her satchel, she carried a couple of books for him, carrots for Prometheus, and a small jar of milk for Romeo. She'd missed them terribly the past two days, too busy with dress fittings and ball preparations to steal away for a few hours. And so, this morning, she'd seized the opportunity to spend time with them, in spite of the gray clouds gathering in the western morning sky.

As she walked into the stable, the familiar smells of horses and hay tickled her nose. She looked around for Charles's shock of blond hair, topped by the brown cap that was always slightly askew. He wasn't there, and yet his presence filled the place. His overcoat hung from a peg beside the door, and a pair of work gloves lay on the ledge of an empty stall beside an open, facedown book. She glanced at the spine and smiled at his choice of reading material: *Annals of Agriculture and Other Useful Arts.*

One morning, over a game of chess, he'd shared his dream of owning land. Selfishly, she hoped he wouldn't leave Huntford Manor anytime soon. She withdrew the volumes of mythology and Grimms' fairy tales from her bag and placed them beside his book.

The half dozen stalls to her right were occupied by thoroughbreds—the very best a duke's money could buy. In a smaller stall to her left was Prometheus, a faithful old draft horse of questionable breeding. His ears perked up when he saw her, and she dug into her satchel for the carrots. He slurped them from her hand, then gave a haughty snort, gloating for the benefit of the thoroughbreds.

Rose wished she could ask Prometheus where Charles was. And where Romeo was, for that matter. The fluffy gray cat was usually the first to greet her, twisting around her ankles, shamelessly crying for attention and treats. She peeked into the empty stall beside Prometheus—the one Romeo had usurped shortly after Rose found him—and checked the dry trough where the cat liked to nap. Empty. Only one thing was sure to bring her fickle friend out of hiding. She poured his milk into a tin bowl and waited.

"Lady Rose?"

She turned as Peter, the freckle-faced stable hand who worshipped Charles, shot her a grin. "Are you looking for Mr. Holland?"

She nodded.

"He went searching for Romeo."

Rose tilted her head in a silent question.

"The cat wandered off two days ago and hasn't been 'round since."

Oh dear. Rose frowned.

"Don't worry, Mr. Holland will find him."

She walked to the back door of the stable and gazed at the thick woods that lay beyond. Peter stood beside her and pointed to a dirt path that led through a clump of trees and disappeared in the brush. "He went that way—not long ago."

Rose gave the boy a grateful smile and headed down the trail.

A sudden gust of wind plastered the skirt of her green morning dress to her legs, and she glanced at the darkening sky. Romeo had seemed well enough during her last visit, but what if he'd gotten sick? Or ventured into the woods and foolishly tangled with a snake or fox? She picked up her pace, ignoring a rumble of thunder so low she could feel it in her belly.

She followed the path as it meandered around the trunks of towering elms and twisting oaks, looking for Charles or Romeo. Once, she would have called out to them, her words floating through the forest. Now she was as silent as the hare that trembled in the hollow log near her feet. She'd forgotten the sound of her own voice.

And sometimes feared she'd never hear it again.

A familiar but unwelcome thudding began in her chest. She mustn't dwell on her troubles, mustn't dwell on the past. She walked faster, as if putting distance between her and her worries were just that easy.

Low-hanging branches grabbed at her hair and thorny underbrush scratched at her ankles. The woods blurred past her, muddy green. Her ragged breathing echoed in her ears and the pungent smells of damp soil and leaves closed in around her, almost suffocating in their intensity. She picked up the front of her skirt and ran, looking down and dodging the stones and sticks in her way.

The toe of her boot caught on a gnarled root. Her satchel sailed through the air and the ground rose up to meet her.

Until a pair of strong arms caught and steadied her.

"Rose?"

Blinking, she looked up at Charles. He searched her face, his expression a mixture of concern and wonder.

"What's happened? Are you hurt?"

His hands easily encircled her arms above her gloves, his palms warm against her bare skin. His light brown eyes crinkled at the corners, letting her know he was happy to see her.

Was she well? She took a deep breath and felt the tension in her body uncoil. The forest came back into focus and her breathing slowed. Her heart still beat fast, but for possibly different reasons. She nodded.

Charles looked at her arms where he clasped them, frowned, and released her quickly, as if his hands had betrayed him. He raked his fingers through his sun-streaked hair before retrieving his cap from the ground and stuffing it into the back pocket of his trousers. Then he scooped up her satchel, handed it to her, and led her toward a small clearing several yards away.

"I found Romeo," he said. "The only problem is, I don't think we can call him Romeo anymore. Look."

He pointed at a nest of leaves on the ground, protected by a log on one side and a large rock on another. The cat rested there, sprawled on his—no, *her*—side, two tiny black kittens nursing under her watchful, weary gaze.

Delighted, Rose clasped her hands beneath her chin and knelt for a closer look.

The babes climbed and tumbled over each other, greedy for their mother's milk and attention. But as Romeo licked the back of one's head, her leg twitched and lifted. Another kitten.

Charles's brow creased. "You might not want to watch this, Rose. It's, ah, messy. Let's return to the stable. I'll do a few chores, and then you can beat me at chess."

She shook her head firmly. *Nothing* could drag her away.

Chuckling, Charles sank to his haunches beside her, so close that his thigh brushed the skirt of her gown. "Amazing, isn't it?"

Rose watched transfixed as the third kitten's hind paws emerged first, followed by a rounded belly and pointed face. The tiny creature resembled a bat wrapped in cobwebs, eerily still.

Romeo stretched, and her foot sent the newest kitten rolling like a mummy. It landed several inches from the leafy nest, and Rose's fingers itched to nestle it beside its mother's warm body. She took off her gloves.

"Patience," Charles whispered. "It's best if we let Romeo take care of this herself."

However, the gray cat was distracted and tired. Rose didn't blame her one bit, but after a minute passed, she shot Charles a pleading look. The newborn kitten, trapped in a thin film, looked so lifeless compared to its fuzzy siblings.

She reached out, unsure how to help but knowing she had to try.

"Wait. The less we handle the kitten the better." Using a handkerchief pulled from his pocket, he carefully broke the membrane and wiped the kitten's face.

Though its body unfurled slightly, it didn't move. Didn't breathe.

Charles's mouth was pressed in a thin line, and Rose wanted to scream at Romeo. *Take care of this one. It needs you.*

"If it doesn't start breathing soon, it's not going to survive." He swept the kitten into his handkerchief, laid flat on his palm. "Come on, little one."

Tears gathered in Rose's eyes. The creature looked so small, so helpless, with its eyes closed tight and its chest motionless. She leaned over Charles's hand, wishing she could somehow breathe life into the kitten.

Desperate, she lifted a corner of the handkerchief and rubbed it over the kitten's belly. The fur there turned soft as down, but her patient remained in a precarious twilight—not quite alive, not quite dead. Several drops of crimson stained the crisp white cotton handkerchief. That couldn't be good. Tears rolled down her cheeks, and because she didn't know what else to do, what else to try, she rubbed the kitten's chest harder.

Charles clasped her wrist, stilling her. "I'm sorry, Rose."

No. This kitten was like her. Fragile and broken, but *not* dead.

She closed her eyes and made one last, fervent wish.

Overhead, thunder cracked, sending birds fluttering. Raindrops pattered on the canopy of leaves, searching for a path through the dense foliage. Several drops plunked on her head, streaked down her forehead, and mingled with her tears. But Charles's warm strength flowed through her, and she willed it to flow through the kitten as well.

"Rose. Look, he's moving!"

Unbelieving, she opened her eyes. The kitten yawned and stretched its paws, writhing on Charles's hand.

He gazed at her with wonder. "You did it."

His words made her glow on the inside, but then his face dimmed.

"He's not out of danger, though. It shouldn't be bleeding this much." He pointed at the kitten's belly. "See where the cord ripped? We need something to tie around it. Do you have anything in your bag?"

Frowning, she shook her head. She had string at the house, of course, but by the time she ran there and back, it could well be too late.

Where to find string or thread? She flipped over the edge of her gown, hastily yanked a thread from the hem, and held it up for Charles to see.

"Perfect. I'll hold him while you tie the strand tightly around the cord. Don't worry, you won't hurt him. Or her," he added with a heart-stopping smile. "We'll have plenty of time to figure that out later."

Her hands trembled so badly that the thread missed its mark and she tied a knot in the air.

But Charles spoke softly, his breath warm near her ear. "Take your time. This one's a fighter. You're almost there."

The rain fell harder, plopping on the backs of her hands as she worked. Charles held his cap over the kitten to shelter it, and Rose remained focused on the task before her. She pressed on, ignoring the thunder, the kitten's blood, and, most daunting of all, her self-doubt.

At last, she pulled the strands tight and looked at Charles triumphantly.

"Well done." The approval in his voice and in his eyes made her belly flip—in a strange and pleasant way.

She held up the ends of the thread, each several inches long.

"Here, hold our patient. I've got a knife." In one smooth motion, he snapped open a pocket knife and cut the extra lengths off the thread. "Let's return him to Romeo and his siblings. See if he can hold his own."

Gingerly, Rose placed the kitten in the nest, just under its mother's chin. He huddled close to her neck, nuzzling against her fur and soaking up her warmth.

Romeo remained vexingly aloof.

"The kitten won't take no for an answer," predicted Charles. "Watch."

Refusing to be ignored, the runt crawled his way on top of his mother's head and slid down her nose. At last, she began to lick his fur.

"Thank God!" Charles jumped up, lifting Rose and

spinning her till she was breathless and dizzy. Lowering her slowly to the ground, he added, "He's going to be fine."

The kitten *would* be fine. And maybe—just maybe—she would be, too.

Because standing there in the rain, with Charles's hands firmly on the curve of her hips, she felt strong enough to face anything. Even her past.

His chest rose and fell as rapidly as hers did—faster than it should. His amber eyes turned a rich chestnut, and his gaze dropped to her mouth. Like he wanted to kiss her.

There was a long list of reasons why she shouldn't let him.

She was a lady; he was a stable master.

She was gently bred; he bred horses.

She was expected to marry a gentleman; he came from a long line of servants.

And yet, in spite of all that, she placed her hands on his chest and lifted her chin, inviting him to kiss her. It was, perhaps, the most daring and reckless thing she'd ever done.

Charles was worth it.

He wrapped his hands around her wrists, tugged her closer, and gazed at her with an intensity that burned her to her very soul. "You tempt me, Rose. But you must understand. There's a line here, and if we cross it, there will be no going back to how things were."

Maybe she wanted to cross the line. Jump right over it. But he was right. Charles wasn't the sort to do something halfway. If they kissed, she would be forever his. And that was a very long time.

She frowned, willing him to understand.

"I know what I want." The desire in his eyes left no doubt as to his meaning, and the low, gravelly timbre of his voice promised all manner of wicked delights. "What do *you* want?"

I want you to heal me, to make me whole, to make me feel alive. I want you to kiss me.

She held her breath as he searched her face. His chest rose and fell as though he'd run a mile; beneath his wet, almost transparent, shirt, his shoulder muscles tensed.

He'd never failed to understand her before, but with every second that passed, she sensed his frustration growing. He wanted something more from her.

And she was unable to give it.

Releasing her, he looked away.

For once, her silence had disappointed him. *She'd* disappointed him.

He took two steps backward, but they might as well have been a mile. "If ever you need a friend, you may depend on me. But I think it's best if you don't visit the stables for a while."

She gasped, reached for his arm, and opened her mouth.

He froze, expectant. Hopeful.

And all the things she wanted to say to him, all the feelings she wanted to confess, died somewhere between her heart and her throat. She pressed her lips together.

He nodded, as though he should have known better than to wish for more. "Good-bye, Lady Rose."

And he turned and walked away, leaving her sobbing, silently.

Chapter One

Rearing: (1) The act of a horse rising up on its hind legs.
(2) The raising and nurturing of a child, as in
A gently reared, well-bred young lady would
never loiter about the stables daydreaming
of the handsome stable master.

Winter 1818

London's elite could not fathom why a young, eligible miss like Lady Rose Sherbourne, who happened to be the Duke of Huntford's sister, would choose to travel to Bath, playing the part of companion to the esteemed—but famously cantankerous—Lady Bonneville.

Rose had her reasons.

The first—which everyone rightfully suspected—was that she wished to escape the constant pressure from her well-meaning family to fall in love with a respectable gentleman and marry. As if she could, with a mere snap of her fingers, command her heart to desire a suitable sort of man. Her heart had proven to be less than docile.

The second reason, *no one* suspected.

Which was for the best.

Because her brother and sister, Owen and Olivia, would never approve of her plan to discover the where-abouts of their mother, who'd disappeared six years ago. According to rumor, Mama had left her husband and chil-dren to run off to the Continent with her lover.

But as far as Rose's siblings were concerned, their mother was dead. No, worse than dead. It was as though her very existence had been erased.

No one spoke of her. Most of her personal things had been sold or given to the poor. Owen and Olivia would deny that they'd been born from her womb if they could, preferring a mythical sort of creation involving Zeus's head or sea foam.

But as the youngest child, Rose couldn't quite forget Mama. She couldn't forget the tea parties where Mama carried on silly conversations with her doll guests, or the cozy evenings when Mama let Rose wear her silky ball dresses and prettiest slippers. There had been lazy after-noons when Rose and Olivia had stayed in their dressing gowns and listened to Mama read stories as they ate bis-cuits. A mother who'd done all those things couldn't be *all* bad—even if she had abandoned her three children.

Owen and Olivia didn't agree, however. Just the casual mention of Mama's name darkened their moods, and for their sakes, Rose had tried to keep the past buried. But the older she grew, the more she needed to understand. And she couldn't quite resist the urge to dig—to find out what had become of the mother she'd once adored.

So here she was, in a coach rumbling over the frozen ground toward Bath, grateful for the warmed brick beneath her feet and the whisper-soft fur lining her muff. Lady Bonneville sat beside her, snoring softly. The viscountess's maid sat on the seat opposite them, gazing out the window and enjoying the few minutes of peace in much the same way a mother blissfully relishes her infant's naptime.

The trip had been enjoyable thus far. Lady Bonneville was one of the few people who didn't coddle Rose. Everyone else assumed she was fragile, on the verge of shattering if someone mentioned an unpleasant matter or looked at her askance. She *had* been fragile once, but no more. Indeed, she could feel herself becoming stronger every day.

Charles had provided the catalyst that helped her recover her voice. Even now, her palms grew clammy as she remembered that terrifying, momentous day. Her brother had learned of her secret visits to the stables and her intimate—if innocent—relationship with Charles. Enraged, Owen fired Charles and ordered him to leave Huntford Manor immediately. And Rose simply couldn't let that happen.

So she'd uttered a single word. *No.*

She'd spoken millions more words since then, but none had been as difficult, as necessary, or as impassioned. She'd saved Charles's job, and she'd saved herself from a life without him. At least temporarily.

But that was Rose's problem—she was always so preoccupied with the past.

She was a grown woman now, and a completely different person, ready and able to take matters into her own hands. Somehow, she knew that if she were able to find her mother, she would finally be able to put her difficult past behind her and embrace the opportunities that lay before her. Something she hadn't quite been able to manage heretofore.

Outside the foggy coach windows, miles of frostbitten pastures gradually gave way to cozy cottages blowing smoky tendrils from their chimneys. The dirt road widened into a city street with shops along either side, and an arched bridge ferried the coach across the River Avon, where ducks bobbed in the cold gray water. "We'll be there soon," Rose said to the maid. "Shall we wake her?"

Audrey molded her face into a stoic expression, nodded, and touched the viscountess's arm with the caution one might use when petting a sleeping lion. "My lady, we shall arrive shortly."

Lady Bonneville bolted upright and blinked. "It's about time. Between the cold and the cramped conditions, sleeping is nigh impossible."

Though Rose could hardly imagine a conveyance more luxurious than the viscountess's coach, she offered a sympathetic smile. "You'll soon be in Lady Yardley's drawing room, enjoying a cup of hot tea."

Lady Bonneville yawned and felt around on the velvet squabs beside her. "Audrey?"

"Here you are, my lady." The maid proffered a lorgnette, which the older woman snatched and peered through, taking in the pinkish-orange sunset with apparent distaste.

Facing Rose, Lady Bonneville said, "Well then. This is your last chance. Are you sure you wouldn't rather take a room at the White Hart?" The viscountess wrinkled her powdered face in concern. "Staying with an old friend of your mother's is bound to resurrect some unpleasant memories."

Rose's heart beat rapidly, but she gave Lady Bonneville a reassuring smile. "Do not worry. I've made my peace with the past." A small fib. "Besides, Lady Yardley is expecting us. It would be rude to decline her hospitality." Even as she spoke, their hostess's manor house came into view. Tall windows and iconic columns graced its honey-colored limestone walls.

"Rude? I should think not. When a woman is of a certain age"—Lady Bonneville lifted her chin proudly—"rude behavior is merely considered eccentric." She narrowed her eyes, blatantly assessing Rose. "What is the real reason you decided to accompany me to Bath?"

The pulse at Rose's throat beat like a hummingbird's wings. "What do you mean?"

"Gads, gel. It's a shame you are so kind, so... guileless. You really are transparent, you know. It was obvious from the moment you volunteered to be my companion that you wished to escape London and your matchmaking relatives. Your sister-in-law, Anabelle, and her sister, Daphne, are quite determined. And I've no doubt that Olivia will join their ranks as soon as she returns from Egypt."

"Yes. They mean well, but—"

Lady Bonneville held up a gloved hand, heavy with sparkling rings. "You needn't defend them. There's nothing so tiresome as blissfully happy newlyweds. Although I suppose new grandmothers are almost as tedious. My dear friend Marian can hardly tear herself away from her granddaughter—as though the little cretin will forget who she is if she goes out for one evening to play bridge."

The viscountess snorted indelicately. "In any event, I don't object to being your excuse for fleeing London. However, that does not mean I'll allow you to hole yourself up in Lady Yardley's gauche manor house all month with only a pair of older ladies and a stack of dull books for company. If you are to play the part of my companion, you shall have to try to keep up with me and my social engagements."

"I'll do my best."

Rose intended to be a dutiful, pleasant companion. She only required a little time alone with their hostess—an old friend of Mama's, and the one person she could think of who might know where to find her.

The coach glided to a stop in front of the house. Flanked by a line of servants, Lady Yardley stood ready to welcome them.

"Ah, here we are," said the viscountess. "Let us hope my legs haven't frozen all the way through. I should hate to have to ask a footman to carry me." She shot Rose a mischievous grin. "Unless he was handsome—then I shouldn't mind it at all."

A half hour later, Lady Bonneville was sufficiently thawed to have tea with Rose and Lady Yardley in their hostess's pale green drawing room. Despite Lady Bonneville's warning, Rose could find nothing remotely gauche about the manor house. The drawing room's thick carpet in muted creams and blues felt soft beneath her slippers, and the settee was angled in front of a flickering fire. Sconces on the wall lent a warm and inviting glow to the room.

Holding her lorgnette to her face, Lady Bonneville

glared about as though a lady of ill repute might pop out from behind a sofa.

"It was good of you to come." Lady Yardley smiled warmly, and the lines on her otherwise youthful face became more pronounced. She'd aged gracefully, just as Mama would no doubt have done. A familiar pang went through Rose.

"The house is so large, so empty," Lady Yardley continued. "I haven't entertained much since Roger passed, and I've missed it. Your visit gave me an excuse to bring out the fine china and silver."

Lady Bonneville eyed the Wedgwood bone china, clearly unimpressed.

"Thank you for making us feel so welcome," Rose said. "Shall I pour?"

"Please, dear."

As Rose tipped the steaming pot over a delicate teacup, she felt Lady Yardley measuring her.

"So much like your mother. Not in the coloring, of course—your particular shade of red hair is utterly unique— but you *do* resemble her. It must be the high cheekbones and delicate chin. Wouldn't you agree, Henrietta?"

The viscountess seemed to consider the question carefully, and Rose held her breath as she awaited the answer, conflicted about the response she hoped for.

"The more I get to know young Lady Rose, the more I think she is like her hair. Unique."

Rose suspected *unique* was simply a polite way of saying *odd*. Then again, no one could accuse Lady Bonneville of being polite.

"Here, this will warm you." Rose handed the viscountess her teacup.

Lady Bonneville grimaced. "I am warm enough. I require my footstool."

"Ah." The viscountess never went anywhere without the red velvet ottoman on which she rested her feet—a peculiar habit for which she was rather famous. "I believe Audrey is putting your things away. Shall I retrieve the stool for you?"

"I should think not. Simply tell Audrey that if my ottoman is not here within five minutes my legs will turn into sausages from the knees down—and that *she* shall be to blame."

Rose spotted at least two other perfectly good footstools in the drawing room, but knew better than to suggest that Lady Bonneville use one till hers could be located.

"I'll check with Audrey at once." Rose smiled at Lady Yardley. "Excuse me."

She glided out of the room and up the grand staircase. Though her visit had just begun, Rose felt hopeful. Lady Yardley had already mentioned Mama, so perhaps the topic wasn't taboo, as it was at home. Still, she couldn't imagine that Lady Bonneville would approve of her quest to discover Mama's whereabouts. She was, in her own ornery way, very protective of Rose's family—a fact she'd probably deny with her dying breath.

Lady Bonneville had been assigned the bedchamber next to hers. Rose knocked on the door and peeked inside, but the lady's maid wasn't there. Rose looked about for the red velvet ottoman. It had definitely been on the coach, hadn't it? She had a small jolt of panic, the kind she imagined a mother must feel upon discovering she'd left her child's favorite toy at home.

"Oh, Lady Rose. May I help you?"

Rose turned to find Audrey standing in the doorway, slightly breathless.

"I'd come looking for—"

"Her ladyship's ottoman? I just took it to her." She smiled apologetically. "You'd think I'd know better by now than to keep Lady Bonneville waiting."

"Do not fret. I suspect that she derives a great deal of pleasure from complaining—you would not wish to deny her that, would you?"

"You're very kind," the maid said gratefully. "You should return to the drawing room and finish your tea. Meanwhile, I'll go next door and unpack your things. Hopefully you can have a rest before dinner."

Rose was already looking forward to an hour of solitude. Humming to herself, she made her way back down to the drawing room. She was about to enter, when something made her freeze just outside the door. From where she stood, she could see Lady Bonneville, slippers perched on her bright red footstool. She was leaning forward, serious and thoughtful as she listened to Lady Yardley. Their hostess stood beside a desk, glancing down occasionally at a paper she held. "Such a pity," she was saying. "Who would have thought?"

A chill ran through Rose and the back of her neck prickled. Somehow, she knew Lady Yardley was talking about Mama. She debated whether to remain there, eavesdropping, or to boldly walk in, asking for answers. In the end, she compromised, clearing her throat before walking toward the settee. "Have I missed anything?" she asked innocently.

The paper Lady Yardley was holding fluttered from

her fingers and landed on the desk. She opened the drawer and stuffed it—a letter perhaps?—inside before shutting it with considerably more force than was necessary. Her face flushed. "No, not a thing."

Rose looked at Lady Bonneville, who suddenly seemed fascinated with the vase sitting on the table beside her. "Come have a crumpet, dear."

Anger flashed through her. If Lady Yardley knew something about Mama, Rose had a right to know it, too. Why did Lady Bonneville think she could placate her with a pastry? Though tempted to protest and make a scene, Rose refrained—as she'd learned to do so long ago.

She had to keep her emotions in check, needed to maintain her sense of calm. If she let go, even the slightest little bit, she might unleash all the anguish that had built up inside her—a terrifying thought if ever there was one.

And so she obediently took her seat and pretended that she wasn't at all curious about the conversation she'd almost overheard. She poured herself tea and even had a bite to eat, as Lady Bonneville had suggested. She made polite small talk with her hostess and acted interested in all the upcoming engagements on her social calendar, many of which she and Lady Bonneville would attend as well. A serene smile in place once more, Rose smoothed over the viscountess's rough edges, which also seemed to endear her to Lady Yardley.

And all the while, she plotted how to get her hands on that letter.

Chapter Two

*L*ater that evening, Rose waited in her room, listening intently. When Audrey knocked on Lady Bonneville's door and began to help her dress for dinner—a rather involved process—Rose stood and took a deep, fortifying breath.

She was determined to retrieve the letter from Lady Yardley's desk. It was wrong, of course, a clear invasion of privacy, but for once, Rose shushed her conscience. The anger she'd felt before had waned a bit, but her need to know had not. She feared that the longer she waited, the less likely the letter would be there. Lady Yardley might move it to a more secure spot or, worse, burn it. Perhaps she already had.

Hopefully, Lady Yardley had forgotten about the letter and was also dressing for dinner. Rose needed only five minutes. And a bit of good fortune.

She slipped out of her room and down the corridor, grateful that she was quite alone. The house was so sprawling, so devoid of humanity, that she could almost hear her frantic heartbeat echoing off the walls.

As she entered the drawing room, a shiver ran through her. She was afraid of being discovered—and even more afraid of what she might discover.

Secrets. Her mother had been full of them. At a young and fragile age, Rose had come face-to-face with Mama's most scandalous and shameful secret. It had been the reason she went silent for so long. Even now, she wished she could unsee it.

As she approached Lady Yardley's feminine mahogany desk, she doubled her resolve. Mama had already disgraced and abandoned her family. She'd chosen a life of excess and pleasure over responsibility and *them*—her children. Rose couldn't imagine it was possible for Mama to hurt her any more than she already had.

Besides, the whole point of coming to Bath was to discover the truth. No matter how ugly it might be.

The servants had already cleared the tea tray, and the fire burned low in the grate. The room was quiet but for the soft sizzle of the log and the ticking of the clock on the mantel.

Rose pulled open the drawer.

There, on top of a stack of correspondence, was a slightly crumpled letter.

Written in Mama's handwriting.

The cheerful, flowing script was perfectly matched to her lilting voice and twinkling eyes. It was more of her mother than Rose had seen or felt in six years, and the force of it hit her solidly in the belly.

Just holding the letter unleashed a rush of memories so sweet that they hurt. Mama's golden beauty and contagious smile. Her soothing touch on Rose's fevered brow. The way her exquisite French perfume lingered after she'd tucked Rose into bed.

Of course, Mama hadn't written *her* a note, and that knowledge stung.

But there was no time for self-pity or hurt. The letter Rose held was a clue, and she'd be a fool not to read it—quickly.

She lifted the paper, but the words swam before her. Sniffling, she swiped at the corners of her eyes.

"What are you doing?"

The voice was authoritative, rich, and deep. And hauntingly familiar.

She turned, hiding the letter behind her. She made a clumsy attempt to shove the drawer shut with her bottom but succeeded only in bumping the desk, which rocked on spindly legs. The man must be a servant. If she could manage a haughty tone, she could probably talk her way out of the situation. But she'd never been particularly good at haughty. Her face burned.

"I was looking for something." She looked at the man, hoping he wasn't half as intimidating as he sounded, and froze.

Dear God. It couldn't be.

"Rose?" He blinked, clearly as stunned as she, then quickly corrected himself. "Lady Rose?"

"Charles." The sound of his name on her lips was surreal. She'd thought that her feelings for him had withered, dried, and blown away like dead leaves.

She'd been wrong.

He was the same as she remembered—confident, solid, and steady. But he was different, too. His hair had turned a darker shade of gold, and he seemed to have grown all over. His neck was thicker, his jaw stronger. He'd traded the patched trousers and threadbare shirt that he'd worn in the stables for buckskin breeches and a nicely tailored jacket, both of which showed his strong physique to advantage. But the biggest change in him was the way he looked at her.

And it nearly broke her heart.

For instead of looking happy to see her, like he was anticipating a few stolen moments of summertime bliss, he looked suspicious. The laughing amber eyes that had always welcomed her to the stable glowered, chilly and remote.

She choked out the obvious question. "What are you doing at Lady Yardley's?"

"I could ask the same of you." The words, formal and clipped, didn't fit with the Charles she knew.

She raised her chin and matched her tone to his. "I'm acting as a companion to Lady Bonneville, and we're guests of the countess."

"You're a companion?" He raised a brow, skeptical.

"Yes."

"Why?"

Once, she would have willingly explained everything to him. For even before she'd regained her voice, she'd shared her whole being with him—she'd been as honest and open as it was possible for her to be. But now, his question irritated her. It presumed too much—a connection, a trust, a bond.

"I don't see that it's any concern of yours."

"Forgive me." But the look he leveled at her belied his apology. It said, *Fine. We can play it that way if you'd like.*

Fighting the urge to shiver, she folded the letter behind her back. She felt for the drawer, slipped the note through the crack, and slid the drawer shut. "You're no longer a stable master." It was an idiotic thing to say, but she had to say something—anything—to fill the vast and unnatural gulf between them.

"No." His stiff smile didn't reach his eyes.

"And I think it's safe to presume," she stated saucily, "that you're not Lady Yardley's companion."

"I am not." This time, his smile was genuine.

Dangerous, that. She gripped the edge of the desk behind her to keep her knees from wobbling.

He took one step toward her. "I'm her steward."

Ah, he'd been too busy moving up in the world to reply to her letters. She couldn't blame him for wanting to better his station in life—that had always been his dream. Perhaps he wanted no reminders of the days he'd spent mucking out stables. But those days happened to be the ones she most treasured.

"Congratulations are in order then."

"I'm grateful to Lady Yardley for giving me the opportunity." He took another step toward Rose. "And I am in her debt."

The show of loyalty to his employer stung—especially since he seemed to have forgotten the sultry summer days and the confidences they'd shared. "I've no doubt you've proven yourself worthy."

He strode closer, till only an arm's length separated them. His clothes might have been more refined, but the man beneath them was not. He looked like he'd be more at ease chopping wood and hammering nails outdoors than reviewing ledgers and attending to correspondence in a study. The merest shadow of a beard covered the lower half of his masculine face, but his lips, soft and full, captured her attention. She'd imagined kissing him so many times that she could almost convince herself she had.

"I need to ask you again," he said evenly. "What are you doing in here?"

"We had tea here earlier. I left something behind."

"In Lady Yardley's desk?" he asked doubtfully.

Drat. She'd rather hoped he hadn't seen her rummaging through the drawer. "No, of course not. I, ah, simply noticed that the drawer was open and thought I'd close it." Heat crept up her face—the curse of being a redhead. Even the tops of her ears burned.

"I see." His cool, assessing gaze raked over her. "Did you find it?"

"Pardon?" Her mouth went dry. Had he seen her holding the letter?

"The item you left behind."

She laughed a bit too loudly. "No. That is, perhaps it's in my room after all."

He nodded—as though he didn't believe a word she said.

"In fact, I'm sure I left it there. I feel quite foolish for coming here to search for it. I don't suppose we could pretend that I didn't?"

Rose held her breath as she awaited his response. Asking him to overlook her snooping was like asking him to put her before his employer, Lady Yardley. He'd always been very dedicated to his job, the most conscientious of workers, and yet, there was a time when Charles would have put her ahead of anyone. She wouldn't have even had to ask. But that was years ago, and he wasn't the same. *She* wasn't the same.

He inclined his head politely. Distantly. Like they were barely acquainted. "I hope you find what you're looking for, Lady Rose." With that, he stepped aside and glanced at the door, dismissing her. He might be willing to forget about this incident, but he wasn't about to leave her to her own devices in Lady Yardley's drawing room.

She thought of the letter with her mother's handwriting, still sitting in the desk drawer. It could hold all the answers Rose was seeking. Who knew when she'd have another chance to peek at the letter, or whether it would still be there when she did? Surely *that* was the reason her feet refused to move.

The stark physical change in Charles made her realize just how young he'd been the summer that she'd met him. Back then, she'd thought him terribly mature and experienced, but the truth was he'd been little more than a boy himself. She should never have placed so much hope in him. She should have known they'd grow apart—that he'd leave, just as Mama had. Papa, too. No, it wasn't Charles's fault that she'd been so naïve. She always expected too much from people . . . and was inevitably disappointed.

"You should leave now." His voice was deeper but still achingly familiar.

Hurt, and determined that he should not see it, Rose lifted her chin. "I was just about to return to my room to dress for dinner."

"I think that would be best."

She should have simply nodded and taken her leave. But that one simple statement, uttered with such frosty detachment, wounded her to the core.

She was tired of being dismissed, deserted, and forgotten. Years might have passed, but the ache in her chest was a permanent, palpable thing. Mama was missing; Papa was dead. And now Charles was here, in the flesh, exposing all the hurt and grief once again.

She couldn't walk away.

"Why do you want me to leave, Charles? Does it make you uncomfortable that the girl who once visited you in the stables has made an appearance in your new life?"

"No." His brows, several shades darker than his golden hair, drew together. It was a glimpse of the old Charles— the one who would sooner die than hurt her, the one who looked at her with undisguised longing. "I heard some of the staff in the hallway. I didn't think you'd want to be discovered here. With me."

Well, that did make sense...but wait. As of this moment, she was through with giving people the benefit of the doubt. Especially the ones who'd let her down.

"If you are truly concerned for my reputation," she said, "why don't *you* leave? It's what a gentleman would do."

She regretted the words the moment she'd uttered them. She'd only meant to point out that his behavior was less than gallant, not to belittle his station or to wound his pride.

Throwing off the mask of polite behavior, he leaned toward her and curled his mouth into a wicked smile. "You should know, Rose, that I'm no gentleman."

His breath was a caress on her neck, his words a heady elixir. This was the closest he'd ever come to flirting with her. And she had to admit...she liked it. So much so, that she almost forgot he had caught her brazenly riffling through the contents of his employer's desk drawer.

But the suspicion in his beautiful brown eyes told her that *he* hadn't forgotten.

"What were you *really* doing in here?" His whispered question invited her confidences and promised understanding.

But this was not the Charles she'd known before—predictable, solid, and safe. As his heavy-lidded gaze drifted over her, her pulse leaped in her throat, confirming her thoughts. There was nothing safe about him.

"Excuse me. I must go." Just as she started to sweep past him, footsteps sounded in the hall. Charles grasped her upper arm, pulled her away from the desk, and almost carried her to the shadowed area between the large open door and a bookcase. He pressed her back against the shelves and held a calloused finger to her lips.

Rose's whole body tingled.

It sounded as though a maid had entered the drawing room and was lighting a few lamps. She proceeded to plump the pillows on the chairs and settees, timing each *thump* of the velvet pillows to the beat of the waltz she was humming.

Meanwhile, Charles stood very close, his torso a mere inch from Rose's. It was too dark to see his face—to see anything, really—but somehow she felt the intensity of his gaze upon her, heating her skin. The air fairly crackled around them. And his finger still rested on her lips.

It was funny how one little transgression led to another. Her heart pounded in her chest from fear, desire, and delight at her own daring. No one—not even her dear sister, Olivia—would believe that the always obedient and demure Rose was hiding in the shadows of Lady Yardley's drawing room. With a man. The same virile, breathtakingly handsome man whom she'd once believed she loved. The man she'd never been quite able to forget.

Charles felt as though he'd stumbled into a strange dream. He shouldn't be hiding behind a door with Rose or touching her mouth. And he *certainly* shouldn't be thinking of all the wicked things he'd like to do to her.

Seeing her, after so many years, was a punch to the gut. The flimsy lies he'd told himself—*it was a youthful infatuation, you'll forget her in time*—didn't begin to hold up now that she was in his arms. Her creamy skin, fine features, and slender frame would drive any man to distraction, but for him, the pull was greater. He knew that her delicate beauty hid deep wisdom and quiet strength. He knew *Rose*.

And the truth was that he'd never stopped wanting her.

He peered around the edge of the door. The maid knelt before the fireplace, adding a few sticks of kindling to the grate. She was probably preparing the room for a before-dinner gathering.

Somehow, he had to make sure Rose escaped from the room unseen—or at least unseen *with him*.

The maid's back was to the door. He could whisk Rose out of the room in two seconds and the servant would be none the wiser.

"Follow my lead," he whispered.

Slowly—reluctantly—he let his finger drop and placed his hands on Rose's slender shoulders.

She nodded. At least she wasn't resisting him. He slipped an arm behind her and prepared to guide her around the door and out of Lady Yardley's drawing room. He checked once more to ensure the maid was still tending the fire, but she'd moved. She was wiping her hands on her apron as she walked directly toward the doorway—and Rose and him.

He hauled her lithe body against his and pressed her against the wall of bookshelves, trying to make their entwined bodies as small as possible. Her sharp intake of breath reminded him she wasn't accustomed to being manhandled, and he supposed he should be grateful she hadn't slapped him across the face—not yet, at any rate.

The maid's humming grew louder as she approached the door, but then her singing and her footsteps halted suddenly, as though she were pausing to listen. Perhaps she was simply giving the room one last check...or maybe she'd sensed something was not as it should be. Charles watched her shadow glide toward Lady Yardley's desk and listened as she moved something—probably the small portrait that sat on top of it.

Charles didn't breathe, didn't flinch. Rose was a statue in his arms—a very beautiful, warm, soft statue.

At last, the maid hurried out of the room, humming once more as she walked down the corridor.

And still, neither he nor Rose moved. Her dress was silky beneath his arm, and the faint scent of summer wildflowers filled his head.

"The maid's gone," he said. A statement so obvious and mundane should have broken the odd spell that had settled over them in their hiding spot. It didn't.

"Yes," she said breathlessly. "That was frightfully close." And still she didn't pull away.

"Rose," he began, uncertain of what he wanted to say and even more uncertain of what he *should* say. He couldn't believe she was there. He'd glimpsed her auburn hair as he'd walked by the drawing room earlier, and it had stopped him dead in his tracks. That distinct, fiery shade could have been only hers.

Having Rose here at Lady Yardley's was everything he'd hoped for and everything he'd feared. He'd liked and admired her from the first day he'd met her. And then came the summer he'd begun to look at her differently—the summer he'd started to fantasize about kissing her. Which he definitely could not do. Not then, not now.

"It's good to see you, Charles," she whispered. "I should have said that before."

"I'm sorry if I—"

"There's no need to apologize—for anything."

But there was. He really should explain why he'd left Huntford Manor without a word and why he hadn't replied to dozens of her letters. The problem was that all the explanations in the world couldn't change the truth.

"I hope I didn't hurt you." He let her go and instantly felt a strange sense of loss.

She walked out of the shadows and smoothed her skirts. "You didn't. I'm stronger than I used to be." Her smile said she wasn't talking just about physical strength.

"That's good."

She stood there as though she expected him to say more. If he were nineteen again, he might invite her on a picnic or ask her if she'd like to meet him at the stables and feed apples to the horses. But he wasn't the same lad. And she sure as hell wasn't the same girl.

After a year of working on the docks and another assisting the steward of a gentleman he'd met in a pub, he was finally on his way to achieving his dream. He couldn't let this beauty distract him from his goals, no matter how much she tempted him. And he couldn't let her riffle through his employer's personal papers either.

"I must go and dress for dinner." She headed toward the door, paused, and turned to look at him. "Thank you for understanding."

"But I don't." He didn't understand why she had become Lady Bonneville's companion or what she'd been doing looking in Lady Yardley's desk. He most definitely didn't understand what had just transpired between them.

"Then I thank you for your discretion."

With that, she glided into the hallway and out of sight. Charles stood there stunned. The desk drawer beckoned, tempting him to look at its contents and discover Rose's secrets. However, that would have amounted to a betrayal of her... and Lady Yardley. Besides, he had no legitimate reason to be near the desk—or even in the drawing room.

No good could come of pursuing answers where Rose was concerned. They had grown apart over the last few years, and that was as it should be. If all went according to plan, he'd be heading to America within the year— far from England's civilized shores and far from Rose's knowing gaze.

Chapter Three

*Snort: (1) The loud sound a horse makes by forcing air
through its nostrils. (2) The unladylike noise a
viscountess makes when surrounded by idiots.*

You look positively wretched this morning." Lady
Bonneville nibbled delicately on the corner of her toast
as she eyed Rose from across Lady Yardley's breakfast
table. "Your face is pale and your eyes are puffy. Was
your mattress as hard as mine? I might as well have
been slumbering on sarsen stone. Be a dear and pass the
jam."

"Oh." Lady Yardley coughed and touched a hand to her
throat, like her last bite of ham had gone down the wrong
pipe. "I shall have Mrs. Seymour look into it at once."

"Please do not trouble yourself," Rose said quickly.
"Our rooms are lovely and our beds are quite comfortable."

Lady Bonneville squinted at Rose, her displeasure
etched in the deep lines framing her mouth. "I hardly
think you an authority on the comfort of *my* mattress."

Rose ignored this and smiled at Lady Yardley. "If I

look tired, I'm sure it's due to the hours we spent traveling yesterday."

It was a lie. Her sleepless night was due to one stable master–turned–steward. Thoughts of him had troubled her throughout the night. She wondered what had brought him to Lady Yardley's house in Bath and whether he'd report her suspicious activities of the night before. She wondered if he remembered the golden summer they'd spent at Huntford Manor and whether any remnants of their improbable but cherished friendship had survived their separation. But mostly she wondered what it would be like to kiss him—to surrender to the desire she'd felt when he held her.

Of course, he hadn't meant to hold her. It was more of a necessity, an act of desperation in order to avoid discovery. But whatever the circumstances, having his hard, large body pressed against hers had been...unsettling. And not the least bit unpleasant.

His torso was a wall of muscle, broad and unyielding, and his arm had easily circled her waist, holding her snug against him. With any other man, she imagined she'd have felt trapped and suffocated. However, with Charles she felt safe and slightly woozy at the same time.

"Rose!" Lady Bonneville was clearly cross, and she startled Rose so badly that she almost tipped over the cream. "You haven't heard a word I've said."

Rose searched her memory for some thread of the conversation but found nary a trace. "Forgive me. What were you saying?"

"Why haven't you touched your food?" The viscountess looked down her nose at the runny egg on Rose's plate. "Never mind, I think I know the answer. At least we shan't grow too plump during our stay."

Lady Yardley whimpered into her teacup.

"Everything looks delicious," Rose assured their hostess. "I haven't much of an appetite this morning."

"Heed my advice," Lady Bonneville said to Rose, "and go back to bed—it's what I intend to do. Before you retire to your room, however, would you fetch my book from the drawing room? I left it on the table beside the settee last night."

"Of course." Rose checked the urge to leap out of her chair. She'd been trying to think of an excuse to return to the room so that she could retrieve her mother's letter, and Lady Bonneville had unwittingly provided it. "If you'd like I could read to you while you're resting."

"I suppose I can let you attempt it. I'm rather particular about the way in which books are read aloud. Too much expression vexes me; too little bores me."

Rose stood and placed her napkin on the table. "I shall endeavor to do my best. If you'll excuse me, I'll fetch the book and meet you in your room in a few minutes."

For a few minutes was all she'd need.

She glided from the breakfast room and down the chilly corridor, wrapping her shawl more tightly about her. The drawing room door was open, and sunlight streamed through the tall windows, banishing the shadows of the previous night. Standing in the bright room, it was hard to believe that she and Charles had managed to hide by the bookshelves.

But Rose had no time to linger, no time to contemplate that unexpected, intimate encounter. She spotted the viscountess's book across the room, went to pick it up, and tucked it under one arm. Then she strode directly to the desk, eager to see her mother's familiar handwriting once more.

She'd already decided she wouldn't read the letter right away. She would slip the folded paper into her pocket and wait until after Lady Bonneville was napping to read it. She suspected it would take some time to digest, and she wouldn't be able to do so while she was reading to the viscountess.

Rose's hand trembled as she opened the desk drawer. Just like last night, it was full of letters and writing supplies...but something was different. The papers were neatly bound in string or ribbon. Several ink pots sat in a row with quills nestled beside them. Rose set down the viscountess's book and frantically flipped through the bundled papers in the drawer, hoping against hope that her mother's note—the one she'd held in her hands just hours ago—would be there.

It was not.

Anger, hot and fierce, welled up inside her. Somebody had removed the letter to ensure that she could not read it.

And there was no doubt who that somebody was, for only Charles had seen her snooping.

She'd thought she could trust him. She'd thought he was on her side.

But perhaps he was not the man she'd imagined him to be.

She checked the other desk drawers, but didn't really expect to find the letter there. If she wanted to get it back, she was going to have to find Charles and either convince him that she deserved to have it or take it without his consent—and if it came to that, she would.

No one had ever accused Rose of being unscrupulous, but she knew in her heart that she'd do anything to obtain that letter—that little piece of Mama.

Lord help the handsome steward who stood in her way.

• • •

Charles divided his duties into two categories. The first, which he vastly preferred, were the physical sorts of activities. Riding around the estate, seeing to repairs, and visiting tenants took up much of his day. He knew he should delegate more of the work, but he liked the satisfaction of mending a fence or patching a leaking roof. Anything to get him out from behind a damned desk.

Which brought him to the second, reviled group of tasks: reviewing ledgers, ensuring accounts were up-to-date, and meeting with Lady Yardley. Not that she was a particularly demanding employer—he just felt trapped if he had to spend more than a few hours sitting indoors.

Today in particular he would avoid the manor house. He needed to lose himself in his work.

Because the one woman he'd always wanted was here in Bath—staying on the estate where he lived and worked.

During his last summer working at Huntford Manor, he and Rose had forged an unlikely bond. He'd been a sullen nineteen-year-old with a huge chip on his shoulder and every reason to distrust Rose. As the sister of a duke, she stood for the very things he resented: wealth, privilege, and power.

But damn it, she hadn't looked like a spoiled debutante when she came into the stables, sat on an upside-down pail, and silently pet Romeo behind his mangy ears. Animals loved her, and he'd respected that. Besides, the loneliness and sadness in her eyes would have crumbled anyone's defenses.

The connection was more than that though. She'd seen something in him that no one but his father had. She believed he could do anything—break the wildest stud colt, heal the sickliest mare, and manage the finest stables in all of England. He might have been a stable master on her brother's estate, but she'd made him feel like a king.

It had been only a matter of time before he'd wanted more than friendship. Her beauty was ethereal and earthly at the same time. Lips he was sure had never been kissed taunted him with their ripe fullness. Hair the color of a perfect sunset begged to be touched. He'd desired her with every fiber of his being. And she'd desired him, too.

But he would never have been content with a part of her. Or a few passionate kisses. He wanted all of her— and it was the very thing that drove him to make something more of himself.

Now she was here, even more beautiful than he'd remembered. And the chasm between them seemed wider than ever.

So he'd decided to spend the bitterly cold afternoon inspecting the garden and noting items to discuss with the head gardener. He strode over pebbled paths, welcoming the brisk breeze that stung his face and the little clouds that appeared when he exhaled.

Winter was a fine time to see to the garden's structural elements. With the branches stripped of their green finery, imperfections in the architecture stood out. The trellis required painting and some of the border stones along a path needed replacing. As he walked down a narrow pathway, one of the large flat slabs of slate beneath his boots wobbled. He crouched to inspect it more closely.

Some of the dirt under one corner of the stone had shifted—either from erosion or a burrowing creature. A hazard such as this was best dealt with immediately, before someone tripped on the stone and took a tumble into the rosebushes. He hadn't brought a shovel or any other tools, but this wasn't a difficult job.

He gripped the edges of the rock and grunted as he hoisted it aside, then exhaled as it thudded on the grass. The soil where the rock had been was compacted—except for one spot where a small animal had dug out a home. Charles frowned. He loved animals more than he did most people, but this creature was going to have to relocate. He'd probably have to come back with a shovel to get the ground completely firm and level, but for now, he stood and dug the heel of his boot into the ground to push dirt into the hole.

"You're a difficult man to find."

Startled, Charles turned to see Rose standing on the walkway. She wore a long, midnight-blue hooded cloak trimmed in snow-white fur, but her cheeks and the tip of her nose were pink from the cold. Tendrils of her fiery hair peeked out from beneath her hood, instantly adding color and life to the dreary garden.

"It's rare that anyone comes looking for me." He brushed off his gloves and stood. "Least of all a beautiful young woman. How can I be of service?"

She raised her chin. "I think you know."

"I'm afraid I don't. Is this about last night?"

"What have you done with it?" she asked.

"With what?"

She opened her mouth, then looked away as though she didn't trust herself to speak.

"Are you referring to the paper that you attempted to take from Lady Yardley's desk last night?"

"Where is it?" Her eyes flicked to the loose dirt beneath his foot. "Surely you didn't . . ."

"What, bury it?" he asked incredulously. "*No*. I don't even know what that paper was or why you wanted it."

"Please don't pretend with me, Charles. I'm sure that you feel allegiance to Lady Yardley, and—"

"I'm not pretending. I'm willing to help, but first I need to understand."

She shook her head and the loose, strawberry spirals around her face fluttered gracefully. "I'm afraid I can't discuss it."

"Then I'm afraid I can't help you." He looked down at the stone and the dirt, doing his best to appear uninterested.

"It's complicated, and..."

"You're not sure if you can trust me?"

She shrugged guiltily. "It's been a long time. Much has changed."

He nodded and waved her toward a bench a few yards farther down the garden path. "Come."

She followed him, and just as she was about to sit on the cold stone, he stopped her, took off his greatcoat, and folded it before laying it on the bench.

Her face clouded with worry. "You'll freeze."

"No, I won't. Unless this conversation takes all night," he teased. "Then I might."

She shivered a little as she sat on the bench, and he checked the urge to rub her fingers between his palms.

"Here," she said, spreading the edge of his greatcoat out beside her, "you sit, too."

"I can see that you're upset, Rose," he began. "And I—"

"It was a letter from my mother," she blurted. "I need to read it." The anguish in her voice caused him pain, as real as if he'd slammed his fist into a brick.

"Your mother? Are you sure?"

"Yes. I didn't have time to read it before..."

"Before I walked into the drawing room and found you?" he offered.

She nodded. "But I recognized her handwriting at once."

"Why are you so desperate to have it?" If she had resorted to rummaging through other people's desks, she was desperate indeed.

"I hoped that it might..." Her voice trailed off, thin and forlorn. "It doesn't matter. I can see that I was wrong to think you'd taken it." She stood, signaling that their conversation was over.

"Wait. Why would you assume that I'd take it? I was trying to protect you last night—don't you remember?"

She turned away as though searching the pale gray sky for answers. "Perhaps. But you were also trying to protect yourself and your position."

She had a point. But it stung that she'd jumped to the worst conclusion about him. "Our friendship still means something."

As she whirled to face him, her hood fell back, unleashing a riot of auburn curls. Unshed tears shone in her eyes. "How dare you speak to me of friendship?"

He swallowed and rose slowly, the same way he'd face a beautiful but untamed horse. "We *were* friends."

She shook her head. "I once thought so. But you left Huntford Manor without so much as a word. And the letters I wrote to you afterward...all of them went unanswered." Her lip trembled.

Jesus.

"Rose, I'm sorry." He'd told himself it was for the best.

That she'd forget about him a few days after he was gone and that she'd be better off in the long run.

Right now, however, a tear trickled down her cheek, making him feel like the worst kind of scoundrel. He felt inside his jacket for a handkerchief and offered it to her wordlessly. She took it and dabbed at her face, looking at him expectantly. She wanted an explanation for his behavior, and he supposed she deserved one.

But what could he say?

Certainly not the truth—that despite years of trying, he hadn't managed to learn to read and write properly. That after endless hours spent staring at books, he still labored to make sense of the simplest of sentences.

No. He couldn't reveal the truth, especially not to Rose. Better she think him a heartless bastard than the hopeless idiot that he was. He clenched his fists, wishing he could punch something. Hard.

Rose sniffled and her teeth chattered. "I should return to the house."

"Yes, you're half frozen." He moved closer and pulled the hood of her cloak over her head. "Go sit by the fire and have some tea."

"Please, don't do that."

"What?"

"Don't make kind gestures and say nice things. Don't pretend that you care when you don't."

His control snapped like a dry twig. He reached for her hands and pulled her closer, forcing her to face him. "Listen to me, Rose. I may not be the most faithful of correspondents. I may not be the most skilled conversationalist. But I will tell you this: I don't have to pretend when it comes to caring about you. Some things come naturally, and caring for you ... well, that's one of them. If you want to know the truth, it wounds me to think that you would doubt that."

"You have an odd way of showing it." She glanced over her shoulder at the manor house. "I really should go."

"Meet me later." The words were out of his mouth before he had the chance to realize what he was asking. But he had to see her again and try to explain.

For the space of several heartbeats, she looked into his eyes, then nodded. "Where are your quarters?" she asked. "Do you live in the manor house?"

"No, I'm staying in a cottage on the other side of the duck pond." He pointed in the general direction. "But we can't meet there." The idea was preposterous. Surely she understood the grave risk to her reputation.

"Then where?"

"There's a folly by the pond—a miniature replica of a Greek rotunda. It's covered and affords some privacy. Can you meet me there at this time tomorrow afternoon?"

She hesitated for a fraction of a second. "I'll be there."

"You must take precautions to ensure no one knows where you're going," he warned. "If we're seen together, you'll be ruined."

"I'm not ashamed to know you."

"Don't be foolish," he chided. "You're no longer a girl. If we're discovered alone together, you'll be shunned from polite society for the rest of your days."

She shrugged and gave a hollow laugh. "There are worse fates."

Damn it.

He squeezed her shoulders, forcing her to look into his eyes. "Don't say that—not even in jest. Do you think

I'd be able to live with myself if your good name was destroyed on my account? Because I wouldn't."

A storm of emotion swirled in her eyes and their breath mingled in the small white clouds between them.

"I'll be careful," she promised. "But I must go now."

Slowly, he released her.

"Until tomorrow." With that, she glided away, her cloak billowing behind her in the breeze.

Chapter Four

Rose sneezed into her handkerchief as delicately as possible. Lady Bonneville raised her lorgnette, her horrified expression suggesting that she feared her young companion had contracted the plague.

"It's a good thing we're here," the viscountess muttered. She sipped from her glass and grimaced at the taste of the Pump Room's warm mineral waters. "You require the curative waters more than I do. Drink up."

Rose did as she was instructed. Actually, she only pretended to drink, but Lady Bonneville was mollified nevertheless.

It was Rose's first time in the Pump Room, and though she'd heard much about it, she was still surprised by the number of people milling about the large, elegant chamber and the cacophony of conversation and the music from the orchestra. The warm waters flowed from a fountain at one end of the room, where a pumper handed glasses to guests.

Light poured through the tall windows, creating sunny patches on the floor. Ash, the cat who frequented the stables at Huntford Manor, would have loved to claim one of the spots as his own. Of course, Ash made her think of Charles and the day they'd helped the kitten make its entrance into the world. She shook off the thought, resolving to have a pleasant and productive morning. Later, she would meet Charles.

Rose offered the viscountess her arm as they strolled around the perimeter of the room. Lady Bonneville was not so feeble that she required assistance with walking, but she found it rather convenient to have someone—namely, Rose—on hand to listen to the insightful, if occasionally biting, remarks she made.

Lady Yardley, who'd accompanied them as well, greeted several acquaintances and friends. She seemed to know everyone and was gracious to all she met—just as Mama had been. And that encouraged Rose to try a new tack in her search for her mother's whereabouts.

Rather than attempt to look for the missing letter, perhaps she'd simply ask Lady Yardley what she knew about Mama. Maybe her hostess would produce the letter and let Rose read it, as well as any others that existed. But she didn't dare ask in front of Lady Bonneville, who clearly intimidated their hostess—and most mere mortals.

Lady Yardley approached, eyes alight with mischief. "Henrietta," she said breathlessly, "you must allow me to introduce Rose to a young gentleman."

"Must I?" Lady Bonneville asked incredulously. "And who is this gentleman? Don't you think I should meet him as well?"

"Of course. I shall introduce you both. However, you

mentioned that Rose should have an opportunity to mingle with people her age, and Lord Stanton seems an ideal
candidate." She winked conspiratorially at Rose, who felt
a vague sense of alarm at the word *candidate*. Candidate
for *what*, precisely? She'd thought Lady Bonneville was
her ally in avoiding the matchmaking efforts of well-
meaning family and friends—but the calculating gleam
in her sharp eyes made Rose shudder involuntarily.

"Aha. It's just as I suspected," the viscountess announced
to Rose. "You're taking a chill."

"Not at all. I—"

Lady Bonneville released Rose's arm and took the pre-
caution of moving a few steps away. "Go with Diana to
meet Lord Stanton. Do try to refrain from sneezing on
him, dear, as it tends to make a horrid first impression.
Afterward, you may report back to me. I shall be sitting
on the side of the room opposite the orchestra, for obvious
reasons. I trust Audrey has seen to my footstool?"

"She has. Allow me to escort you to it."

"No need." She shooed Rose in the direction of Lady
Yardley, who seized her wrist, apparently undaunted by
threat of disease. "Lord Stanton is the son of the Mar-
quess Holdsworth. I think you'll find him quite charming.
Handsome, too. He accompanied his mother here today."
As they approached a dark-haired gentleman and an older
woman, Lady Yardley gushed, "Ah, here we are."

Rose resisted the urge to cringe, for she felt rather like
a stuffed partridge on a platter just before the footman
prepared to remove the cover.

"Lady Holdsworth, Lord Stanton," said Lady Yardley,
"may I present Lady Rose Sherbourne, sister of the Duke
of Huntford."

The moment Lady Yardley uttered the word *duke* the level of interest in Lord Stanton's eyes went from mild to keen. But perhaps that was a coincidence. Rose generally believed in giving people the benefit of the doubt, so she made the most graceful curtsey she could manage and decided to withhold judgment.

As they exchanged niceties, Lord Stanton assumed the bored, brooding air that she supposed was currently in fashion. A silly affectation, but she had to admit he was handsome—in a polished, arrogant sort of way.

"Is this your first visit to the Pump Room, Lady Rose?" he asked.

"It is indeed."

"What do you think of the refreshments?" He raised his glass of mineral water and arched a dark brow.

"I think…" Oh dear. There was no way to respond both truthfully and politely, so she opted for candor. "I think that I'd vastly prefer tea."

"As would I." The baron flashed her a disarming smile, then continued in a stage whisper, "Not even cream and sugar could save this dreck."

"I should think they'd only make matters worse," she said.

He laughed at that and turned to Lady Yardley. "I must thank you for the introduction. Your young friend is a delight."

Lady Holdsworth tittered at her son's comment, and her highly rouged cheeks turned even pinker as she addressed Rose. "I do hope we shall see you both at the Assembly Rooms—perhaps at the ball next week?"

"That depends," Rose began. "You see, I'm acting as a compan—"

"Of course you shall see us at the ball," Lady Yardley interjected. "We wouldn't miss it."

"I look forward to it," Lord Stanton said meaningfully. His gaze lingered on Rose for a bit longer than was proper before he smoothly steered the conversation to the unusually cold winter.

When both parties at last said their farewells, Lady Yardley swept Rose aside. "You needn't mention to everyone you meet that you're Lady Bonneville's companion."

"But I *am* her companion."

"Of course you are." Though clearly exasperated, Lady Yardley smiled as she spoke, so much so that her lips barely moved. "But you are also a young, eligible lady. You mustn't forget that."

As if she could. Still, Rose nodded obediently.

"Now then," Lady Yardley said, "no harm done. I do believe Lord Stanton was taken with you in spite of your slip. We must tell Henrietta the details."

"Wait." Rose had their hostess—her mother's close friend—all to herself for the moment. No time like the present. She took a deep breath. "May I ask you something?"

"Certainly, my dear. What is it?" Lady Yardley glanced around the room, vaguely distracted.

A drop of sweat trickled down Rose's spine, but if she truly wanted answers, she had to ask questions. The brave and courageous kinds of questions.

So she asked the one that was in her heart, as simply and as clearly as she could. "Will you tell me what's become of my mother?"

The color drained from Lady Yardley's face. "What?"

"You were a good friend to Mama. I thought you could

tell me what's happened to her." Her voice shook with desperation. "I need to know."

Lady Yardley looked at the orchestra, the ceiling, and through the multipaned windows. Anywhere but at Rose. "Of all the times...why would you ask such a question *now*?"

Perhaps she hadn't chosen the ideal time or location, but Rose had the distinct feeling that Lady Yardley's reaction would have been the same anytime and anywhere. "There is always a reason to put off difficult conversations," Rose said. "I've put off this one for far too long."

Lady Yardley reached for the reticule dangling from her wrist and withdrew a handkerchief. She patted her brow and gazed at the door as if she were praying the cavalry would charge through it and spare her from this inquisition. "But it's been years. Surely, some things are better left alone."

"It *has* been years," Rose said softly. "I've thought about Mama every day."

"No good can come of digging up the past, my dear. You are much better off moving forward. Think of the bright future you could have with someone like Lord Stanton." Lady Yardley beamed, as though happy to be back on solid matchmaking ground.

"I must know what's become of Mama." Panic gripped her, and she fought back tears of frustration. "Could we speak later, at the manor house?"

Lady Yardley shook her head, her delicate features awash in regret. "I don't think so. I understand you are curious, and I suppose that's natural. However, I'm afraid I can't help you. I know nothing, you see. I'm sorry."

She gave Rose the same patient, pitying look one might

give a child after informing her that her beloved puppy has died.

Indeed, Lady Yardley was a fine actress. But the claim that she knew nothing was false, and Rose couldn't pretend to believe it. "But you must know something."

"No more than you do, darling."

The old Rose would have accepted the falsehood gracefully and let the matter drop. There in the Pump Room, the rules of polite society bound her as surely as ropes on her wrists. Summoning courage, she mentally wriggled free from one. "What about Mama's letter?"

In one measure of music, Lady Yardley's demeanor shifted. She narrowed her eyes and pinned Rose with an icy stare. "I'm sure I don't know what you're talking about."

However, her high color and flared nostrils suggested that she did.

Rose's own heartbeat thundered in her chest. "Why do you wish to keep the truth about Mama from me?"

Lady Yardley looked down her nose. "So this is why you accompanied Henrietta to Bath. Does she know that she is merely an excuse for your snooping and prying?"

"I'm not certain. Lady Bonneville knows more than most people give her credit for."

"That is true." Lady Yardley looked at the glass in her hand like she desperately wished the mineral water were sherry, or perhaps something stronger. She took a deep breath and exhaled slowly, till she was composed—the picture of calm and reason. "I am sorry to disappoint you, Rose, but I have no information about your mother. I sincerely doubt that anyone does. The sooner you are able to accept that, the better off you shall be." She looked away, clearly signaling not only that the discussion was over, but that she had just put the whole nasty business to bed. Forever.

Rose tried to keep her expression impassive, but with one brief conversation, Lady Yardley had effectively trampled all her hopes and plans. "I believe I understand your feelings on the matter."

"Excellent. Now, let us turn to happier subjects. We must go to Henrietta and tell her all about your introduction to Lord Stanton."

Rose had little choice but to follow. The binds of polite behavior dug into her wrists, pinching and chafing once more. Lady Yardley may have subdued her for the moment, but if she thought Rose would surrender so easily, she was mistaken. If anything, her hostess's vehemence that Rose was better off not knowing made her more determined than ever to discover the truth.

It also made her rather terrified of what that truth might be.

Later that afternoon, Lady Bonneville was in bed, her head propped on three silk pillows as she dictated a letter intended for her niece. "You would do well to heed my advice and not your mother's."

Rose sat at a small table, transcribing.

"I can't believe I even have to state such a thing," the viscountess muttered, "but I'm afraid my niece is nearly as addle-brained as my dear sister."

Rose lifted her quill, looked up, and noted Lady Bonneville's drooping eyelids. "Shall we finish the letter after you've had a rest?"

"No, we must press on," the viscountess said dramatically,

as if the future of England depended upon her advice. For all Rose knew, it did.

"Very well. We left off with 'and not your mother's.' "

The viscountess cleared her throat and continued, "Under no circumstances should you take a position as a governess. Especially for a man such as . . ."

Rose scribbled furiously to catch up, then waited, quill poised, for Lady Bonneville to complete her sentence.

She began to snore instead.

The timing was perfect. Rose set down her pen and put the stopper on the ink bottle. Quietly, she drew the curtains and slipped out of the viscountess's bedchamber. She went to her own room to retrieve her cloak and fur-lined gloves before informing Audrey that she was going for a walk.

And then she was on her way—to meet with Charles.

She'd had plenty of time to think about what she wanted to ask him and what she wanted to say, and yet she still wasn't sure how much to reveal. She had to trust that when she saw him again, somehow she'd know.

The air was as crisp and cold as it had been yesterday, and Rose walked briskly, hood up and head down. The edges of the lake were frozen and ducks swam in vigorous circles, occasionally diving below the surface in search of supper. The folly stood proudly on the far side of the lake, perhaps a hundred yards away, and Rose could see why Charles had designated it as their meeting place.

A tall cylinder of stone with four pointed, narrow archways spaced around its base, the folly had a magical, almost mystical air about it, with vines crawling around the openings and sunlight glinting off the ancient rocks. She looked for any sign of movement within, but it was almost impossible to see inside the structure from her vantage point.

Upon reaching the threshold of one of the entrances, she paused and let her eyes adjust to the dimmer light. Charles was sitting on a bench but stood the moment he saw her. He seemed to take up much of the interior, and the whole folly was probably only twice the span of his arms. She entered, surprised to find it several degrees warmer than outside. The curved walls and picturesque views created an inviting, intimate space.

"Rose." He waved a hand toward the bench. "Come, sit. I've brought some quilts for you."

She smiled. He seemed impervious to the cold but had thought to bring along the blankets so she'd be more comfortable. He'd always been thoughtful that way and more of a gentleman than most earls and viscounts of her acquaintance.

He arranged a soft, thick quilt for her to sit on, then draped another across her, tucking it beneath her arms as he sat beside her. "I've been thinking about you." The admission, uttered so simply, warmed her more than the blankets.

"Have you?" she said.

"Why are you so determined to find your mother?"

"I adored her, Charles. She was the center of my world before she left. If she was a bit distant sometimes, it only made me more eager to please her. All I wanted was to grow up to be like her—beautiful, poised, confident."

He snorted and shook his head. "You have already surpassed her."

Rose waved off the compliment. "In spite of all she's done, I...love her. I harbor no illusions of a heartwarming mother and daughter reunion. I just want to know what's become of her. I need to understand *why* she left. Why she's never come back."

"Doesn't your family know where to find her? Surely your brother could find out if he wanted to."

"That's the problem. Owen doesn't want to. He and Olivia would prefer never to see her, think of her, or speak of her again."

"I cannot blame them."

Charles had witnessed the devastating effects of her mother's abandonment. After Mama ran off with her lover, Papa had been so grief-stricken that he...well, he couldn't bear it. Then he was gone.

"I didn't know you then, when your family—you—suffered that heartbreak," he said. "But I heard the rumors, and I saw enough. After your mother left and your father died, you were shattered. A shadow of the carefree girl you were before. Your brother and sister don't want to lose you again."

She nodded. That was indeed the scandal that had shaken her world and almost crushed her soul. But there was more to it.

Rose had walked into her parents' bedchamber and unwittingly caught her mother and her lovers in the act, effectively setting the whole chain of events into motion. *She* was the reason her mother had fled. And if Mama hadn't left, Papa might still be alive today. The whole tragedy was her fault. That knowledge was like an immovable weight on her chest. Why did she have to walk into Mama's bedroom that day? The memory would forever haunt her, pinning her down and making it difficult to breathe every time it resurfaced.

"Mama's disappearance changed all of us. Owen and

Olivia see no point in trying to find her. They think that doing so could only cause more strife. I'm certain they wish to protect me from any unpleasantness, but I'm not the same distraught girl that I was when Mama left—and I don't need protecting."

Charles grunted. "Your brother is right to want to protect you. If I were in his place I'd do the same."

Rose couldn't decide if she was frustrated or touched by the declaration. "Well, I realized that if I wanted to discover Mama's whereabouts—and I do—I would have to proceed without their help."

"And without their knowledge?"

"Yes," she admitted. "I knew that Lady Yardley was a close friend of Mama's and suspected that she'd know how to reach her."

"Did you ask her?"

"Actually, I did, earlier today. It didn't go well."

His brow creased. "She must know something."

"She says that she does not. However, I'm almost sure she does. On the first evening I arrived, I saw her with the letter. That's why I was looking for it when you caught me in the drawing room."

"And I prevented you from reading it."

"Yes. I was so shocked to see you there. I feared you'd tell Lady Yardley."

"I would never betray you."

"I wasn't sure what to think." She tossed the quilt aside and stood. "After the first two brief letters, you never wrote back to me. What happened?"

He ran a hand through his longish, wavy hair. "It's complicated, but I asked you to come here today so that I could explain—and I will."

Chapter Five

*Balk: (1) When a horse stops short and refuses to
obey a rider's commands. (2) When a lady stops being
agreeable and refuses to obey society's strictures.*

Charles swallowed as he looked at Rose's earnest face.
She wanted to know the truth about why he hadn't written
to her.

He'd told her it was complicated, but it wasn't. Not
really.

It was simple. *He* was simple. And too proud to admit
the real reason.

He stood and leaned against the arched opening that
faced the pond. "I disappointed you, and you deserved
better." That much was certainly true.

They'd spent too much time together that summer. In
the beginning he'd thought her a sad, frail lass who'd suffered a tragic loss. He'd seen no harm in letting her hang
about.

But with each visit she made to the stables, Charles
grew to understand and respect her more. He found

himself glancing up at the manor house as he worked, hoping to see her walking across the lawn toward him, her auburn hair glinting in the sun.

He could remember the precise day that their friendship developed into something more—at least for him. He'd been repairing a saddle when she walked into the yard, her thick strawberry braid swaying to the rhythm of her hips. She held a bunch of yellow wildflowers that she'd picked, and her eyes glowed with mischief as she sauntered up to him and brushed the soft petals under his chin. He jumped and she laughed—a rare and beautiful sound that stirred a dangerous desire inside him. Her fragrance mingled with the wildflowers', creating an intoxicating mixture. She stood close, her gown revealing the smooth expanse of creamy skin above her breasts.

In that moment he realized that she was more than a girl—and that he wanted her.

But setting aside the fact that she was the duke's sister, what kind of man—even a young man of nineteen—desired a girl who was so troubled that she didn't speak? So he kept his baser impulses in check. That entire, long summer.

And when it was time for Rose and her family to return to London, he knew he'd miss her. But mostly he was relieved that he no longer had to ignore the heat in her beautiful eyes or the enticing curve of her lips or the fierce arousal he felt whenever she was near. He'd planned to focus on building the future he'd dreamed of.

Still, he would have written to her. If he could have.

He sensed her behind him even before she spoke. "Don't spare my feelings. Even if the truth stings, the pain will eventually subside. It always does. Besides, I would rather feel pain than nothing."

Dried leaves swirled in an eddy on the stone path, completely at the mercy of the fickle winds. But he was not. Though he hadn't been born to a privileged family of means, he meant to take his place in the world. And he intended to do so with his integrity intact.

Responding to Rose—honestly—was a good beginning. "There are two reasons I didn't reply to your letters," he said.

"Go on, please."

"First, because our friendship seemed to be developing into something altogether different. Something that could never be. I thought it would be easier if we made a clean break of it."

"I understand. I had those feelings, too." He noted that she'd used the past tense and mentally slapped himself for wishing she hadn't. "When you didn't write back to me," she continued, "I felt as though I'd lost my best friend."

"I didn't mean to hurt you."

"But you had to know it would."

"Yes." There was no use denying it.

"You said there was another reason, too," she prompted.

He faced her, determined to speak the truth no matter how humiliating. Because even though she didn't feel the same way about him that she once had, hearing his explanation would make her understand that his failure to correspond had absolutely nothing to do with her.

And everything to do with his own shortcomings.

"The reason I didn't write after the first letter or two is because...it's because I am an awful writer." A gross understatement, but a start.

She blinked. "That's it? I wouldn't have cared, Charles. That is, I'm not particularly skilled with a pen, either, but—"

"Rose, compared to me, you're Shakespeare."

She placed her palm on her forehead, clearly confounded. "But I was desperate to hear from you. I wouldn't have given a fig about a few misspelled words or grammatical errors. Do you think me such a snob?"

He laughed—an empty, hollow sound. "You don't understand. I'm not talking about minor mistakes. I can write only the simplest, most basic of sentences. Most children over the age of seven could do better."

The confusion in her eyes gradually changed...to something resembling pity. He swallowed the bitter taste in his mouth and pressed on. "But it's worse than that. Your letters, though rarely longer than a page, usually took me several hours to decipher."

"What do you mean?"

Good God, it was mortifying to admit. "I can't read. At least not well, though it's not for lack of trying. It can take me an hour to work through a paragraph, trying to put the words together."

"I hadn't the faintest notion," she said thoughtfully, then looked up as though she'd been struck by a realization. "My letters must have seemed a chore. Like a dreaded school assignment."

"No," he answered quickly. "Never. I was always happy to receive news from you." He'd saved every letter she'd ever sent him. "I only regretted that I wasn't able to reciprocate."

"But I did receive two letters from you. How did you manage those?"

"My father wrote them for me."

"But then you left Huntford Manor."

"Yes. My father forwarded your letters to me in London. I thought about asking one of my friends to write for me, but our conversations seemed too personal to share with anyone else. Besides, you would have noticed the different handwriting."

She walked back to the bench, sat upon the quilt, and patted the space beside her, inviting him to sit. He joined her and, noting her pink nose, tucked the extra quilt around her. "So now you know the sordid truth." He shot her a wry grin. "No chance of me wooing women with poetry."

"I should think you'd do just fine without the poetry." Her gaze drifted to his lips for a moment, then slid away. "There's something else I don't understand."

"What? You may ask me anything."

"When I'd visit you at the stables, I'd often see books there—books I'd assumed you were reading. I even lent you books from my brother's library."

"I loved the books you brought—especially the myths of gods and monsters. But I didn't read them myself. My father read those stories to me in the evenings—sometimes over and over, at my insistence. I'd bring them with me to the stables each day, intent on making sense of a page or two if I had some spare time. But the main reason I carried those books around was…"

"Go on." She leaned into him, blue eyes rapt. God, she was beautiful.

"I carried those books to impress you."

"*You* wanted to impress *me*?" The look on her face was incredulous.

"Of course."

She wriggled her arms free from the quilt, reached out, and placed her gloved palms on his cheeks. "You were the center of my world, the one person who recognized that I was more than a sad, damaged girl. You made me smile, and you gave me something to look forward to. You were strong and caring and smart. Other people tried to make me feel better, but you were the only one who could. The only one who *did*."

Her fingers slid slowly downward, caressing his jaw and neck. She couldn't know what that one innocent gesture did to him. His heart pounded and his lips tingled with the desire to kiss her.

"Rose..."

"You have no idea how grateful I am. I shall be indebted to you forevermore."

He didn't want her gratitude—he wanted *her*. "You don't owe me anything. But now you know why I didn't write. I hope you'll forgive me."

"There is nothing to forgive," she said, smiling at him like he was some sort of damned hero. "Your confession has made me feel two stone lighter, for now I know that our friendship was true. That it wasn't a figment of my youthful, troubled imagination. That you felt something, too."

She was so close that he could feel her breath against his cheek. "What if I still do?"

Her eyes widened and her pupils darkened. "Charles..."

With a growl, he cupped her face in his palms and pressed his forehead against hers. The soft fur of her hood brushed his skin, and her breath warmed the tip of his nose. Her plump bottom lip taunted him like a ripe strawberry, and he barely resisted the urge to capture it between his teeth.

His heart hammered against his chest. "Damn it, Rose. Tell me to stop."

In a breathless whisper she said, "Never."

His restraint shattered. Years of pent-up longing pounded through his veins as he slanted his mouth across hers. His tongue traced the seam of her lips, and she opened to him, sighing as he explored the warm, smooth contours of her mouth. God, but she tasted good—like a mixture of honey, spice, and woman.

He pulled her closer, and her hood fell back, exposing inches of creamy skin at her neck. Groaning, he dipped his head and kissed a path from the sensitive spot beneath her ear to the hollow at the base of her throat. Her pulse fluttered beneath his lips, mimicking the erratic beat of his own heart.

He traced a path up her neck and nibbled lightly on her earlobe. In response, she moaned softly and leaned into him. It was his undoing.

Cursing, he hauled her onto his lap and speared his fingers through her hair.

This was madness. He'd thought that one taste of her would quench his curiosity and sate his hunger, but it only made him want her more.

Everything about her felt right. The soft weight of her bottom pressed against his thigh. The featherlight touch of her fingertips on his face. The silky strands of her hair beneath his palms.

Why did she have to be so gloriously passionate? And for the love of God, why hadn't she told him to stop?

Reluctantly, he slowed the pace of his kisses, lifted

his head, and soothed her swollen lips with the pad of his thumb.

Her breath hitched in her throat and she smiled at him, eyes shining. "That was..."

"Beautiful," he murmured.

"Yes."

But to him it was more than that. It had changed everything.

"I need to return to the house soon," she said regretfully, "but there's something else I'd like to know."

"What is it?"

"Why did you leave Huntford Manor? And how did you become Lady Yardley's steward?"

He'd never shared the specifics of his dreams or plans with her. Once, it had seemed foolhardy to want so much, but he'd replaced doubt with determination. "We'll have to save that conversation for another day."

Disappointment dimmed her smile. "I cannot meet tomorrow, as I'm to accompany Lady Bonneville to the Pump Room again. Shall we plan to meet here the day after tomorrow?"

He captured the auburn curl that dangled beside her cheek and rubbed it between his fingers. "Very well. But be careful. Do not come if the viscountess seems suspicious or if you think someone might follow you."

She released a long breath, creating a small misty cloud between them. "I won't."

He pulled her hood over her head and wrapped her cloak more tightly around her.

Smoothly, she slid off bench and stood in front of him. Before he could stand—before he even knew what she was doing—she placed her hands on his shoulders and leaned toward him. The hood of her cloak blocked out the world, and suddenly, only the two of them existed. He dared not move for fear of breaking the spell.

He sat motionless as Rose's lips slowly glided from one side of his mouth to the other, like she was learning the territory and mapping it for future reference. Then, with a small sigh, she breathed his name and pulled away. "Thank you for confiding in me. I'm glad we don't have any secrets."

But they did. "You don't know everything about me."

She shrugged. "I know enough." Shyly, she added, "I shall see you again in two days' time."

Yes. And then he would have to tell her about his plan to set sail for America, leaving his father, his country—and her—behind. She would no doubt come to think of him as the latest in a line of people who'd abandoned her. But there was no future for him here, and certainly no future with her, even if he wished it.

He could imagine a life with Rose in America...he just couldn't imagine asking her to leave behind everything and everyone she loved.

He stood and took her hands in his. "If I can help you find your mother, I will." It seemed important to her, and even though he had every reason to despise her mother, the duchess, it was the least he could do for Rose.

Beaming, she said, "I knew you would understand." With a graceful swirl of velvet and fur, she left him there thinking how very, very little he understood.

Chapter Six

$\mathcal{W}$hat, exactly, transpired between you and Diana?"
Lady Bonneville peered through her lorgnette and across
the coach at Rose, her expression more intrigued than
annoyed.

Caught unaware, Rose blinked. She and the viscountess had left the Pump Room and were on their way to pay
a visit to a friend of Lady Bonneville's. A moment ago the
viscountess had been sharing the latest gossip about Lord
Stanton spending too much time at the gaming tables
and playing too deep. Rose had been unable to tell if the
tidbit was meant to be a warning or a hint that the viscount might be uncharacteristically amenable to the idea
of marriage at the moment. Rose rather hoped it was the
former.

But now, out of the blue, the viscountess was asking if
Rose and Lady Yardley had had some sort of a row, which
suggested that she knew very well that they had. And that
she wanted a recounting of any salacious details. Rose

opened her mouth to reply truthfully, for Lady Bonneville was bound to learn Rose's true motivation for coming to Bath sooner or later, but then a prickling sensation stole over the back of her neck, and she reconsidered.

If she told Lady Bonneville that she was trying to locate her mother, the viscountess might insist that they pack up and return to London, where Rose would once again be under the watchful eye of her brother. Which would also mean she'd have to say good-bye to Charles— and she wasn't ready to do that yet.

"It's not a difficult question," Lady Bonneville mused. "I simply wish to know what happened between you and our hostess."

Rose snapped to attention. "Nothing untoward—that I'm aware of, that is. Did she mention anything?"

Lady Bonneville sucked in her cheeks as if to say, *So that's how it's to be then.* Placing her lorgnette on her lap, she said, "On the contrary. She seems delighted to have you at Yardley Manor and rather eager to match you up with Lord Stanton."

"I cannot pretend to share her enthusiasm for Lord Stanton," Rose offered, happy to change the subject.

Lady Bonneville's wry smile, however, said *not so fast.* "Ever since our last trip to the Pump Room, there has been some tension between you and Diana. I would not go so far as to call it animosity...more like distrust. You're like two animals circling each other."

"Pardon?"

"Trying to size up the competition."

Rose laughed a bit too loudly. "What a fanciful notion."

"Don't make the mistake of underestimating Diana. Though she may seem meek at times, she can be a formidable opponent. She'll stop at nothing to get what she wants."

Touched by the viscountess's rare display of affection— or at least as close an approximation as she was capable of—Rose leaned across the coach and patted her knee. "Don't worry. Lady Yardley is not my opponent, and I can't imagine I have anything that she covets."

"I'm not entirely sure about that, my dear. It may be something you don't even realize that you have." Lady Bonneville sighed as the coach slowed. "Ah, we have arrived."

When the coach halted, a footman opened the door. "Audrey, do go ahead with my stool. Rose and I shall follow momentarily."

As the viscountess turned her gaze upon Rose, another shiver raced down her spine. "What is it, my lady?"

"I noticed that you have been wandering on your own in the afternoons."

Rose swallowed. "Yes, perhaps once or twice."

"I trust that you are, indeed, alone?"

"I was in the garden one day. I took a stroll by the lake on the other."

"You did not answer my question, and that in itself is an answer, is it not?"

"I…"

The viscountess held up a hand. "How old are you?"

"One and twenty."

Lady Bonneville nodded firmly. "Plenty old enough to understand any risks you might be taking and the consequences of improper behavior."

Rose lowered her head. "Yes, of course."

"Do not make the mistake of assuming that being

away from Town is some sort of protection. News of a good scandal can travel from Bath to London at the same speed as a bullet shot from a dueling pistol."

"I understand."

"I'm glad that's settled. Now let's get this visit over with. You'll like Lord Haversall. He was a friend of my late brother's. I'm afraid he's always been rather taken with me."

Rose brightened a little. "And do you return his affections?"

The viscountess made a face. "He's too old and stodgy for me. Life's is far too short to follow the rules all the time. I like a man who's a bit of a rogue."

"I see," Rose said with a smile. Lady Bonneville was full of contradictions. Which made Rose like her all the more.

After returning to Yardley Manor, Lady Bonneville retired to her bedchamber for a predinner nap and Rose availed herself of the library. Lady Yardley had an impressive collection, with shelves nearly covering three walls from floor to ceiling. The room smelled of lemon wax and leather and ink—a bit like heaven. A settee and a pair of wingback chairs anchored the center of the room and created a cozy area in front of the flickering fire, perfect for losing an hour or four in the pages of a book. But it wasn't the gold silk cushions on the settee that tempted Rose.

Rather, it was the desk behind it.

Could Lady Yardley have stashed some of Mama's letters inside its drawers?

Rose walked directly to the desk, slid open the top

drawer, and peered inside. Sealing wax and seals, a few sketches of the garden and grounds, three random pieces of sheet music. Nothing resembling a letter.

She shut the drawer and opened the one beneath it. Folded maps, drawing charcoal, and blank sheets of vellum. Blast. She thrust her knee at the drawer in a clumsy attempt to shove it closed. Predictably, it jammed, and the heavy desk shook. Tears welled, and not just because of her stinging kneecap.

This was hopeless.

She'd been reduced to snooping around the manor house on the off chance that she'd find a small trace of her own mother's existence. But Lady Yardley clearly didn't want to share whatever information she had, and now that she knew Rose was looking, her chances of finding anything were slimmer than ever. Mama's letter seemed to have disappeared. What if Lady Yardley had burned it?

The very thought angered Rose. She jiggled the desk drawer until it finally slid shut with a satisfying *thud*. Who cared if someone heard her? What did she have to lose?

She spun to face the section of shelves behind the desk. Rows of leather-bound tomes were punctuated with the occasional knickknack—a cut-crystal vase, an ivory carving, a polished wooden box. Boxes could hide things—things like letters—and one caught her eye. It was painted to resemble a large book that sat on turned legs. The hinged top begged to be opened. Rose prayed the small chest wouldn't be locked.

Before she could change her mind, she lifted the cover and peered inside the velvet-lined box. Her heart sank, for there were no letters inside—at least none resembling the letter she'd seen from Mama. Instead three small scrolls, each tied neatly with a string, lay nestled inside.

The scent of rosewater tickled her nose, and she stifled a sneeze. No, whatever these papers were, they didn't belong to Mama, who had always favored expensive French perfume.

Feeling rather daring, Rose reached into the box, picked up a rolled piece of parchment, and slid the string off one end. She walked back to the desk where the light was better and spread the curled paper flat beneath her palms, slowly revealing a sketch—a portrait of some sort.

Her heart hammered and her mouth went dry. This was not just any portrait.

This was *Charles.*

It was a rough sketch, and yet Rose would have recognized those soulful eyes anywhere. With nothing more than a bit of charcoal, the artist had captured Charles's wavy, slightly too-long hair, the corded muscles in his neck, and his granite cheekbones. Even his beautiful mouth.

Rose ran a finger over the paper, tracing the curves of his upper lip, then his lower. She'd tasted those lips, felt the light stubble on his jaw against her cheek.

She would have liked to stare at the drawing forever, but she was suddenly self-conscious. Whoever drew the sketch appeared to have feelings for Charles—feelings similar to her own. Rose would have been hard-pressed to explain how she knew this, but she did. The evidence was right there on the parchment, in the laugh lines around his eyes and the hint of a smile playing on his lips.

Reluctantly, she rolled up the sketch and returned it to the box. Unable to resist, she peeked at the other two rolls.

As she'd suspected, they both depicted Charles as well. Like the first sketch, they showed him from the chest up, gazing off to one side, looking impossibly handsome, confident, and strong.

Rose carefully checked the backs for initials, a date, anything, but the sketches contained no clues as to the identity of the artist.

At least she could ask Charles about the drawings when she saw him tomorrow.

But *should* she? She had no right to pry into his personal affairs. He could pose for sketches if he chose to, and he certainly didn't owe her an explanation.

Still, she hoped for one.

How well did she really know Charles, after all? Yes, she'd listened to his stories and memorized every nuance of his voice. She'd watched him in the stables, appreciating the sure, confident movements of a man who embraced hard work. He was as far as one could get from the effeminate gentlemen who worried that their hair was tousled just so and spent an hour to ensure their cravats were tied in a fashionable knot. The perfect male specimen, Charles scoffed at fashion like a fish scoffs at swimming lessons.

But there was more to him, as Rose well knew. He could swing a hammer like a blacksmith one minute and cradle a newborn kitten in his palm the next. And he'd never judged her. Not when she was mute, and not when she spoke. Kind and true, he'd been a rock when the world she'd known was falling apart.

But time had passed. People changed. Maybe she didn't know him as well as she thought.

She'd assumed that he wasn't involved with anyone,

but something about the sketches she'd found made her question that. What if she'd kissed a man whose attentions were already otherwise engaged?

She should have been humiliated by her own brazen behavior by the pond, and she was—a little. But what she mostly felt was a venomous combination of hurt and anger. A new and foreign emotion, she nonetheless recognized it for what it was. Jealousy.

A powerful thing, for it had even made her momentarily forget that she was supposed to be searching for information about Mama. Inhaling deeply, Rose composed herself as best she could. She tucked the sketches back into the wooden box on the bookshelf and gently shut the lid. That was enough exploring for today.

Charles owed her nothing. But she would ask him for the truth.

Tomorrow.

"I've decided to host a ball." Lady Yardley sat on the edge of her seat in the drawing room, excitement oozing out of her. "It's been an age since I've entertained in grand style, and your visit provides the perfect excuse for a celebration. What do you think?"

Lady Bonneville shrugged. "I am generally in favor of parties thrown in my honor—as long as they are not dreadfully boring."

"No, boring would never do. It must be the event of the season!" Lady Yardley turned and clasped Rose's hands. "Won't it be wonderful? You shall have the opportunity to dance with Lord Stanton, and other young gentlemen as well."

Rose dragged her gaze away from the clock on the

mantel. She'd planned to meet with Charles in a half hour. Smiling at Lady Yardley, she nodded and tried valiantly to summon a bit of enthusiasm for the ball. "I look forward to it and will be happy to help with the preparations."

Lady Bonneville piped up, "Preparations can be as diverting as the ball itself—if done properly. One must employ an abundance of strategy if one wishes to host a memorable affair, and that is the goal, is it not?"

"Indeed!" Lady Yardley agreed. "The true measure of a ball's success is how unforgettable the evening is. I shall defer to your expertise on all matters."

The viscountess rolled her eyes but did seem to perk up at the idea of orchestrating the social event of the season. "There's much to be done and not a moment to spare. Rose, fetch some paper and prepare to take notes."

Now? Charles was probably already making his way to the folly. "Are you sure you wouldn't like to rest a bit before dinner?"

The viscountess lifted her lorgnette. Slowly. "I find myself suddenly energized. Have you something else to do? Somewhere else to go?"

Rose hesitated, but she couldn't very well tell the truth. "No."

"Excellent," pronounced Lady Yardley. "I'm going to ring for more tea. Shall we begin by discussing the decorations? Or perhaps the menu?"

"On the contrary." The viscountess's eyes gleamed as she tapped her lorgnette lightly against her palm. "We start with the guest list—the cast of characters. For we must know our actors and actresses before we can envision the scenery."

Lady Yardley placed her hand on her chest, clearly awed by this bit of wisdom.

"There's a daunting amount of work to be done." Lady Bonneville spoke with the command of a general rallying the troops. "We may have to forego our predinner naps for the next several days."

As the older women began making lists of Important Personages, Esteemed Ladies, and Eligible Gentlemen, Rose's heart sank. She imagined Charles standing just outside the rotunda, his body silhouetted against the dusky purple sky, waiting for her in the cold.

With a sigh, she picked up her quill and, like the good soldier she was, dutifully awaited her marching orders. But even as she wrote, her mind was busy devising a way to speak with Charles. She had to tell him that she was sorry for not showing at the appointed time. She had to ask him for his help with discovering Mama's whereabouts. And she had to find out what he knew about the sketches—the very thought of which made her heart beat faster.

Chapter Seven

Habit: (1) Ladies' riding attire, including: a fitted jacket, skirt, gloves, boots, and hat. (2) An almost involuntary, oft-repeated behavior, as in Their secret rendezvous were becoming something of a habit.

Sleet pelted Charles's face as he strode up the stone path to his cottage. In the thought-numbing cold, the freshly painted blue door looked more inviting than usual. He liked living alone, and Lady Yardley had seemed more than happy to have him occupy the abandoned structure, which had been nothing but an eyesore before he'd moved in.

Within a week of arriving at Yardley Manor, he'd rethatched the cottage's roof, cleaned the chimney, and hung new shutters on the windows. Some old furniture had been stored inside, so Charles repaired anything worth saving and used the rest for kindling.

It was tidy and comfortable and a space of his own. But it wasn't home because it wasn't really *his*. And neither was the land. He was content living here now, while he learned all he could about running an estate, but he had much bigger plans. Bigger dreams.

In America, he'd be free to pursue the life he wanted. Land of his own, and someday, a grand house to rival Huntford Manor—a house worthy of a woman like Rose.

There was little to keep him in England. He's miss his father, of course, but Charles would send him money and buy his passage to America as soon as he could. He suspected, though, that his father would choose stay in his cottage, close to the cemetery where his mother had been laid to rest after she'd died so suddenly—and needlessly.

Mama's tormented screams still haunted him. Even as a lad of eight, he'd known the birth of his baby brother or sister wasn't going well. Papa—his strong, stoic father—knelt at Mama's bedside, crying. Frantic, the midwife grabbed Charles by the collar. "Doctor Bentham is at the manor house. Bring him here," she'd said, shoving him out the door of their cottage. "Run!"

He'd flown across the vast lawn, his boots churning up grass. Breathless, he'd pounded on the servants' entrance and gasped out his request. "Mama needs Doctor Bentham...right away...it's an emergency."

The frazzled kitchen maid had whispered to the cook and the cook wiped her hands on her apron as she bustled toward the housekeeper's small office. But they all moved much too slowly for him. Didn't they understand that Mama was in excruciating pain? And that every second they dallied prolonged her misery?

He paced as he waited, his stomach clenching with dread. When the housekeeper returned, the doctor wasn't with her. "He'll be along shortly. He's attending the duchess right now. She's suffering from the devil of a cold."

"But they said to hurry." Shaking with frustration, Charles burst into tears. "They said to hurry."

The cook clucked her tongue in pity and handed him a small pastry. He hurled it across the kitchen and ran home, hoping to be of some use there. But he wasn't. He was only in the way as the midwife worked and Mama clung to life as long as she could.

Bentham had been too late. While he'd been treating the duchess—Rose's mother—for the goddamn sniffles, Mama had bled to death. The infant—a wee girl who would have been his sister—was gone, too.

Charles shook off the memory and shrugged off the pain. Grief and bitterness wouldn't get him anywhere. Only ambition and hard work would. Mama would have wanted him to make something of himself, and, by God, he wouldn't let her down. Not again.

When Rose hadn't met him at the folly, he'd taken a brisk walk to the nearest pub, where he ate dinner and drank three large glasses of ale.

Rose had been wise not to meet him. He would only demand more than she could give. Perhaps she already regretted their kiss.

The kiss he hadn't been able to forget.

He'd waited at the folly by the lake for a full hour. The cold didn't bother him, and if Rose came late, he didn't want her to think he'd given up on her. But after darkness fell, he knew she wasn't coming.

And now, as he kicked the snow off his boots on his front stoop, all he wanted was to light a fire, crawl into bed, and give himself up to dreams of a redheaded beauty with eyes that saw into his soul.

He cracked the door, startled to see a lamp burning

on the small plank table beneath the window. Suddenly wary, he reached for the dagger he kept in his boot, swung the door farther, then stopped.

"Charles." Rose was perched on a bench, petting his cat, Ash.

Dear God. He swiftly tucked the dagger away. "Rose."

Annoyed at the interruption, Ash stretched on the bench and yawned.

Charles's heart raced as he closed the door against the biting chill. "Is everything all right? What are you doing here?"

She blew out a breath slowly, as though calming herself. "I wanted to apologize for this afternoon. I tried to go to the folly, but the viscountess—"

"You don't need to explain," he said gently. "And I hope that's not the reason you risked coming here in the dark and the cold. I don't blame you for reconsidering."

"That's just it—I didn't. I would have met you if I could have. I just wanted you to know."

"How did you find my cottage?"

"You'd mentioned it was by the pond. I took a chance."

"I'll say." He glanced around the room, seeing the stark quarters as they must look through her eyes. Plain, primitive. He hung his greatcoat on a hook by the door. "How long have you been here?"

"Only a few minutes. I told Lady Bonneville's maid that I wanted to take a walk before I retired for the evening."

"She didn't find that odd?"

Rose gave a wan smile. "I'm sure she did; however, she was too kind to say so. She's accustomed to my slightly unconventional behavior. It's a benefit of being eccentric, I suppose. No one really questions my peculiar tendencies."

She lifted the cat and nuzzled him against her cheek, making Charles oddly jealous. "Isn't that right, Ash?" she cooed. "We both know how it feels to be a bit of an outcast."

"You are *not* an outsider." She shouldn't even joke about such things.

"So, you brought this little one with you." She scratched the spot just between Ash's ears, and he purred appreciatively.

"He's family." And a shared memory with Rose. That stormy morning in the woods at Huntford Manor had brought them closer…and driven them apart. The cat was a connection to her he treasured.

He knelt before the hearth to start a fire, then asked, "Would you like a blanket?" He wished he could offer her something more—but it wasn't as though he had a china serving set and freshly baked scones on hand.

"No, thank you." She clasped her hands contentedly. "Everything about this place is cozy and quaint, like a woodcutter's cottage out of a fairy tale. I confess I'm a bit envious. I'd love to have a refuge such as this."

He looked up from the grate to see if she was teasing, but she was gazing around the room like she'd discovered a secret pirate's cove.

Once the flames in the fireplace were flickering several inches high, he joined her on the bench. "You cannot stay long."

"Heavens, Charles," she teased. "That's no way to greet a guest." Ash settled himself in her lap, giving him yet another reason to be jealous.

"Yes, well, I don't do much entertaining. In fact, you're my first guest ever."

"Ever?" Her wide smile warmed him to the core.

"Yes. But that doesn't change the fact that you should not be here. A bachelor's residence is no place for a lady."

"I wish you wouldn't think of me that way."

"As a lady?" He arched a brow at her. "I wouldn't think of you any other way."

"I just meant... are you not glad that I came? Even the tiniest bit?" Her eyes crinkled at the corners and twinkled in the firelight.

"I *am* glad," he admitted. More than he had a right to be. "Now that you are here, what would you like to do?" He hadn't intended for the question to be wicked or suggestive, but it hung in the air between them, giving off more sparks than the crackling wood in the fireplace.

Blushing furiously, she took a deep breath and said, "You were going to tell me why you left and how you ended up here, at Yardley Manor—don't you remember?"

He did. And he had to tell her about his plans before things between them went any further.

"As I mentioned, you were part of the reason I left. It seemed prudent to put some distance between us." Her cheeks flushed pink again, and he continued. "But the truth is that I always planned to leave Huntford Manor."

"You always aspired to be more than a stable master," she said. "Even as a girl, I knew you'd succeed—at whatever you wished to do."

Touched by her confidence, he smiled. "You may have been the only one—besides my father. He taught me all he knew, and after I'd learned all I could about horses, I began spending time with the head gardener and the butler. Anyone who'd let me hang about—even the cook. I asked scores of questions and begged them to let me help.

I needed to make something of myself—not only for my own sake, but also for my father's. We both wanted to honor my mother's memory."

"She'd be proud of the man you've become," Rose said softly.

Charles nodded. "Perhaps. But I'm not yet the man I want to be." Damn. He shouldn't be having this conversation after three glasses of ale.

"You're not content being a steward?"

"I don't want to work for anyone else. It has nothing to do with my employers. I know I was fortunate to work for the duke. Your brother was fair, decent, and honorable. Lady Yardley has been kind to me also."

"But you are not happy being in service to anyone."

"Not for my livelihood." Under different circumstances, and in different ways, he could be very happy being in Rose's service. But that wasn't what she was asking. "I want to work for myself. I want land of my own."

"An admirable goal, but I can't imagine it will be easy."

Charles gazed into her sparkling blue eyes. "Nothing worth achieving is easy."

"That is true."

"You may remember that I had taken over as head groom when my father was thrown from a horse and badly injured. But after a few years he recovered, at least enough to oversee the stables again. I decided it was time for me to make my own way. I went to London in search of work and ended up on the docks."

"Ah, that would account for your shoulders."

"Pardon?"

"When I first saw you again, you seemed so much bigger to me. It must have been grueling labor."

Her admission warmed him. "It paid well. I saved every shilling I could. I earned a reputation as a hard worker who could be trusted, and I started getting different kinds of assignments."

Her nose wrinkled. "Different, as in more dangerous?"

He shrugged. "Sometimes. Higher paying."

"But you're not doing that kind of work anymore. What happened?"

"I met a man—Lord Landridge—in a pub near the shipyards."

"Landridge," Rose mused. "The name sounds familiar, but I can't quite place it. Go on."

"He wanted help locating a former servant who'd absconded with his wife's jewels. I found one of her necklaces at a pawnshop and was able to track down the thief and the rest of her valuables. Landridge paid me for my efforts but asked if there was anything else he could do for me. I declined his generosity at first, but he pressed me to think of something. So I told him I wanted to learn how to run an estate."

"And he hired you." Rose's eyes shone with something akin to pride, warming him inside.

Charles nodded. "He let me work beneath his steward and learn the ropes."

"That's wonderful."

"It was the opportunity I needed. I felt guilty about hiding my lack of reading ability but tried to make up for it by working longer and harder than anyone else."

Rose squeezed his hand. "I'm certain you did."

"About a year later, Lady Yardley attended a house party at his estate. She mentioned to Landridge that she needed a steward. Her former one had been stealing from her ever since her husband died. Landridge told her that though I had limited experience, I was trustworthy, and a quick study.

"The idea of me acting as the steward of a grand estate seemed far-fetched at first, but Lady Yardley met with me and offered me the position. I arrived here almost nine months ago."

"And how do you like it here?"

"I've learned much, and Lady Yardley is pleased with the improvements to the estate, but I must confess... I'm more eager than ever to strike out on my own."

"Where would you like to settle? Kent? Somerset? Hampshire?"

Charles hesitated a split second. "America."

Rose raised a hand to her mouth, then slowly lowered it to her lap. "America?" Her voice trembled. "But... why?"

"I'm sure you can guess. Lots of land. Cheap. And there, no one will care that I wasn't born into the nobility." Maybe they wouldn't even care that he couldn't read. "I'm sorry if I've shocked you."

She blew out a long breath and swiped at her eyes. "It makes perfect sense, actually, and I'm glad you told me. I just wish..."

"What?"

A tear trickled down her cheek. "That you didn't have to cross a vast ocean in order to achieve your dream."

"I don't relish the thought of leaving behind my father and friends." He wiped away her tear, hoping she understood that he'd miss her. Probably more than she knew. "England is my home... but it's not my future."

She closed her eyes briefly, then pasted on a brave face. "I think I understand."

Charles released the breath he'd been holding. Now Rose knew everything. And yet, her forehead wrinkled as though she still had questions. "What is it?" he said. "You may ask me anything."

"I am curious," she began slowly, "as to whether there's another reason you took the position as Lady Yardley's steward."

"Aside from the salary and the experience?"

Rose nodded soberly.

"I suppose it's more respectable than my previous position, but I'm not concerned with impressing anyone." Except Rose, perhaps. "Why do you ask?"

She stood and wrung her hands. "I came across something yesterday. I was somewhere I shouldn't have been, doing something I shouldn't have been doing."

The conversation was growing more interesting by the minute. "That's not like you at all, Rose," he teased. "I'm intrigued."

"It will probably sound silly to you." She faced the fire, as though she couldn't bear to look at him. "But I found some sketches."

"I see." In truth, he was as perplexed as ever. "Drawings?"

She turned and looked at him. "Yes. Three of them."

He nodded thoughtfully. "Were they . . . alarming?"

"Not particularly."

"Er, indecent?"

"No," she answered quickly. "Nothing like that. They're quite proper, but . . ."

"But you find them troubling. Why?"

"They're of you."

"*Me?* Why would someone want to draw me?"

She blushed prettily. "Well, you are quite . . . handsome."

"You must be mistaken. It's probably just an odd resemblance."

"I'm certain it's you."

"It can't be. I've never posed for a drawing."

"Still, someone could have sketched you as you worked. Or perhaps from memory."

He shook his head. "Do you have the drawings? May I see them?"

"I put them back where I found them. I didn't want Lady Yardley to know I'd been snooping around her library."

He rose from the bench and paced. "So you were doing a bit of investigating. Looking for clues as to your mother's whereabouts?"

"Yes." She hung her head. "I know I shouldn't have, but I'm growing increasingly desperate. Then I came across the sketches . . . and I didn't know what to make of them."

Understanding dawned—slowly. "Did you think that Lady Yardley and I were . . ."

She wrung her hands. "I thought it would explain why you'd accepted the position as her steward."

"You mean, why she'd offered it to me." He tried to ignore the stinging in his chest. Rose believed that he and Lady Yardley had an arrangement of some kind. He couldn't blame her for jumping to that conclusion. "Clearly, there were men more qualified for the job. Even if one ignores my difficulties with reading, I have little in the way of experience."

"I wasn't suggesting that was the reason she hired you, Charles. Everyone must know how capable and hard-working you are. She is lucky to have you on her staff."

"Even if I'm not in her bed?"

A crease appeared between her eyes, and pain flicked across her face. "I think I should go."

God, he was an ass. "Wait. I shouldn't have said that." He guided her toward the bench and sat beside her. "I don't know who drew the sketches or if they're even of me. But I can tell you that I'm in no way involved with Lady Yardley."

"I realize it's none of my concern," she said. "But I confess I'm relieved."

Odd, she sounded almost...possessive. A ridiculous thought, and yet it made his heart beat faster.

"While you were in the library," he said, "did you find any information about your mother?"

"No." Her voice was flat. "Nothing."

"You mustn't give up. Lady Yardley knows something...otherwise, she wouldn't have acted so strangely when you inquired about it."

"Do you want to know what hurts the most?"

He laced his fingers through hers and nodded.

"Mama took the time to write to Lady Yardley. And yet, in the six years since she left, she hasn't had the inclination to write to me—her daughter. She hasn't inquired about Owen, Olivia, or me. She probably doesn't even know she has a granddaughter. I think that's so sad."

The anguish on her face gutted him. "It *is* sad. But you must not take her lack of correspondence for lack of caring. My own behavior is a prime example. I didn't write to you even though I care about you. Very much."

She gave him a watery, grateful smile. "Mama can't use the excuse of being a poor reader and writer."

"There could be other reasons why writing to you is difficult for her. The most important and courageous conversations are often the most difficult to initiate. Your mother must know something of the pain she's caused you. Perhaps she doesn't know how a letter from her would be received. Maybe she thinks that you're better off without her."

"I want to believe that her lack of communication doesn't denote a lack of concern... but I'm not certain. I thought I knew her, but I really didn't."

"Why do you say that?"

"I thought she loved Papa. And us. But then I saw her... with another man... and woman." She blushed scarlet. "That's not the behavior of a loving wife and mother."

Jesus. No wonder Rose had been so troubled and withdrawn. "She wasn't faithful to your father, true. And perhaps she hasn't exactly been the model of a loving mother. But that doesn't mean she didn't love you, or that she doesn't still. She is human—just like the rest of us."

Confusion marred her beautiful features. "It almost sounds like you're condoning what she did."

"Not at all. Betraying one's family is the worst sort of offense. I'm only saying that her disappearance has less to do with you than it does with her. I suspect she's fighting her own demons."

Rose slouched a little, as though she were suddenly exhausted. "You may be correct. Somehow, no matter how anxious I feel, you've always been able to bring me a measure of peace."

He slipped an arm around her shoulders, and she leaned into him. The downy-soft fur of her collar brushed his neck, and a few tendrils of burnished hair stroked his cheek. "I'm glad you feel a little better. And there's no need to despair. After all, you've only just begun your search. Don't forget, I'm here to help you."

"At least until you set sail for America." Her voice cracked on the last word, breaking his heart.

"I won't leave until I've helped you find the answers you're looking for."

It was a promise he had no business making. He'd been saving for the journey for years, looking forward to starting his future. The last thing he needed was something—someone—holding him there on England's fair shores.

Rose shook her head. "I would never ask that of you. This is my quest, not yours, and who knows how long it will take?"

"It doesn't matter. Finding the truth about your mother is important to you. And you...well, you're important to me."

Her eyes widened, and the trace of a smile played around her mouth. Damn, he'd revealed too much.

"Thank you," she said simply, then stood. He expected her to pull on her hood and prepare to leave, but instead, she pointed at the ladder across the room that led to his loft. Eyes alight with curiosity, she said, "Another room?"

"Just a small loft."

"It looks so cozy. May I see it?"

He tried to remember if he'd folded the quilt on his mattress that morning, and shrugged. "If you'd like—as long as you won't be offended by a man's sleeping quarters."

She glided to the ladder and poised her foot on the first rung. "Hardly. I have a brother, after all." He walked to the base of the ladder as she began climbing, and she spoke to him over her shoulder. "I'm not likely to swoon if I catch a glimpse of your nightclothes on the floor."

"You don't need to worry about that," he said.

"Ah, you're the tidy sort."

"Not exactly—I sleep naked."

Chapter Eight

Naked? Dear Jesus.

Rose couldn't even pretend to be unaffected by Charles's casual revelation. Her mind filled with images of him sprawled on a mattress with nothing but a thin linen sheet twisted around his hips...if there even *was* a sheet.

She gulped and stepped onto the next ladder rung. Or, rather, she tried to.

The toe of her boot caught in the hem of her woolen skirt and she stumbled, falling forward. Her chin smacked a rung, jarring her teeth. Her legs tangled in her heavy cloak and skirts, and her heart pounded, spurred on by a potent combination of embarrassment and fear.

Just before she would have landed in a heap on the floor, Charles leaned forward and swept her into his arms. She gasped and clutched at his jacket, suddenly secure against the solid, warm wall of his chest.

"Are you all right?" His low, soothing voice calmed her nerves.

Pain radiated from her chin, but her pride was the real casualty. "Just rather embarrassed."

"Don't be." He carried her back to the cozy spot in front of the fireplace and slid the bench aside with his boot. Then he sat near the fire, letting her rest comfortably on his lap. Actually *comfortable* wasn't the correct adjective to describe what she was feeling. Though several layers of wool separated her bottom and his thigh, it felt very wicked to be perched on his leg. And also very wonderful. Her face was level with his, their noses just inches apart. She wanted to lean in, touch her forehead to his, and trace his lips with her fingertip.

"Where does it hurt?"

"Hmm?"

He gently placed his hands on either side of her head and narrowed his eyes as his gaze roved over her face. "Your face hit the ladder, didn't it?"

She sighed. She wasn't normally prone to accidents. Of all times, why did she have to be so clumsy tonight? "The side of my chin."

He touched the right side of her jaw. "Here?"

Wincing, she said, "It's just a little tender." In truth, it throbbed like the devil.

"Let me see." He angled her head toward the fire to get a better look, then brushed his fingers lightly over the sore spot. "Can you open and close your jaw?"

She did a fish imitation and immediately wished she hadn't.

"That's very good." His eyes gleamed with mischief, stirring strange feelings in her belly.

"Your bedside manner leaves something to be desired." She pouted to show her displeasure, but it was difficult to be angry with him when he looked so...so...delicious.

"Forgive me." Turning serious, he brushed a tendril of hair behind her shoulder and slid his fingers down her neck. "The injury isn't serious, but it'll leave a nasty bruise."

She shrugged. "Perhaps. A little powder should cover it."

"That's just like you." A heart-stopping smile spread slowly across his face.

"What do you mean?"

"You are brave. It's what you invariably do—cover up the hurt and press on."

She swallowed hard. "It's just a little bump on the face, for goodness sake."

"I know. But it's okay to tell me if it hurts." With that, he cupped her cheek in his hand, leaned in, and brushed his lips over her bruised chin. He lingered there for several seconds, nuzzling her neck and sprinkling kisses over her flushed skin. "How does that feel?" he whispered against her throat.

"That... doesn't hurt a bit."

"Ah, then my bedside manner is improving?"

"Markedly."

He lifted her off his knee, placed her gently on the small rug in front of the fire, and sat facing her. "Good. Because it's very important that you follow doctor's orders."

"I see." She gulped. "And what might those be?"

"First, you must absolutely avoid ladders from here on out."

"I'm afraid I cannot make any promises where that is concerned." Now that she knew what Charles wore to bed—or rather, didn't wear—she was more determined than ever to see the loft. "What other course of treatment do you recommend?"

"A little snow applied to the bruise will keep it from swelling."

"Snow?"

"Allow me." With panther-like grace, he sprang to his feet, pulled a handkerchief from his pocket, and strode to the cottage door. He ducked outside and returned a moment later with his handkerchief knotted around a snowball.

He returned to her side and placed the cold bundle against her chin. Ash crawled into her lap, nestling his head against her knee.

"He definitely remembers you."

"That day, the storm—it was so long ago."

"Maybe. But you're not the sort of person who's easy to forget." His low, gruff voice sent delicious shivers through her limbs. He set down the cold compress and took her face in his hands. "I know it isn't right for me to want you, but God help me, Rose, I do."

His admission thrilled her to the core. "I want you, too."

"Then you are as much a fool as I." He rained kisses over her cheeks, brow, and neck as if he didn't want to miss a single spot of exposed skin. His lips hot against her temple, he murmured, "The hour grows late. I should walk you back to the house."

The regret in his voice mirrored her own. "I have a little time."

"Excellent." With skilled fingers, he undid the clasp at the neck of her cloak and pushed yards of heavy velvet off her shoulders. His gaze raked over the revealing neckline of her gown, heating her skin and leaving her breathless.

As he swept a stray curl off her shoulder, he growled. The cat leaped out of her lap and scurried away.

"*Tsk*. You frightened Ash," she teased.

"What about you?"

"You could never frighten me." Reaching out, she touched the longish hair above his collar, loving the way it curled around her fingers.

Heat flared in his dark eyes—and for a moment she thought she'd offended him. "Don't make the mistake of thinking you're safe with me, Rose. I would protect you from all else—fire, storms, and any evil that might harm you—but I can't protect you from me. And I may be the biggest danger of all."

"Nonsense." She leaned forward, wantonly brushing her breast against his arm and savoring the tingling sensation it stirred. "You would never hurt me."

"True. But you and I together—we are trouble."

As if to demonstrate, he pressed his lips to hers and took her mouth, plundering with his tongue and leaving her dizzy from desire. With a tormented moan, he wrapped an arm behind her and hauled her body flush with his. As though intent on proving how dangerous he was, he slid his hand over her shoulder, down her breast, and tweaked a taut nipple through her bodice. She gasped, wishing he'd do it again, but his hand roamed lower, over the curve of her bottom. Boldly, he pulled her hips against his, letting her feel the evidence of his desire.

Which only served to stoke her own.

With calloused fingers, he traced the neckline of her gown, lingering on the swells of her breasts until she was boneless from the pleasure of it. The teasing little circles he made on the skin just below her ear left her dizzy . . . and longing for more.

She lay back on the soft rug and Charles followed.

Their mouths and bodies seemed perfectly fitted for kissing—and more. The leg he slung over hers, so muscular and male, made her want the weight of his entire body on hers, with nothing—not even a scrap of clothing—separating them.

Inexperienced and unschooled in passion, she simply surrendered to her instincts. Arching toward him, she grabbed fistfuls of his jacket and pulled him closer still.

He moaned softly into her mouth, sending ripples of delight coursing through her limbs. Somehow, she'd broken down the fortress surrounding this virile, handsome man. She'd made him forget all the reasons they shouldn't be together—even made herself forget. He cupped the back of her head and slanted his mouth across hers like he was a starving man ... and she was a feast.

"Rose," he murmured into her neck, "I want you so badly that I forget myself."

"As do I." Her voice was raspy to her own ears. "When I'm with you—no matter where I am—I never want to be anywhere else."

Charles lifted his head and glanced around the room, as though he'd momentarily forgotten they were sprawled on the floor of his cottage, their legs entwined. "Damn it." He closed his eyes for a moment, clearly disgusted with himself and with what he'd done.

With what *they'd* done.

Sitting up, he said, "Look at this place and see where you are." He seemed angry with himself and at her—but why?

She pushed herself to sitting and, suddenly chilly, turned her body toward the fire. "As I said, I would be happy anywhere with you. The place matters not to me."

"It *should*. A lady like you shouldn't have to endure advances from the likes of me. Especially not on the cold floor of an old cottage."

"I was not 'enduring' anything, and I love your cottage. I came here of my own accord. If I didn't want to be here with you, I'd simply leave."

"Actually, I think it is past time I walked you home." He stood, unceremoniously brushed off his trousers, and extended a hand to her.

She allowed him to help her up so that she'd be able to look him in the eye. Well, more or less. She wasn't about to be so easily dismissed. "I want to make sure that you understand exactly what just happened here."

"I'm all too aware." His eyes still flashed with the desire he was trying to ignore. "I think that you are the one who's acting blindly."

Drat, he did have a point. Passion was not exactly her area of expertise. However, she knew a few things. "You kissed me and I kissed you back. There was nothing unseemly or tawdry about it." Was there?

"No, but that's not the point. You deserve more respect, Rose. You should demand it."

"I think you are mistaken. I didn't feel disrespected just now." But part of her wondered if she should have. Charles acted as though he'd done something to earn her ire. Perhaps she *should* be scandalized...but she just couldn't summon anything approximating outrage. Did proper ladies normally eschew such behavior?

Her mother certainly had not. Rose had been shocked when, at the confused age of fifteen, she'd accidentally witnessed her mother's intimate encounter with an earl and a maid. It had horrified her then, for she'd never before

seen her prim mother with so much as a hair out of place.
Though Rose now understood a bit more about passion,
she couldn't help but judge Mama harshly for betraying
Papa and succumbing to her own wicked desires.

But an uncomfortable thought niggled at Rose. Maybe
she was more like her mother than she wanted to admit.
After all, she'd snuck out of the house, broken into a
cottage, and kissed Charles with no small amount of
abandon.

He eyed her thoughtfully as he scooped up her cloak
from the floor and draped it around her shoulders. "Come.
I'll take you back to the house."

She opened her mouth to inform him she didn't require
an escort, but he held up a palm. "I insist."

Silently, they prepared to brave the wild winter night.
She slipped her hood over her head while he swung his
greatcoat around his shoulders and tugged on gloves.
Wordlessly, they left the cozy comfort of the cottage and
stepped into tundra-like conditions.

The wind whipped Rose's skirts around her ankles,
and Charles tried to shield her with his body.

During the short walk to the manor house, light snow
swirled around them, floating more than falling. It would
have been magical if Rose didn't feel so...so...ashamed.
When they were a few yards from the back door, she
turned and faced him, wishing she could see more than
the vague shadow of his features.

"Shall we meet at the folly tomorrow?"

Charles looked away. "I don't think so."

"The next day then?"

"Rose, it kills me to say this...but we can't meet
anymore."

Her heart dropped. "Not at all? I was going to bring you some books, work with you on developing your reading skills."

"That's very kind of you," he said formally. Too formally. Like he was a stranger and not the man who'd been passionately kissing her only minutes before. "But it's not necessary."

"I want to help," she pleaded.

He shook his head, anguish written plainly on his handsome face. "I don't think we should be alone together—at least not for a while."

"But I only just found you." Her eyes stung—from the wind and the pain and the unjustness of it all. "And your time in England is limited. Would you say good-bye so soon, even before you leave for America?"

He clasped her hands tightly between his. "You're one of the wisest people I know. Surely you understand that I'm trying to do the honorable thing here."

She sniffled, dash it all. "Yes."

"If I should uncover some piece of information about your mother, I'll get word to you somehow. Trust me."

She did. More than he knew. And certainly more than he trusted himself.

With a slight nod, she withdrew her hands, picked up her skirts, and made her way to the door at the rear of the house. Though she felt Charles's gaze on her back, she never turned around, never waved good night. It was her little protest, her way of showing that even as her heart was breaking, she had her pride.

He could say good-bye if he wished, but he couldn't make her say it back.

Chapter Nine

*Pedigree: (1) The documented lineage of a horse,
especially a purebred. (2) A family tree, especially one showing
an impressive ancestry, as in* What he lacked in pedigree
he made up for in character and substance.

Charles avoided the manor house the next morning and
most of the afternoon. Rose's kisses were seared on his
lips, and worse, on his heart. The passion that constantly
sparked between them was dangerous—as unpredictable
as a brush fire. Someone had to stamp it out before it raged
into a blaze that consumed them both, and it appeared as
though the job would fall to him.

Pushing her away had been the hardest thing he'd ever
done. She was all he'd ever desired, warm and willing in
his arms. Last night, in the light of the fire, her blue eyes
had simmered with a passion that matched his own. Every
little moan, every hitch of her breath, betrayed her state of
arousal. He'd wanted to make her his, completely.

But he couldn't seduce her knowing full well that he'd
soon set sail for America. He'd be the worst kind of cad.

And yet, he'd been tempted—so very, very tempted. One more innocent brush of her palm over his chest, one more intoxicating taste of her tongue, would have pushed him over the edge and past the point of control.

And that was why he couldn't continue meeting with her. He didn't trust himself around her—not when they were alone. But he'd promised to help her locate her mother, and he wouldn't renege on that.

Fortunately, Lady Yardley's butler had mentioned yesterday that the ladies would be going to the Assembly Rooms for tea at four, which would give him a window of at least two hours in which to do a bit of investigating.

He waited until Lady Yardley's coach rumbled down the drive, then set off toward the manor house. Rose's footprints from the night before were etched in the snow along the path, and he trampled over them, dragging his boots to wipe out the evidence of her late night visit. He tried not to think about the sadness in her eyes when he'd pushed her away or the anguish in her voice when she'd said she'd only just found him.

Of course he didn't want to stay away from her. Everything in him longed to claim her, to make her his, now and forever. But one of them had to be sensible. The sooner Rose accepted that she'd be better off without him, the sooner she could begin looking for a suitable husband—one who was rich and titled and intelligent. Someone who could give her everything she deserved without uprooting her to a distant and foreign land.

Swallowing the bitterness in his throat, he approached the front door and waited for Evans to admit him.

The butler opened the door with the haughty glare Charles had come to expect. Most of the staff accepted him as one of their own, grateful that he'd replaced the former steward whose corrupt dealings had threatened the entire estate, but Evans remained aloof and vaguely suspicious.

"Lady Yardley and her guests are out, Mr. Holland. I presume you've come to review the books?"

Charles glared back at the butler and angled his shoulders through the doorway. "Yes. I think I'll work in the study."

"Very good," Evans said, in a tone suggesting the visit was anything but. "Would you like anything? Tea or refreshments?"

"No, thank you." He didn't want interruptions while he searched on Rose's behalf. Reading random correspondence, without any context, would require his full attention. At least he'd have no trouble identifying the words *Sherbourne* and *Huntford*. Those were in his mental lexicon, imprinted on his memory. If he could explore freely for one hour, surely he'd turn up some scrap of information. Something that would be valuable to Rose.

He made his way to the study, which boasted a wall of built-in shelves, floor-to-ceiling windows, and a massive desk. The centerpiece of the room, the mahogany desk was designed to instill power in whomever sat behind it and to impress whomever sat in front of it. A small globe sat on one corner and a pristine blotting mat lay in the center.

He left the door open so as not to raise suspicion and immediately pulled three volumes of ledgers from a shelf behind the desk. He stacked two on the side of the desk and opened one so that if anyone entered the room it would look as though he were examining the books.

Then he sat in the chair and began exploring.

Though he couldn't give Rose everything she wanted, he could do this one thing. For her.

The heated brick beneath Rose's feet did nothing to warm the cold, hollow feeling inside her. After taking tea in the Upper Assembly Rooms, she, Lady Bonneville, and Lady Yardley were now in the coach, rolling toward the manor house. Snowflakes danced by the window like fairies celebrating the arrival of winter. Meanwhile, Rose mourned for summers past and the long, carefree days she'd spent with Charles. She'd taken those days for granted, never realizing what a gift they were—

Ouch. Lady Bonneville had poked her knee with her lorgnette, and now glared at her from her seat across the coach. "Ye gads, gel. You are not attending to this conversation in the least."

"I believe she's tired, Henrietta," Lady Yardley said in a stage whisper. "Look at the dark smudges beneath her eyes. Perhaps we should wait and have this conversation at another time."

Her curiosity piqued, Rose rubbed her knee and sat up straighter. "Forgive me, I was woolgathering. What is it?"

Lady Yardley cast a questioning look at Lady Bonneville, who nodded solemnly, sending a chill skittering down Rose's spine.

"Henrietta and I have been discussing this...this... quest of yours to locate your mother."

Lady Yardley had discussed Mama with the viscountess? Hope flared in Rose's chest. "Do you have news for me?"

"Patience, my dear." Lady Yardley's words were kind, but there was a slight edge to her voice. "It is just this sort of overzealousness that gives me pause. However, Henrietta feels you are entitled to know what has become of your dear mother, so I will tell you."

God bless Lady Bonneville. She might be a far cry from a fairy godmother, but in this instance, she'd certainly worked a little magic. Rose would have leaped across the coach and hugged her if she hadn't known the viscountess would detest any show of affection.

"Please," Rose said.

"Very well." Lady Yardley raised a gloved hand and pointed her finger. "But first you must promise me that you will accept what I'm about to tell you with the grace and dignity befitting the sister of a duke."

She would have promised anything in that moment. With a calmness that belied the churning of her belly, she said, "Of course. I promise."

Lady Bonneville nodded approvingly. Not unkindly, she said, "I remember how close you were to your mother, Rose. You must understand that things can never be as they were before."

Rose wanted to yell *Why not*? Instead she bowed her head demurely. "I understand."

Lady Yardley cleared her throat. "I did, in fact, receive a very brief letter from your mother several months ago. I do not know her specific address, but she wrote that she was living in a villa in the French countryside. Apparently, she's quite happy."

Several seconds passed as Rose waited for more information. Surely, there was more. When none came, her questions rushed out. "Who is she living with? How long has she been there? Does she ever plan on returning to England?"

Lady Yardley raised an elegant brow. "Remember—grace and dignity."

Rose checked the impulse to throttle her. "I am grateful for this news and beyond relieved to hear that Mama is well. I'd just like to know a bit more about her situation."

"I'm afraid I've told you all that I know."

"But you must have some idea of whom she's staying with. Did she mention any names at all? Or perhaps give a hint of the village or town she's in?"

"No and no," Lady Yardley said smoothly. She turned to the viscountess. "I do hope this wasn't a mistake."

"It wasn't," Rose protested. "I have a right to know what's become of my mother. And I don't think there's anything wrong with asking questions...especially if they lead to the truth."

"The truth is often unkind," Lady Bonneville said softly. "You are not a child. You've heard the rumors about your mother. Her scandalous behavior has made her—and anyone who would dare associate with her—a pariah. She made her bed, so to speak. I know this is difficult, but it is time for you to let go of the past."

Difficult? It was nigh impossible.

Closing her eyes, Rose whispered. "I'm not sure I can let go."

Lady Bonneville leaned forward and patted her knee. "Diana has shared all that she knows. We must leave it at that."

Rose nodded. What choice did she have? In as gracious a tone as she could muster, she addressed Lady Yardley. "Thank you for telling me about the letter. Just knowing that Mama's alive and well is a comfort and a weight off my shoulders."

"I should imagine it is." Lady Yardley smiled a bit too sweetly.

Rose turned again toward the small window. As she watched the sun sink in the sky, she tried to picture Mama living in a villa. It wasn't difficult to imagine her in a beautiful house complete with elegant furnishings and stunning views of the lush countryside. Such a place would be the perfect backdrop for Mama's beauty and charm. But who was she with? And how could she be content to live there so distant from her children—even if they were grown?

As though privy to her thoughts, Lady Bonneville said, "You will never have all of your questions answered, Rose. That, unfortunately, is a fact of life. But at least you know more than you did this morning, and the news is heartening. I do hope that you will begin to think of your future."

Ah, yes. That had been Rose's plan all along, hadn't it? To discover what happened to her mother so that she could make her peace with it and move on. Why, then, did she still feel so unsettled?

The viscountess stared as though she were seeing through Rose, to her very center. She barely resisted the urge to squirm.

At last, Lady Bonneville said, "Your future shall be happy. I'm almost never wrong about these things, you know."

Rose rallied a smile for the viscountess's sake. "Yes, your record is impressive." She'd been credited with predicting several great matches, including the one between Anabelle's sister, Daphne, and her handsome war hero, Ben. But Rose wasn't like Daphne, beautiful and determined. She wasn't like Olivia either, passionate and headstrong.

She was the quiet one, content as long as she could be near her family. Until recently, spinsterhood had seemed a perfectly acceptable option. But now that she'd tasted passion with Charles, she yearned for more—companionship, pleasure, love.

"Time is of the essence," Lady Yardley warned. "With each season that passes, the field of suitable, prospective husbands narrows. You would be wise to devise a strategy and employ it at once."

"Strategy?"

Lady Yardley sighed as though she found the depths of Rose's naïveté thoroughly dismaying. "Too many young ladies rely on fate to deliver them into the arms of the proper husband. A romantic notion"—Lady Bonneville snorted, indicating her agreement—"but a foolish one. You must give fate some assistance. Take matters into your own hands...with Lord Stanton, for instance."

Rose glanced out the window, hoping to see evergreens lining the drive that would signal they were close to the manor house. They couldn't be more than a few minutes away, and she desperately wished this conversation would cease. But now that Lady Yardley had begun to impart helpful advice, she did not seem inclined to stop.

"He is a fine, proper sort of gentleman. You couldn't do much better than him, dear."

Rose noticed Lady Bonneville rolled her eyes slightly at the declaration. Rose couldn't help thinking that she *could* do better than him. Not in the way that Lady Yardley thought—richer, more respected, or in possession of a better title. Only that there was someone better for *her*—if only Charles were open to the possibility.

But after last night, Rose had to accept that he was not.

He wanted to avoid her, keeping matters between them uncomplicated. He wanted to keep a razor-sharp focus on his dream of sailing to America and becoming a wealthy, respected landowner.

She couldn't—wouldn't—begrudge him his dream.

Even if she longed for the young man who'd been happy lying in the fields and looking up at the sky . . . with her.

"Lord Stanton will attend our ball three days hence," Lady Yardley rambled on. "He's already quite smitten with you. With a modicum of encouragement, you could have him courting you by the final dance and proposing before Christmas. Imagine how delighted your sister and brother would be to hear the happy news." As if it were all but accomplished. But Lady Yardley was correct—Olivia and Owen *would* be thrilled to learn she was happily engaged.

They only wanted what was best for her . . . and Rose wanted to please them. Perhaps it was time for her to take the advice everyone was giving her, to try to fit the mold for once, and embrace the opportunities she'd been given. It was time to find a husband.

She took a deep, heartening breath and resolved to let go of the hurt and longing of her past. Attempting a bright smile, she said, "It seems we have a bit of strategizing to do in the next three days."

"That's the spirit," Lady Yardley said approvingly. "I believe the first and most pressing matter we must address is your ball gown."

Charles had methodically checked each desk drawer in the study. He'd looked inside every book, every cubby, on the shelves behind him. He'd examined every decorative item, from bookends to vases to sculptures, in case there was a false bottom or a hidden compartment that could house a letter. He'd even checked the floorboards beneath the thick carpet to see if they were removable.

He'd found nothing.

Discouraged, but unwilling to give up, he closed the ledgers, returned them to the shelf, and quietly made his way to the library. A glance at the grandfather clock in the foyer told him he had at least a half hour before the women returned, and he didn't intend to waste it. If Lady Yardley had hidden sketches in the library, perhaps she'd hidden other items there as well.

Charles hoped that she had, because the two other likely possibilities were less than optimal. The first alternative was that she'd destroyed the duchess's letters, and Rose would never get to read them. The second was that Lady Yardley had removed them to her bedchamber, which would make them extremely difficult to retrieve— he couldn't exactly claim to be reviewing ledgers at her dressing table.

No, the library was infinitely more accessible. If a servant questioned his presence there, he'd just say that he was searching for a volume on flora so that he could identify a specific tree on the outskirts of Lady Yardley's land. That was plausible enough. Still, he hoped to slip in and out undetected.

His shoulders tensed as he opened the door and entered. Seeing hundreds of book spines lined up and flaunting mostly indecipherable titles made him uncomfortable. It was like walking into a gathering where everyone knew a secret but him.

Illuminated only by the waning daylight, the room was

gray and chilly, but he didn't want to risk lighting a lantern, much less a fire. He'd search for a few minutes and when light ran out, he'd know his time had as well.

He didn't waste time on the desk or any other obvious spots, since he trusted Rose had already covered those. Instead, he flipped up the corners of the rug and lifted the cushions off footstools. He checked small drawers in side tables and the tops of shelves.

And then he saw the box that Rose had described—the one that held the sketches.

Through the multipaned windows he glimpsed the sun sinking into the tree line, but this wouldn't take long. And he simply couldn't resist the chance to see if Rose had been correct—if the subject of the sketches was him.

He flipped the box's lid open, found the scrolls inside, and plucked one from its velvet bed. He slid the string off and unrolled the paper.

Holy hell.

Unless he had a secret twin brother, the drawing was of him. Or, rather, some romanticized version of him. The clothes worn by his charcoal likeness were more elegant than anything Charles actually owned or wore, and his hair looked like it had been intentionally tousled and arranged to curl in front of his forehead. He was more of the towel-dry-and-forget-it sort of chap.

But the shape of the face, the eyes, and the torso— those were unmistakably his.

That realization stunned him to the core, for this was no simple, straightforward, unassuming portrait. The tone of it was intimate, personal.

And he suddenly understood why it had affected Rose so much that she felt the need to seek him out at his cottage.

He moved toward the window and inspected the drawing more closely, looking for a signature or some clue as to where and when it might have been drawn.

Damn it all, he didn't want to admit the most obvious possibility—that his employer had drawn it. He knew nothing about her hobbies or if she was artistically inclined, but it was her library, after all.

He scanned the room for other artwork. A gold-framed oil painting hung between the windows. The landscape of muted browns and greens featured a lone rider on a horse, but at some distance. It was difficult to say if the artist's style was similar to the sketch—they were too different in composition and medium.

The only other artwork in the room was a large portrait above the fireplace. Charles had never studied it before, but he recalled Evans mentioning it was Lady Yardley's late husband. The earl relaxed on a stone bench beneath a tree, wearing the smile of a man who hadn't a care in the world. Like the sketch, this portrait had an air of intimacy about it. Merely viewing it made him feel as though he'd intruded on a private moment.

He moved closer to examine the lower right corner and found a scrawled signature, but it was difficult to make out in the waning light. He held the corner of the frame and leaned forward, hoping to decipher a few letters—

And the painting moved. Not side to side, as he would have expected, but toward him, as though it were a door on hinges. His first panicked reaction was to return the painting to its former position. He had no legitimate reason for being in the library, and if someone discovered he was responsible for damaging Lady Yardley's portrait of her beloved late husband he'd be sacked on the spot.

But wait. There was something very strange about the way the painting had moved, almost like it was intended to swing outward. Cautiously, Charles pulled on the right side of the frame once more. With an eerie creak, it glided toward him.

In the shadows behind the painting, a small cabinet was nested in the wall, its face flush with the library's brocade wallpaper.

Good God. It was the stuff of spy stories—the sort of fantastical tales his father had read to him as a boy.

He hesitated. A cabinet like this one was likely designed to hold valuables, and Charles was no thief. He only wanted to help Rose find her mother. Now that Lady Yardley knew Rose was searching for information, she could well have hidden letters there.

Though his conscience niggled, he couldn't pass up an opportunity like this—especially since it might never present itself again.

So he reached for the small knob on the cabinet door, expecting to find a hidden lock or some other obstacle to opening it. When he tugged on the handle, however, the door easily opened, revealing the cabinet's contents.

There was a velvet box, a small pistol, a large drawstring purse, a stack of legal-looking papers, and—right in the front—a small bundle of letters.

The notes could have been from anyone, but the prickling sensation on the back of Charles's neck told him they were from Rose's mother, the duchess. There was one way to confirm his suspicion. He reached into the cabinet but froze at the sound of throaty laughter coming from the corridor.

Damn. Heart pounding, he grabbed the top letter from

the bundle and stuffed it into his jacket pocket. He swung the portrait back into place, effectively closing the cabinet door at the same time. Then he scooped up the sketch of him—which he'd set on the mantel—and rolled it as he darted across the room toward the shelf where he'd found it. He barely had time to slip the string back on the scroll, drop it in the wooden box, and close the lid before Lady Yardley swept into the room.

He quickly yanked a book from the shelf in front of him and pretended to examine the spine.

"Why, Mr. Holland," she purred. "Evans said you were working in the study. I didn't expect to find you in here... all alone."

Chapter Ten

I hope it wasn't too presumptuous of me." Charles bowed politely to Lady Yardley, wondering if his face looked as hot as it felt. What was his excuse for being in the library? Oh yes, the tree. "I was looking for a book that might help me identify a certain tree."

Eyeing the volume in his hand, she arched a brow. "And so you picked up Byron's poetry?"

"I, ah . . . I suppose I became distracted."

Lady Yardley glided closer and shot him an assessing look. "I would not have taken you for a lover of poetry."

"I'm not," he said quickly. "It just happened to catch my eye."

"I confess, I'm intrigued by this side of you, Mr. Holland. You and I normally discuss such mundane topics. The effects of the dry weather on the fields, the larger repairs required about the estate, accounting matters. It's all so dreadfully boring, isn't it?"

"I don't think so, no."

"Tell me, what is your favorite poem?"

"I don't have one."

"Don't be coy." Stepping closer, she smiled suggestively, and there was no mistaking the look in her eyes. It invited him to forget that she was his employer, to think of her purely as a woman. An interested, willing, and available woman.

This was bad. Not because he was tempted to accept her unspoken offer, but because he wasn't. He didn't want to hurt her feelings. She'd been kind enough to hire him, to give him a chance in a position for which he had little experience. And she'd lost her husband just a couple of years ago. It had to be difficult, becoming a widow at a relatively young age. She couldn't be more than forty years old. Maybe Rose's suspicions were correct and Lady Yardley *had* hired him because she was interested in him—not as a steward, but as a man. But no matter the reason, he'd gotten the job—he couldn't afford to lose it.

He sensed he was perilously close to jeopardizing his position at the moment.

So Charles ignored her invitation and tried for a change of subject. He pointed at the picture above the mantel. "Did you paint that? Your husband's portrait?"

Her eyelids drooped as she stared across the room at the likeness of the man she'd married. "I did. I still miss him."

"I'm sorry." He hadn't intended to make her sad. "It's a wonderful portrait. I never had the pleasure of knowing him, and yet I can see that he was kind ... and very much in love with you." He shouldn't have added that last part, but she looked so dejected, so forlorn, and he thought it might cheer her.

It had the opposite, unintended effect of making her burst into tears.

In a matter of seconds, her face turned red as a beet and tears streamed down her cheeks and off her chin.

"Forgive me." Charles fumbled in his pocket for his crisp handkerchief, found it, and thrust it at her. "It's none of my affair, I shouldn't have said anything." He wanted nothing so much as to slink out of the room and to forget the entire encounter.

"No, no," she gasped. "I am glad that you mentioned him. It seems I never get to talk about him anymore. This house...it's desperately lonely without him. And I...I see him, not just in his picture, but in his things...everywhere I look."

With this, she began to cry even harder, sobs racking her body.

Charles stood there stiffly, unsure what to do. "Shall I call someone for you?"

"No, I—"

She staggered and quickly gripped the edge of the shelf, but then her legs buckled and she crumpled to the floor.

Good God. He fell to his knees beside her and searched her face. She had not fainted exactly, for she was still alert and crying. "Let me help you sit up," he suggested.

Sniffling, she nodded. He slipped an arm around her and helped her to sit upright, her back against the bookshelves. As he knelt beside her, her sobs subsided a little.

"I'm going to ring for your maid to assist you."

"Please, no." She stared up at him with red, watery eyes. "I don't want anyone else to see me like this. Just help me to the sofa over there. I only need a few moments to compose myself."

"Very well." He held out a hand and she took it, but when she attempted to stand, her legs wobbled like a newborn colt's.

"You'll have to carry me," she said breathlessly.

Warning flares shot off in his head, but surely she was too distraught to have wicked intentions.

Shaking off his doubts, he crouched and lifted her in as gentlemanly a manner as he could manage. With one arm behind her back and another beneath her knees, he stood, strode across the room to the sofa, and leaned over to deposit her on the gold silk cushions.

Except that, when he let go—she didn't.

He reached behind his neck to unclasp her hands, but she kept them locked tightly together. He would have yanked on one of her arms to free himself if he wasn't afraid he'd snap one of her bones in the process. "Lady Yardley," he began.

"Please, you must call me Diana." Her breath, smelling faintly of wine, wafted over his face. "It feels so wonderful to be in your arms."

"You're not," he said firmly. "I thought you were hurt, so I carried you."

Still clinging to his neck, she said, "So easily, too. I admire that about you, you know—your strength, your masculinity."

Bloody hell. "I must go now."

Ignoring this, she ran a hand down his arm, arched her back, and thrust her breasts toward him. "You have the body of a Viking, you know. I would not mind seeing more of it."

Dear Jesus. How much wine had she had?

She reached for his shirt as though she meant to tear

it off him. He backed away quickly and stood, but she launched herself at him. Her torso collided with his and when she started to bounce off, he caught her so she wouldn't end up on the floor. Again.

"Ahem." Evans, the butler, stood in the doorway wearing a look that was half disgust and half amusement. "Is everything all right, Lady Yardley?"

She immediately put some distance between her and Charles, then smoothed the front of her skirt. "Quite. Just a bit clumsy, I fear. I almost tripped. Thank heaven Mr. Holland was here to steady me."

The butler arched a brow at Charles as though he were putting all the pieces of a perplexing puzzle in place. "Very well then. I heard some...commotion, but if I'm not needed here, I'll return to my duties."

"Thank you for your concern, Evans." Lady Yardley patted her hair, the dignified countess once more.

The moment the butler left, Charles bowed politely. "Good evening, Lady Yardley."

"It's just Diana, remember...Charles?"

"I'd prefer to address you properly, my lady."

She sauntered closer, and when he took a step back, she chuckled softly. "Call me whatever you like," she said breathlessly. "We can continue our...conversation another time."

"As you wish." He would have said anything to extract himself from the library—and her company—at that moment.

He was almost to the doorway when she called out, "Did you find what you were looking for?"

Stopping dead in his tracks, he swallowed. The letter he'd swiped was still in the pocket of his jacket. He hoped. But she couldn't be referring to that. Ah, the *book*. "I did not," he said smoothly. "Perhaps next time."

"Yes, surely you shall have better luck next time." Lady Yardley cast him a wicked smile. "I am certain we both shall."

Rose's morning had included a trip to the bustling milliner's shop and calls to three of Lady Bonneville's acquaintances in Bath. It seemed there was no one the viscountess didn't know. Upon returning to Yardley Manor, the butler presented Rose with a stack of replies about the ball— which was only two days away. To date, only one person had sent his regrets. Actually, his daughter sent them as he was unable to reply himself, on account of his being deceased. Everyone else had responded in the affirmative.

All the shopping, visiting, and planning had left Rose frazzled. The constant conversation sapped her energy. More than anything, she craved solitude, so when Lady Bonneville announced she was retiring to her bedchamber for a nap, Rose seized the chance to escape to the garden for a rejuvenating walk.

The moment she stepped outside, the fresh, if chilly, air soothed her frayed nerves. Alone with her thoughts, she strolled through the mostly dormant garden, pausing now and then to imagine what it would look like in all its midsummer glory.

Unfortunately, every curve of the path reminded her of Charles and the day that they'd met in the garden—the day he'd said he cared for her.

Only, it seemed he didn't care enough. The distance he was putting between them hurt more than she'd thought possible. She'd been left before—first by her mother and then by her father—but her relationship with Charles was not based on blood. They had an emotional connection so strong she would have sworn it was physical. Even now, as she thought of him setting sail for America, her head pounded and her chest ached.

But she'd healed before. She would again. She had no choice.

Pushing thoughts of him from her mind, she walked to the far corner of the garden where a few evergreens created a secluded spot. She sat on a bench, intending to formulate a plan for finding Mama—or to at least decide on her next steps.

Meow.

Rose leaned over and peeked beneath the bench. Ash stood, stretched, and rubbed himself affectionately against her ankles.

Laughing, she scratched the top of his head, just between his ears. "What are you doing here? Looking for a peaceful spot, too? Sorry to disrupt your nap."

The cat meowed his forgiveness, then closed his eyes in purr-filled bliss as she stroked his back.

"What shall become of you when Charles leaves?"

The cat paced before Rose's feet, as if he, too, worried about the prospect of being alone.

"You'll always have a home with me," she whispered.

"Am I interrupting?"

Rose jumped as Charles walked down the stone path, closing the distance between them in a few powerful strides.

"I was hoping Ash would help me find you," he said.

"You were looking for me?"

"Do you have a moment to talk?" His tone turned serious, sending chills through her limbs.

"Of course."

They settled themselves on the bench, and the cat leaped up and nestled himself against Rose's hip, as though he sensed she needed a warm companion.

"First, I want to apologize for my behavior the other night at my cottage. I handled every aspect of that evening badly."

"You needn't apologize for being truthful. Or for following your dreams. I envy you, you know."

"You do?" His forehead crinkled. "Why?"

"Because you needn't bow to others' expectations of you. You can live your life the way you want to."

Nodding thoughtfully, he said, "That's true."

"Please, don't misunderstand. I know I'm awfully fortunate. Being born to a duke and duchess has given me every advantage. And I'm doubly blessed to have a brother, sister, and even a half sister whom I adore."

He raised an eyebrow at the mention of her half sister, Sophia. She'd forgotten he didn't know about her. All the gossip rags had reported that the former Duke of Huntford had fathered a child with a bookshop clerk, but Charles wasn't versed in the latest scandals, and Rose had no wish to steer their conversation off course. "I'll have to tell you about Sophia another time. The point is, I'm extremely fortunate."

"But...?"

"But now I must play the part I was born to."

Frowning, he asked, "Which means?"

"I must enter the social whirl, marry well, and become a respectable member of society." But perhaps not right away—not if she could help it. "I owe that to my family."

He pressed his lips together in a thin line. A muscle ticked along the left side of his jaw. She sensed he wanted to say something... but he didn't.

"It won't be a bad life," she assured him. "I'm sure I shall be content."

"But that's not the same thing as being happy."

"No, it is not." Her words echoed in the silence that followed. She rubbed Ash beneath the chin, grateful for his camaraderie.

At last, Charles said, "So you have decided to marry a wealthy, titled husband and live the life you were meant to." She didn't think she imagined the barely contained jealousy that seethed beneath his skin, but it was little consolation.

She wanted to tell him that she'd change her mind in an instant if she could spend a lifetime with him. "Yes."

"Does that mean you've given up on the idea of finding your mother?"

"No," she said quickly. "I'm more determined than ever. Just yesterday, Lady Yardley told me that Mama's living in the French countryside, but she couldn't be more specific than that."

"Couldn't or wouldn't?"

"I'm thinking the latter. I'm almost certain that Lady Yardley knows more than she's telling me, and I'm not going to be satisfied with half-truths. If I never learned what happened to Mama, I think I'd go quite mad. I must find her. Or at least learn what's become of her."

Charles took a deep breath. "In that case"—he withdrew a paper from the breast pocket of his jacket and held it out—"this is for you."

Chapter Eleven

Filly: (1) A female horse under four years of age.
(2) A spirited young woman, as in Young bucks prowled
the ballroom in search of wide-eyed fillies.

Rose stared at the paper in Charles's hand. "What is it?"

"A letter. From your mother."

Blood pounding in her ears, she pressed the folded sheet of parchment against her chest. "Where did you find it?"

"In Lady Yardley's library."

"Have you read it?"

"No. I only looked for the signature at the bottom, and when I saw her name I folded the letter and put it away until I could give it to you. I don't know if it will answer any of your questions, but I thought you'd want to find out for yourself."

She cast him a grateful smile. "I do. I hope you didn't put yourself or your position at risk in order to obtain the letter for me."

He glanced away, providing her answer. "It was the least I could do. I want you to have your answers, to be happy."

How easy he made it sound. "Where did you find it? Was this the only letter?"

He hesitated briefly, then said, "There's a small cabinet hidden behind the portrait above the fireplace where Lady Yardley keeps a pistol and valuables. Other letters were stashed there, but I only had time to grab the one."

Rose blinked. "Lady Yardley has a secret cubby?"

"So it would seem. But promise me that you won't try to access it. The less you are involved, the better."

She chafed at his words. "I disagree. This has to do with my mother, and I *should* be involved. Of all people, I thought you understood."

"I do. All I ask is that you give the letter to me when you're finished with it. It should be fairly simple for me to slip into the library and return it to the cabinet before Lady Yardley realizes it's missing."

"Very well." But she was glad to know about the hiding spot. If the letter she held failed to shed light on Mama's whereabouts, she could likely find others.

As though he'd read her thoughts, Charles said, "If you need me to retrieve additional letters, I will."

"I wouldn't ask that of you. You've risked enough already."

His eyes drifted downward, to the letter she still clutched to her breast. "Are you going to read it now?"

"I don't think so. I doubt my ability to remain composed."

"Do you think that it will contain bad news?"

"Yes. And I fear that it will contain all good news. For if I discover that Mama is happy living her life without me—her daughter—then I shall be sadder than ever."

He frowned. "The letter is bound to bring you pain then, no matter what it says."

"Yes."

"And yet you're determined to read it."

"I must."

He folded her into his arms, instantly enveloping her in warmth and strength. She leaned into him as though it were the most natural thing in the world, and when he brushed his lips across her forehead, her heart did a cartwheel.

"I hope you get your answers, Rose." Charles's voice, low and gravely, washed over her like a healing rain. "But more than anything, I hope you realize that no matter what you learn about your mother, you deserve love. She may be able to give it...she may not. But one thing I know for certain is that you *deserve* it. And more."

Sniffling, Rose folded the letter and tucked it deep into the pocket of her cloak. "You say that, and I believe that you mean it."

He pulled back to look at her face, his expression slightly offended. "Of course I do."

"Then why do I feel so alone?" So pathetically unwanted.

"Because some mothers—and fathers—just don't have the right instincts. I've seen it dozens of times with animals." Ash flicked his tail, right on cue. "It's not fair, but that's the way of the nature. Don't let your parents' failings define you."

He was right.

In that very moment, with Charles's arms securely around her, she made a silent vow. If any failings were going to define her, they were going to be her own. And if she failed, she planned to do so spectacularly.

No time like the present.

"When I mentioned earlier that I'd decided to begin the search for a suitable husband I left out an important detail."

Charles's raised brow was one part curiosity, two parts suspicion. "I'm listening."

"I'm not quite ready to shackle myself to a man in a loveless marriage."

"It certainly doesn't sound appealing when you put it like that."

"No. That's why I've decided that before I marry I shall experience pleasure."

Charles nearly choked. "Pleasure?"

"Yes. Passion, physical love, coupling—"

He held up a hand. "No need to elaborate."

"Does this make you uncomfortable? Because I'd rather hoped—"

"Don't say it."

She blinked innocently. "What? That I hoped you would be my guide?"

"Jesus. We're not talking about a bloody tour, here."

"That's precisely why I need someone whom I trust and . . ."

"And?"

"And someone who makes my heart beat fast with every touch."

Charles swallowed. "Rose."

Soberly, she took his hand and tugged off his glove. Then she guided his hand beneath her cloak and placed it on the left side of her chest. His warm, calloused palm skimmed the swell of her breast, sending delicious tremors through her. "You see? No other man has this effect on me."

"You don't know what you're asking."

"Perhaps the idea of me seeking an introduction to pleasure seems rash to you."

"You could say that."

"But it makes perfect sense. I don't think I've imagined the unique attraction between us...have I?"

He closed his eyes briefly. "God, no."

"Excellent. Then you won't find the task terribly unappealing or taxing?"

"On the contrary. Loving you could never be a hardship." He slid his hand down, cupping her breast and grazing her nipple with his thumb. "That's the problem, you see. I think I might like this task...too much."

Desire and delight swirled in her belly. "Oh," she said breathlessly, "this is proving to be an excellent first lesson."

With a low growl, he hauled her against him. "Here's the second."

His kiss was raw and wild, designed to deter her current reckless course of action.

It didn't.

Everything Charles did thrilled her. He had one hand on her nape, tugging on the curls dangling there. He let his other hand roam beneath her cloak, over her breasts, hips, and between her thighs. When he pulled her onto his lap, she had to resist the very unladylike urge to straddle him. The evidence of his desire pressed against her bottom and she had a second improper urge to strip off his clothes, which she also managed to resist.

But only barely.

She adored seeing Charles so passionate, so out of control. Nothing about his kiss was expected. He explored her mouth with abandon, his tongue tangling with hers. The light stubble on his upper lip and jaw abraded her skin, leaving a tingling sensation in its wake. Every nerve ending in her body felt intensely alive, making her wonder if she'd been in a trance for the first twenty-one years of her life.

The feeling was too magical to ignore, too rare to suppress. Even her genteel upbringing and years of cautionary tales were no match for the thrill of being in his arms. She had to experience more of passion, and she couldn't imagine being intimate with anyone but Charles.

The best part was that he seemed similarly affected by their kiss. He held her like he wanted her for himself, like he never wanted to let her go.

Which would have been perfectly acceptable to her.

She poured all the happiness and heartbreak of the past week into her kisses. He needed to know that she would never shy away from him. That she was stronger than the girl he remembered. That she was a woman with desires of her own. She speared her hands through his hair and wriggled her bottom against his erection, loving the tortured groan it earned her.

"You're going to be the death of me, you know." But he didn't sound as though he minded.

"Then you'll help me?" She gazed into his beautiful, heavy-lidded eyes, willing him to say yes.

"I *should* say no."

"But you won't?"

"I think we should wait and see how you feel in a week or so."

"A week?" It may as well have been a lifetime. "I'm not going to change my mind about this."

"Then a few days won't make a difference."

"Our time together is finite. I'll be here with Lady Bonneville for only another fortnight. You'll likely be on a ship bound for America before we meet again. We don't have time to waste."

"That is true."

"So why would you delay?"

"It's easy to be carried away in a moment. But memories last. Actions have consequences."

She shook her head, confused by his platitudes. "What are you saying?"

"Our lives are leading us down different paths, and we can't change that, even though we might like to. Years from now—hell, *days* from now—I don't want you to think back on me as a regret."

Solemnly, she took his face between her palms. "I could never." Frowning, she added, "But perhaps *you* have doubts."

He turned his head, pressing his lips to her wrist. "Understand this, Rose. If you and I were to make love, it would be imprinted on my heart and soul as the best day of my godforsaken life. But you have more at stake, more to lose. That's why I want you to have time to think about it."

She couldn't say exactly why, but it felt as though he were slipping through her fingers. Panic, her familiar foe, rose in her chest.

But then he brushed her cheek with his thumb, soothing her with his touch and his words. "I'm not going anywhere anytime soon. I promise."

Rose smiled, appreciating his attempt to calm her. And she believed him. The problem was, people *always* left her. Eventually.

Reluctantly she slid off his lap and stood before him. "Three days."

Chuckling, he said, "You have mastered the art of persuasion. Very well—I'll meet you at the folly at sunset, three days hence." He stood and slipped her hood over her head. "If you should need anything before then, just send word."

"How?"

He thought for a moment, then said, "Hang a handkerchief outside the window of your bedchamber if you want me to meet you here. I'll come at dusk."

She narrowed her eyes. "Have you done this before?"

"Never." But he shot her a wicked grin. "Return to the house and read your mother's letter. I'll be thinking of you."

She pressed her hand over the pocket that held the letter. "Thank you for finding it."

"Remember what I said, earlier. Her failures are not yours. Nor are they a reflection of you." With a tenderness that made her ache, he kissed her cheek. "I shall see you in three days."

Just knowing that she had their meeting to look forward to eased some of the apprehension she felt about reading the letter. She knelt to pet Ash, then walked back toward the house. After a few steps she spun around. "I almost forgot to ask. Did you see the sketches?"

"Yes. One of them, anyhow. You were right—it was of me."

Rose tried not to gloat, but "you were right" had to be three of the sweetest words in the English language. "And do you know who drew them?"

"I have a pretty good idea," he said. "And I wish it were anyone but her."

Chapter Twelve

*E*ven with Mama's unread letter waiting for her upstairs, Rose found herself swept up in the excitement of planning. She'd decided to read the note after everyone retired for the evening, in case it contained news that was upsetting—or worse, no news at all.

After dinner, Rose, Lady Bonneville, and Lady Yardley discussed the details of the impending ball. Extra staff had been hired, the menu had been set, and an orchestra had been secured for the evening.

"How many guests are we expecting, Diana?" Lady Bonneville squinted at the paper in front of her face.

"Eighty." Turning to Rose, she continued, "Including several eligible, titled gentlemen. Some of them are rich as well," Lady Yardley assured her. "However, wealth is not an absolute requirement, is it? Your brother will no doubt provide an excellent dowry."

"He is very generous," Rose agreed, wishing Lady Yardley wasn't so intent on finding her a husband at the ball.

Yes, Rose had resolved to find a husband, but perhaps this was best accomplished once she returned to London. As long as she was in Bath, she'd naturally be inclined to compare any prospects to Charles—and she was certain no other man would measure up in her eyes.

Perhaps she'd delay her husband search for a bit and spend the evening of the ball at the viscountess's side, fetching drinks and listening to her colorful narrations of the evening's events.

As though Lady Bonneville had been privy to Rose's thoughts, she raised her lorgnette and glared through it. "I shall not consider the evening a success unless Rose dances every set."

"I shall do my—"

"I do not ask much, my dear," she said dramatically. "With striking looks such as yours, a full dance card is easily accomplished. See that you manage it."

"Yes, my lady."

Satisfied at last, Lady Bonneville yawned. "I'd forgotten how exhausting hosting a ball could be."

"Shall I help you to your room?" Rose asked.

"Yes, and you should retire soon as well. Your face is drawn, and too thin. You should eat a scone or two."

Rose held out an arm for her. "I shall, in the morning."

Lady Bonneville grunted as she grasped Rose's elbow, then bid a good evening to Lady Yardley. A few moments later, the viscountess was in Audrey's capable hands, and Rose was in her bedchamber. Alone. Holding Mama's letter.

She turned it over a few times, noting the elegant stationery and careful, even fold in the center. Mama had always believed in keeping up appearances.

Rose took a deep breath and opened the letter.

Dear Diana,

Though I confess I had hoped to receive your reply by now, I do not blame you in the least for being slow to respond. Perhaps what I have asked is too great an imposition, but we are the closest of friends—or at least we once were. I pray you will find it in your heart to visit me so that I may convey a few personal items to you. In the event that I never leave this awful place, at least I'll have some peace of mind knowing that you'll deliver my effects into the hands of my children.

You know I would never ask for your help if I wasn't quite desperate. Even in my pitiful state, however, I have a modicum of pride. So if you should choose to ignore this letter, I shall neither beg for assistance nor bother you again.

I am acutely aware that the sad situation in which I find myself is of my own making. Whatever you decide, I beg you to keep my plight a secret. I wish to spare my children further shame and pain, and selfishly, I want them to remember me as a young and beautiful duchess—and not the disgrace that I've since become.

Anxiously awaiting your reply,
Lily

The letter fluttered from Rose's hand to the velvet quilt on her bed. Mama was in trouble, trapped in a horrible sort of place.

She trembled at the thought of her sophisticated, privileged mother locked away in a ghastly place like a prison or an asylum for the insane. It was too terrible to imagine.

Although Rose hadn't seen her mother in six years, the news that she was alone and in need made her almost physically ill.

And yet a part of the letter sparked hope, for Mama hadn't forgotten about her, Olivia, and Owen after all. She'd wanted to spare them something—but what?

Rose picked up the letter and skimmed it once more. The date revealed Mama had written it three weeks ago, shortly before Rose had arrived in Bath. The note bore no address, provided no clue as to where it had come from.

One thing was certain: it didn't sound like Mama was frolicking in the French countryside. Lady Yardley had lied...but why?

Perhaps she was simply honoring Mama's request to keep her circumstances secret, especially from her children.

But Rose couldn't help thinking that Lady Yardley had her own interests at heart. Rose's chest tightened, simmering with anger. Clearly, Lady Yardley had ignored Mama's first—and perhaps second—plea for help.

Rose jumped off the bed and paced, bemoaning the late hour and the great distance from London. Olivia was still on her honeymoon in Egypt, due back in a couple of weeks. Rose longed to talk with her about her discovery. Even Owen, stubborn as he was, would likely feel her urgency, the need to do *something*—and fast. He said he'd never forgive Mama, but things had changed. He had a daughter of his own. Surely he'd want her to know her grandmamma.

It was true Mama had never been the model of a loving mother, but she'd had her moments. She'd pushed them on the swing hanging from the big oak tree in the field.

And she'd laughed good-naturedly as she taught a scowling ten-year-old Owen how to dance a reel.

Of course, there'd also been dark times, when she locked herself in her room for days on end. She wasn't the perfect mother, but she was the only one they had. That was reason enough to help her.

Unfortunately, Rose now knew enough to be worried but not enough to solve anything. Most vexingly, she still didn't know where to begin to look for Mama.

She wanted to run to the library, locate the cubby behind the painting, and search for more of Mama's letters. Immediately. It seemed the only way to discover the entire truth. But Charles had asked her not to attempt it, and she wouldn't do anything that would make trouble for him if she could avoid it.

She'd been in the dark about her mother for years, and one more day was not likely to make a difference in Mama's fate. A good night's sleep would clear Rose's head and let her determine the next steps.

In the meantime, the need to confide in someone— namely, Charles—was strong. Rose considered hanging a handkerchief out of her window, but even if he could see it in the dark of night, it was too late for her to leave the house. No, she'd signal him tomorrow and meet him at the folly at dusk.

Charles had been thinking about Rose ever since saying farewell to her the night before. Giving her the letter had been the right thing—he was sure of it—but he hated that the news was also bound to bring her pain.

The wounds of her childhood appeared healed on the outside, but he feared that her mother's hastily scrawled words could rip open those wounds, exposing the hurt that lay beneath. Still, she didn't want to be shielded from the truth. And he respected that. She'd emerged from the heartache of her youth stronger and wiser.

No one who met her today would dream that only a few years ago she was mute and painfully shy. True, she was still a bit reserved and might never be as outgoing as her sister, Olivia, but then, few people were.

Of course, there was another reason she'd occupied his thoughts all morning—her request that they share a night of passion.

One night, before he left for distant shores and she resigned herself to a lifetime of fulfilling others' expectations. Here, it was harder to know what was right. And damned difficult to be objective in the face of such temptation.

From the moment he'd first seen her here in Bath—nicking a letter from Lady Yardley's desk drawer—he'd been attracted to her. Hell, he'd been attracted to her long before that. Fantasies of her filled his dreams at night and his thoughts during the day. Knowing that she wanted him, too ... well, it was too much to hope for.

She'd said that it was to be one night. A good-bye.

That's how it had to be, but his chest still ached at the thought of leaving her.

The best thing to do was to keep busy. He ventured out into the cold, crisp morning, and prepared to ride into Bath to conduct some estate business at the bank. After mounting his horse, however, he decided to take the long way around Yardley Manor, just to glance at Rose's window and check for the handkerchief.

As he rounded a corner of the house, sunlight lent a golden glow to its limestone walls. His gaze scanned rows of windows before settling on the pair that belonged to Rose's bedchamber. Squinting against the glare, he spotted it. Beneath the sash of one of her windows, a small white square fluttered like a trapped dove.

Damn. The letter must have contained upsetting news, and he didn't want to wait until dusk, the appointed time, to know that she was all right. He stared at the window, searching for some sign that she was in the room. If she could give him a little wave, just to indicate she wasn't completely distraught, he'd feel much—

"Why, good morning, Mr. Holland."

Startled, Charles turned to find Lady Yardley atop her marc, looking elegant in her green riding habit and black velvet cloak. A wide-brimmed bonnet shaded her face from the sun.

"Good morning," he replied, with a smoothness that belied the prickling sensation between his shoulder blades.

"What a pleasant surprise," she cooed. "I confess I'm delighted that our paths have happened to cross once again."

Charles smiled, hoping to distract her from following the direction of his gaze. If Lady Yardley happened to glance up and see the handkerchief hanging out of Rose's bedchamber window, she could easily jump to the wrong conclusion.

Or, worse, the right one.

Waving in the general direction of town, he said, "I'm on my way to visit Mr. Davies at the bank. Are there any other errands you'd like me to see to while I'm there?"

She smiled, a cat contemplating a bowl of milk. "How very kind of you to offer. I cannot think of anything at the moment, but there *is* something I should like to ask you."

He swallowed guiltily. What if she knew that he'd discovered her secret cabinet—and taken something? Or maybe she could tell that the sketches of him in the library had been disturbed. Keeping his voice even-keeled and nonchalant, he responded, "Of course."

"This may seem like an odd question."

"I'm sure it's not."

"You must withhold judgment until I ask it."

He arched a brow. "Very well."

Her cheeks, already flushed from the brisk breeze, turned pinker. "I'm sure you're aware that Lady Bonneville and I are hosting a ball tomorrow night."

He would have to have been living in a cave not to notice the flurry of preparations of late. "I'm certain it shall be the event of the season."

This earned him another—even brighter—smile. "I appreciate your confidence and . . . would like to extend an invitation to you."

He blinked. "Pardon me?"

"To the ball. I'd like you to come. As a guest."

Attend the ball? Oh, *hell* no.

"It's very kind of you to invite me, but I don't think it would be proper. I'm just a steward, after all."

Her horse danced in place, as eager to escape this awkward encounter as he. Lady Yardley shrugged off Charles's concern. "It's not as formal as a London ball. Wear your finest jacket. You'll blend in well enough."

With dukes and earls? Not likely. "I'd planned to rise early the following morning. I have much to do."

Clearly exasperated, she huffed. "You're always working so hard. Take the day off."

"I'd rather not," he said. "I enjoy my work."

"And you are very good at it. In fact, I am in your debt. Say you'll attend. It's a chance for you to mingle with important people. If you were wise, you'd take advantage of the opportunity."

"I..." The very idea of a ball made his cravat feel tighter. "I... will think about it."

"Very well. I'm sure you'll come to the right decision." She adjusted her skirts so they cascaded down the side of the mare like a green velvet waterfall. "Be sure to save me a dance, Mr. Holland." With that, she gave the horse a kick and rode off.

Charles arrived at the folly early, and the half hour before dusk seemed an eternity. When at last Rose hurried up the path, his heart leaped in his chest. There was a determination in her eyes that he'd begun to see more and more of late. He took it as a sign that she would not be pushed around by life anymore, that she would take control of her fate.

The minute she walked into the folly, he clasped her hands between his. "How are you? Did you learn anything?"

"A bit. Mama is in trouble, but I don't know what sort."

"Where is she?"

Rose shook her head sadly. "I don't know that, either. In the letter she asked for Lady Yardley's help. But she must have provided details in a previous note. I need to find that letter. The urgency of her plea suggests time is of the essence."

"The note I gave you—it gives no clues?"

She reached into the pocket of her cloak and produced the piece of parchment. "Here, you may read it for yourself."

How simple she made it sound—and it *should* have been. Not for him though.

The moment she realized what she'd said, she pressed her fingertips to her forehead. "How thoughtless of me. I'm sorry, Charles."

"Don't be." He was actually gratified to know that she'd forgotten. That she didn't think of him as a caveman.

Recovering quickly, she hooked a hand around his elbow and led him to the bench. "Let's sit for a minute so I can catch my breath. Then we'll read the letter together and try to determine Mama's predicament. It's entirely possible I missed something in my frantic state."

They sat shoulder to shoulder, and Rose held the letter between them, a slender index finger trailing beneath each word as she read it. The handwriting, a tangle of loops and humps, seemed to taunt him, so he closed his eyes and focused on the clear, lilting sound of her voice.

Upon reaching the closing, she sighed and folded the note. "What do you make of it?"

He thought her mother was in prison, an asylum, or worse. She'd probably already reached the same conclusions and didn't need him to give voice to them. Speculation along those lines was certainly not going to make her feel better. "I think we need to retrieve another letter."

She nodded. "I was sorely tempted to sneak into the library last night and look behind the portrait for the secret cubby, but I told myself that one night was unlikely to make a difference. I hope I wasn't mistaken."

"You were wise to wait. It will be easier for me."

"I didn't ask you here because I wanted you to steal another letter on my behalf."

He quirked his mouth in a half-smile. "Then why *did* you ask me here?"

Her blue eyes sparkled, melting something inside him.

"Because you're my friend. You understand, and I trust your advice."

"Very well. My advice is that you let me retrieve another letter for you."

"You don't think I can manage it?" Huffing, she crossed her arms and tilted her head to one side. "How difficult can it be?"

"Retrieving the letter is not difficult," he reasoned, "if you're tall enough to reach the hiding spot. I think you'd need a stool."

She shot him a sweet—and completely insincere—smile. "Stools are hardly in short supply. If I'm not mistaken, the library has three."

Good point. "I suppose the tricky part is not being caught. Or, if you are, being able to talk your way out of it. You're not very good at lying."

"Neither are you."

"How do you know?" he teased.

"I can read every emotion on your face," she said quite seriously.

"Very well. What am I thinking right now?"

He was thinking about the night they'd agreed to spend together, and that he cared for her a lot more than he ought to, more than he had a right to. That he was probably going to have his heart broken.

But he couldn't very well let her know that. So he let his gaze drift over her lips, the hollow at the base of her throat, and the swells of her breasts before meeting her eyes once more. He shot her a wicked smile and heard her breath hitch.

"Tell me," he encouraged her. "What am I thinking? Here. I'll even give you a hint." He laced his fingers through hers and pressed a kiss to the back of her gloved hand.

Her lips parted. "I think you must be thinking the same thing I am."

"Which is?" What he'd give to hear her say it. That she desired him. That she wanted his body pressed to hers, with nothing between them.

She blushed prettily but did not look away. "That the attraction we feel toward each other is powerful, almost frightening in its intensity."

"You are very good."

"I believe I warned you." She shot him a sultry smile that heated his blood. "As for retrieving another letter, it will be easier for me. You don't spend nearly as much time in the house, and I have more opportunities to be in the library alone than you do."

"True..." But he didn't like the idea. If Rose was caught, Lady Yardley was not likely to be very forgiving. Indeed, she seemed a bitter sort of person, inclined to be irrationally resentful of anyone younger and more beautiful than she. Rose was correct, however. It would appear suspicious if he started spending more time at the house...

Unless.

"Actually," he said. "I'll have the perfect opportunity tomorrow night."

"You will? When?"

"During Lady Yardley's ball. She's invited me. I'd planned to decline, but..." But for Rose, he'd do anything.

She blinked. "You'll be at the ball? How wonderful, but..."

"Odd?" he suggested. "I couldn't agree more. However, it works to our advantage."

She gazed thoughtfully at the ground, where broken bits of leaves swirled at her feet. "Lady Yardley drew the sketches. She's in love with you."

Love wasn't the right word. She didn't want *him* so much as she wanted a tumble in the sheets. "I wouldn't hazard to guess the nature of her feelings, but I do think it's likely the sketches are hers."

"That complicates things." Rose frowned.

"Not really. I'm only going to put in an appearance at the ball," he said. "Once everyone is caught up in the music, dancing, and conversation, I'll slip out of the ball-room and into the library. It should be an easy matter to retrieve another letter. Then I can return to the party and give it to you without anyone being aware."

She nodded. "That could work. If all goes well, I'll know what happened to Mama by tomorrow night."

He squeezed her hand. "You'll have your answers."

In the waning light, she looked impossibly lovely—as ethereal and as intricate as a snowflake. She looked up at him then, her blue eyes full of trepidation. "There's one more thing I need to ask you."

Chapter Thirteen

*Saddle: (1) A seat placed on a horse's back to help a
person ride astride. (2) To impose a responsibility or burden,
as in The viscountess had no wish to be saddled with a
crotchety, old husband, vastly preferring beaus of
the younger, more spirited variety.*

Rose shivered, less from the cold than from apprehension. She didn't have a right to ask Charles such a personal question, and yet, she had to know.

As though he'd read her jumbled thoughts, he said, "You can ask me anything."

Swallowing the knot in her throat, she said, "Do you care for her—for Lady Yardley?"

His brow furrowed. "What? No!"

He seemed sincere, but perhaps he hadn't yet admitted the truth of his feelings to himself. "If you did, I would not judge either of you," she said. "I realize there are reasons you might want to keep a relationship with her secret—"

"Rose. There is no relationship."

"But she would clearly like one."

He looked up at the domed ceiling of the folly where painted-on stars had faded on the weathered stone. "I suppose so."

"If there's a chance that something could blossom between you, I don't want to interfere. You deserve happiness."

He stood abruptly, anger rolling off him. "Lady Yardley is my employer, and that's all she'll ever be. Besides, you already know my future is not here."

Rose sprang to her feet. "Yes, but love—when it happens—has a strange way of changing people's plans. Look at Olivia. She never dreamed she'd go on an expedition to Egypt, but she did. For James."

"I'm not changing my plans," he said firmly. "For anyone."

His meaning couldn't have been clearer. She'd known this, and yet the crippling sort of pain that his declaration had exacted suggested that some naïve part of her had held out hope that—

Foolishness.

"I understand," she said.

He clasped her shoulders and looked at her earnestly. "Do you? It may sound selfish, and I suppose it is. But I'm also thinking of you."

"How so?"

He shook his head as though words eluded him. At last he said, "You're a gently bred young lady. You need a husband who fits into your world."

"No. Don't presume to tell me what I am or what I need." She slid her arms around his neck and leaned in to him.

Dusk's shadows accentuated the angles of his cheeks

and jaw and his curls rustled in the evening breeze. He looked devastatingly handsome, so much so that she nearly trembled with wanting.

"Fine," he said gruffly. "I won't presume. You tell me... what do you need?"

"This." Rising on tiptoe, she molded her mouth to his, kissing him with everything she felt—fear, desire, and yes, love. She let her hands roam beneath his jacket, over the hard planes of his chest, the taut ridges of his abdomen, and the firm contours of his bottom. She was no delicate, whimsical butterfly, and her kisses, full of raw, potent need, would surely prove it.

He seemed stunned by her sudden, heated display of passion, momentarily frozen by the urgency in her touch. She pushed him back until his shoulders collided with the stone wall, then pressed her body against his, giving him no room for escape.

He didn't seem to mind. Moaning softly into her mouth, he pulled her hips toward his, letting her feel the long, hard length of him.

"This," she breathed hotly, "this is what I need." Burying her face in his neck, she savored the taste and scent of him.

"God, Rose." In one smooth, lightning-fast move, he spun her around, reversing their positions. As he plundered her mouth, he eased up the front of her skirt—and the petticoat that she wore beneath it. Cold air rushed around and between her legs, reminding her just how exposed, how vulnerable, she was.

Charles slid his warm, rough palm up her leg and gently kneaded her inner thigh. His thumb circled closer and closer till at last he brushed the sensitive folds between her legs.

Her knees wobbled, but his chest firmly pinned her to

the wall, allowing her to concentrate on the sweet, intoxi-cating effects of his touch. She leaned her head against the stone and savored the slightly abrasive feel of his hot, possessive kisses along the column of her neck.

She was floating, suspended by desire and pleasure, and spiraling higher by the minute. His wicked fingers teased and tempted, pushing her past mild arousal into raw need. Her whimpers echoed in the stark winter land-scape and swirled around them in a rhythm matching his sensuous strokes, taking her higher... and higher...

"Charles!"

She shuddered, stunned by the power and sweetness of her release. Even a minute afterward, delicious tremors radiated through her, leaving her breathless, weak, sated.

He let her skirts fall back into place and kissed her softly as she floated back to earth.

"That was..." At a loss for words, she framed his handsome face with her hands. "Thank you."

"Oh, Rose." Chuckling, he nuzzled her neck. "You always surprise me—in the most delightful ways."

She blinked. "*You're* surprised? I honestly never knew..." And it was only the beginning. She had so much to learn and experience, a lifetime of loving ahead of her.

The problem was, she couldn't imagine that kind of passion—that kind of intimacy—with anyone but Charles.

"We can't stay out here much longer," he said. "Some-one might come looking for you."

"But I'll see you tomorrow night, at the ball?" How strange it would be to see him in Lady Yardley's ballroom, with both of them dressed in their finery, awkwardly unable to acknowledge their feelings for each other.

"Yes, briefly. I'll look for an opportunity to escape to

the library, and if I'm able to retrieve a letter, I shall return to give it to you."

"If you are discovered accessing the secret cabinet…it would look very bad."

"Indeed. But I won't be caught. Do not worry about me."

"Until tomorrow, then," she said.

He took her hand, pressed a kiss to her wrist, and shot her a knee-melting grin. "At the ball."

She turned to go, surprised her legs still supported her, then stopped just outside of the folly. Facing Charles once more, she said, "The night of passion you promised me— I haven't changed my mind about that. After this evening I'm looking forward to it more than ever."

"So am I, Rose." His voice, deep and promising, drifted over her, and her skin tingled in its wake. "Good night."

Snow began to fall as the first guests arrived, and it didn't stop. Outside the floor-to-ceiling windows of Lady Yardley's spectacularly lavish ballroom, small flakes waltzed in an impressive imitation of the couples on the dance floor inside.

Rose wore a gown that her sister-in-law, Anabelle, had made for her. It was the most beautiful one she owned, a stunning pale blue silk creation. The shimmering dress draped across her arms, Belle had presented it to Rose solemnly. "You must never again think of yourself as an ugly duckling," she'd said. "You are a swan to outshine all others."

Ridiculousness, of course, but Rose loved Belle for believing it. And even though Rose was a far cry from swan material, she had to admit the gown made her feel graceful—gloriously so.

She'd started the evening at Lady Bonneville's side,

but the viscountess would not allow her to remain there. "I don't need you hovering about," she'd said, "fetching me tepid drinks and engaging me in inane conversation."

"No? I'd rather thought that was what companions did."

Rose's quip had earned her a hearty cackle and an unceremonious shove toward the dance floor.

She was the odd debutante who wasn't enthralled with dancing. She disliked the crowded jostling, the awkward hand holding, and the uncomfortable eye gazing. At least here, in Bath, Rose felt less on display than she did in London. Perhaps the thought was naught but a comforting fallacy, but if it helped her through the evening, she would happily delude herself. At the very least, dancing would take her mind off Charles and the risky mission he was undertaking for her sake.

He hadn't yet arrived, and Rose couldn't help noticing that Lady Yardley's gaze was on the ballroom entrance almost as often as her own. Possibly more.

Confident that he'd show as promised, Rose dedicated herself to playing the part of a normal young lady enjoying a winter ball. Her first dance partner, Lord Westman, was a jovial, older gentleman who expounded on the snowy weather with great enthusiasm. "The almanac said nothing about snow this month, but mark my words! This will be a storm to remember if my aching knees are any indication."

"If the dancing is making them worse—" Rose began, perhaps a bit too hopefully.

"Not at all!" Lord Westman bellowed. "Dancing is the best medicine for old joints, don't you know."

Rose was inclined to believe him, as he moved with the agility of a man two decades younger, leaving her slightly winded at the end of the first set. Gallantly, he insisted upon returning her to Lady Bonneville's side before going in search of his next partner.

"A pathetic start," the viscountess said.

"Pardon?" Rose blinked slowly.

"You aren't even trying. Westman is too old, even for *me*."

Rose gave the viscountess a mildly scolding look. "I cannot afford to be choosy when it comes to dance partners. It was kind of him to ask me."

Lady Bonneville raised her lorgnette and squinted at Rose. "What utter nonsense. I expect your next dance partner to be both handsome *and* eligible."

"What about wealthy? Shall I require him to provide a banker's recommendation?"

"If you can manage it."

Valiantly attempting not to roll her eyes, Rose said, "I will do my best." She headed toward the perimeter of the dance floor.

"Not that way."

Rose faced the viscountess. "Pardon?"

"That's the old codger section. There's more gray over there than in a London fog."

A glance in that direction confirmed Lady Bonneville's observation. "Where would you like me to go?"

The viscountess waved her lorgnette like a sorceress's wand, pointing to a crowd of younger gentlemen standing near the front of the room, a mass of stylish jackets and colorful waistcoats.

Rose gulped.

"Hurry, gel," Lady Bonneville urged. "The second set's about to begin."

Just to vex the viscountess, Rose moved at a leisurely pace, smiling sweetly over her shoulder as she made her way—along with every other young lady—toward the group of eligible bachelors.

She wished Olivia, Belle, or Daphne were here with her—there was nothing quite so humiliating as lingering on the edge of the dance floor by one's self, desperately trying to appear as though one wasn't, well, desperate. She looked forlornly at the entrance to the ballroom, wondering when Charles would finally appear.

"Lady Rose." Lord Stanton glided to a stop in front of her. "I've found you at last."

"Good evening." She dipped a curtsy and tried to hide her disappointment that he wasn't Charles.

"Would you care to dance?"

Rose could feel Lady Bonneville's lorgnette trained on her, just between her shoulder blades. Although something about Lord Stanton made her skin prickle, she couldn't very well decline. And at least she'd be spared the awkwardness of being a wallflower for the next set. "That would be lovely."

As they slowly paraded to the dance floor, Lady Yardley nodded a greeting, smiling approvingly. She looked especially beautiful this evening. With her slender form wrapped in green silk, and her hair styled in cascading ringlets, she looked bubbly and youthful.

Rose knew precisely whom Lady Yardley hoped to impress—and couldn't blame her.

When a flush stole over her cheeks, Rose followed the direction of her gaze...and saw him.

Charles hesitated at the entrance and let his eyes sweep over the crowd. Rose's knees wobbled a little at the sight of him. Though his jacket wasn't the finest in the ballroom, the shoulders filling it most definitely were.

When he spotted Rose, he gave an almost imperceptible smile. His gaze flicked to Lord Stanton's hand at the small of her back, and his smile tightened. Rose had no wish to make him jealous . . . and yet it was rather thrilling to note that perhaps he was.

Before he'd taken two steps into the room, Lady Yardley waylaid him, smoothly steering him toward the dance floor. When the first strains of music began moments later, Rose whirled in Lord Stanton's arms. Lady Yardley twirled in Charles's.

Rose tried to focus on the steps rather than the unfairness of it all, but she stumbled twice. She couldn't help but search for Charles in the throng. He towered above most of the guests and, while not the most accomplished of dancers, moved with an athletic ease and confidence that made him the object of many a longing sigh.

If Lord Stanton noticed Rose's inattentiveness, he didn't mention it. Feeling guilty, she resolved to be a better dance partner for the remainder of the set.

"Do you think it will snow all night?" she asked, grateful that the weather was a mildly interesting topic of conversation, for once.

"I hope not. Mother doesn't like to travel in it and has warned me that she shall want to leave immediately if it starts to pile up."

"I see." Rose smiled sympathetically. "And you would rather not?"

"Not when this ball has so much to recommend it," he purred with a hint of a slur. "I would not be denied a moment of the pleasure of your company, Lady Rose. Not if I could help it."

He arched a brow, and Rose had the feeling he'd half

expected his passionate declaration would cause her to swoon, or to blush at the very least. But as he leered at the swells of her breasts, all she felt was mild revulsion.

She was more than relieved when the dance ended and Lord Stanton reluctantly returned her to Lady Bonneville, who'd watched the proceedings with her feet perched on her red tufted stool. "You do not like him," she pronounced.

"I don't care for his company," Rose said as diplomatically as possible.

The viscountess sucked in her cheeks. "Be that as it may, it is inadvisable to burn any bridges." Pointing her lorgnette toward the dance floor, she added, "Lady Yardley certainly seemed to enjoy her partner. Mr. Holland, isn't it? The steward?" The viscountess's deceptively casual words were accompanied by a shrewd stare.

Rose knew better than to feign ignorance. "They make a striking couple." Though it pained her to admit it, it was true.

"Just because one reaches a certain age," the viscountess mused, "doesn't mean one is through with passion."

Good heavens. "Lady Bonneville, would you like me to fetch you something to drink?" She prayed for an affirmative response—some excuse to flee this conversation, fraught with equal measures of awkwardness and agony.

Ignoring her question, the viscountess continued. "Those of us with more years to our credit may not have the advantage of youth; however, we do have the advantage of experience."

Rose didn't want to think of Lady Yardley exercising her "experience"—or anything else—on Charles. But she did agree with the viscountess's sentiment, in a general sort of way. "Every age is deserving of happiness . . . and love."

Lady Bonneville nodded emphatically and focused on a spot somewhere behind Rose. "Well, well," she said under her breath, "here comes the source of Lady Yardley's happiness now."

Rose turned as Charles strode toward them, and a surreal haze descended. Her two worlds—the real, intimate one with Charles, and the proper, apparent one with Lady Bonneville—collided in that moment. She was not ashamed of Charles or what she felt for him, and yet, there were reasons they had been meeting secretively, in the dark of the night.

"Good evening, Lady Rose." His smooth, assured bow could have put a duke's to shame.

"Mr. Holland." She inclined her head, trying to contain the smile that threatened to spread across her face, then introduced him to Lady Bonneville.

The viscountess's gaze flicked from Charles to Rose and back, and she arched a snowy white brow. "I presume you have come to ask Rose to dance."

"I have, my lady."

"Well then, I suggest that you do not dally. There are any number of gentlemen hoping to claim her. Go on."

Rose refrained from rolling her eyes at the gross exaggeration. Men hadn't exactly been swarming.

"It is easy to see why," Charles said, the sincerity in his amber eyes nearly taking her breath away. Offering his hand to her, he said, "Would you care to dance?"

"I should be delighted." Rose took his hand, catching a glimpse of the viscountess's smug expression as they made their way toward the dance floor.

When the music began, they moved together—tentatively at first, adjusting not to each other so much as to the public setting. Soon, however, Rose was oblivious to everything but the pressure of his hand on her back, the nearness of their bodies, and the heat in his eyes. For a few blessed moments, she was able to forget about Mama's troubling letter, Charles's risky mission, and her own breaking heart.

She was just a girl, dancing at a ball, with the man she loved.

And then the music ended.

In the mild eruption of clapping, laughter, and conversation that ensued, Charles leaned close to her ear. "Keep dancing. I'll return shortly."

Her belly sank.

Sensing her anxiety, he squeezed her hand and grinned. "Don't worry. It's not as though I'm on an espionage mission for the king."

She smiled and relaxed. "I wish you luck."

Neither of them spoke as he returned her to Lady Bonneville. Rose was strangely reluctant to release his arm, but she did.

With a reassuring smile, he strode into the crowd... and was gone.

Chapter Fourteen

Charles slipped out of the ballroom and headed down the corridor toward the library, apparently unnoticed. If he happened to encounter anyone in the hallway, he'd pretend to be foxed and claim that he'd lost his way while in search of a drink. Members of the staff seemed to expect and tolerate such behavior from the guests. Sad, but it served his purposes nicely.

He reached the library without seeing another soul, stepped into the darkness, and shut the door behind him. It took a moment for his eyes to adjust. No lamps lit the room, but light from the ballroom spilled onto the snow-covered lawn outside the library's windows. Flakes continued to fall steadily, flying sideways when the winter wind howled.

Silently, he glided around the desk and seating area to the fireplace mantel. A quick glance over his shoulder confirmed the door was still shut, so he reached for the portrait of the late Lord Yardley and pulled on the corner.

It swung open with an eerie creak that echoed off the book-filled walls. The cabinet door opened easily as well, only it was too dark to see anything inside. He reached in, relying on his memory and hoping that the contents hadn't been moved since his last visit. He felt a stack of papers, grabbed the entire bunch, and stalked to the window in order to examine them.

Even an expert reader would have had difficulty finding a particular letter in the dim light—at least, that's what he told himself. But for him, it was nigh impossible.

Note by note, he searched for the duchess's expensive stationery, her dainty handwriting, her distinctive signature.

And there it was.

At the very bottom of the stack, as though someone wished to bury it and forget it existed.

He shoved the letter into the pocket of his jacket, hastily coaxed the rest of them into some semblance of a stack, and returned the pile to the cabinet.

It took only a moment to close the door and return the portrait to its original position, and then the room looked just as it had before he'd come.

He exhaled slowly. Rose would be so relieved. Not only had he managed to retrieve the letter, but it was easier than he had even hoped. He walked to the door, smoothed a hand over the front of his jacket, and placed a hand on the knob. Which unexpectedly turned.

Before he could hide, the door swung open, admitting a shaft of light—and Lady Yardley.

"Charles," she breathed, closing the door. "I was wondering where you'd gone. Something told me I might find you here."

Damn. He wobbled and leaned against the wall in his best drunk but not yet annihilated impression. "Forgive me. I was looking for a spot of brandy."

"And did you find one?"

"No, but maybe that's for the best."

"Nonsense." She walked across the room, opened a cabinet beneath a bookshelf, and pulled out a decanter and two stacked glasses. She set them on a table and plopped onto a settee, a cloud of green silk billowing around her. "Come, sit and pour." She patted the cushion beside her, and though sorely tempted to dash from the room, he knew he could not.

Instead he sauntered over, sat, and splashed a finger of brandy into each glass. Handing one to her, he raised his in a toast. "To your ball, Lady Yardley—a smashing success, by all accounts."

She took a sip of brandy, eyeing him seductively over the rim of her glass. "Is it truly, Charles? A success, that is?"

"I'm hardly an expert, but it seems so to me. Your ballroom is bursting at the seams with fine ladies and gentlemen. Everyone's dancing and enjoying themselves. What else could you possibly need to consider the ball a success?"

"Funny you should ask." She threw back the rest of her drink and set the glass on the table with a *clunk*. "For one, I should like you to stop calling me Lady Yardley. It makes me sound so very...old."

"I must respectfully disagree."

"That's the problem with you, Charles."

"Pardon?"

"You're always so *respectful*." She scooted closer to

him on the settee, draping an arm over the back as though making herself comfortable for a long, cozy chat. Which was the very last thing he wanted.

"You're a lady and my employer," he said, because she seemed to need reminding. "Of course you have my respect."

"You asked me what I required to consider the ball a success."

Yes. And he had a feeling he was about to regret that question. "Speaking of the ball, shouldn't we return to your guests?"

Waving off the suggestion, she continued, "It would be an unqualified success if only"—she removed an invisible piece of lint from the shoulder of his jacket—"you would kiss me."

Damn. He placed his glass on the table—an excuse to inch away from her. "You don't mean that. I wouldn't dream of taking such a liberty."

"You and your damned sense of honor." She pouted.

"Allow me to escort you back to the ballroom." He started to stand, but the yank she gave his arm was so unexpected that he fell toward her. She grasped his lapels and leaned back on the settee, pulling him with her.

He managed to brace his arms on either side of her so that their bodies didn't collide, but his face was a mere inch from hers.

"I've watched you working—thatching roofs, breaking stallions, even moving boulders. There's something so very attractive about a man who's good with his hands. I bet you know how to take care of a woman."

Holy hell. "Actually—"

Before he could finish his sentence, she grabbed a

fistful of hair on either side of his head, pulled him toward her, and planted her lips on his mouth.

Rose danced the next set with Lord Avery, a nice young gentleman who had clammy hands and a tendency to blush each time she attempted to start a conversation. She sympathized with him—it was rare she encountered someone even shyer than she was. As they circled the dance floor, she tried not to crane her neck looking for a pair of broad shoulders angling through the crowd. As soon as he was able, Charles would return and let her know if he'd had any success in the library.

It was so nice to have someone to depend on besides her family. Olivia and Owen were very good to her, as were Belle and Daphne. But they were her relatives and saw her as a girl who needed protection and coddling.

Charles was different. He was more like a partner, someone she could share her worries and dreams with. Someone whom she could count on.

When the music ended, Lord Avery seemed both disappointed and relieved. "I hope I didn't trample your feet too badly," he said.

"Not at all," she assured him. "I enjoyed our dance—and your company."

The compliment caused his cheeks to turn bright pink, and he was still attempting to regain his composure as he escorted her to Lady Bonneville.

Rose was expecting the viscountess to chide her for not attracting a more seasoned dance partner, but she hardly seemed to notice Lord Avery. In fact, she looked a little pale.

"Are you feeling unwell?" Rose asked. "If you're tired, I'd be happy to take you to your room."

Lady Bonneville shot her an affronted look. "You're certainly eager to cart me off, aren't you?"

"Hardly. I just want to make sure you're comfortable."

"It's too warm in here. Someone should open a door."

Rose blinked. "But it's frightful outside. The snow hasn't stopped. Shall I fetch your fan for you?"

"Yes, the Chinese silk with the bright blue tassel. Audrey will know where it is."

"Very well. I shall return shortly."

"If you hurry, you should be able to make it back in time to dance the next set."

Rose nodded obediently but decided to make the errand last as long as possible. She hadn't ever danced so much in one night. Her feet ached and her head throbbed, but she suspected a few minutes away from bustle of the ballroom would work wonders.

She exited through a side door, slipped into a corridor, and tried to get her bearings in this unfamiliar part of the house. The sitting room was at one end of the hallway, she was fairly certain, and from there she could easily navigate her way to the stairs and the corridor where their bedchambers were located. Her sense of direction was appallingly bad, however, and if getting lost meant she had a longer respite from dancing, she'd gladly lose her way.

Turning right, she glided down the elegant hallway, savoring the relative silence and the dim light from the sconces on the walls. With every step she took, the cacophony of music, laughter, and conversation in the ballroom grew more distant. It seemed that all the staff and activity were focused on that part of the manor house, leaving the rest blissfully deserted.

Portraits of austere-looking gentlemen lined the hallway, and she suddenly recalled where she was—the wing of the house where Lady Yardley's study and library were located.

The library.

She halted, the heels of her slippers suddenly glued to the floor. The library door was only a few yards away.

Charles could be in there now, searching the hidden cabinet.

She shouldn't go in. She'd only startle him or distract him from the task at hand.

But how she'd love a few stolen moments, alone, with him.

The pull was strong, almost irresistible. And she had to admit to being curious about the cabinet. How she'd love a peek at it.

She walked up to the door and paused, her hand on the knob. She pressed an ear to the thick oak panels but heard nothing save her own rapid breaths. A quick glance inside couldn't hurt. If Charles was absorbed in his task, she'd simply retreat and leave him to it. But maybe he could use her help, an extra set of eyes to scan the notes.

Holding her breath, she eased the door open.

Her gaze flew to the far wall where the portrait hung. Charles wasn't there. Disappointment washed over her, but she shoved it aside. There could be any number of explanations. Perhaps he'd already found a letter and had left the room. She should hurry to retrieve Lady Bonneville's fan and return to the ballroom in case he was there looking for her.

She took a step back, about to close the door, when a movement on the settee caught her attention. Though the room was mostly dark, she would have recognized Charles's wavy, collar-length hair anywhere. And those shoulders...they could only be his. He appeared to be kneeling on the sofa.

Odd. Perhaps he wasn't feeling well. Only the groan that echoed through the room wasn't his. It was distinctly female. And the woman wasn't in pain.

Dear God. All the air rushed from her lungs and she swayed on her feet. Clutching the door frame for support, she backed up, then slammed the door.

As fast as her feet would carry her, she ran. The corridor sped by in a blur of wallpaper and portraits. She passed the study, sprinted by the sitting room, and stumbled her way up the stairs toward her bedchamber.

Charles had been kissing someone. Heatedly. And Rose knew who.

She burst into her room, closed the door, and locked it.

Her stomach in knots, she staggered to the chamber pot and retched.

It was just like before—that night six years ago, when she'd discovered Mama in bed with the greasy earl. And the maid.

Why did the people she loved the most always betray her?

And why did she have such a knack for witnessing their hurtful behavior firsthand?

She stalked to the escritoire beneath the window and snatched up the cut-glass vase holding a few festive sprigs of holly. Water sloshed out of the top as she faced the opposite wall and drew back her arm, anticipating the oh-so-satisfying *crash* of glass against plaster.

As anger boiled over, her eyes burned and her hands

trembled. She had the primal need to destroy something, and she would. No matter that the vase wasn't hers or that the noise could draw the attention of the staff.

She was weary of being good—of containing her emotions and avoiding unseemly behavior. For once, she wanted to make a scene.

Chest heaving with determination, she adjusted her grip. The traitorous vase slipped through her fingers and landed on the plush carpet with a soft thud that mocked her rage.

She sank to the floor, next to the soggy spot on the carpet and the prickly holly and the uncooperative vase, where she was forced to confront the truth.

She wasn't angry, so much as heartbroken.

She wasn't tired of being good, so much as tired of being gullible.

She'd thought Charles was different, but he wasn't.

And in spite of his offer to help her, he didn't owe her anything. She should never have relied on him, believed in him, fallen for—

Ridiculousness. That's what it was. She stood, brushed out her skirts, and smoothed her hair. She kicked the vase, and it rolled across the floor, stopping just before the wall, vexingly intact.

Who cared? She didn't need to smash vases or howl in misery. Those were the actions of a woman whose world was crumbling around her. And she didn't want anyone—especially Charles—to think that her world was crumbling, even if it was.

No. What she needed was to show him absolute, bone-chilling indifference.

She went to the washbasin and splashed cool water on

her face. Her reflection didn't show a fraction of the hurt inside her—that was good. If her eyes were too bright and her cheeks too flushed, no one was likely to notice.

She would fetch Lady Bonneville's fan and return to the ballroom. And if Charles and Lady Yardley should have the gall to rejoin the festivities, they wouldn't have an inkling that they'd almost made her forget what she'd survived . . . and who she'd become.

Chapter Fifteen

Stud: (1) A stallion intended for breeding.
(2) An especially attractive, virile man.

Even before the library door slammed, Charles had been trying to untangle himself from Lady Yardley's grasping hands. It took him longer than he would have liked to pry her fingers from his hair and shove himself off the settee—and her—only because he didn't want to physically hurt her. "No," he said, simply but firmly. "I'm sure you realize it is a bad idea, for many reasons."

With a little cry, she sprang to her feet. "I disagree." Pouting, she grasped one side of his jacket, snaked a hand inside his waistcoat, and unabashedly stroked his chest.

"Lady Yardley," he said sternly, "I am trying to be a gentleman, and I must ask you to stop."

With a frustrated growl, she yanked his jacket open, popping off a button. "I don't think you understand. I'm willing to do anything you want. Anything," she added meaningfully. "It's been so long since I've . . ."

She broke into pitiful sobs then, clinging to his cravat,

shirt, and waistcoat as she slid down his body, crumpling into a heap at his feet.

He considered leaving her there, not because he was a heartless bastard, but because it might well be his best chance at escape. However, a deeply ingrained sense of honor would not permit him to walk away from a woman sobbing on the floor.

"Allow me to help you." He leaned down and offered his hand.

As she sniffled and reached up, the duchess's letter fell out of his pocket and landed on Lady Yardley's lap.

Damn. He swooped down to scoop it up, but she grabbed it out of his fingers.

"What's this?" As she turned the note over, her eyes narrowed and her brows knit in suspicion. She hoisted herself to her feet and stood toe to toe with him, all traces of the pitiful, devastated woman gone. "Where did you get this?"

There was no use lying. "I think you know."

"I want to hear you say it."

"I took it from the cabinet behind your late husband's portrait."

"You did it for Lady Rose, didn't you?"

He stood there, stone-faced, unwilling to implicate Rose.

"Your silence is answer enough. She's been badgering me for information about her dear Mama. Of course you're doing it for her—the beautiful, young damsel in distress." Her face twisted in an ugly sneer. "I hope you don't think you're going to win her heart. Surely you're not that naïve. She has manipulated you into doing her bidding, has she not?"

His jaw clenched. "I acted on my own."

She snorted. "And for what? A chaste kiss on the terrace? Once she has what she wants, she'll toss you aside like last year's gown. She would never risk her future for someone like you."

"Someone like me," he repeated, his fists clenching involuntarily. "What, precisely, does that mean?"

"You needn't become agitated. I think you know what I mean."

He threw her words back at her. "I want to hear you say it."

Lifting her chin, she said, "Very well. Lady Rose will never settle for a poor, untitled man born to two uneducated servants. She may flirt with you. Indeed, I'm sure she enjoys the attentions of a strapping young buck like yourself. But that doesn't mean she cares for you. The minute she has the information she wants, she'll wash her hands of you. Forever." Her nostrils flared and she placed a hand on her hip, challenging him to deny the truth of her claims.

He closed his eyes for the space of three heartbeats, suppressing his anger and summoning his control. "You have no right to besmirch my parents—whom you know *nothing* about—or Lady Rose," he said slowly. "I'm tendering my resignation." He moved toward the door, but she leaped into his path, placing a palm squarely on his chest.

"Don't be so hasty," she said. "You still want the letter, don't you?"

He did. He'd promised Rose that he'd help her, and she deserved to know what had become of her mother. "Yes."

"Well then, I think there's a way we can both get what we want."

"I'm listening."

Coyly, she folded the letter lengthwise, swept it along the edge of his jaw, and then slid it into the front of her gown, deep into the crevice between her breasts.

"It's yours for the taking." She slid the small puffed sleeves of her gown off her shoulders and arched her back. "All of it."

He stood still as a statue as he contemplated her offer. He had enough money saved for passage to America, and he could earn a little more working for a few weeks on the docks. This job had served its purpose. Now he could walk away.

If it weren't for Rose.

More than anything, he wanted to give her the answers she sought.

So he unceremoniously grabbed the neckline of Lady Yardley's low-cut gown, pulled it forward, and reached down into her chemise till he felt the letter between his fingers. With one swift move, he freed it from the sweaty depths of her cleavage and held it high, above her grasping reach.

"That's not fair," she protested. "We had a bargain, and now you must deliver."

"I promised you nothing."

Her gaze turned icy. "I want you gone by morning, Mr. Holland."

"At last, a request I'm happy to oblige."

She gaped at him as he stalked past, leaving her uncharacteristically speechless and unquestionably alone.

Upon reaching the corridor, he walked in the direction of the ballroom. Lady Yardley would likely be on his heels, and he had to give the letter to Rose before he returned to the cottage and packed his things.

He imagined the shock and utter dismay on her beautiful face when he told her the news that he was leaving and that they'd likely never see each other again.

With the ballroom door just a few paces away, he came to a dead stop. He couldn't bear to say good-bye in such a public venue, didn't trust himself to keep his composure. And what if Lady Yardley chased him in there, creating even more of a scene and humiliating Rose further?

Though he longed to see her one last time, he couldn't risk it. So he strode past the entrance, down a parallel corridor, and up a staircase that led to the wing of the house where the bedchambers were located. He'd never been in that section of the house, but he knew the layout, and he'd seen Rose's room from the outside.

With the boldness of a man who has absolutely nothing to lose, he stalked directly to her door and bent to slide the note under. But he couldn't resist a peek inside, just to be certain he'd chosen the right door. That's what he told himself. The truth was he couldn't resist the chance to feel close to her, just briefly, before he left.

He swung open the unlocked door and took in the room. When he spotted the glass vase toppled on the floor and two small cuttings of holly littered on the carpet, his gut clenched. What if Rose had been involved in some sort of struggle?

But thankfully there were no other indications of foul play—just reminders of Rose everywhere he looked. Books on the table by her bed, a chessboard set for a match, a rainbow of ribbons hanging from the full-length looking glass. He walked to the mirror, fingered a silky ribbon the same shade of blue as her eyes, and slid it off its hook into his pocket.

Though he would have liked to linger, time was running short. He pulled the duchess's letter from his jacket and placed it on Rose's pillow. If he had any semblance of skill with a pen he'd write her a note to leave beside her mother's. He would have told her that he was going to miss her and asked her to take care of Ash. He would have told her that she deserved every happiness and teased her about her freckles, which he happened to adore.

He might have even told her he loved her.

But he couldn't.

So, he picked up a sprig of holly and set it next to her mother's letter, hoping that somehow, the simple gesture would convey all he'd meant to say.

Sighing, he left her room, made his way down the stairs, and walked out of the grand doors of Yardley Manor into the blinding snow.

Rose spent the rest of the ball in a fog. She danced with two more gentlemen, surprised her feet would move in time to the music, amazed that her face could smile in response to a compliment. Each time she thought of Charles with Lady Yardley, she wanted to run from the room and find a dark, quiet corner in which she could cry to her heart's content.

But she'd suffered similar heartaches. Not exactly the same, for Charles was her first love. Her only love. Still, no matter how dark things seemed at the moment, she knew she'd survive. She just had to keep moving forward and acting as though everything were normal. One day—perhaps months or years from now—she'd wake up and things *would* be normal.

For now, she'd simply pretend.

She attempted to make polite conversation with Lady Bonneville and her friends, but unfortunately, they seemed to prefer *impolite* conversation.

Behind her fan, Lady Napier managed to whisper indiscreetly to the viscountess and two other respected ladies of the ton. "What can Mrs. Seaton be thinking? Someone with her girth should not attempt to dress like a debutante. Perhaps I should inform her. After all, she is a dear friend."

Rose shuddered to think of the remarks she'd make about enemies.

"Where has Lady Yardley been, I wonder?" said Lady Bonneville to everyone and no one in particular. "I haven't seen her in at least an hour."

The anger and hurt welled up again, but Rose blinked them back into submission.

"How very odd," Lady Napier mused. "She is the hostess of this event, is she not?"

Rose felt the viscountess's lorgnette trained upon her but didn't dare to look at her. It would have been as foolish as staring directly at the sun.

"Do you know something, Rose?" Lady Bonneville asked.

"Hmm? Pardon?"

"Have you seen Lady Yardley?"

"Not recently, no."

The viscountess pursed her lips. "Fascinating. If she doesn't return soon, I shall have to send out a search party to locate— Well, would you look at that? There's our hostess now."

All heads swiveled to the opposite end of the ballroom, where Lady Yardley hurried in and gave instructions to a passing footman. She patted the back of her head, assuring herself that her elegant hairstyle had not been unduly compromised. Rose suspected a maid would find a few extra pins beneath the cushions of the library settee tomorrow.

"Are you quite all right, Rose?" Lady Bonneville's jowls shook with genuine concern.

"Yes, a bit tired is all," she lied. "I know I ought to enjoy the revelry all night, but I am unaccustomed to keeping these late hours."

"Woefully so," the viscountess remarked. "Fortunately, you have me. Crotchety old ladies make the best excuses for leaving early. You can avoid all the tedious good-byes."

"I wouldn't say you're crotchety," Rose lied again.

Lady Napier pursed her lips. "What would you call her?"

"Opinionated," said Rose. "Delightfully so."

"Keep this up," the viscountess announced, "and I shall have to speak with my solicitor about writing you into my will. For now, however, I require you to help me to my bedchamber. Audrey can take over from there. She's adamant that I adhere to my nighttime routines, and I find it easier to indulge her than argue."

Rose learned something new about Lady Bonneville every day. "You are more soft-hearted than you admit."

"Nonsense. And I take back what I said about my will."

A quarter of an hour later, after Rose had delivered Lady Bonneville into Audrey's capable hands, she limped to her bedchamber on swollen, aching feet.

All she wanted was to remove her gown, collapse on her bed, and slip into the oblivion of sleep.

But there, on her pillow, was a note.

Charles had not let her down—at least not in this.

He'd retrieved Mama's letter, just as he'd said he would.

She sat on the edge of the mattress, pondering the scene in the library, desperately wishing there could be some other explanation for what she'd seen. He had been lying on top of Lady Yardley. In the darkness Rose hadn't been able to assess their state of undress or discern their expressions, but she had definitely heard a moan. All in all, a rather damning set of circumstances.

Though her heart had been trampled and bruised, she couldn't help but feel a flicker of hope that she'd soon have answers about Mama's whereabouts. Summoning courage, she picked up the letter and opened it.

Dear Diana,

I am writing to you with grave news—the sort that no one ever wishes to share. As you know, I have suffered from a variety of maladies of late. After consulting with two physicians, I have at last received a diagnosis. And now I wish that I had not.

It seems I am afflicted with consumption. My prognosis is not favorable, and given the severity of my symptoms, I fear the worst.

Suddenly, I find myself quite alone. Companions who were once delighted to dine and dance with me now treat me as an outcast. I am hopeful that you will prove to be different, however, for I am in dire need of a friend.

I am in London, in St. Bartholomew's Hospital, a far cry from the sun-soaked, luxurious French mansion where I used to laze about, indulging my every desire. The knowledge that I could well spend the rest of my days here frightens me to my core.

I suppose that a mother who abandons her children to pursue a life of debauchery deserves no less.

However, I now must prevail upon our longstanding friendship and beg three favors of you.

First, I would ask for news of Owen, Olivia, and Rose. Knowing that they are well and happily settled in spite of my maternal deficiencies would be a great comfort.

Second, I'd request that you keep my condition a secret. My name is already tarnished beyond repair, and if the ton learns that I am back in London, my children shall know no peace. I have no wish to burden them with this news or humiliate them further.

Last, I'd implore you to visit me here—at your earliest convenience. Though I'm surrounded by patients and nurses, I confess to being desperately lonely. In addition, I'd like to give you a few personal items for safekeeping.

> *Sorrowfully yours,*
> *Lily*

Rose's pulse pounded in her ears. Consumption.

Regardless of what Mama thought, no one deserved that.

Mama had said her prognosis was not favorable, but perhaps something could be done for her. Maybe there was reason to hope.

One thing Rose knew for sure was that she had to share this information with Owen and Olivia as soon as possible. They had a right to know about Mama's condition.

What they decided to do with the knowledge would be their decision, but Rose already knew what *she* needed to do.

She would go to St. Bartholomew's and help her mother in any way she could.

She sprang off the bed and paced the length of her room. Lady Bonneville planned to return to London the following week, but perhaps Rose could persuade her to make the trip earlier—she gazed at the veritable blizzard outside her window—if the roads permitted.

Clenching her fists, she struggled to come to terms with the horrible vision of her beautiful, vibrant mother, neglected and withering away in a crowded hospital ward. It was almost unfathomable.

Did Charles have an inkling of the sad news in the letter he'd delivered? Even if he hadn't had the time to decipher it, Lady Yardley might have enlightened him. Indeed, she seemed eager to share all sorts of things with him.

Swallowing the bitterness in her throat, Rose glided toward the bed and swept the holly sprig off her pillow. She twirled it between her finger and thumb, then held it to her chest, ignoring the pricks of the leaves against her skin.

The lovely memory of her encounter with Charles in the folly the day before was sullied by what she'd seen in the library earlier that night. She just couldn't reconcile the two incidents with what she knew about Charles. She had so many questions.

And she would have answers.

She kicked off her delicate slippers and donned her warmest, sturdiest pair of boots. Without bothering to change out of her ball gown, she threw on her fur-lined cloak and gloves. The walk to Charles's cottage wasn't long, but any distance in a half foot of snow was bound to present a challenge.

Rose exited her room and made her way to the back staircase. Most of the staff were still tending to guests at the ball. She suspected that the rest were getting some much-deserved sleep.

No one saw her tiptoe down the stairs or sneak out of the servants' entrance.

The moment she left the protection of the manor house, whirling flakes assaulted her face and fallen snow drenched the hem of her cloak. Rose pulled her hood over her head and trudged forward.

Chapter Sixteen

Charles shoved the last of his clothes in a bag and glanced around the cottage for any belongings he might have overlooked. He'd set out a large bowl of water and a plate of leftover chicken and fish morsels for Ash, who strutted back and forth, flicking his tail as though demanding an explanation for the packing.

Pointing to the heaping plate, Charles warned, "Make this last for a few days, or else you'll be reduced to catching your own food."

The cat let out an indignant meow.

Chuckling, Charles crouched and rubbed Ash's head, just between his crooked ears. "Take care of Rose. And if one day you crave adventure, you could always stow away on a ship and join me in America."

Ash yawned and plopped himself on the rug in front of the fireplace, indicating the likelihood of that particular scenario.

Charles hoisted a large bag onto one shoulder and

slung a smaller leather sack over the other. It would be a long, arduous walk to Bath, but he didn't want to wait till morning. The sooner he put Yardley Manor behind him, the better.

He'd find an inn where he could warm up with a pint of ale, then depart for London on the first mail coach that came through town. If he took two or three lucrative jobs on the docks, he'd soon have enough money to buy a parcel of land. Then he could leave England's shores forever.

Leaving Yardley Manor was easy. Leaving Rose... well, nothing could be bloody harder.

But it was also inevitable.

"Good-bye, Ash." Bracing himself for a bitter blast, Charles opened the door, and froze.

There, shivering on his doorstep, stood Rose, her hand suspended in mid-air as though she were about to knock.

Jesus. Her teeth chattered and her lips had turned blue. Her hand dropped and her gaze flicked over him, his luggage, and the empty cottage behind him. Damn.

He dropped both of his bags, kicked them aside, and hauled her inside. Firmly shutting the door behind her, he pulled her toward the fireplace and warmth of the embers that still glowed there. "What are you doing here? You shouldn't be out on a night like this."

She blinked slowly, her lashes glistening with icy crystals. "Y-you were about to leave."

Guilty. He turned toward the hearth, threw another log on the grate, and blew life into the fire. "I was going to call on you once you returned to London. You're supposed to be at the ball right now, and trudging through the snow to come here was foolish—not to mention dangerous."

"I had t-to know."

"I . . . I don't understand." He guided her to the bench, tugged off her gloves, and rubbed her hands between his own. "What do you need to know?"

"What happened in the library—w-when you went to retrieve the letter?"

He looked away, reluctant to relate the whole of it. "It doesn't matter, does it? It's now in your possession, as it should be. Did you read it? Did you learn anything helpful?"

"It matters to me," she said simply. "I must know what you did in exchange for the letter."

Puzzled, he dragged his hands down his face. "In exchange for the— Wait. Did you happen to wander into the library? Slam the door perhaps?"

"I was fetching Lady Bonneville's fan. I passed by . . . and c-couldn't resist a peek."

Good God. "Rose, it may have looked bad, but whatever you may have seen—"

"It's not as though you owe me your loyalty. I understand that. I just believed, perhaps incorrectly, that what you and I had was . . . special."

No wonder she was distraught. Lady Yardley's groping might well give him nightmares, too. He looked into Rose's eyes, past the hurt and doubt, willing her to believe what he was about to say. "I was not engaged in a tryst with Lady Yardley."

She raised her chin. "What would you call it then? I desperately want to believe there's another explanation for what I saw. Truly, I do. But please don't mistake me for the naïve girl I once was. I'm strong enough to hear the truth."

He'd hoped to spare her all the sordid details but couldn't—not unless he wished her last impression of him to be that of a cold and calculating rake.

So he sat on the bench beside her and recounted everything, starting with Lady Yardley discovering him in the library and ending with him stuffing his hand down her dress. That part even made her smile a little.

The sympathy in her eyes told him she believed him, took him at his word. Thank God.

"It seems so unfair," she said. "That you should lose your position just because you don't return Lady Yardley's feelings."

There was the small matter of him stealing her letters as well, but mentioning it would only make Rose feel worse. "She didn't fire me; I quit. All things considered, it's for the best. The sooner I begin working for myself— instead of someone else—the better."

"Still, I can't believe you were going to leave without saying good-bye." The pain in her eyes, raw and intense, echoed in his chest.

"That wouldn't have been my choice. I never wanted to hurt you . . . and I'm sorry that I have."

"Please don't leave tonight," she pleaded.

"I must. But first I'll deliver you safely back to the manor house."

"Couldn't I just stay here?"

"Impossible. But I think we could give you an hour to thaw before we brave the blizzard again."

"An hour."

"I wish we had more time," he admitted. He would have liked a lifetime with her. "But I suppose we should be grateful for what we have."

She reached for his hand and laced her fingers through his. "Yes."

"Did you read the letter?"

"I did. But I don't want to discuss it right now—not because I don't trust you, but because if we have only one hour left together, I want to spend every minute of it focused on you and me."

The sentiment, so sweet and sincere, warmed him to the core. He wrapped an arm around her and pulled her close so he could memorize the scent of her skin, the color of her hair, the curve of her hip. She leaned her head on his shoulder and sighed softly.

As they listened to the crackle of the fire in the grate and the patter of flakes on the windows, he twined a damp curl around his index finger, mesmerized by the way it reflected light, just as she did.

The two of them existed in a strange twilight where they both knew they'd soon have to go their separate ways—and where neither was prepared to let go. Not yet.

"I feel as though I've been robbed," she said softly. "Of the time we were supposed to have together. I know it would have been only a few more days, but I would have savored each one."

"I would have, too."

"Do you want to know what I think?"

"Hmm?"

Color rose in her cheeks. "That we should make this a night we will remember always."

"I'm not likely to forget it," he said with a smile.

"True. But for all the wrong reasons. We must make happy memories." Still holding his hand, she stood and tugged him toward the ladder to the loft. "Come with me."

Dear God. "Rose, I don't think we should—"

She placed his hand on her chest, over her rapidly beating heart. "Do you feel that? I want to be with you. And I think you want to be with me."

He'd never wanted anything more. "Yes, but—"

"We planned to share a night of passion, and as it turns out, this is our opportunity. Our only one." Her voice caught on the last word.

He swallowed. "I know. It just doesn't seem right to lay with you, to love you, and then walk away forever. You deserve more."

"I deserve to make my own choices. And I choose you. I choose *this*." Twining her fingers in his hair, she pulled his head lower and melded her mouth to his. Her lips, cool at first, warmed on contact. Her tongue was insistent, exploring his mouth, demanding his surrender.

His body responded instantly and powerfully. Every muscle tensed in anticipation and his breath caught in his throat. Blood thrummed in his veins and rushed to his cock. He was gone.

He undid the tie at her throat and shoved her cloak off her shoulders. The silky blue gown she wore glowed like the moon. Its low, square neckline and barely there puffed sleeves framed her pixie-like face. The sash cinched below her breasts revealed their fullness while accentuating her slender frame. Yards of glistening satin skimmed over her hips and legs, hinting at her lithe but sweetly curved body.

"When I first saw you in the ballroom tonight, you took my breath away. Your gown...it's beautiful," he said, aware of the inadequacy of his words. "*You* are beautiful."

She looked down, admiring the dress. "Thank you. Belle made it. She has a gift."

"Perhaps," he said, "but you are beautiful apart from the gown. Your beauty is in your kindness and compassion. It's in your wisdom and grace. It's as much a part of you as your heart. And it's why I adore you so."

"Oh, Charles," she breathed. "I adore you, too. I think I've always known that we were meant for each other. We may not have a lifetime together, but the days we've had have *counted*. They're the days that the sun has felt warmer, the fields have looked greener, and the birdsong has sounded sweeter. If I live to be one hundred, the days I've spent with you are the ones I'll treasure most."

A lump lodged in his throat, and he looked at the ground, not trusting himself to speak. When the stinging behind his eyes subsided, he met her steady gaze, cupped her face in his hands, and brushed his thumbs across her impossibly smooth skin. "You said earlier that you thought we had something special. We do. It's a connection that transcends words and distance and even time. No matter where I go or what I do, you'll be a part of me—the best part of me."

A tear spilled down her cheek, and he kissed it away, tasting the salt and sharing her emotion. But now was not the time for crying. She was right. If they had only an hour together, he didn't want to fill it with tears or rage or angst.

No. They'd drive all that away with passion, pleasure, humor . . . and love.

With a grin, he said, "You did want to see my loft."

"I did." She managed a watery, wobbly smile.

"And do you always get what you want?"

"I'll have to let you know after tonight."

Chapter Seventeen

Harness: (1) A type of tack used to hitch a horse to a carriage or wagon. (2) To gain control over, as in After years of denying their passion, they could no longer harness it.

They didn't go to the loft right away.

Rose pushed Charles's greatcoat off his shoulders and then removed the jacket beneath it. After that, they played a tantalizing little game in which each took a turn at removing an article of clothing from the other. Plenty warm from the fire and their desire, she savored every round.

Charles patted the bench, directing her to sit. When she did, he removed both her boots, cradled one of her feet in his hands, and pushed her skirt up past her knee.

Smiling wickedly, he rubbed her heel, massaged her arch, tugged lightly on her toes. Her whole body melted a little, relaxing under his expert touch. He treated her other foot to the same pampering, then kissed his way from her ankle to her calf to her knee, sending sweet shivers through her body.

He pushed the hem of her dress higher, letting it glide over her thighs, and though the unmistakable hunger in his eyes thrilled her, she stopped him.

Because it was her turn, after all.

She rose and smoothly guided him to sit, switching places. When he reached for her hips, she skirted his grasp and moved behind the bench. The white cloth of his shirt stretched across his muscled shoulders and clung to the contours of his back. With a fingertip, she traced the indent of his spine all the way to his waistband. Heady with anticipation, she grabbed a fistful of shirt and pulled it up, exposing his tapered torso inch by inch. He lifted his arms, freed his head and hands, and tossed the shirt aside. When he would have turned to embrace her, she placed a firm hand on each of his shoulders, stilling him. For she wanted to explore.

His body was breathtaking, more stirring than any painting or statue. She glided her hands over the breadth of his shoulders and down his upper arms, skimming her palms over hard muscles. Unable to resist the temptation of his neck, she leaned forward and kissed the soft skin near the curve of his shoulder. She tasted him, nipping at his neck and shoulders, wondering if she pleased him half as much as he pleased her. In answer, he moaned and gripped the front edge of the bench as though she'd pushed him to the very limits of his control.

Emboldened, she slipped her arms around him, raining kisses on his back as she caressed his chest, smoothed her palms over his nipples, and felt the downy hair on his hard, flat abdomen. When she dipped the tips of her fingers below his belt, he seized her wrist and stood, freeing himself from the circle of her arms.

"My turn." A feral grin lit his face as he led her around the bench, directly in front of the crackling fire. His heavy-lidded gaze raked over her, lingering on her lips, her breasts, her hips.

Slowly, as if he were unwrapping a long-awaited gift, he reached behind her and tugged on one end of her silk sash, releasing the bow. The ribbon pooled on the floor, and her dress loosened—a gloriously liberating feeling. Charles moved behind her, swept aside the tendrils of hair at her nape, and bent his head to her neck. As he kissed her, the slight stubble on his jaw prickled her skin, leaving her breathless. She closed her eyes and leaned back against him, reveling in the warm, solid wall of his chest.

Impatiently, he pushed her sleeves off her shoulders and down her arms. When they would go no farther, he found the laces of her dress and worked them loose. All the while, he whispered in her ear, nibbled on her lobe, and kissed the column of her neck, driving her dizzy with desire. At last, her gown fell away, a puddle of silk at her feet.

Charles spun her around and growled, running his rough palms over the sensitive skin of her arms. "I've wanted you for so long," he said. "I wouldn't even admit it to myself, but I've wanted you since that summer. Dreamed of you. Longed for you."

His words, coupled with the tender look in his eyes, thrilled and humbled her. "I've wanted you for . . . forever."

He reached for the laces of her corset then, and even though it was supposed to be her turn, she allowed it, for denying him would have been denying herself. He separated the halves of her stays several inches, and she raised her arms as he gently lifted the corset over her head, leaving her wearing nothing save her thin chemise.

The corset fell from his fingers as he stepped back and blinked. "My God, you're beautiful." He started toward her then as though he'd devour her, but she halted him with a raised hand.

"It's my turn," she said. "Let's take off your ... boots."

"I have a proposition for you," he countered.

"I'm listening."

"I'll take off my boots, if you'll take down your hair. It will save time."

She barely flinched at the mention of time, even though she resented every relentless tick of the clock. "You have a deal, Mr. Holland."

He sat on the bench like he was taking the front row seat at an opera, eager for the performance to start. She waited for him to begin pulling off his boots, then reached up to remove the pins from her hair.

Long, heavy curls tumbled free, tickling her back. As she shook them out and massaged away the tightness on her scalp, a sigh of pleasure escaped her. "That's better," she said.

"Indeed." The approval in his eyes warmed her exposed skin.

He'd removed his boots, leaving only his trousers.

She was down to one garment as well.

The game had reached its final round—only it was no longer a game.

He stood, enveloped her hand in his, and looked at her with a tenderness that almost made her weep. "I want you to know," he said, "that if things were different, I'd give you the world. I'd spend my entire life—"

"Stop." Each word he spoke brought exquisite, excruciating pain. She couldn't endure torture wrought by visions of what might have been. "At this moment," she said, "I'm exactly where I want to be, where I need to be—with you. That's all that matters."

He hauled her close and covered her mouth with his, pressing his hips against hers and running his hands over her body. A minute later they were both breathless and wild with wanting. "It's time for your tour of the loft."

Charles went up the ladder first, and Rose followed right behind. She waited on the third rung and watched as he lit a small lamp and covered the pallet with a soft, thick quilt. Then he extended a hand to help her climb the rest of the way. The ceiling slanted above their heads, much too low to allow them to stand. But the cozy quarters made for an inviting bedroom. Light from the lamp flickered low on the wooden walls, and the heat from the fire rose up to warm them. Two books sat on a crate next to the pallet.

Rose nodded at them. "You were going to leave them?"

"They're of little use to me." He stared, challenging her to contradict him. Though tempted, she didn't take the bait. Oh, she didn't doubt he possessed the drive and determination to succeed in whatever he wished, but she wouldn't let him think she measured his worth by his ability to read, because she didn't, any more than she measured it by his wealth, social standing, or even his knee-melting good looks.

"I like it up here." She lay on her side, leaning on an elbow and propping her head on her hand. "It feels like a retreat from the world."

He stretched out beside her. "I've slept here for months

but never thought of it that way. Now that I'm here with you, I like it a lot more."

The lamp's glow illuminated the contours of his chest, defining every muscle and indentation. The sprinkling of hair covering the center of his torso proved irresistible, and she glided her palm over it, then down his side and over his hip.

At his sharp intake of breath, she met his gaze.

"You know," he said gruffly, "we don't have to make love. We could lie here with each other and talk and kiss."

A touch of anger ignited within her and she sat up abruptly. "No. I want everything with you. I want your skin against mine. I want to taste you. I want to be as close to you as a person can be." To be sure he understood the sincerity of her words, she pushed him flat against the pallet, straddled him, and kissed him with all the passion pent up inside her.

A glorious curtain of red hair surrounded Charles's head. He inhaled the scents of oranges and soap... and Rose. The night had a surreal quality—as though the snow had stopped time and created a haven where his wildest fantasies could come true.

Rose was here with him, in the flesh. He savored the weight of her on his hips and the view of her breasts above her loose, white shift. Thus far, he'd maintained a scrap of control, but her kisses intoxicated him and her touch seduced him, stripping him of everything but desire and—he couldn't deny it—love.

He pulled the flimsy tie at her neckline and tugged the fabric lower, exposing her breasts. Moaning, he flipped her onto her back and removed the chemise entirely.

With her auburn hair fanned out behind her and her pale, smooth skin glowing, she resembled a wanton goddess. Her sultry eyes shone with complete trust and her pink, swollen lips smiled in wicked invitation.

Which he readily accepted.

He hauled off his trousers and, at last, no barriers existed between them—at least, not the physical kind. She gave herself completely, sighing as he suckled her breasts and arching her back as he traced circles on her inner thighs. She seemed eager to explore, too, running her hands over his buttocks and tentatively circling her fingers around his—

Dear God.

He gasped, struggling to deny his body the release it suddenly demanded. More than anything, he wanted to make the experience pleasurable for her, but she looked, felt, and tasted so impossibly good. Too good.

"Rose," he choked out, "I don't know if I can...wait."

Tangling her fingers in his hair, she shot him a pleased smile. "You don't have to. *We* don't have to."

He swallowed the curse on his lips. He hadn't been with many women before, and they were generally more experienced than he. The thought of causing Rose pain... well, it sickened him. "I'm afraid it might hurt at first."

"I'm not," she breathed. "When you kiss and hold me, I feel only pleasure."

Jesus, she was amazing. Speechless, he poured his emotions into every kiss, every caress. When he positioned himself at her entrance, she wrapped her legs around him and threw her arms around his neck. "I want you, Charles. I have no doubts, and I'll have no regrets."

He touched his forehead to hers, slipped his hands

beneath her soft bottom, and slowly eased into her. At her sharp intake of breath, he stilled, his muscles quivering with restraint. He wanted to lose himself in her—to let go of all his ambitions and shortcomings, his dreams and failures—and steal a few moments of blissful contentment. With her.

"Are you all right?"

In answer, she wrapped her legs more tightly around him and drew him in. Deeper, harder, faster.

Over the blood pounding in his ears, he heard her whisper, "Yes, yes." And that was his undoing. Release barreled through him, stripping his soul of doubt and worry, leaving only the brief perfection of him and Rose together.

Much too brief.

He pulled out, spilling his seed on the quilt. It was bad enough that he'd taken her virginity. He couldn't leave her with child as well. She made a little cry of protest when he rolled away, and he knew that he hadn't brought her pleasure. Yet.

He lay next to her, and as his heartbeat slowly returned to normal, traced lazy swirls on her belly. "How do you feel?"

"Like I've been ravished," she teased. "In the best possible way."

"It wasn't the best, I fear."

"No?" She looked surprised—and a bit hopeful.

"I should have taken more time," he admitted. "When it comes to you, my control is in short supply."

"I wouldn't have it any other way."

"But now," he said huskily, "I want to see you let go."

A fetching blush stole across her cheeks. "Let go?"

"Mmm."

"Like the other day in the folly?"

"Exactly. Except maybe better."

"Better?" Rose could hardly imagine. But she was more than happy to let Charles do his best. He kissed her…everywhere. The hollow of her throat, the undersides of her breasts, the base of her spine. The brush of his lips across her skin made her burn with desire, made her want him more. He let his hands roam free as well, teasing her taut nipples, stroking the backs of her legs, and gently touching the still-tender folds at her entrance.

She didn't close her eyes, for she loved watching his handsome face and seeing the intensity with which he devoted himself to the task of pleasuring her. He seemed in tune to her every sigh, quiver, and moan, doing the things that she liked the best till the sweet pulsing began in her core, drowning out her troubles and sweeping away her doubts.

But just when she was on the brink of something spectacular, his wicked fingers stilled.

He trailed kisses down her belly, alternately licking and nipping until she thought she'd go mad with desire. His head dipped lower then, and he parted her legs, seemingly intent on…

And then he *was*. His tongue, warm and wet, brought her to new heights. Every wicked stroke brought her further, enticing her to forget everything but this, everything but him. Every muscle in her body tensed, on the edge of ecstasy. Her fingers clutched the quilt, grasping for anything to keep her from plummeting too fast, too hard.

As though he sensed her need for something solid to

hold on to, he reached for her hands and laced his fingers through hers. He squeezed tightly, encouraging her to trust him, to let go.

And for him, for herself, she did. Spasms rocked her body and her cries filled the cottage. The force of her release, so exquisite and so raw, was almost too much, but Charles wouldn't let her flee from it. Instead, he stayed with her, ensuring she rode out every wave, seeing her pleasure to its completion.

He lay beside her once more, swept the damp tendrils from her cheeks, and kissed her with heartbreaking tenderness. "*Now* you've been properly ravished," he whispered.

"It certainly feels that way." Her limbs had turned to jelly, and glorious tremors still echoed softly in her core.

"I shall return in just a moment," he promised, and he did. Using the damp cloth he'd fetched, he gently washed away the evidence of their lovemaking from her body first, then his. Afterward, he pulled a blanket over them, hauled her close, and held her tight, like he never wanted to let her go.

Her cheek pressed to his chest, she breathed in the scent of him and committed it to memory. The steady rhythm of his breathing lulled her into a dreamlike state, and her eyes fluttered shut.

His voice heavy with regret, he said, "We must go soon."

"Mmm," she murmured, just short of agreeing.

For she had the sinking, certain feeling that the best night of her life was about to become the worst.

Chapter Eighteen

Rose didn't sleep, and she doubted Charles had either. They lingered in the loft longer than they should have, and yet not nearly long enough.

When the sun's first rays reflected off the snow and penetrated the cottage's threadbare curtains, they descended the ladder and dressed. Charles gathered up all the pins he could find on the floor and handed them to her. He had neither a hairbrush nor looking glass in the cottage, so she twisted the heavy length of her hair into a bun at her nape and secured it as best she could. Frowning, she asked, "How is this?"

"Beautiful." His soft, sincere expression almost made her believe it—in spite of her matted hair, wrinkled gown, and puffy eyes.

It didn't matter anyway.

The flakes had stopped falling and the wind had ceased blowing, but a foot of fluffy snow covered the ground. Frigid air seeped beneath the door and around the windows, and last night's crackling fire had turned to cold, gray ash.

Even after Rose slipped on her cloak, she couldn't help shivering. Charles shrugged into his greatcoat, looked into her eyes, and held her hands in his as though he meant to say something sweet and tender.

So she cut him off. She had to. "If you don't mind, I think I'd rather not say good-bye." If she started crying, she wasn't likely to stop, and she didn't want to make this harder than it already was.

He nodded. She'd known he'd understand. He always had.

He left his two bags just inside the door. "I'll return for these after I see you safely back to the manor house. Ready?"

No, she wanted to scream. *And I never will be*. But instead of shouting, she summoned all the courage she possessed and gave him a small smile. "Yes."

She took the hand he offered as he opened the door and followed him across the vast frozen lawn. He packed down the snow, making a path for her, and she tried valiantly not to think of him walking all the way to town in the bitter cold. She tried not to think about Mama's horrid illness. She tried not to think about anything except putting one foot in front of the other.

Too soon, they reached the servants' entrance. He stepped aside so that she could walk past him to the door. She couldn't bring herself to look at him, but when she would have released his hand, he refused to let go. "Wait."

She knew gazing into his amber eyes was a bad idea, that it would only prolong the inevitable, and that it would increase the pain for both of them. But she was powerless to deny him.

He grasped her arms and pulled her forward, touching his nose to hers. "Rose, there's something I must say. I—"

"I need to go."

"Please. This is no way to—"

Dear God, he was killing her. "Don't you see? There's no point in saying anything."

"Fine." He clenched his jaw. "No words. But hear this."

He pressed his lips to hers, lifting her off her feet, and robbing her of breath. He kissed her like he wished she were his.

That was the irony of the whole thing.

She *was* his. And she always would be.

When at last he released her, she dashed for the door, relieved to find it unlocked. She didn't dare look back, but stepped inside, shutting the door on the only man she'd ever truly love.

Inside the servants' entrance, maids and footmen bustled to and fro, preparing breakfast and performing their morning chores. Upon seeing Rose, a couple of them froze as though stunned. Another covered her mouth, clearly horrified.

Rose stomped her feet on the mat, shook the snow off her hem, and held her head high. "Good morning," she said. Then she walked by them as though it were perfectly normal for a young lady to sneak into the house through the back entrance in the wee hours of the morning.

She might be heartbroken, but she refused to be ashamed.

Luncheon was an awkward affair. Rose pushed the food around on her plate, and Lady Yardley was uncharacteristically quiet. Both women were the objects of Lady Bonneville's shrewd gaze.

"In my considerable experience," the viscountess began, "I have found that the conversation on the morning after a ball is often more entertaining than the ball itself."

Rose and Lady Yardley nodded halfheartedly.

"Very well." The viscountess rolled her eyes dramatically. "I see it is up to me to begin. I noticed that Rose had many dance partners, including a couple who could arguably be considered dashing."

Rose forced herself to swallow a morsel of ham. The ball seemed a lifetime ago.

Lady Bonneville sighed in exasperation. "So now you must tell us, Rose, which of the gentlemen was your favorite partner and why."

Her dance with Charles had been magical, but she couldn't very well admit that in front of Lady Yardley. "Each of the gentlemen was kind and chivalrous. I enjoyed their company."

"Spare no details. Did any of them trample your feet or have horrid breath?"

"No," Rose said.

The viscountess frowned. "How dreadfully untitillating. However, since you look as though you're about to fall off your chair from exhaustion, I shall forgive it." She turned her attention toward Lady Yardley. "Now then, as hostess of the ball, you must be privy to all manner of gossip. Which of the guests imbibed too much? Who overstayed their welcome?"

Lady Yardley set down her fork. "Lord Westman and his daughter were the last to leave. His coach became stuck in the snow halfway down the drive. I invited him to stay here for the night, but he insisted they could make it home. I sent out three footmen with shovels and a half hour later, the coach was on its way."

"Westman is a mulish sort," Lady Bonneville mused. As though suddenly inspired, she sat up taller. "What about trysts?"

Lady Yardley blinked nervously. "Pardon?"

"Rendezvous, assignations," the viscountess replied.

Rose nearly choked on her sip of tea.

Lady Bonneville shot her a fleeting look of concern before proceeding with her interrogation. "Did the staff witness anything of a scandalous nature? Did they notice whether any of the guests made use of other rooms in the house for their indiscretions?"

Blushing, Lady Yardley shook her head. "Not that I'm aware of. There was one incident that was rather troubling."

"Oh?" Lady Bonneville's brows shot up her forehead.

"It involves a member of my staff." She shot a brief, accusatory look in Rose's direction. "I'd rather not elaborate until I have all the facts, but it appears I'm the victim of a robbery."

"How awful!" Lady Bonneville exclaimed with delight. "What was taken? And by whom?"

"The investigation has just begun. However, I've already taken steps to ensure this sort of thing doesn't happen again."

Rose simmered with barely contained anger. Charles was no thief. Well, perhaps in the strictest sense of the word, but it wasn't as though Mama's letter had any intrinsic value—at least not to anyone but her. Lady Yardley was not the victim here.

In fact, Rose was glad that Charles was leaving. If he wasn't already on his way to London, he soon would be.

Lady Yardley's vindictive and false accusations were unlikely to follow him there, and if they did, they certainly wouldn't follow him across the Atlantic to America.

"Are you quite all right, Rose?" Lady Bonneville asked. "You have the murderous look of someone who's had a pot of tea spilled on your favorite gown."

Oh, it was worse than that. Far worse. She took a couple of deep breaths through her nose to compose herself. Then, looking directly at Lady Yardley, she said, "I suppose it's just that I find dishonesty deeply disturbing."

"As do I," Lady Bonneville quickly assured her. "As do I." Once again, she leveled assessing glances at Rose and Lady Yardley. "Fortunately, the truth has a way of coming to light, eventually."

"I do hope so," Rose murmured.

"I trust you will let us know how it all turns out if we are not here to see for ourselves," Lady Bonneville said to their hostess. "For I fear Rose and I must soon return to London."

If there was one thing that could have cheered Rose that morning, leaving Bath was it. Now that Charles was gone, their departure couldn't come soon enough.

"We can't leave immediately, of course," the viscountess added, dashing Rose's hopes. "We've promised to attend the ball at the Assembly Rooms two days hence. But I see no reason we can't return home the following day—assuming the snow has melted sufficiently."

Two days. They'd feel like an eternity. Now that she knew Mama's plight, Rose wanted to go to her immediately. And she wanted to put distance between her and this place and all its blissful, torturous memories. She wanted to go home.

• • •

Charles was numb. From the cold of his journey and from the pain of leaving Rose.

The trek from his cottage to Bath had taken him all morning and would have taken longer if a farmer hadn't offered him a ride in the back of his wagon.

Bone weary, Charles took a room at the first inn he came to, the White Lion, and inquired about the mail coach. Though it normally arrived in the late afternoon, the innkeeper predicted a delay due to weather.

Either way, Charles figured he had some time. He staggered up the stairs to his room, threw down his bags, and fell onto the bed, hoping exhaustion would give him a few hours of oblivion.

Bang.

Pulse pounding, Charles bolted upright in bed and scrambled toward his ladder. Except this wasn't his loft and he wasn't in his cottage. He blinked at the bags on the floor. Ah yes, the White Lion. Outside the room's only window, darkness loomed. He must have slept for hours.

Bang, bang. "Mr. Holland?"

He couldn't imagine who would know that he'd taken a room at this particular inn, much less who would care.

Part of him longed to cover his head with the pillow and remain in bed. But from the sound of the pounding, the person on the other side of the door was about to break it down. "I'm coming."

He unlocked the door, cracked it open a few inches, and two burly men muscled their way into the tiny room, nearly trampling him. "Are you Charles Holland?"

"Why do you ask?"

The two men exchanged a brief look, and the taller one nodded. Before Charles knew what was happening, the shorter, stockier one slammed him against the wall and wedged his forearm under Charles's chin. The other man pulled a pistol from his waistband and aimed it at Charles's head.

Holy hell. The arm jammed against his throat made him gasp for breath, but he managed to choke out, "What do you want with me?"

"So you *are* Holland."

There was no use denying it. "I think you've made a mis—"

"You're under arrest."

"What?" He shoved himself away from the wall but froze when he felt the cool barrel of the pistol pressed against his temple. "I haven't done anything."

"No?" The one with the gun arched a brow as though he'd heard the same yarn countless times.

And then Charles realized why they'd come for him. The letters. Lady Yardley must have reported him to the magistrate. The pistol aimed at his head and the bursting into the room seemed a bit overmuch, considering all he'd taken were a couple of sheets of paper, but surely the matter could be resolved with a calm explanation of the facts.

One thing he knew with certainty: he would not implicate Rose in any way, or under any circumstances.

"You're coming with us," the taller man said.

"Fine." The sooner the matter was straightened out, the sooner he could be on his way to London . . . and then America.

Each of the men grabbed an arm and started hauling him out of the room.

"Wait. My bags."

The men exchanged another look, and for a heart-stopping second, Charles thought they'd refuse to let him keep them—all he owned in the world.

"Search 'em," said the tall one.

He kept his pistol trained on Charles while the stocky man rummaged through the bags. He found a knife, held it up for inspection, and confiscated it, sticking it in his belt. "Nothing else in here," he said, pushing aside Charles's clothes, the lone miniature portrait of his parents, and the ribbon he'd taken from Rose's room.

"Good, then he can carry them."

Charles picked up a bag in each hand and nodded at the hook beside the door. "What about my coat?"

The tall one grunted, checked the pockets, and tossed the coat at him. "No more delays. Let's go."

The men threw him into a coach waiting in front of the inn and sat on the bench across from him. It was too dark to discern much, but he could feel the pistol trained on him and could imagine the disgusted glares they shot his way.

"Where are we going?"

"Not Carlton House—that's for damn sure."

"What, exactly, is the charge against me?"

"Larceny."

Even though he'd expected it, hearing the word spoken made his stomach sink like a stone.

Good God, he was in trouble.

And facing the very real and terrifying possibility that he would spend the rest of his life in a prison cell.

Why would Lady Yardley want to destroy him? Even in the confines of his mind, he recognized the naïveté of his question. He'd scorned her. She meant to exact revenge.

But the countess didn't know who she was dealing with. The good-natured, accommodating steward she'd once given orders to was gone—for good. From now on, Charles worked for no one but himself. And he'd come too far to let her ruin his plans.

She had no proof of his guilt, but if it was to be a case of her word against his, he didn't like his chances.

No, he wouldn't hang about a prison waiting for a sentence he didn't deserve. Somehow, he would be on a ship bound for America before the trial ever occurred.

As the coach rumbled through the dark streets carrying him closer and closer to Bath prison, Charles looked out the window, carefully tucking away any information that might be useful.

For it was never too soon to devise an escape plan.

Chapter Nineteen

Muzzle: (1) The part of a horse's face comprised of the nostrils, mouth, and chin. (2) To restrain from speech, as in The viscountess would have sorely loved to muzzle her vindictive, devious adversary.

The next morning in the drawing room, Rose sat across the chessboard from Lady Bonneville. Sad and anxious, Rose fought the urge to withdraw. It would be so easy to shut herself off from the world again, to retreat from the pain and sadness.

But she couldn't do that anymore. Wouldn't. She had a responsibility to Olivia and Owen, to Charles—and to herself.

So she forced herself to sleep, dress, eat, and converse as though her heart hadn't been shattered into a million pieces.

Fortunately, the chess match did not require much of her concentration. Lady Bonneville would have been a capable and skilled opponent if she cared about the outcome. But she couldn't be bothered to expend her limited

energy on a trifling game. She never thought more than a
move or two ahead. At least in chess.

Social matters, on the other hand, were a completely
different matter. In those, she was a formidable strate-
gist, employing all manner of strikes and counterstrikes.
Whenever the viscountess steered the conversation to
eligible gentlemen, formal balls, or morning calls, Rose
knew she had better be on her toes.

"I heard a rather shocking piece of news at breakfast
this morning." The viscountess cavalierly moved her
pawn directly into the path of Rose's rook.

"News . . . or gossip?"

"Pfft. A useless distinction. I think it may interest you."

Rose thought it highly unlikely but knew better than to
say so. She pretended to study the board. "Why is that?"

"What, precisely, is your relationship to Mr. Holland?"

Rose's gaze snapped up. "You have news of him?"

The viscountess leaned back in her chair and slowly
raised her lorgnette. "I do. It seems we each have information the other desires."

"Charles—er, Mr. Holland—and I are friends. Or,
we were. He once worked in the stables at Huntford
Manor."

"Friends?" Lady Bonneville arched a brow. "Do not
forget that I observed you dancing together. I would not
describe the way you gazed at each other as *friendly*."

Heat crept up Rose's neck, but she did not look away.
"I won't deny that I care for him, but you needn't worry.
He's gone. He resigned over a disagreement with Lady
Yardley."

"Yes, she mentioned that. And here I thought that she
was fond of him."

"Perhaps he did not return her feelings." Unseemly though it was, Rose couldn't help feeling a bit smug.

"It would have been an unlikely match, but stranger things have happened."

"I suppose they have." Rose's brother, a duke, had married a poor seamstress. The difference was that Belle was lovely and sweet—not vindictive and manipulative. "In any event, I don't think his lack of affection for Lady Yardley was a proper reason to fire him."

"She claims to have other reasons."

Rose narrowed her eyes. "What do you mean?" It was bad enough that Lady Yardley had driven him away. She wouldn't tolerate slanderous gossip about Charles on top of it.

"She says that your Mr. Holland stole items of considerable value from a secure location in the library."

"That's preposterous." He'd taken a few letters. For her. What value could they possibly have? "Did she happen to mention what the items were?"

"Personal correspondence. Letters of a private nature."

Rose crossed her arms. "What if I told you that I was the one who took the letters?"

The viscountess pursed her lips, as though fascinated in spite of herself. "Go on."

"I was desperate to know what had become of Mama, so I searched the library and took the letters. Lady Yardley must have confronted Charles about the missing letters…he probably confessed in order to protect me."

"Impressive." It was impossible to tell whether the viscountess referred to Charles's gallantry or Rose's lie.

For a full moment, neither woman spoke.

"Am I to assume you took the jewels as well?"

Rose shook her head. "What?"

"Your mother's letters weren't the only items missing, apparently."

Her fists clenched, Rose stood. "That's a lie!"

Lady Bonneville's gaze flicked to the door behind her. "Sit and lower your voice."

"I won't allow her to make such horrible, false accusations."

"I'm afraid she already has, dear gel." The viscountess set down her lorgnette and sighed as though suddenly weary. "Are you quite certain that the steward is as blameless as you say?"

"I'd wager my life on it." Rose's eyes burned and a huge knot lodged in her throat. "He would never steal. Lady Yardley is angry with Charles because he rejected her advances. This is her way of punishing him. And he doesn't deserve any of it."

"Perhaps not," Lady Bonneville said noncommittally, raising Rose's ire even further.

"Thank goodness he's gone," she said. "The gossip is unlikely to reach him in London, and by the time it does, he'll be on his way to America."

"I don't think so."

"Pardon?"

"I'm afraid Mr. Holland has been detained…in the Bath prison."

The room began to spin, and Rose gripped the arms of her chair. "Prison?"

"Yes."

"How can they lock him up? They have no proof of any wrongdoing."

"According to Diana, there's a witness. Someone who

saw Charles attack her in the library on the night of the ball."

"Who? They're lying."

Lady Bonneville's expression held equal measures of sympathy and pity. "How can you be sure?"

"I saw them in the library that night. She was clearly the aggressor." Although Rose had been fooled at first, too.

"It will be very difficult for Mr. Holland to clear his name. Lady Yardley is a respected member of the ton. If she wishes to destroy him, she will."

"But that's so unjust. Surely my word must count for something."

The viscountess tented her fingers and pressed them to her lips. "It does, but she'll just say that the incident occurred later, after all the guests had left and you had gone to bed."

Rose drew a long deep breath. "I can prove Charles's innocence."

"How?"

She swallowed and looked Lady Bonneville directly in the eye. "I was with him. All night. In his cottage."

Through multiple layers of face powder, the viscountess's cheeks shone red. Her chest heaved, her mouth gaped, and for several surreal seconds she was speechless.

When at last she spoke, her eyes blazed with frightening intensity. "You will listen to me very carefully, Rose."

Not trusting herself to speak, she nodded.

"You must never—ever—repeat what you just told me."

"But it's the—"

She held up a bejeweled hand. "*No.* You must trust me on this. You are young, and you may even fancy yourself in love, but I will *not* let you ruin your life for a man who worked in the stables."

"That's not fair."

Lady Bonneville snorted. "That's life, my dear."

"It's no fault of Charles's that his parents were servants. And it's no accomplishment of mine to have been born to a duke and duchess. Charles is smart and hardworking, and yet you'd judge him harshly?"

"You are so naïve, Rose. I don't judge him because of his station in life."

"Then why? Why do you speak of him with such disdain?"

"Do you really want to know?"

Rose wasn't sure. She closed her eyes, inhaled, and opened them. "Yes."

"I judge him because he seduced you—an innocent— knowing full well that he intended to leave England forever. *That* is not the behavior of a gentleman."

Rose wanted to defend him but doubted anything she said would change Lady Bonneville's opinion. "What's going to happen to him?"

The viscountess didn't respond immediately. At last she said, "I *should* tell you that what happens to Mr. Holland is no concern of yours. But I have a strong suspicion that you will disagree. Your notions of justice and fairness can be terribly inconvenient."

"I must go to him."

"Absolutely not. I forbid it," Lady Bonneville snapped. "You cannot help him."

Rose ran her hands down her face and sprang out of her chair. "I can! I'll convince the authorities of his innocence."

"I fear the only thing you'll accomplish is your own ruin."

She paced beside the chessboard. "I don't care. I won't let him languish in a prison cell—it would kill him. He has dreams, and he values his freedom above all else."

"So it would seem," the viscountess said dryly.

Rose ignored the barb. "There must be something I can do."

"Perhaps."

She spun to face Lady Bonneville, desperate for a scrap of hope. "What?"

"I think that our best chance at helping the steward lies in convincing Diana to drop the charges." Touched by the use of the pronoun *our*, Rose had the sudden and strong urge to hug the viscountess, but she frowned upon overt displays of emotion.

"That's an excellent idea. Lady Yardley acted in the heat of the moment. Now that a little time has passed, we can reason with her."

"*We* will not do anything. *I* will."

"But—"

"You are the competition, the enemy. She is not going to acquiesce to anything you suggest, especially if you attempt to appeal to her sense of justice. In her mind, she is the only party who has been injured."

"Then how will you convince her?"

"She must be made to see that freeing Mr. Holland is in her own best interests. That it is necessary to preserving her reputation and pride." Lady Bonneville rubbed her gloved palms together and curled her lips in a chilling smile. "Such matters happen to be squarely within my area of expertise."

Rose almost—but not quite—felt sorry for Lady Yardley. If anyone could persuade her to give up her ridiculous vendetta against Charles, the viscountess could, masterfully bringing to bear every sort of societal pressure. "Thank you," Rose said sincerely. "But I still feel helpless. I wish there were something I could do myself."

"If you want to help the cause, do not attempt anything. If you do, you risk raising Diana's ire. Then all will be lost."

Rose swallowed. "I understand."

"Two days should be sufficient for me to make her see the light of reason. We will return to London the morning after the ball at the Assembly Rooms, regardless." The viscountess emphasized the last word, her meaning clear. They would leave Bath whether Charles had been freed or not. And she expected Rose to accompany her without argument.

"Very well."

"Did you find the answers you sought?"

"Pardon?"

"In the letters," Lady Bonneville clarified. "Did you learn what became of your mother?"

"Yes." But she wasn't ready to discuss it—not even with the viscountess. "At least I know where to find her."

Lady Bonneville nodded but did not press for more information. "Let us hope that all of your machinations were worth it."

Chapter Twenty

Rose had agreed not to interfere with Lady Bonneville's plans, and she was all too happy to avoid Lady Yardley. But she couldn't forget about Charles. She simply had to know how he fared. And she knew just who to ask.

Shortly after the viscountess retired for her afternoon nap, Rose spied Audrey in the corridor, carrying Lady Bonneville's red tufted footstool.

Rose stopped her and, pressing a finger to her lips, waved the maid into her room.

"My lady," Audrey whispered, "what can I do for you?"

"I have a favor to ask. It requires your discretion."

The maid frowned but nodded.

"Do you know Mr. Holland?"

"Aye. Lady Yardley's steward. The one she sacked. He was the main topic of discussion at luncheon today."

Of course the staff knew what had transpired. Rose tried not to dwell on what they all surely knew about her own recent behavior.

"I don't know if you're aware, but Mr. Holland is now in even more trouble."

"How so, my lady?"

"He's . . . in prison."

Audrey dropped the footstool with a *thud*. "What? Such a nice man. What could he have possibly done?"

"I don't believe he's done anything wrong. That is why I'm asking the favor. Could you talk to the staff and inquire whether anyone has been in contact with him? I'd like to know how he's faring." It sounded like a polite, proper inquiry, devoid of desperation. Her words gave no hint of how much she longed to go to him, to hold his hand, to cry over the injustice of it all.

"Aye, I will. They were all fond of him and upset to see him go, except perhaps for Mr. Evans, the butler. But he doesn't seem to approve of anyone. I'll see what they know downstairs." The maid's gaze flitted to Rose's hands, clenched with worry. "Do not despair, my lady. Mr. Holland is as strong as an ox and as clever as a fox. He can take care of himself."

"Thank you, Audrey." Rose mustered a small smile. "And one more thing. If, by some chance, someone is able to visit Mr. Holland, I have a message for him."

The maid tilted her capped head. "Yes?"

Rose swallowed. There was so much she wanted to say to Charles. "Please just tell him not to give up hope, and that help is on the way."

"We'll do our best," Audrey assured her. "I'll stop by after dinner this evening to let you know what I've learned." With that, she bobbed a quick curtsy, picked up the unwieldy footstool, and angled her way through the door.

Rose walked to the bed, sank onto the mattress, and exhaled slowly. Audrey was right—Charles could take care of himself. But knowing he was caged like an animal made her sick. She'd forced herself to say good-bye to him because she'd thought he'd be able to achieve his dream of owning land in America. She couldn't let all her heartache—and his—be for naught.

But there was nothing else to be done right now. She had to trust Lady Bonneville and Audrey. And she had to exercise patience, something she normally excelled at.

But she had the dreadful, sinking feeling that the virtue would elude her. Until Charles was free.

Charles's first-floor cell was only slightly warmer than the frigid air outside and reeked of unwashed bodies. Some of the cells housed two men, but he was alone in his. He hadn't slept much the night before, thanks to his lumpy pallet and the snores of his fellow prisoners. He'd spent most of the morning and afternoon futilely walking from one side of the room to the other, wearing out the stained floorboards. But now the small window at the top of the back wall revealed the setting sun, and he sat on a wooden bench near the iron bars at the front of his cell, watching and listening.

The men who'd burst into his room at the inn and dragged him here were gone. Only one man—Wescott was his name—stood guard in the center of the prison floor this evening. Young and fit, he walked to each of the cells, which were laid out in a large U shape, and eyed the inhabitants suspiciously. The morning guard had spent his time nipping drinks from a flask and playing solitaire, but Wescott's pressed uniform and businesslike posture suggested he was cut from different cloth. He took his job seriously. Under different circumstances, Charles would have admired that trait.

Wescott paused in front of Charles and shot him a long, assessing stare. Charles stared back. "How long until I can go before the magistrate?"

The guard shrugged. "The weather's made travel difficult. Could be a couple of days, could be a week."

"My bags"—Charles nodded toward the rough wooden table in the center of the floor where his two bags sat, their contents spilling out—"contain everything I own. The watchmen already took my knife. You can search my bags, too. But let me keep them in here." When the watchmen had discovered Charles's heavy pouch of coins, their eyes had lit with greed. He'd resorted to mentioning his connection to a duke. It was admittedly tenuous, but when paired with the deadly look he'd given them, it had been enough to deter them from stealing the coins—for the time being. But the longer his bags sat in the center of the prison floor, the greater the likelihood that his hard-earned money would be pocketed by the corrupt officials who imprisoned others for theft. Hypocrites. Charles suspected that Wescott had integrity few of the others possessed.

The guard turned to look at the bags and rocked on his heels, thoughtful. "You were planning on leaving town?"

"I was. Not because I did anything wrong," Charles added.

"Of course not." Wescott rolled his eyes but nodded. "I'll consider the request—after a thorough search." He began rummaging through Charles's bags.

"Thank you."

"Does your family know you're here?" the guard asked.

"No." Charles thanked God that his father was blissfully unaware of his current predicament. Pa was powerless to help anyway.

After Mum died, he'd aged ten years overnight. His smile was never as bright as before, his shoulders never as straight. While his grief took the form of sadness, Charles's turned to rage. He couldn't forget the wounded sound of Pa's sobs as he bent over the bed where his wife lay, pale and lifeless. Nor could he shake the feeling that Mum's death was somehow his fault. He should have run faster, pleaded harder. He should have forced the doctor to come to her aid.

Their family, which should have grown to four, had shrunk to two—him and Pa. They had only each other now, and Charles needed to make his father proud and spare him further pain. He owed him that much.

Charles wouldn't burden him with his current predicament. Neither would he involve Rose. She couldn't be tainted by this—by him—any more than she already had been.

"I can give you some paper and a pen if you'd like to write to someone and inform them of your circumstances," the guard said.

Charles thought about his friend, Harry, whom he'd met while working on the docks. Harry had surprising connections to all sorts of influential people and a knack for employing coercion. If anyone could find a way to have Charles released, he could. But writing a letter explaining his situation took more skill than he possessed.

"No need," Charles said. "I can handle my own affairs. But I appreciate the offer."

Wescott raised a brow as he unlocked Charles's cell and kicked his bags through the door. "Let me know if you change your mind. You have plenty of time to think things over."

Indeed, and he'd started to formulate a plan. Now that he had his bags, he had money. And the morning guard was lazy, greedy, and frequently foxed, which provided another key component of his plan—opportunity. "I think I'd like that paper after all."

After dinner that evening, Rose pleaded a mild headache and went to her room so that Lady Bonneville would have ample time to help Lady Yardley see the error of her ways. Or at least convince her that dropping the charges against Charles would work to her own advantage. The viscountess had given Rose a confident, encouraging nod as she left, bolstering her drooping spirits.

But time ticked away, and when at last Rose heard Lady Bonneville in the corridor, she dashed out of her room. "Were you able to convince her?"

The viscountess blinked and rubbed her forehead. "Not yet. But not for lack of trying." She looked weary and almost...defeated. Which frightened Rose even more.

"What shall we do?"

"You must be patient, my dear. Persuasion is best accomplished slowly and in almost imperceptible increments."

Rose wrinkled her nose. "I don't understand. We haven't much time, remember?"

The viscountess sighed dramatically. "A lady does not bash in a brick wall with a sledgehammer," she said slowly. "Rather, she chips away at the brick, bit by bit, until the wall crumbles."

Perhaps, but Rose rather liked the sound of the sledge-hammer. "You are right, of course. My concern for Charles is overpowering my good sense."

Lady Bonneville clucked her tongue. "I cannot imagine what that man did to inspire such devotion. I cannot think him worthy of it."

Rose swallowed. "I'm afraid I do not agree with you. He is one of the finest people I know."

The viscountess laid her fingers on Rose's cheek. "Never fear, my girl. I shall chip away some more tomorrow, and then we must hope that Diana does the right thing."

Rose didn't want to leave Charles's fate to hope, but she nodded obediently. "Shall I come in and read to you for a bit?"

"No, I wouldn't hear a word of it, as I am sure to be snoring the moment my head hits the pillow. I suggest you get your rest as well. Good night."

Rose smiled wanly as Lady Bonneville shuffled into her room. "Good night."

But she had no intention of resting. Not until she received the rest of the news she awaited.

It was almost eleven o'clock when a faint knock sounded at Rose's door. She leaped up to open it, relieved to see Audrey standing outside.

The maid swept into the room breathlessly, bobbed a curtsy, and without preamble said, "The Bath prison's on Grove Street, my lady. No one has been to see Mr. Holland yet, but one of the footmen, Edward, and the kitchen maid, Shirley, plan to visit tomorrow. They're going to sneak out immediately after luncheon while Mr. Evans is preoccupied with his weekly inventory of the silver and take a wagon into town. I've given Shirley your message, and I'm sure she'll convey it to Mr. Holland if she's able. She's a fine girl, even if she does always manage to burn the toast."

Rose sat on the edge of her bed, absorbing the news. "That's good. At least he'll have some visitors." But she couldn't help feeling a bit jealous of the footman and kitchen maid. If they could visit Charles, why couldn't *she*?

She stood, took a fortifying breath, and looked directly at Audrey. The maid was about her height. "I must ask another favor of you."

"Anything, my lady."

"Would you lend me one of your dresses?"

As soon as the morning light filtered through the dirty window of his cell, Charles threw off his rough wool blanket and retrieved a book from his bag. Grimms' fairy tales. Rose had given him the volume years ago, and he'd kept it with him always. Not because he'd spent much time rereading the stories, but because it reminded him of her and of his father, who'd often read them aloud after dinner.

He opened to one of his favorites, *The Fisherman and His Wife*, and read the first line.

There was once upon a time a fisherman who lived with his wife in a hut beside the sea.

He repeated it to himself quietly, over and over, studying each word's shape, sound, and size. He memorized the way his mouth moved when he said each word out loud. Then he took the paper and pen that the guard had given him and slowly, carefully, at the top of the page began to copy the sentence. When he'd finished, he wrote it again.

And again. By the tenth iteration, his hand remembered the words and the pen flowed smoothly across the paper. The left to right movement, the loops and bumps of the letters, and the crosses and dots created a rhythm in his head. If it wasn't exactly soothing, at least it took his mind off his current predicament.

So he repeated the process with the next sentence.

He discovered that when he placed the edge of his paper under the line of text he was reading, the letters didn't seem to move as they usually did. The paper was like an anchor that kept the text above it from rocking wildly. And for the first time, he began to think—to believe—that reading was not beyond him.

When the morning guard grunted and slid a breakfast tray into Charles's cell, he placed Rose's ribbon between the pages before closing the book and choking down a few bites of cold gruel. After he ate, he continued writing, and when he ran out of space on his paper, he made a trade with the solitaire-playing guard, exchanging a couple of coins for several clean sheets and an additional pot of ink.

As Charles read and wrote, he could almost forget that he'd been accused of theft and imprisoned. That during his one night with Rose he'd tasted heaven...and then been cast into this hell.

He shook his head, erasing those sorts of dangerous thoughts. Instead, he let his eyes make sense of letters and his fingers glide across the page. Having something constructive to do kept his anger at bay, and that was a necessity. If he allowed rage to surface, he'd only appear guiltier, digging himself deeper into trouble.

Lunch bore an uncanny resemblance to breakfast, but Charles forced himself to eat it all. When he was done, he did forty push-ups, which served the dual purposes of maintaining his strength and warming his blood. He was just about to open his book when a small commotion in the guards' area distracted him—and every other prisoner on the floor.

He slid his bags into the corner, covered them with his brown blanket, and walked to the iron bars at the front of his cell. Three visitors, still bundled in their coats and hats, conferred with the morning guard, who looked annoyed at the interruption of his daily rituals—playing cards and swilling liquor from his flask.

"What's your business here?" the bleary-eyed guard demanded.

"We've come to visit Mr. Charles Holland."

He blinked. The man who'd spoken was Edward, a footman from Yardley Manor—he recognized the voice. The two women with him wore plain gray cloaks and hats and were almost surely maids. One carried a small basket that the guard snatched from her hands.

"What's this?"

"Some food for Mr. Holland." Edward took a step forward and scowled. "They told us downstairs that we could give it to him."

The guard snorted, unimpressed. "After I have a look." He unceremoniously dumped the contents of the basket on the large table, picked up one of several apples, and bit into it. Juice trickled down his chin, but he didn't bother to wipe it. "Holland is over there," he said, jerking his head in Charles's direction. "Give him the food. You have ten minutes. I'll be watching." But he plopped down on his stool, munched on the apple, and turned his attention back to his card game.

The trio of visitors gathered the items on the table and rushed over. Edward, followed by the kitchen maid, Shirley, and—

Dear God.

Rose pushed the dingy gray hood off her head and curled her gloved hands around the iron bars that separated them. "Charles." Her eyes shone and her hair glistened, brightening the whole damned place. He wanted to reach between the bars and touch her face, haul her close, and breathe in her scent.

"What are you doing here?" he asked. "This is no place for you."

"It's no place for you, either," she retorted. "And you wouldn't be here if you hadn't been trying to help me."

Edward and Shirley stood on either side of Rose. "We were sorry to hear that Lady Yardley fired you and even sorrier to learn that she accused you of stealing."

"She didn't fire me—I quit."

Edward shook his head. "It's just not right."

"Thank you," Charles said. "It was good of you and Shirley to come."

"The whole staff would have joined us if they could," the maid said. "Everyone but Mr. Evans. He's taken Lady Yardley's side."

Rose turned to Shirley, her brow wrinkled. "What do you mean?"

The maid flushed scarlet. "Mr. Evans claims he witnessed Mr. Holland stealing Lady Yardley's possessions from the library."

Rose gasped. "But that's not true."

"None of us believes it," Edward interjected, "but Mr. Evans says he's been asked to testify on Lady Yardley's behalf, and he intends to. He'd say or do anything to ingratiate himself to her. Blasted idiot. Begging your ladies' pardon," he quickly added.

Rose's face turned ashen. "I was hopeful that you could convince the magistrate of your innocence," she said to Charles. "After all, truth is on your side. But if Mr. Evans corroborates Lady Yardley's story..."

The anguish in her eyes shredded him. "Do not worry. I will find a way out of this." He shot a wary look at the guard. "I'm already working on it."

"We brought you some sustenance." Shirley offered him an apple, a loosely wrapped loaf of bread, and a wedge of cheese.

"This is awfully kind of you—and it means the world to me." He reached through the bars and took the items one at a time. He broke off a piece of the bread and a hunk of cheese, then handed the rest back to Shirley and Edward. "Would you mind sharing these with the other prisoners? They've been here much longer than I."

"Of course," Edward said. He put a protective arm around Shirley and led her toward the next cell.

Once they were alone, Rose exclaimed, "This is awful."

"True, but it's wonderful to see you." His chest was nearly bursting with the need to hold her, to kiss her, but he kept his distance, aware of the guard's periodic glances.

"You must not despair. Lady Bonneville is doing her best to persuade Lady Yardley to drop the charges and have you released. She can be quite formidable."

"I don't doubt it." He'd seen the way the viscountess glared through her lorgnette. "But why would she try to help a lowly steward?"

"Perhaps she knows that I care for you."

"Rose," he said firmly, "I appreciate what you're trying to do. But my welfare is not your concern. We had our reasons for parting ways. You need to forget about me and...move forward with your life."

Her chin dropped and she took half a step back as though he'd offended her deeply. "We may have said good-bye, but things were different then. You're in trouble now, and I would never walk away from someone that I... from someone that I care about."

He hung his head, gutted. "What if I told you that it would be easier for me?"

"I don't understand."

"It's hard to explain, but I'd feel better if you weren't wasting your time worrying about me. I want you to be happy, to enjoy your family, to find someone who..." *Loves you like I do.* "...will be the kind of husband you deserve."

She reached through the bars and grabbed his wrist, sending a frisson of longing through him. "I refuse to accept that," she hissed. "Perhaps you have already managed to put our relationship behind you—wrapped it up in a tidy package and stored it away. But I haven't. I can't bear to. Not yet."

He freed his wrist from her grasp and laced his fingers through hers. "Make no mistake. I will never forget you." She was part of him. Body, heart, and soul. "I just don't want to worry about you doing something foolish for my sake."

"Like disguising myself as a maid and coming to visit you in prison?" The hint of a smile played about her lips.

"Precisely." He grinned, then sobered. "You're leaving

for London in two days." It was both a statement and a plea.

"As it stands now," she said noncommittally.

"I'm glad you came to see me. But now you must stop worrying and leave matters to me. When I tell the magistrate that I plan to leave for America, he'll probably be more than happy to release me." In truth, Charles hoped to be gone long before that. "We must believe that justice will prevail."

Rose shook her head slowly. "I wish I shared your faith and optimism, but I do not. I believe our best chance lies with Lady Bonneville. I'll place my faith in her."

Chapter Twenty-One

Buck: (1) To jump with an arched back, often unsaddling a rider. (2) A gentleman who pursues pleasure and enjoys debauchery, as in As the viscountess propelled Rose across the ballroom toward a group of young bucks, she couldn't escape the sensation that she was being fed to the lions.

Lady Bonneville pinched the bridge of her nose and raised her brows as though a headache were coming on. "I'm afraid there's nothing else I can do."

Behind the viscountess, Audrey whisked back and forth across the bedchamber, gathering Lady Bonneville's things and efficiently folding them before placing them in her trunk.

"But you can't just give up," Rose protested. "Charles is counting on you, and so am I."

"I know, dear gel. I tried every possible tactic to persuade Diana to drop the charges. I even made a thinly veiled threat to ruin her reputation myself."

"But why? *Why* would she seek to destroy him?"

"It is a truly curious thing," the viscountess said thoughtfully. "She is quite aware of the risk to her own good name and is determined to proceed with her false accusations in spite of it. Perhaps her feelings for Mr. Holland ran deeper than we knew. Many a scorned woman—and man—have behaved irrationally, and I fear it's true in this case. Logic is useless."

Rose thought of the sketches. Clearly, Lady Yardley was more than a little infatuated with her steward.

"Not only does Diana refuse to drop the charges," Lady Bonneville continued softly, hesitantly, "she says she wants him to hang for his offense."

"What?" Rose's knees wobbled, and she sank onto the edge of Lady Bonneville's bed. Her heart pounded as if it would burst, and her throat constricted painfully. "Surely, the magistrate wouldn't sentence him to hang. He hasn't done anything wrong."

"You and I are not in complete agreement on that point. However, even *I* don't believe the young man deserves to die. Let us hope that the magistrate is not swayed by her lies, beauty, and wealth. The fact remains, Rose. We've done all we can."

The slump of Lady Bonneville's shoulders and the defeat in her voice chilled Rose to the bone. If the viscountess had given up the fight, Charles had no one left on his side—no one but Rose.

And she wouldn't let him down. She'd stay up all night, examine their options, and visit him again tomorrow. Together, they'd work through it all and figure out something.

The viscountess cleared her throat. "I am sorry that things didn't turn out as you'd hoped."

"I know you tried your best," Rose choked out. "Thank you for that."

"Everything will seem better in the morning. It always does."

Eager for the solace of her room, Rose stood on shaky legs, then blinked. "Wait. Why is Audrey packing your things at this late hour? We have all day tomorrow to pack."

"Unfortunately, we do not. I cannot stay under this roof for one more night," the viscountess declared. "You must go now and gather your things together as well. We shall leave as soon as the coach is loaded and take a room at the White Hart for the evening. We'll return to London first thing in the morning.

"We're leaving Bath tomorrow?" Rose had been counting on a couple of more days. She needed time to devise a plan to help Charles. She'd be useless to him in London. Desperate, she grasped at the only straw she could think of. "But I told Lord Stanton that I'd be at the ball."

Lady Bonneville raised her lorgnette suspiciously. "The ball? I had not realized that it was a priority for you."

"I confess to being less than enthused initially, but we did say that we'd attend. Besides, it would be rude to leave town without warning."

The viscountess shrugged, unconcerned. "If I offend a few sensitive souls, all the better." Rose had forgotten that rudeness was an integral part of her carefully cultivated, formidable reputation.

She scrambled for something else. "What about Lady Yardley?"

Lady Bonneville narrowed her eyes. "What about her?"

Treading lightly, Rose continued. "If we leave before

the ball, she'll be gloating for everyone to see. She'll let it be known that there was a falling out and make it seem as though we ran away, scared. But then perhaps that is true..."

"Nonsense!" the viscountess snapped. "I would never run from the likes of her."

"*I* know that," Rose assured her. "However, I could see how some might jump to the wrong conclusion."

"We will attend the ball tomorrow night." The viscountess craned her neck in search of the maid. "Audrey, where is my fan?"

The maid produced a fan with impressive speed. Lady Bonneville snatched it, snapped it open like a switchblade, and waved it with force sufficient to power a small windmill. "We will leave Yardley Manor this evening, not because we wish to flee the premises, but because we cannot abide the company and do not tolerate untruthfulness. That said, we will not alter our plans to attend the ball. We shall go, you shall dance the entire evening, and then we shall leave for London the next afternoon. At our leisure."

Rose nodded solemnly. "If you think that's best."

"I do. Go pack your things, and Audrey will be along to help as soon as she's done here. The sooner we remove ourselves from this odious place, the better."

"Yes, my lady." She scurried out of the room before the viscountess could change her mind.

But she didn't go to her own bedchamber as Lady Bonneville had instructed. She stood in the corridor for a moment. Her back pressed to the wall, she closed her eyes and breathed. There was no time for elaborate plans, no time for indecision. And though tempting, falling apart was a luxury she definitely could not afford. Not when Charles could hang.

An idea flashed in her mind. An ill-advised, utterly mad idea. But patience and good sense had not served her well—at least not in this instance. Drastic measures were required.

With renewed determination, she straightened and strode toward the staircase. There were two tasks she had to accomplish before leaving Yardley Manor.

The first was relatively easy. She walked directly to the servant's quarters and stopped the first maid she encountered.

The young woman squeaked, clearly startled. "My lady! May I help you with something? Are you lost?"

"I need to speak with Shirley, immediately."

The maid glanced up and down the empty hall and gulped. "Follow me."

She led Rose past several doors, then stopped and knocked on one. When Shirley opened the door, Rose swept into the room without hesitation. Another maid sat on one of the two small beds, braiding her hair. When she saw Rose, her fingers froze.

"Would you give us a moment, please?" Rose asked.

The maid scurried out of the room, her braid unraveling, and shut the door behind her.

"Lady Rose." Shirley wrung her hands. "What brings you here?"

"It concerns Charles. I may require your help tomorrow night. Edward's, too."

"Has something happened to Mr. Holland?"

"Not yet. But I'm afraid his life is in danger." Rose kept her voice even despite the panic that fluttered in her chest.

The maid blinked, and her face turned white. "I will help if I can, and I'm sure Edward will, too. What would you like us to do?"

"I should tell you that there is risk involved. I promise that I'll do everything I can to ensure you are not implicated in any trouble that arises out of this plan." And there was sure to be trouble.

Shirley nodded bravely. "Mr. Holland is a good man. He doesn't deserve to die."

Rose managed a grateful smile. "I need to visit the prison again, in the evening this time, while Lady Yardley is attending a ball. You mustn't tell anyone about the visit or that you've spoken to me—for your sake and Edward's, the fewer people who know about this, the easier it will be for me to protect you."

Shirley nodded soberly. "Yes, my lady."

"Lady Bonneville and I are leaving Yardley Manor tonight and will be staying at the White Hart Inn in Bath. I must go now, but I'll send word to you tomorrow morning and provide further instructions."

"I'll speak with Edward tonight." The maid pressed her lips together and inhaled deeply. Her forehead wrinkled in concern, she looked directly into Rose's eyes. "Be careful. When Lady Yardley is defied, she's often unpredictable and . . . cruel. I would not wish to see you hurt."

Rose reached out and clasped the maid's hands in her own. "Thank you. You needn't worry about me, but do take care of yourself." She released Shirley's hands and walked toward the door. "Good night."

Now for the second task. Rose left the servants' quarters and headed toward the library, praying that she wouldn't encounter Lady Yardley. A hush seemed to have settled over the main rooms of the house. Perhaps in the aftermath of the verbal clash with Lady Bonneville, Lady Yardley had retreated to her bedchamber to lick her wounds and await the viscountess's departure. Rose hoped so.

The library was dark, except for the light of a single lamp on a small table beside the door. Rose picked up the lamp and moved it to the mantel. She placed an ottoman on the hearth and stepped on it. With trembling fingers, she reached for the painting above the mantel and swung it open.

The pistol was still there.

Rose had never held one, but she'd witnessed a gun's powerful effects. She swallowed hard. With one irreversible pull of the trigger, Papa had taken his life, leaving her, Olivia, and Owen essentially orphaned and very much alone.

Since the day that she and Olivia had found him lying on the floor of his study in a pool of blood and brains, she'd had a revulsion for guns. A disgust for them that affected her on a physical level, turning her stomach and plucking at the memories of that horrid day. This pistol, dainty as it was, struck her as all the more abhorrent. Even its elegant scrollwork and pearl handle couldn't fool her, couldn't disguise the evil it could do.

But there was no time to debate the moral implications of what she was about to do or all the spectacular ways in which her plan could fail.

Carefully, she removed the pistol from the cabinet and held it near the light of the lamp. Cool and heavy in her hands, it glowed ominously. She tucked the pistol into her bodice between her breasts, shivering at the foreign sensation of iron against her skin.

Now for ammunition. She reached behind the letters and ornate boxes and found a velvet pouch. She loosened the drawstring, peered inside at the small lead spheres, and released the breath she'd been holding. Part of her wished the bullets hadn't been there. But they were, and she knew what she must do if she wanted to rescue Charles. The pistol, the bullets—they were just a last resort, to be used if all other measures failed.

She pulled the drawstring tight and tucked the pouch into her pocket. It weighed down her skirt and bumped against her thigh, clunking softly as she moved. As quickly and quietly as she could manage it, she returned the library to order and made her way back upstairs to her bedchamber.

Audrey was there, removing a gown from the armoire and hastily folding it before placing it in Rose's portmanteau on her bed. "I believe that's the last of your things," the maid said. "Lady Bonneville's eager to leave. Are you ready?"

With a gulp, Rose nodded. "I'm ready."

Chapter Twenty-Two

The Upper Assembly Rooms sparkled with silk gowns, dazzling jewels, and crystal glasses. The guests had braved the unusually cold evening in order to dance and be merry . . . or, in Lady Bonneville's case, to make a point.

"Though I enjoy a holiday respite in Bath," she was telling another matriarch, "its entertainments simply cannot compare to London's. Rose insisted we stay for the ball tonight, but we shall return to Town tomorrow."

Rose smiled dutifully at the viscountess, who sat in a plush chair, her feet propped on her red stool. "Thank you for agreeing to come tonight," Rose said, for the benefit of Lady Bonneville's friend.

The frail, gray-haired woman waggled white brows. "You and Lord Stanton make a striking couple."

Rose lowered her eyes demurely. "That's kind of you to say." She had felt obliged to dance with him but couldn't wait for the music to end. He'd held her a little too tightly, spoken too familiarly. After he'd returned her to Lady

Bonneville's side, he'd asked Lady Yardley to dance. Now that she thought on it, Rose thought them rather well suited. She wouldn't miss either of them when she returned to London.

If she returned to London.

She cast a surreptitious look at the grandfather clock beside the door, and her heartbeat kicked into a gallop. It was time. "Would you ladies please excuse me while I freshen up?"

"Oh, of course." The gray-haired woman waved a bejeweled hand. "Never fear, we shall keep an eye on Lord Stanton for you."

The viscountess raised a brow as Rose headed in the general direction of the water closet. But once she was out of Lady Bonneville's sight, she changed course and located Audrey sitting on the other side of the room with another maid. Each woman stood ready to fetch anything her mistress might need, whether it be a glass of champagne, a fan, or a peacock feather to adorn her turban.

"Lady Rose," Audrey said with some surprise. "May I help you?"

"No, thank you. I only wanted to let you know that I've a bit of a headache and am returning to the hotel. Lady Bonneville says she wishes to remain for another hour or two."

"You poor dear," Audrey exclaimed. "Let me retrieve your cloak."

"No need," Rose said, amazed by her ability to spout one lie after the other. "I've already asked a footman to fetch it and escort me to the coach. He's probably waiting just outside the ballroom as we speak."

The maid frowned. "Very well. Try to rest. I can't imagine the viscountess will want to stay much longer."

"Oh, but she's having a grand time over there. We mustn't spoil her last evening in Bath. In fact, it's best if she puts me out of her mind and enjoys the company of her friends."

"If you're certain."

"I am," Rose said firmly. "Now I'm off to the hotel—and my bed."

"Sleep well, Lady Rose."

Rose glided out of the ballroom and down the stairway. In the Lower Rooms she intercepted a maid, who went in search of her cloak. It seemed an eternity before the woman returned but it was more likely three minutes. Rose slipped her arms into the sleeves and pulled the fur-lined hood over her head not only to keep her warm, but also to conceal her identity.

She stepped into the frigid night, walking purposefully past the fancy coaches waiting by the curb. Escaping the ballroom had been shockingly easy, but her most daunting challenges still lay ahead.

The ground beneath her delicate heels was icy and slick. With each step she took away from the Assembly Rooms, the street grew darker and the air grew colder. She navigated the slippery walkway down the block and rounded the corner where she prayed that Edward and Shirley waited with the wagon.

When she reached their arranged meeting spot, however, she saw nothing but shadows and darkened storefronts. Perhaps they hadn't received the note or hadn't been able to leave Yardley Manor. Perhaps they'd simply—and wisely—decided that helping Charles wasn't worth the risk of losing their jobs.

Rose huddled against a stone wall, pulled her cloak

more tightly around her, and waited. She kept a wary eye on the occasional passersby, taking comfort in the heavy reticule dangling from her wrist. She possessed the means to defend herself—but hoped to God it wouldn't be necessary.

At last, she heard the creaking wheels of a wagon approaching. When it passed beneath a street lantern, she saw Shirley and Edward bundled on the front seat. The moment Edward pulled the horses to a stop, Rose gathered up her skirts and climbed inelegantly onto the back of the wagon.

Edward turned his head and spoke over his shoulder. "I'm sorry we're late. The roads are still a bit difficult to travel."

"I'm just glad you're here," Rose said. "Let's be on our way."

"The items you requested are in a satchel beneath the blanket," Shirley said.

"Thank you." Rose pulled the blanket over her lap and placed the satchel at her side. It contained everything she and Charles would need.

Everything, that is, but luck. They'd need quite a lot to see her plan through.

Charles had used all his paper. Most of the sheets were covered in sentences he'd transcribed from his book of Grimms' fairy tales, but not the one he now held between ink-stained fingers.

No, this last page was filled with nothing but Rose's name. Rose Sherbourne. He hadn't even been aware when he'd first begun writing it . . . over and over. But just the look of the letters on the parchment and the sound of them in his head made him think of her and gave him comfort. He folded it and stuck it deep into the pocket of his trousers.

The floor was quiet this evening. Half of the prisoners were already asleep. The loudest one, an old man named Howard who claimed the devil routinely visited his cell and stole his drawers, had been literally carted off to Bedlam that afternoon. He'd seemed harmless to Charles, but the guards had grown weary of his constant shouting and decided he was better suited for the asylum than their jail.

Which meant that the prison was eerily silent, with nothing to distract Charles from the *what if*s that haunted him. *What if his plan to escape early tomorrow morning failed? What if the morning guard arrived for duty less inebriated than usual? What if the key ring on his belt didn't hold the key to the side door that Charles intended to slip out of? What if he was destined to spend the rest of his life within these stone walls and ended up like poor old Howard—stark raving mad?*

Shaking off the thought, he put away his ink and pen, dropped to the floor, and did push-ups until sweat beaded on his forehead and his arms trembled from the exertion. When he collapsed onto the floor, spent, the night guard, Wescott, snorted but shot him a look of grudging admiration.

Charles felt in control once more. His plan would succeed. It had to.

Using the water in a small, cracked basin, he washed up the best he could. He was about to remove his boots when a commotion from the staircase outside the main door brought him and every other prisoner who was awake to his feet. Grasping the iron bars at the front of his cell, he craned his neck for a better look at the door.

Instantly alert, Wescott drew his gun and took aim at the door, waiting. With his left hand, he reached for the club on the table beside him and clenched the handle in his large fist.

Several of the prisoners, delighted at the prospect of violence, let out whoops of excitement.

"Shut up," the guard growled.

But then the door swung open, slowly, revealing a woman in a cloak.

Charles knew that cloak. And he knew that woman.

What on God's sweet earth was she doing there?

Wescott dropped the baton and fumbled the gun.

Charles slammed into the iron bars in a wholly futile attempt to protect Rose from the guard's carelessness. "Rose!" he shouted.

Rose stepped back, and the guard set down his weapons, recovering his wits if not his manners. "What in the bloody hell are you doing here?" he demanded.

She pushed the hood off her head, revealing a crown of gleaming auburn hair, adorned with a sparkling silver ribbon. Beneath her black velvet cloak, she appeared to be wearing a glittering ball gown, of all things. She looked like a princess—strikingly beautiful against the stark, grim backdrop of the prison.

"Jesus," muttered one of the jailed men. Several others made lewd comments—the kind that made Charles want to break someone's nose.

Ignoring their taunts, she shot the guard a confident, dazzling smile. "Allow me to introduce myself." In spite of her bravado, Charles detected a slight tremor in her voice. "I'm Lady Rose Sherbourne, sister to the Duke of Huntford."

Wescott frowned, skeptical. "If that's true, I can only conclude you're lost."

"I assure you that I *am* the duke's sister and that I'm exactly where I intend to be." She cast a brief, indecipherable glance at Charles, then devoted her full attention to the guard.

"Do you mind if I sit, Mr. . . . ?"

"Wescott." He hastily cleared a spot at the table and dragged a chair over. "Be my guest." His tone, however, suggested he was less than thrilled at the prospect of entertaining anyone—especially a gorgeous young woman who could disrupt his orderly jail floor.

Rose lowered herself onto the wooden chair gracefully, as though she were in an elegant drawing room and not a squalid jail. "Mr. Wescott, I can see that you are a busy man with an important job to do, keeping our citizens safe."

"How did you manage to make it up here?" the guard asked.

"I simply explained my business to your colleagues, and they graciously allowed me to pass."

Wescott grunted. "I know my colleagues. They're more likely to be persuaded by bribes than by reason."

Rose inclined her head. "But you are not, are you? I respect a man with integrity. I regret to inform you that one of your prisoners, a Mr. Holland, has been unjustly imprisoned. The Duke of Huntford has requested that you release him to his custody."

Good God. What was she doing?

The guard made a great show of looking over and around Rose. "I don't see a duke anywhere." Bastard.

"I should hope not," Rose retorted. "I'm afraid my brother has been detained by business in London and simply could not come himself. That is why he's sent me."

"I don't care if your brother is the prince regent," Wescott spat. "Mr. Holland isn't stepping foot outside of his cell until it's time for him to go before the magistrate."

Rose flinched but quickly masked her fear. "I admire your adherence to the established procedures. I find that there's an appalling tendency in today's society to flout the rules. Your commitment to upholding them is… refreshing."

"And yet terribly inconvenient for you," the guard quipped.

Charles's grip on the iron bars tightened. Wescott would pay for his insolence.

"That is true," she said. "You must grant that there are some cases—and this is one of them—in which the rules must be bent in order to prevent a greater injustice. My brother, the duke, is prepared to vouch for Mr. Holland's character. He will ensure that your superiors know that you released the prisoner at his request and see that you do not suffer any negative repercussions."

Wescott glared at her, his mouth open in disbelief.

"I am sure," Rose continued, "that you could make excellent use of the cell Mr. Holland vacates. There must be true criminals out there—"

"Lady Rose," the guard interrupted, "I can see that you are convinced of Mr. Holland's innocence and passionate about his defense. However, it would be irresponsible and reckless of me to release him into your custody."

"The charges against him are false," she said.

The guard raised his brows. "Be that as it may, I cannot take the chance that you will be his next victim."

Her face flushed, and her eyes fairly sparked with anger.

"Rose," Charles warned, wishing she wasn't halfway across the room. "Wescott is right. You shouldn't be here."

Ignoring him, she addressed the guard. "I had thought to appeal to your sense of justice, but perhaps you prefer monetary compensation, after all. I am prepared to pay handsomely for Mr. Holland's release, and no one else ever need know about it."

"I'll know about it," cried the toothless prisoner catty corner from Charles.

"Yes, but no one will believe your sorry arse, Higgins," retorted his neighbor.

Apparently oblivious to the ruckus, Rose cleared her throat, jingled her reticule, and reached inside. "Name your price, Mr. Wescott."

Dear God, what in the devil was she doing, risking her reputation in coming here and bribing his prison guard? Actually, it would have worked splendidly on the morning guard. But not Wescott.

Fuming, the guard pressed his lips together and drew himself to his full height. "I cannot be bought, Lady Rose. Just as I cannot be charmed, blackmailed, or strong-armed. Mr. Holland will not be leaving his cell tonight— not as long as I'm alive."

Rose stood and held her chin high. "That is a shame." She turned as though to leave, then whirled around to face the guard. She pulled a pistol from her reticule, cocked it, and aimed it squarely at Wescott's chest.

"I'm going to need the keys," she said smoothly. "Now."

From his cell, Charles begged Rose to lower the pistol. "Shit." Wescott held out his hands and took a cautious step toward the table, where he'd placed his own gun and his club.

"Stop right there," she warned the guard. She flicked her gaze to the large ring of keys that hung from his belt. "Walk slowly to Mr. Holland's cell and unlock it."

"Like hell I will." Wescott jerked his head toward Charles. "He'd snap my neck on his way out."

"No," Rose assured him. "We only want to slip out quietly. If you'd prefer the hard way . . ."

"Damn it." As the guard shuffled toward Charles, his gaze darted everywhere, looking for a way out or for help from some quarter.

An older, stooped man banged his tin cup on the iron bars of his cell. "Let me out while you're at it."

"Shut yer toothless mouth, Higgins," called another prisoner. "The princess didn't come to save ye."

Rose kept a razor-like focus on the guard and concentrated on keeping her arms from shaking uncontrollably, which was harder than she'd imagined.

Wescott unhooked the ring of keys from his belt, stopped several feet from Charles's cell, and turned to Rose. "Tell him to back away from the door."

"I'm not going to hurt you, Wescott," Charles said evenly. "Not unless you try to hurt her."

Rose looked at Charles, the guard, and Charles again.

Wescott clenched his jaw. "I don't unlock the door unless he steps to the back wall."

She nodded. "Do as he asks, Charles. Please." As the guard glanced at the pistol she held, she deliberately placed her finger on the trigger. Charles took three steps back but stood with his muscles tensed, ready to pounce.

The jeers of the other prisoners suddenly stopped, and

the entire floor fell silent, but for the clinking of Wescott's keys. Swallowing, he placed one in the lock on Charles's door.

Rose took her eyes off him, just for second, to watch as he turned the key. Only he didn't. He let the key ring drop to the floor and lunged for her. She fell backward, landing on her bottom. The pistol slipped from her hands and slid across the floor.

As she and the guard watched it glide beneath the table, Charles sprang forward. His torso slammed into the iron bars, and he reached through, grabbing a fistful of the guard's shirt. With a grunt, he hauled Wescott closer and pinned his back against the bars. Through gritted teeth, he said, "I'll hold him until you get away. Leave now, Rose."

No. *No.* Didn't he understand? "I'm not leaving this prison without you." Dodging Wescott's flailing limbs, she scooped the keys off the floor. "I don't know which one it is."

"You should go, damn it."

There were a dozen keys on the ring. "Tell me."

Charles uttered a curse and tightened his grip on the struggling guard. "One of the black ones."

Her hands shaking, she tried the first black key in lock. No luck. The second, however, fit perfectly. She turned it, and door's latch released. She'd done it. Well, at least the first step.

But what to do about the guard?

She had no wish to hurt him, but he wasn't going to let them just walk out of there.

"Help!" he shouted, before Charles clamped a hand over his mouth.

Charles leaned forward and spoke directly into the

guard's ear. "If you yell again, I'll be forced to silence you." There was no mistaking his meaning. "Don't. Yell."

He pushed his way forward, swinging the door outward and dragging Wescott with him. There was just enough room for Rose to slip through the opening into the cell. "Take the blanket off my pallet," Charles said. "We'll use it to bind him to the bars."

While Charles held the guard, Rose slid one end of the blanket through the iron bars and around him. Squeezing into the space between the men, she tied a loose knot, then Charles quickly cinched it tight. Wescott's arms and torso were bound for the moment but the blanket's knot wouldn't hold the struggling guard for long.

As though he'd read Rose's mind, Higgins shouted from his cell. "Yer gonna have to knock him out if you want a chance in hell of escaping this godforsaken place."

Charles moved in front of Wescott and looked into his eyes. "No. He's just doing his job. But I do need to silence him." He looked around, his gaze landing on a cloth on the table that the guard had been using to clean and polish his gun. Charles grabbed it and stuffed it into the guard's mouth. "Sorry, Wescott."

Rose's heart pounded with fright. What on earth were they doing, threatening and tying up the prison guard? She'd known that getting Charles out of prison would be messy, but she'd naïvely hoped that brandishing the pistol would do the trick. The reality of guns and gags was tenfold worse than she'd imagined—almost enough to make her sick.

And yet, she'd gladly do it again to keep him from hanging.

He grabbed the key ring from the lock and his bags

from beside his pallet. Rose ducked beneath the table to pick up her pistol.

"This way to the exit," Charles said. "Let's go, quickly."

Just as she stood, a portly guard entered the room, a stunned look on his face. He reached for the gun at his waist just as she aimed hers, and—

Pow.

The guard's shot whizzed through the air and echoed through the building.

Terrified, she turned toward Charles, who appeared to be unhurt. And enraged.

He dropped his bags, barreled toward the guard at the door, and slammed him against the wall, jarring the gun from his hand.

When the guard reached for Charles's throat, he grabbed him by the ears and knocked their skulls together. The guard slumped against the wall and crumpled to the floor, out cold.

Charles picked up the guard's gun and jammed it into the waistband of his trousers. Then he hoisted his bags over one shoulder and reached for Rose's hand. "Let's go."

She tamped down the panic that hammered in her chest and followed him out the door and down the staircase, cursing the yards of silk and velvet that tangled around her legs.

At the bottom, she stopped him and pointed to a dark bolted door. "Should we try it?"

Charles smiled, impressed. Quickly, he slid the bolt aside, pried the heavy door open, and peered outside. "It's clear."

They stepped into the night and took deep breaths of clean, crisp, cold air.

He cupped one of her cheeks in his hand and looked at her with a tenderness that made her throat constrict. "You are very courageous—and a little bit mad. I can't believe you risked coming here."

The enormity of what she'd done began to sink in, and a tremor ran through her. "I had to—"

A ruckus sounded inside the prison, cutting her off. Angry shouts pierced the stillness of the night.

He pressed a brief, fervent kiss to her lips. "We need to move quickly. Follow me."

Chapter Twenty-Three

Bridle: (1) A horse's headpiece, including the headstall, bit, and reins. (2) To hold back or restrain. See also unbridled, *as in* He kissed her with unbridled desire. And she rather liked it.

Charles led the way through the shadows, keeping Rose close to the prison wall and shielding her with his body. At the corner of the building, she stopped him. "Wait."

She crouched by a large shrub and leaned underneath.

Fearing she was ill, he dropped to his knees beside her. "Are you all right?"

"There should be a satchel under here. I packed some things we'll need."

Charles still felt like he was in some odd dream. The Rose he knew did not brandish a pistol or orchestrate prison escapes. But now she was implicated in the entire mess—in nearly as much trouble as he was. He ducked his head to search beneath the bush, quickly located the bag, and pulled it out. "Here."

"Thank you. Now we just need to—"

"Find a way out of Bath," he said.

She swallowed. "Without being captured. I brought money. Shall we hire a hackney coach?"

He shook his head. "Too conspicuous and slow. We need horses. Let's head over the bridge to the stable on High Street. Quickly, before the prison guards alert the entire town."

She slipped her hand in his and they hurried along, she in her ball gown and jewels, he in his shirtsleeves. They would appear an odd pair to anyone who spotted them, and he supposed they were. But she'd risked everything for him, and he knew one thing without a doubt. He *had* to keep her safe.

Squeezing his hand as they scurried toward town, she said, "We're going to be all right. I believe in you... and us."

Awed by her faith in him, he smiled. "The stable is just over there." He pointed across the street. "I'll secure horses for us. It's probably best if we're not seen together."

She reached into her reticule. "Take these coins."

"I have money. Stay here. Should anyone bother you, show your pistol and scream. I can be at your side in an instant." She nodded bravely and slipped around the corner of a building into the shadows.

Charles jogged across the road and entered the stable casually. A thin man slouched on an overturned crate, his cap pulled low over his eyes, snoring. Charles cleared his throat loudly and the man sat up.

"I'm bound for London and need two horses," Charles told the stable hand. "I'm in a bit of a hurry."

The stable hand blinked and looked at him curiously, no doubt finding it strange that a man without a jacket would request two horses this late on a winter's night. He ran a hand down his lined face as if to say, either way, it mattered not to him. "I've got this pair."

"They'll do," said Charles. But he sincerely hoped that he and Rose would not have to rely on the tired-looking mares to help them outrun any constables who gave chase.

"Let me saddle them up and you can be on your way."

"I'll give you a hand," Charles offered. He hoisted a worn saddle over the blanket on the horse's back and stooped to buckle it beneath her belly. While the stable hand wrestled with the saddle on the other mare, Charles dug several coins out of his bag and slapped them on the wide beam between two stalls. He hooked his bags onto the back of the saddle, shifted uneasily, and glanced out onto the street. Three men ran down the road, craning their necks from side to side as though they were looking for someone. And gripping their clubs as though that someone might be dangerous.

Holy hell. He had to return to Rose. Now. But the second mare wasn't ready. He hopped onto the mare he'd saddled and took the reins in his hands.

"Wait a second," the stable hand protested, just loud enough to draw the attention of the men—constables—on the street. They immediately turned and headed for the stable. "I'll go around the back," one cried, splitting off from the trio. "You cut him off at the front."

Damn. Charles had no choice. Leaving the second mare behind, he kicked his horse into a gallop and charged out of the stable, darting past the constables toward Rose.

Tentatively, she emerged from the shadows, holding her reticule and satchel in one hand.

When he stopped in front of her, she threw him her

bags, reached for his hand, and allowed him to swing her up into the saddle in front of him.

Behind them, the constables yelled for them to halt and threatened to shoot. Charles wrapped his body around Rose's as he urged the horse into a run, but the mare struggled with the weight of two riders and their bags. She could manage only a fast trot, and with just moonlight to illuminate their way over the frozen ground, that was probably for the best.

The men's shouts subsided once he and Rose crossed the Pulteney Bridge, and they kept riding. Farther and farther from Bath.

"Are the men still following us?" Rose asked breathlessly.

"Probably, but at least we've put some space between us and them." He wished he could give her more reassurance without stretching the truth to the thinnest of threads.

"That's good," she said firmly.

"Can you keep going for a while?" he asked.

"As long as we need to."

They rode another hour. Charles looked over his shoulder every few minutes but could see no one trailing them. He listened for the sound of hooves thundering behind them, but the highway was quite deserted.

When the mare had nothing left to give and slowed, Charles steered her off the road and into an adjacent field. He found a stream where the horse could drink, dismounted, and helped Rose from the saddle.

"Oh, Charles," she cried, launching herself into his arms. "I didn't know what else to do. But I'm not sorry. I'd do it again."

"Shhh." He held her close and smoothed a hand over

her hair, inadvertently freeing the silver ribbon that had adorned her curls.

As he bent to sweep if off the ground, she giggled. "It's absurd, isn't it?"

"Maybe a little. But you look beautiful."

"It's my break-out-of-prison ensemble," she said through chattering teeth.

He looked down at her feet. "Pretty silver slippers can't be much defense against the cold."

"I brought boots. They're in my satchel."

"You should have told me," he said. "I would have stopped sooner. Here." He drew the greatcoat from his bag and spread it out so she wouldn't have to sit on the frozen ground.

"Why aren't you wearing that?" she said.

"I'm not cold." It was true. Maybe he was still in shock, still struggling with the idea of what she'd done. For him.

He handed her satchel to her. "Did you bring another gown?" he asked hopefully.

"I did." She sat, winced as she slid her slippers off her feet, then reached for a boot.

"Wait." He knelt and took one foot in his hands, gently rubbing the warmth back into it before easing it into her boot. He did the same for the other foot, smiling at the little mewling sounds she made in her throat as he caressed her heel, arch, and toes.

He laced the boots and pulled her cloak tightly about her legs. "Better?"

She sighed and stood. "Much."

"Good." He picked up his greatcoat and draped it over her shoulders, but the back dragged behind her like a train.

"Please," she said, pulling it off and handing it to him, "put this on. I won't have you developing frostbite on my account."

"You can use it as a blanket when we're back on the horse." But he had to find some shelter for the night, somewhere she could warm up and he could think about their next moves without fear of being discovered.

"We'll give the mare a few minutes to recover, then go search for a place to rest. I won't let anything happen to you," he said.

She smiled. "I know."

They traveled for another hour, maybe two. Riding under the stars, Rose lost track of time. After all of the evening's excitement, she would have thought it impossible to feel sleepy, and yet her eyelids drooped. She leaned back against the warm, hard wall of Charles's chest and told herself that everything would turn out all right. As long as she was with him, she would be fine. *They* would be fine.

Leaning close to her ear, he said, "There's an old barn ahead. If it's vacant, it should suit our purposes nicely."

He pointed off to the right, and Rose squinted in that direction, barely able to discern the barn's outline in the moonlight. It was large and dark, and if it afforded them a place to hide for the remainder of the night, it was a godsend.

Charles stopped several yards away from the structure and dismounted. "I'll have a look. Stay here, and I'll return shortly."

He disappeared around the front of the barn, and a minute later she heard the rattling of a wooden door, followed by the smashing of a metal lock.

For a moment, all was silent, then the creak of a rusty-hinged door echoed across the field and skittered down her spine. She held her breath, waiting for a signal from Charles.

Soft light spilled from the barn door, and as Charles strode toward her, the silhouette of his broad shoulders and narrow hips made her want to sigh. "Our lodgings for the night," he announced, helping her down from the mare. "Not as luxurious as you're accustomed to, but they'll do." He led her to the door and reached for the dented lantern hanging from a hook just inside. It didn't illuminate the whole barn, just enough for Rose to see some empty animal pens, a pitchfork and some other abandoned tools, and hay. Lots of hay.

He flipped over a crate and set it in an alcove away from the door and the bitterly cold air that drifted through it. "Rest here for a moment while I see to the horse." As she sat, he shrugged off his greatcoat and settled it around her shoulders. Infused with his scent and the warmth of his body, the coat thawed her more quickly than any fire could have. She tucked her feet and hands beneath its folds and watched as Charles led the mare to a pen and shut the door to the barn.

They had so much to say to each other, so much to discuss. But she felt as though she'd used up all her words for the night trying to flee the ballroom and negotiate Charles's release. Besides, there were issues she wasn't quite ready to face.

As though he understood, Charles said, "You must be exhausted."

She nodded, and for the first time that evening, felt as though she might cry. He dropped to his knees and wrapped his arms around her.

She laid her head on his shoulder and breathed slowly until she was calm again. "I brought a bit of food in my satchel, if you're hungry."

"I'm not, but maybe you'd like something to eat?"

"No."

"Very well, then I'm going to make you a bed. I don't suppose you have a blanket in your bag?"

She smiled. "I'm afraid not. I only brought my boots, a change of clothes, money, and some food." Just the things she'd thought they might need after Charles's escape... until he could board a ship for America. "I did pack a large shawl, though. Would that help?"

"It would." He stood, grabbed the pitchfork, and tossed large bunches of clean hay onto the floor beside her. His movements, so easy and familiar, transported her to that magical summer when she'd followed him everywhere. She might have been a girl again, naïve, troubled, and hopelessly in love with the stable master—the only person who truly understood her. She'd thought then that her life couldn't possibly be more complicated. How wrong she'd been.

"How did you hide the satchel outside the prison? Weren't you at a ball earlier this evening?"

"I sent it to Edward and Shirley at Yardley Manor earlier today." It seemed ages ago. "They brought it when they picked me up from the ball in the wagon. They drove me directly to the prison, and I threw the satchel under the shrub. I waited there while they drove out front and yelled at each other as though they were having a row to end all rows. When a couple of guards ran out to see what was happening, I slipped through the side door behind them." She shrugged. "It was shockingly easy."

He set down the pitchfork, went to unhook her satchel and his bags from the horse's saddle, and set them both beside Rose. Gesturing to the large mound of hay, he said, "Not the finest of mattresses, but it will be comfortable enough once we cover it with your shawl."

She rummaged through the satchel and held up the shawl.

"Perfect." Together, they unfurled the soft wool garment and held the corners, letting it billow down over the hay. He slipped his bag under one end of the shawl and punched it a few times. "You can use this as a pillow. Ready to try it out?"

She was indeed. The makeshift bed looked surprisingly inviting. "Only if you lie down, too."

"I'm going to remain awake. We should be safe here," he quickly assured her, "but it's best if I keep an eye out in the unlikely event that someone stumbles upon us."

"You don't have to sleep," she said. "But at least lie down and rest with me. You'll need your strength tomorrow."

"An invitation such as that is nigh impossible to refuse. I'll join you for a bit, just until you doze off."

He held her hand as she sat on the pallet and sank into its softness. She patted the spot beside her, and he stretched out there, compressing the mound of hay beneath him to half its original height. Together they leaned back, resting their heads on his lumpy bag.

"What do you have in your bag?" she asked. "Stones?"

"All my worldly possessions. You've probably got a volume of Grimms' fairy tales beneath your neck."

She turned toward him, her eyes shining suspiciously. "A book. You didn't leave them all at your cottage."

He chuckled. "You don't give up on people, do you Rose?"

She wrinkled her nose. "What do you mean?"

He adjusted his greatcoat so that it covered her like a blanket, from neck to toe. "You didn't give up on your mother, and you didn't give up on me. Any young lady in her right mind would have washed her hands of a man who was imprisoned and accused of theft."

"You were there only because you were trying to help me. It was my fault."

"No," he said firmly. "Everything I did was my choice."

"What shall we do now?" She'd given her future some thought, but the decision was his as well.

"Little has changed for me. I'll still set out for America—just sooner than I'd planned." He circled an arm around her waist and pulled her against the warm, solid wall of his chest. "What about you? What do you hope for?"

"I suppose that, like you, I'm a fugitive now." A thought that was both sobering and frightening. "Strange to think I was attending a ball earlier this evening. I can't imagine I'll be welcomed in many drawing rooms after the salacious gossip about us spreads."

"There is a difference in our situations, though, Rose." He propped himself on an elbow and laced his fingers through hers. "You are a lady, gently born and raised. People will assume—and I'd encourage you to let them— that I forced you to come to my aid. If you go directly home to London and beg your brother to help you clear your name, he will. He adores you and would do anything in his power to protect you and restore your reputation. Truly, it's the only real choice you have."

She frowned. "I disagree. There is another option...I could go to America with you."

"And leave your family three thousand miles behind?" he asked skeptically. "You would never be happy. And I wouldn't be happy knowing that you were unhappy."

"I will miss them." Desperately. In fact, if she dwelled on it she might easily dissolve into a puddle of tears. "But if I stayed here, I'd miss you more."

"Jesus, Rose. I feel awful that it's come to this. You belong in England, living in a stately mansion and dancing in elegant ballrooms."

"I belong with *you*."

"You don't understand, damn it. The selfish part of me wants to pull you close and never let go. To make you my wife and never spend another night without you. But I don't think that's what's best for you."

Though the sentiment was sweet, it still made her hackles rise. "I'm a grown woman. *I* can decide what's best for me. And it's not staying here, hoping my brother can keep me out of prison while the man I love sails to another continent. Owen has a great deal of influence; however, I'm not certain that even he can help me after I threatened a prison guard with a gun."

"You love me?" He blinked, as though awestruck by her confession.

Nestling closer to him, she nodded. "Yes. I only run away with men I love."

"But this idea of going to America with me. Is it born out of love . . . or fear?"

"Love."

He blew out a long, slow breath. "Nothing about it would be easy for you. The journey across the Atlantic will be tedious—dangerous, even. Once we arrive in America, it will take me several months to build a home with basic comforts. It will be a hard life, at least in the beginning."

Rose smiled, because in spite of the concerns he listed, Charles almost sounded like he was envisioning a future with her in it. "I don't need an easy life," she said. "Just a happy one." She gazed up at his handsome face, suddenly shy. "Did you mean what you said earlier? About marrying me?"

He leaned in, touching his forehead to hers. "There is nothing—and I mean nothing," he said slowly, "in this world that I want more than to marry you. And, God forgive me, that's what I'm going to do."

With that, he brushed his lips over hers in a kiss filled with promise and passion—the kind of kiss that curled her toes and left her breathless with desire.

There was no denying that her life was a complete and utter mess . . . but for once, she didn't mind in the slightest.

Chapter Twenty-Four

Charles let his lips linger on Rose's. Hers were cold. The tip of her nose was an icicle, yet she hadn't uttered a single complaint.

He pulled the hood of her cloak over her head, tucking the loose, soft strands of her hair inside. Then he held her close, willing the heat from his body to seep into hers. Her thin silk ball gown didn't provide much protection from the wintry temperatures, and even her velvet cloak was more stylish than warm.

"Maybe you should put the gown in your bag over the one you're wearing," he suggested.

"In the morning," she murmured sleepily. "It's cozy under your jacket, and I refuse to come out from under it until I absolutely must."

Chuckling, he touched his nose to hers. "Very well. Sweet dreams, love."

"Good night," she sighed, and within minutes, her breathing slipped into the even, peaceful rhythm of sleep.

But Charles remained awake and alert, awed by what she'd done for him and what she was willing to do.

"I love you, Rose," he whispered.

As he watched the involuntary flutter of her long lashes and the perfect bow of her parted lips, he made a vow—to spend the rest of his days trying to give her the life she deserved and trying to be the man she deserved.

Morning sunlight slipped through the crack between the barn's large doors, and Rose stirred on her hay mattress. Charles left his post against the wall and went to her, smiling as she stretched contentedly. God, she was beautiful.

"Good morning." He nuzzled her neck and kissed her chilly lips.

Circling her arms around him, she murmured, "Did you sleep at all?"

"Yes," he lied. "I woke just before you."

She raised a brow. "We should be going, shouldn't we?"

"Soon. But you must eat something first. I'm going to collect some snow in the pail I found and set it in the sun. We'll have something to drink shortly."

She smiled bravely. "An excellent plan."

He scooped up the bucket and ventured outside into the gray dawn, scanning the horizon for any sign that they'd been followed. The crisp landscape looked still as a painting, save for the slight rustle of tree branches overhead. He walked around the barn till he found several patches of snow that hadn't melted, then threw a few fistfuls of slush into the pail. He sloshed it around, dumped it, and wiped the inside clean with his sleeve before filling the bucket with fresh snow.

He squinted in the direction of the highway. Before long, he and Rose would be pursued not only by the constables, but by her brother, Huntford, as well. Charles couldn't imagine they'd receive much mercy from either party.

Traveling on main roads was out of the question. They would stick to fields and smaller roads and hope to avoid detection. Rose didn't deserve to live in the shadows, and yet they had little choice. At least for now.

When he returned to the barn, he found Rose moving about in a dark blue, woolen dress. She smiled at him as she rolled the silver gown into a ball, stuffed it into her satchel, and then produced a loaf of bread. "Would you like some?"

"You eat it," he encouraged. "We have many miles to cover today. You'll need your strength."

"I can eat while we ride. I'm ready. So is Pandora."

"Who?"

"The mare. It's an apt name, don't you agree? Although I suppose I'm actually the one who's unleashed all the trouble."

He set down the bucket and caressed the tops of her arms. "You did no such thing. And don't forget the one thing Pandora kept in her box."

"Hope." A tentative smile lit her face. "We still have that."

"Absolutely. Now eat a little, and drink, too. We'll be on our way shortly."

As he pulled a jacket out of his bag and shrugged it on, he debated how to best broach the questions he had to ask her. "I am wondering," he began, "if you still feel the same way you did last night."

"About going to America with you? Yes, of course."

"I would understand if you changed your mind," he said. "After we left the prison, your emotions were riding high. Now, after a few hours' sleep, you may see things differently. I wouldn't blame you." He barely breathed as he waited for her reply.

"I'm going to America with you," she repeated.

Relief flooded his veins even as something in his gut niggled. "I'm glad. But know this. If you change your mind at any time on our way to London, I will understand. I could reunite you with your family before I leave."

At the mention of her family, her face fell, but she quickly recovered. "Thank you, but I'm confident in my decision."

"Are you prepared to leave for America without seeing them again?"

She swallowed hard. "I won't pretend that leaving them is easy for me. That's the only hard part, really. But they have one another, and once we're settled, I'll write and let them know that I'm well."

"They'll be looking for you long before then."

"I know. I hate the thought of them worrying about me."

"They'll be beside themselves, Rose."

"It can't be helped. Last night, before I went to the ball, I left a note on my bed for Lady Bonneville. I told her in the vaguest terms that I had to try to help you and that I was sorry for the scandal that would result. But I also told her that I was safe as long as I was with you, and that she shouldn't worry about my welfare."

"If I were in her shoes, I would not be persuaded."

"She was planning to leave for London today. I am sure that she'll send word ahead to Owen, and he'll be looking for me."

"With good reason. He loves you."

"Yes." Her voice cracked on the word. "And I love him as well. But if I were to take the opportunity to say good-bye to him and Olivia...they'd never let me go. My future is not here—not if you're in America. Once we're there, no one will know what we've done. You can buy up all the land you want and we'll start fresh, making a life together."

A future with Rose was something that he hadn't even dared to dream of, and now she was offering him this priceless gift—a gift that would require her to turn her back on the family that she held dear.

"You once told me something," he said, "something that made a lot of sense. That in order to move forward with your future, you had to first make sense of your past."

She nodded. "My mother. I never told you what I learned about her."

"I'd like to know."

"She's in a hospital in London, all alone, ill with consumption. In the letters she wrote to Lady Yardley, Mama begged her to visit. I think she wanted to get her affairs in order and..." She paused and swiped at her eyes, trying valiantly to compose herself. "I think she wanted to feel as though someone would care enough to mourn her passing."

Charles hugged her tightly and kissed the top of her head, inhaling the clean scent of her hair. "You are the most generous person I know, Rose. Frankly, after the pain your mother has caused you, I'm not certain she deserves your compassion." He thought about his own mother, bleeding to death while the duchess monopolized the doctor's time.

Rose looked up at him, eyes brimming with tears. "It's not a matter of deserving. She is my mother, and she is suffering." She shrugged helplessly. "I would ease her pain and loneliness if I could."

He swiped the pads of his thumbs over her cheeks, drying her tears. And he knew what they had to do. "We can visit her before we go. We'll see that she's getting the care she needs."

"Isn't that risky?" she asked. "Don't you want to board a ship as quickly as possible?"

It was risky as hell. But it was important to her, and he didn't want her mother's desperate written pleas to haunt Rose for the rest of her life. "No one else knows where your mother is, right?"

"As far as I'm aware, only Lady Yardley. I don't believe Lady Bonneville knows the particulars. Mama has been shunned by her former friends, and she didn't want Owen, Olivia, or me to be troubled by the sad news."

That was good. "Then no one will think to look for us in a hospital. We'll slip in and slip out before anyone's the wiser."

She brightened, and he knew he'd made the right decision. "Do you really think we could?" she asked.

"I do. But we'll have to move quickly, covering a lot of ground each day until we reach London."

"Thank you, Charles." She said it like he'd given her the world, and her watery smile warmed him to the core.

"Let's go."

They rode all day, pausing only twice to stretch their legs and to allow Pandora to rest. The sun was dipping behind the fields now.

Rose had never spent so many hours in a saddle. Her bottom tingled with numbness, her thighs ached, and her belly rumbled from hunger.

As though he'd heard her thoughts—or perhaps her belly—Charles spoke in her ear. "We'll stop for the night soon."

"Another barn?" At the moment, even a bed of straw sounded divine.

"Maybe we can do a bit better."

He steered the mare toward a stone cottage with a thatched roof and plume of smoke rising from the chimney.

"It's charming," she said. "Do you know who lives there?"

"Let's find out, shall we?"

They rode up the drive, dismounted several yards from the cheery red door, and tied Pandora's lead to a fence post. "I'm nervous," she whispered. "What if they're angry with us for trespassing?"

He squeezed her hand and gave her a knee-melting grin as he rapped on the door. "Just be your usual, charming self. And follow my lead."

A balding man, perhaps fifty years of age or so, opened the door a crack.

"Good evening, sir," Charles said.

The man took in their rumpled clothes and tired faces. "What brings you young people here?"

"Forgive us for interrupting your evening." Charles swept off his cap and offered his hand. "I'm John, and this is my wife, Edna."

Wife? *Edna*?

"We're heading to Bristol to visit her sister—she has a newborn—and had a minor problem with our wagon, so we had to leave it on the side of the road. It should be easy for me to repair in the morning, but it's gotten too dark for us to travel the rest of the way this evening."

The man's eyes flicked from Rose to Charles and back again. Rose detected some sympathy in the wizened face.

"We certainly don't want to impose, but we'd be grateful if you could give us a place to spend the night. Perhaps a stable or barn loft? We would gladly pay for your hospitality."

"Who is it, dear?" A soft female voice called from inside the cottage. "It's too cold for visitors to stand on the front stoop. Invite them in."

The man stepped aside and waved them into the cozy warmth of the cottage. Charles recounted his story for the woman's sake, embellishing a bit.

The woman clucked her tongue sympathetically. "Well, I'll wager you two could use something to eat. We've just finished our supper and there's some stew left. Warm bread, too. Sit and let me fill your bellies, while we figure out suitable accommodations for the night."

"You're very kind." Charles led Rose to the wooden table in front of the fire and pulled out the bench for her.

"We could make a pallet here on the floor," the man said. "Not the most comfortable of sleeping arrangements, but at least you'd be warm."

"That's very generous," Rose said. "Thank you."

But the woman frowned as she clunked bowls of hearty stew onto the table before them. "Surely we can do better than that, Neville. A young newlywed couple needs a bit of privacy." She turned to Rose. "You are newly wed, are you not?"

"Yes, ma'am." She lowered her eyes and kept her left

hand under the table as she ate a spoonful of the mouth-watering stew.

"We don't have a spare room, Matilda. What would you have me do? Give up my own damned bed?"

The woman shot Neville a scolding, long-suffering grimace. "Heaven forbid." More softly she added, "But you remember how it was when we were their age. What about the cabin you worked on during the summer?"

The man tilted his head. "There's not much there but a couple of chairs and a fireplace."

"I have plenty of quilts and some extra pillows." She patted Rose's shoulder. "How does that sound?"

"Perfect."

"It's an easy walk," Matilda said. "Neville will take you down there right after your supper. You both look like you could use a good night's sleep."

Half an hour later, Neville led the way to the cabin, holding a lantern at eye level to light the path. Loaded down with bedding and their bags, Charles followed behind the farmer, chatting amiably. Rose carried a small basket that Matilda had slipped onto her arm as they were about to leave. Rose wasn't sure what was inside, but the delicious aromas of cinnamon and apple wafted from it.

Nestled between three large trees, the cabin looked as though it might have been home to a band of woodland fairies or sprites.

"It's not much," Neville apologized, but Rose couldn't imagine anything more charming.

"It's lovely."

Neville crossed the tiny front porch, opened the door, and ushered them into the one-room cabin. Two rocking chairs sat in front of a dormant fireplace, and one small window looked out over a field. A narrow shelf on one wall held a lantern, matches, and several candles. Rose breathed in the faint scents of pine and lemon wax and sighed.

"You built this?" Charles asked.

"Aye," said Neville. "We thought it would make a fun hideout for young ones, if were blessed with grandchildren. None so far," he added sadly. "But we're not giving up hope."

"We're honored you'd let us stay here for the night," Rose said.

Charles knelt before the hearth, and Neville handed him some kindling and a match. "It's nice to see it getting some use."

After lighting the fire, Charles stood and reached into his pocket. "We'll most likely head back to our wagon first thing in the morning. Please accept this small token of our gratitude for your generosity," he said, holding out a few coins.

Neville waved his hand away. "Matilda would have my head if I took money from a nice young couple like you. Save it up for the children you'll have one day. You'll need it."

The mention of children made Rose blush, and she was grateful for the dim light in the cabin. "Thank you," she said.

Neville brushed off his hands and reached for his lantern. "Come to the cottage if you need anything else. Otherwise, sleep well."

He left, and as Charles poked at the fire, Rose sank into one of the rocking chairs, relaxing for the first time in what seemed like days. "I think I'm going to sleep very well indeed."

"Shall I take your cloak?"

Though loath to move, she slipped off the cloak and handed it to him. "I think I shall stay in this spot. Forever."

Chuckling, Charles walked up behind her chair, placed his warm hands on her shoulders, and gently kneaded the tension out of them.

She closed her eyes and moaned softly. "That feels heavenly."

"So will a good night's sleep," he said. "Stay here. I'll spread out the quilts and pillows for you."

Turning in her chair, she watched as he layered two thick quilts on the floor and tossed two fluffy pillows against the wall. "You've had less sleep than I in the past two days. You must be about to collapse."

"Not at all." He returned to her, took her hand, and when she would have stood, swept her up into his arms.

"What are you doing?" She kicked playfully, loving the solid strength of his arms beneath her.

"Taking you to bed."

"It's an odd thing," she said, as he gently lowered her onto the quilt. "I suddenly find that I'm not as tired as I'd originally thought."

Charles shot her a grin that melted her insides. "I was hoping you'd say that."

Chapter Twenty-Five

Tack: (1) All the equipment that a horse wears, including the saddle, bridle, and harness. (2) A course of conduct, especially one that is heretofore untried, as in Determined to try a new tack, she slid her hand under his waistcoat, across his hard, flat abdomen.

Rose sat back on her heels and removed the pins from her hair. Charles watched her with an expression of awe, as though she were performing a sacred rite that few mortals had ever witnessed. With each pin she pulled free, the heavy bun on top of her head began to fall, easing the tightness in her scalp. When she'd rid herself of the last one, she tossed them into her satchel and ran her hands lightly through her unruly curls.

He swept a lock off her shoulder and wound it around his finger. "You have no idea what the sight of you like this does to me."

Her heart beat faster. "Why don't you tell me?"

"I'd rather show you."

They couldn't remove their clothes fast enough. He

pulled off his boots while she pushed off his jacket. He wrestled off her dress, not seeming to mind in the least that it was serviceable wool rather than elegant silk. Her boots and stockings were the next casualties, tossed across the small room like the nuisances they were. Before long, she wore only her chemise, he only his trousers. They tumbled onto the makeshift bed in a tangle of arms and legs, skin against skin.

"I hope you don't mind that I introduced you as my wife," Charles said. "I thought it would make things easier ... but I probably should have warned you."

"I like this charade," she admitted. "And truthfully, it doesn't feel like much of a charade."

He turned sober then, his beautiful eyes intense. Almost pained. "How in God's name did I get so lucky?"

"I am lucky, too," she said. "Every minute that I'm with you feels like a gift. And greedy person that I am, I want more. More of you."

"Tonight," he said huskily, "we have lots of minutes together, and you may be as greedy as you like. I'd encourage it, actually." He loosened the tie at the neck of her chemise and tugged the soft linen lower, exposing the swells of her breasts and taut, pink nipples. "I may not be able to give you riches or a title, but I will gladly give you everything I have and everything I am. I promise to provide for you and protect you."

She cupped his cheeks in her hands and brushed her lips over his. "I've never doubted that," she said. "I've never doubted *you*."

His eyes turned hungry—and mischievous. "You trust me, do you?"

"Implicitly."

His gaze lingered on her breasts, heating her skin. "Lie back."

Tingling with anticipation, she lay her head on the down pillow and placed her hands at her sides, resisting the urge to cover herself.

"I'm going to taste every inch of you," he promised. "I should warn you, it's going to take some time."

A delicious shiver stole through her. "I'm all yours."

God, he was handsome. The firelight cast shadows over his body, shading the contours of his chest and abdomen. The muscles of his arms flexed as he moved over her, dipping his head to nibble her shoulder and kiss her neck. With every touch, she slipped further under his spell. Her whole world boiled down to him, her, and the passion that sparked hot between them.

With calloused palms, he caressed her bottom and the soft skin behind her knees. With the stubble on his chin, he skimmed her belly and tickled the insides of her thighs. With his tongue, he teased the folds at her entrance, turning her limbs to jelly and her insides to butter.

True to his word, he took his time, bringing her to the edge of ecstasy and keeping her balanced there for an eternity. "It's been long enough," she said breathlessly. "Even the sweetest torture must end. Please."

"The waiting is almost over, love." He sat up, pulled off his trousers in one fell swoop, and hauled her chemise over her head. "Come with me."

Gloriously naked, he took her hand as he walked to one of the rocking chairs in front of the low-burning fire. He lowered himself onto the wooden seat and tugged her forward, guiding her hips until she straddled him in the chair. Her toes just touched the floor, and if she pressed down, the chair swayed.

She glanced down between them, blushing at the sight of him erect and undeniably aroused.

"I want to memorize everything about you," he said. "The taste of your skin, the sound of your moans, and the softness of your lips."

"I don't think I could possibly forget this night. It feels like a dream I've had a million times before and one I want to live again and again."

She moved over him then, taking him inside and surrendering to the rhythm that her body craved. Each time she lowered herself, taking him deeper, he moaned, and her own pleasure spiraled. His fingers dug into the soft flesh of her bottom, demanding more from her, pulling her closer. His mouth found the tip of a breast, and he sucked hard, sending sweet vibrations throughout her body.

She felt like she was floating, weightless and free. And when he thrust faster, the insistent pulsing began, lifting her even higher. Needing something to cling to, she raked her fingers down his arms and called out his name.

"That's it," he urged. "Come with me."

And then she did. Her head fell back and every muscle in her body tensed in anticipation of pure bliss. She whimpered as the waves rolled over her, overwhelming her body, mind, and soul.

The muscles in his neck tensed, and he gasped as he found his release, too. He held her tightly until she collapsed onto him, deliciously content. They remained there, joined together for several minutes, neither of them willing to move.

At last, he kissed her forehead and gazed into her eyes.

"You're the center of my world, Rose. I tried to pretend that you weren't, that I could go to America and find what I needed there, even while you were an ocean away. But I need you. Your goodness, your wisdom, your kindness. I need you."

She warmed at his words. Being needed was good. People didn't leave if they needed you. If it wasn't quite the same thing as love, well, it was close. It was good enough for her, good enough for now. "I need you, too."

Gently, he helped her stand, then carried her to the quilts. "Rest. I'm going to see what treats Matilda gave us." He peeked into the basket and grinned at her. "Soft cinnamon-apple rolls with butter. Have a bite." They shared one roll and then another, savoring each decadent morsel.

"I think Matilda must have a soft spot for you," said Rose.

"It's my charm," Charles confirmed, licking a crumb off his thumb.

She stretched lazily and yawned. "You have definitely charmed me, Mr. Holland."

He drew a blanket over her and kissed her tenderly. "I've only just begun. Sweet dreams, Rose."

Her eyes fluttered shut, and the weight of the arm he'd draped over her waist made her feel safe and warm. She snuggled closer, secure in the knowledge that there would be no worries tonight. Only intimacy, comfort, and pleasure.

When Charles awoke in the morning, their idyllic hideaway was several degrees colder than the night before. The fire had died, and a chilly draft blew beneath the door and around the window.

Rose slept snugly under the blankets. Her fair skin and auburn hair gave her the look of a mischievous woodland nymph. Though Charles hated to rouse her, they needed to be on their way. He wanted to leave before Neville and Matilda came to check on them. Besides, if they made good time today, they might reach London before nightfall.

"Good morning," he said softly, brushing a tendril of hair off her cheek.

She blinked sleepily, smiled, and arched a brow. "A good morning indeed."

"It's time to get dressed." He shook his head and grinned. "Though I should have my head examined for even suggesting that you put on clothes."

"No, I think clothes are prudent." She sat up, shivered, and pulled the quilt up over her shoulders. "How much longer until we reach London?"

"Tonight, perhaps."

A range of emotions flitted over her face. Relief, apprehension, and resolve.

He squeezed one of her hands and laced his fingers through hers. "You must be nervous at the prospect of seeing your mother after so many years."

"Yes. I'm not sure what to expect, but I know I need to see her."

"I'll tend to Pandora while you dress. There's a bowl of water on the hearth in case you'd like to wash up and a roll in the basket if you're hungry. Is there anything else you need?"

"No, thank you." She sighed as she looked around the cabin. "I confess I'm a bit sad to leave this place."

Charles's heart swelled. Who would have thought that

the daughter of a duke could be content sleeping on the floor of a rustic cabin? And yet there was no mistaking the wistfulness in her voice or the sincerity of her words. They made him want to tug the blanket off her and pleasure her all over again, but he refrained. There would be many other mornings...and afternoons and nights.

"I'll return shortly," he said, kissing her on the cheek before slipping on his greatcoat and leaving her alone in the cabin.

Outside, the sun had just peeked over the tree line, and the first rays glinted off the frosty fields, promising a warmer day was in store. Charles felt lighter than he had in ages. He *could* make Rose happy, and that's what he intended to do. But first he had to see her safely to America. He retrieved Pandora from the small stable where she'd spent the night with Neville's cows, led her back to the cabin, and tied her lead to one of the large trees. When he knocked on the door, Rose answered, "Come in."

Dressed in her dark wool dress and black cloak, she stood in the middle of the room, slipping on her gloves. "I'm just about ready," she said.

She'd straightened the room, and everything was back in its place. The quilts were folded and neatly stacked in the corner, along with the pillows and something else... something silver. "Is that...?" He pointed at the luxurious fabric, oddly out of place among the patchwork quilts and humble linens.

"The ball gown," she confirmed matter-of-factly.

"Did you intend to leave it here?"

She hoisted her satchel onto her arm and walked toward him. "Yes, I thought perhaps Matilda would like to have it."

"Matilda?" It didn't seem polite to mention, but the older lady wouldn't be able to fit one leg into Rose's gown. "She doesn't need a dress like that."

"Then maybe one day her granddaughters will use it to play dress up. It seems silly for me to take something so impractical on our journey. It's not as though I'll have need of it." She spoke without a trace of bitterness or regret, and yet Charles felt as though he'd been punched in the gut.

Because what she'd said was true. Married to him, she would never, ever have use for a gown like that. There would be no balls for her, no house parties, no elegant soirees.

And regardless of what she thought about the matter, that truth struck him as very, very wrong.

Chapter Twenty-Six

Rose and Charles traveled all day, and when darkness fell they took a room at the Pelican, a small inn just outside of London. Once again they pretended to be married; however, this time Charles gave the innkeeper a different name.

Stopping at an inn was risky, and Rose suspected Charles had done so out of concern for her. Her face was so cold that she could barely move her mouth and tongue to talk; her fingers and toes had lost feeling after a couple of hours of riding. So, while the inn was far from luxurious, a warm room and real bed seemed like true decadence.

The minute they walked into their tiny room, Charles set down their bags, shut the door, and pulled her into his arms, kissing her cheeks and rubbing her arms and back. "You're frozen."

"I'm fine," she assured him.

"You should have told me," he scolded. "We could have stopped earlier."

She slipped her hands beneath his coat and jacket and splayed them over his back, savoring the warmth of his body. "I'm thawing nicely," she said, nuzzling his neck.

The look he shot her conveyed an equal mix of affection and skepticism.

"I'm going to ask for hot tea and supper to be sent up. In the meantime, I want you to take off your boots, climb into that bed, and stay beneath the covers until I return."

"And then you'll join me?" she asked with a smile.

"Gladly." He cupped her cheeks and took her mouth in a kiss that banished the chill. "Under the covers," he said firmly. "I'll be back shortly."

Rose sat on the room's one rickety chair and removed her boots, still stiff from the cold. As she rubbed the feeling back into her toes, she gazed out of the window at the stars winking in the ink-black sky.

They were close to Town now. During the last several miles they'd ridden, they'd encountered more travelers and seen more shops and taverns than they had in the two previous days combined. And that meant Rose was closer to home.

Home. With her comfortable bedchamber and her favorite chessboard and shelves of much-loved books.

So close to Owen, Belle, and their little daughter Lizzy; Daphne and Ben; and Sophia. Olivia and James would return from Egypt any day now, too.

She swallowed the sudden, painful lump in her throat and shook her head. The elegant town house in Mayfair was no longer home. Her life was with Charles now, and for all that her childhood home had to recommend it, it didn't have him.

Still, she wondered what her brother and Belle were

doing at that moment. By now, they had no doubt heard the news of the scandal. Owen would be one part livid and two parts frantic with worry. If Olivia had heard the news, she would be sympathetic but distraught over the apparent splintering of their small family. Family was everything to Olivia.

It was to Rose, too.

She took off her cloak, hung it on a hook, and climbed into the bed, fully dressed. She tried not to look at the peeling paint on the walls or the cobwebs in the corners of the ceiling. She didn't dwell on the lumpy mattress or the dingy linens. None of these things troubled her greatly.

But the thought that she might never again see Olivia or Owen... that was enough to break her heart to bits.

She pulled the covers to her chin and trembled with the effort to stave off tears. If Charles saw her crying, if he guessed the depths of her despair, he would return her to Owen immediately and sail away, out of her life forever— a prospect that was equally terrifying.

So she closed her eyes and told herself she was only emotional at the moment because she was cold and tired and hungry... and because Charles wasn't there, circling her in his strong arms.

A soft knock on the door made her gasp and bolt upright in the bed.

"It's just me." Charles opened the door slowly, balancing a tray in one hand. "I didn't mean to startle you. Look, I brought supper."

Rose blew out a long, slow breath. The mere sight of Charles standing there soothed her frayed nerves and distracted her from her sorrow. It was difficult to be sad while she stared at his ruggedly handsome face, broad shoulders, and lean hips.

He stepped toward her and nodded at the tray. "Shall I set this on the bed?"

She shook her head. "On the chair, I think."

Frowning, he did as she asked. "Don't you want to eat?"

"Eventually," she murmured, holding her arms out to him.

A slow, wicked smile lit his face as he rested the tray on the chair seat and eased himself onto the bed beside her. "I approve of your priorities, but will you mind if your food grows cold?"

"I shall be disappointed if it does not." Sighing, she grabbed him by the lapels, hauled him close, and kissed him.

She kissed him till there was no room for pain or homesickness or grief. Till she was dizzy with desire and weak with longing. Till all she could feel was the perfect rhythm of their bodies coming together and the pounding rush of pleasure that overtook them both.

Charles seemed different the next morning. Not distant, precisely, but less playful. More focused on the tasks before them—namely, visiting Rose's mother in the hospital and purchasing passage for them on the next ship sailing to America. They dressed in silence, collected their bags, and left the inn before the sun had fully risen.

Rose sat in the saddle in front of him, enjoying the muted beauty of the frosty dawn. Sore from three days of riding, she was grateful that they'd soon reach London, but apprehensive also. She could no longer pretend that this was simply a grand adventure after which she'd return to her normal life, complete with maids, mansions, and modistes. Her world had changed forever, and though she wanted nothing more than to be with Charles, she couldn't deny she'd miss the life she'd known.

"Our first stop will be the docks," Charles said, "to purchase passage on a packet ship. I don't like the idea of taking you to the shipyards, but I like the idea of leaving you alone even less."

"I'm sure I shall find the experience exhilarating."

He snorted slightly. "Let us hope it's not too exhilarating."

"Do you know when the next ship sails?"

"No, but hopefully in the next day or two. The longer we stay in London, the greater the danger."

One or two days. She tried not to think about how little time that left her to say good-bye to her mother... and to her life. She leaned into his chest and looked over her shoulder, up at him. "Are you worried that we'll be caught?"

Staring at the horizon, he shook his head. "My only concern is keeping you safe."

"You've done a wonderful job protecting me."

"Have I?" He gave a hollow laugh. "What about the night you had to sleep in a barn? Or the three days you had to ride for hours on end in the bitter cold?"

"That couldn't be helped," she countered. "Besides, I don't need to be pampered."

"Perhaps not. But if you think the last few days have been difficult... well, they might seem like paradise after our six-week voyage to America."

"I'm not prone to seasickness," she assured him.

"That's good. Even the best sailors are sick during a strong gale, though. And there will be other hardships.

Awful food—you can expect a lot of herring and garlic bread—and very little privacy."

If Rose didn't know better, she'd think he was trying to frighten her. To make her rethink her decision. She didn't flinch. "I'll manage."

"I'm going to try to purchase a cabin for us, but I'm afraid it won't be first class." He avoided her gaze as though embarrassed. As though he feared he'd disappointed her. Her heart ached for him.

"I wasn't expecting first class," she said. "To tell you the truth, I'm happy to know that we won't be in steerage."

He shook his head, appalled. "I would never subject you to that."

"But if I weren't traveling with you? Would *you* have been in steerage?"

He shrugged. "Probably."

"Then you should allow me to pay for the difference in the cost of our tickets."

"No." It was final. Adamant.

"Why not? That's money that you could put toward purchasing land."

"I won't take money from you, Rose. You freed me from prison and now you're leaving behind everything to come with me. The least I can do is buy your bloody second-class ticket."

Rose gasped, stung. She wanted to shake him and make him understand. Although it occurred to her that kissing might be more effective. Unfortunately, neither was possible while they were riding, so she had to depend on words—a poor substitute for either shaking or kissing. "I didn't mean to offend you or to suggest you couldn't provide for me."

"No? Then what did you mean?"

Tears burned at the back of her eyes. How could she make him understand? "I have some money—not a lot, but if we're going to make a life together, I don't see the point in your refusing it. It doesn't matter whose purse it comes from—we're going to be together forever now. Aren't we?"

He pulled up on the reins, and Pandora lurched to a stop. His lips pressed tightly together, he remained silent for several seconds. At last, he said, "Don't you see? I've already taken *everything* from you. And it kills me. I want to leave you with something of your own... and in doing so, maybe I'll be able to preserve a scrap of my self-respect."

A tear trickled down her cheek. She wanted to take her stupid coins and throw them on the ground for having come between her and Charles and shattering their harmony. "How long do you intend to punish yourself?"

"I don't know."

"Because as long as you do... you're punishing me, too."

He cursed under his breath, wiped away her tears, and hugged her close. It wasn't exactly an apology, but it seemed to be the best either of them could manage at the moment. "I didn't mean to upset you," he said.

She nodded. "I'll be fine." But she wasn't sure she would be—not unless Charles realized she needed him to be more than a protector and provider. More than anything right now, she needed a partner.

"The *Perseverance* leaves in four days." The teller adjusted his spectacles and checked the ledger in front of him. "One private cabin left. No porthole, but of course you'll have access to the deck when you need fresh air."

"Sounds charming," said Charles.

Rose squeezed his hand. "We'll take it."

As Charles handed over the coins, the teller wrote down their names. Or rather, the fake names that Charles had given. She'd had three different married names this week alone...and she still wasn't married.

Charles had said he'd try to quickly procure a marriage license so they could wed in London, but Rose discouraged him. It was too risky while they were trying to avoid detection by constables and her family. There would be time later, she'd told him. Perhaps when they were at sea. It wouldn't be the wedding she'd dreamed of, but as long as she was with Charles, it would be enough.

"Four days," Charles repeated. "I wish we could leave sooner, but this will give us time to visit your mother and to purchase the clothes and other items you'll need for the journey."

Rose frowned. It seemed wasteful to spend money on dresses and undergarments when she had an armoire full of them just a few blocks away, but they might as well have been in India for all her chances of retrieving them. The hurt from that morning's heated discussion hadn't yet subsided, and she had a feeling that if she objected to purchasing a few necessities he would be even more offended. So she sought another topic of conversation.

"Where will we stay while we're in London?" she asked.

"I have a friend who owns a shop a couple of blocks from the wharfs. He lets out the rooms above the shop, and I can count on his discretion."

The prospect of meeting one of Charles's friends both delighted and intrigued her. "What sort of business is it?"

"A pawnshop. Patrick has all sorts of things, but mechanical objects are his specialty. He buys broken watches, music boxes, and the like, repairs them, and sells them for a profit."

"I can't wait to meet him," she said.

"He already knows a bit about you," Charles admitted.

"Oh?"

"He's the one who used to read me your letters."

Charles and Rose stood on Cannon Street outside the pawnshop, he with the brim of his cap pulled low over his face, she with the hood of her cloak drawn forward. While they waited for the lone customer to leave the shop, she admired the tidy storefronts and the colorful wares displayed in their windows. The streets bustled with hackney coaches, folks scurrying to work, boys selling newspapers, and girls selling oranges.

And she realized she'd been here before. Her half sister's bookshop was located less than a block away. With the generous allowance that Owen now gave her, Sophia didn't have to continue to run the store, but she chose to anyway. She was probably behind the counter now, helping a customer or shelving new books. Rose practically ached with the need to see her.

"Are you all right?" Charles asked. "You look a little sad."

Rose knew she should tell him that Sophia's shop was nearby, but then he'd insist on leaving this area, and he wouldn't be able to see his friend, and they'd need to find another—possibly more expensive—place to stay. She would just avoid the bookshop and hide her face whenever she walked outside. It was only four days.

"I am fine," Rose said. "Though I suppose I'm nervous about visiting my mother later today." It was the truth, if not the whole of it.

Charles shot her a sympathetic smile. "I'll be at your side, today and always."

"I know." But hearing him say it aloud still made her heart squeeze in her chest.

"The pawnshop is free of customers," he said. "Let's go."

They crossed the road and entered the store, ringing a small bell above the door. Patrick glanced up from a worktable strewn with metal springs, nuts, bolts, and other parts, looking mildly peeved about the interruption. But his expression changed the moment he recognized his friend.

"Holland!" He wiped his hands on the front of his apron, untied it from his waist, and flung it onto the table. The men shook hands and clapped each other on the back. Their face-splitting grins said they were genuinely happy to see each other, and for the first time, Rose realized that she wasn't the only one who would be severing relationships when they left for America. Charles was making sacrifices, too.

"This is my fiancée, Rose." The fact that Charles introduced her using her real name spoke volumes about the trust he had in Patrick. And yet, he'd left off "Lady" and her surname. Perhaps he felt the formalities would have created an unnecessary barrier between her and his best friend. Whatever his reasons, she rather liked being known just as Rose.

She pushed back the hood of her cloak and extended a hand. "It's a pleasure to meet you." She swept her gaze around the store, stuffed to the gills with trinkets, objets d'art, and the sorts of odd treasures one finds in an attic. "You have a fascinating shop."

Even as Patrick beamed at the compliment, Rose could see his mind at work, trying to determine if she was the same lovesick girl who'd written to Charles over and over again.

"We've known each other for many years," Charles confirmed, "and were only recently reunited. We just bought our tickets for the next packet ship to America. We sail in four days."

"America, at last." Rose detected a hit of wistfulness in Patrick's voice. "Congratulations, my friend." More brightly, he said, "I think this calls for a toast."

Charles held out a hand. "Not yet. For reasons I'd rather not discuss, there are various people who are trying to stop us from going. We need a place to stay...a place to hide."

"You know you're welcome here." He smiled at Rose. "Both of you."

"You're very kind," she said.

He glanced out the front window of the shop and started moving toward the door. "Looks like I've got a customer coming in, but you know the way upstairs. Make yourselves comfortable, and you can tell me more later...or not." He raised a brow at them, then turned his attention to the gentleman who ambled into the store.

Charles swept aside a heavy curtain at the rear of the shop, revealing more shelves, more antiquities, and a narrow staircase to the upper floors. "This way to your suite, my lady," he said.

She followed him up the stairs, glad that she hadn't mentioned Sophia or the bookshop to him. He deserved some time with his friend before he left England.

As for her, she took a bit of comfort from knowing that Sophia was close.

She wouldn't think about the rest of her family, at least not at the moment.

For the next few days, she would focus on staying hidden, and hopefully, making peace with Mama...and the past.

Chapter Twenty-Seven

Broken: (1) Referring to a horse that is accustomed to a saddle and rider. (2) Damaged, often irreparably, as in The heartache and grief of her childhood had left her broken—but not without hope.

Rose stood in the hallway of St. Bartholomew's, just outside of a room with a dozen beds. The head nurse near the front entrance had told her and Charles that patients in advanced stages of incurable diseases were in the north wing of the first floor. Suddenly hot and clammy all at once, Rose loosened the tie at the neck of her cloak and fanned herself with her gloved hand.

Charles wrinkled his forehead in concern. "Shall I take your cloak?"

She shook her head and began to pace. "I've waited so long to see her, to speak with her. And now that I'm here, I don't know what to say."

"Just tell her . . . what's in your heart."

She wrung her hands. "What if I don't know what's in my heart?" But that was not truly the problem either. The frightening thing was that she had no idea what was in *Mama's* heart. "What if she refuses to see or speak with me?" Her lower lip trembled at the thought. All of this trouble could *not* have been for nothing.

Charles smoothed his palms down her arms. "You read her letters. She sounded lonely. I don't think she'll turn you away."

"She might be too weak to speak... she might not even be conscious."

He wrapped her in an embrace and pressed his lips to the top of her head. "Perhaps not, but the important thing is that you are here, with her."

She swallowed the lump in her throat. "I pray I'm not too late."

"As do I." He held her shoulders, looked into her eyes, and coaxed a smile from her. "Ironically, while you are worried that she won't know you're here, I am worried that she'll realize you're with me—and disapprove of your betrothal to her former stable hand."

"We don't require her approval," Rose said. "Or anyone's." Though it would be nice if *someone* in her family was on their side.

"Let's go, then, so that you can finish what you set out to do."

"My past is a part of me," she said, more to herself than to him. "But it's not who I am."

"Precisely," he said approvingly.

"I'm ready."

Holding her head high, she entered the room in front of Charles, nodding to the nurses who scurried down the aisles while she scanned the beds for a petite blond woman with elegant bearing.

One woman cried out—clearly in pain, out of her mind, or both. When Rose looked at her face and realized she was not Mama, relief coursed through her with guilt following closely on its heels.

She walked faster, and near the far end of the room heard another voice call out. "Rose? Can it really be? Is that... you?"

A frail woman with disheveled hair and hollow cheeks sat up in her bed, a bony hand clasped over her mouth. Dear God. Mama.

Somehow, Rose dragged her leaden feet to the bedside. "It is I."

"I can't believe it. How did you know I was...?" Her thin voice trailed off into nothing.

Rose took a deep breath. Her mother looked so different, so old. "There's a rather long answer to that question, but suffice it to say that I wished to find you. I'm glad that I have; however, I'm sorry that you are ill and confined to this place."

Mama clutched the covers to her chest, concealing the stained gown she wore, and patted her hair as though it were a source of extreme embarrassment. "It was good of you to come." She looked away. "But I confess part of me wishes that you had not."

Rose touched her fingertips to her throbbing temples and momentarily closed her eyes.

She could turn around and walk out of the room, out of the hospital, and out of Mama's life, forever. It would be the easiest thing for her, perhaps for them both.

Then Charles's steady, warm hand came to rest at the small of her back, infusing her with strength and confidence. Opening her eyes, she said, "Well, I am here, and as long as I am, I think we should try to have a pleasant visit, don't you?"

Mama coughed into a handkerchief and nodded. "I suppose."

Rose linked her arm through Charles's and pulled him forward. "Mama, do you remember Mr. Charles Holland?"

She hesitated, as though she were trying to figure out what the stable hand was doing with her daughter, then smiled weakly. "Of course. It was kind of you to accompany Rose."

Rose breathed a small sigh of relief. Perhaps there was still a glimmer of hope for their mother-daughter relationship.

"I'm certain you both have much to discuss," said Charles. "I'll bring a chair over," he said, "and give the two of you some time to talk."

Rose stood there feeling awkward for a moment, then decided that the faster they both conquered that feeling, the better.

"Owen and Olivia don't know I'm here. They don't even know that *you're* here."

Mama nodded slowly. "I see. Perhaps that's for the best."

"Yes, I think so—for now."

"I wanted to spare you all from my illness...and the shame associated with my past actions." She patted at her head again, pushing a matted lock of hair behind her ear. "But I won't pretend I'm not delighted to see you. What a lovely woman you've become."

"Thank you."

Charles returned with the chair then, which he placed at an angle to the bed.

When Rose sat, he leaned over her shoulder and whispered, "If you should need me, I'll be just outside, in the hall. Take all the time you'd like."

Left alone, she and Mama sat in silence, as though they were each letting the import of the moment sink in.

"Are you in great pain?" Rose asked.

"Sometimes," Mama admitted. "They give me laudanum when the coughing fits are too much to bear. But this week has been tolerable."

"That's encouraging," Rose said hopefully.

"Oh, I shan't recover," Mama said. "Some people manage to survive this disease, but I know I will not. I can feel my body failing, a little more each day."

"I'm sorry." Rose squeezed her hand.

Mama's head dropped and her hair fell into her eyes. "After what I did—being unfaithful to your father and abandoning you—it's no more than I deserve."

Rose blinked back her own tears. It was so odd, the way the tables had turned. Throughout her childhood, Mama had been in control. Poised, composed, and dignified. Rose had always felt so small and inconsequential in her presence. She'd yearned for Mama's approval, lived for a moment of her attention. But Rose had learned to survive without her mother's love. She'd relied on Olivia and Owen. More important, she'd relied on herself.

And now, Mama was the one to be pitied. She seemed to have withered to half her original size, the disease effectively obliterating all traces of the elegant duchess she'd once been.

Rose was in control, and what's more, she had the answers she'd come for. She might not know all the details of Mama's life, like whether she had missed pretend tea parties with Olivia and her, or whether she remembered the lullaby she used to sing to them at night. She didn't know exactly what Mama had been doing for the last several years, where she'd been, or whom she'd lived with. Those sorts of questions had once kept Rose awake at night, but no longer.

She looked into Mama's eyes and saw the regret there. She had her answers.

The question was, what to do now?

Rose did not owe Mama anything. She appeared to be receiving adequate care, and Rose doubted anyone would blame her if she chose to wash her hands of the situation, say good-bye to Mama, and walk out of the hospital forever. It might even spare them both some heartache in the end. What was the point of salvaging a mother-daughter relationship just to sever it when she left for America a few days later?

But Rose remembered all too well how it had felt to be abandoned and apparently forgotten. And she couldn't do that to Mama.

"Do you want to know what I think?" Rose asked.

Mama blinked her bloodshot eyes and nodded.

"No one deserves an illness such as this. And we all deserve a second chance. We all deserve forgiveness."

Mama blinked several more times, then covered her face with her hands and sobbed. Though Rose was tempted to do the same, she decided they simply didn't have time to be maudlin.

"I'll be in London for only a few more days," Rose continued. "But while I'm here, I think we should get to know each other again. I can tell you all about Owen, his lovely wife, Anabelle, and their darling baby—your granddaughter. I can tell you about Olivia and her dashing husband and their expedition to Egypt."

"Goodness." Mama sniffled. "And what about you? Are you happily settled as well?"

"I fear my own situation is a bit more complicated," she said vaguely. "Sometimes life forces us to make difficult choices."

"The difference between you and me," Mama said, "is that I made decisions selfishly, thinking only of my own desires and whims. You, Rose, are generous to a fault. You give no consideration to your own needs and far too much to the needs of others. That fact that you're sitting here beside me now is proof."

Rose swallowed the knot in her throat and blew out a long breath. "I suppose we could debate these sorts of things all morning, and I'm more than happy to do so. But I think we must put first things first."

Mama's brow wrinkled.

"Let's fix your hair, shall we? I should probably fix my own while I'm at it. Have you a brush?"

Charles tried not to disturb Rose as he climbed out of the bed the next morning. She'd spent three hours at her mother's bedside yesterday, and the reunion had left her happy, contemplative, and exhausted. After the physical and emotional demands of the last week, she could probably use an entire day of sleep. He tiptoed around the tiny room they'd let above Patrick's shop, gathering his clothes and dressing as quietly as possible. Rose lay on her side, an auburn halo of curls on her pillow. Her slightly parted lips begged to be kissed, and he was sorely tempted to forget about his plan and climb back into bed beside her.

But he wanted to do this for her—to let her know what she meant to him. And he couldn't get started soon enough. Shrugging on his jacket, he stole one last look at her, angled his shoulders through the doorway, and closed the door behind him. He felt his way down the dark stairway to the ground level and swept past the curtain into the dimly lit shop. Patrick was hunched over his table, examining the inner workings of an intricate mechanical toy by the light of a candle.

He glanced at Charles out of the corner of his eye and waved without looking up. "You're up and about early. Preparing for your journey?"

"Not exactly. I, ah, actually could use your advice."

Patrick set down his tweezers, pushed his spectacles onto the top of his head, and shot him a quizzical look. "Advice? About what?"

"Two things. First, I need a job for the next couple of days. It doesn't matter where it is or how much sweat is involved, but I need some quick money."

"I could give you a loan," Patrick offered.

"No," Charles said. Too harshly, perhaps. "I need to earn it."

"I thought you were trying to remain out of sight."

"I am. I'll use another name, do my work, and get paid."

Patrick nodded thoughtfully. "I have a few contacts. You said there was a second matter. Would it perchance pertain to a certain red-haired beauty?"

Charles resisted the urge to punch the knowing grin off Patrick's face. "I want to buy a wedding ring. Something unique and . . . special."

"Ah, I think I can help you there." Patrick walked

behind the counter, unlocked a safe, and withdrew a velvet drawstring pouch. "These three are the finest I have," he said, spilling a trio of rings onto a cloth on the counter. Charles moved the candle closer and looked helplessly at the sparkling, jewel-adorned bands.

"This one," Patrick said, holding out a ring topped with a square-shaped emerald, "came in just last week. The baroness said it had been passed down to her by her mother-in-law, and since she couldn't abide the woman, she'd just as soon be rid of it."

Charles took the ring and turned it over in his hand. The stone would complement Rose's coloring, and he could picture it on her slender finger, but something about it wasn't *her*. He set it down and shook his head. "I don't think so."

Patrick picked up another band, gold and crowned with a fat ruby circled with diamonds. "A courtesan brought this in. It's a very valuable piece, and she assured me that she earned every diamond on it—the hard way. I'd give you an excellent deal on it, of course."

It looked too garish for Rose, too showy for her personality. "I appreciate that, but it's not right either."

Patrick raised a brow and picked up the third ring. "How about this one? The design is elegant and classical."

Charles inspected the tasteful, rectangular shaped sapphire, flanked by a pair of diamonds. "Where'd it come from?"

"A gentleman sold it to me. He needed the blunt to pay off a gambling debt. I bought it for a steal."

"It's nice..." Charles frowned.

"But not for Rose," Patrick guessed.

"No."

His friend rolled his eyes. "Maybe while you're out working today, the prince regent will waltz into my shop with something from the queen's personal collection."

Charles jammed on his cap. "Give him my regards."

"You'll find work at 56 Sawbush Street. Tell Jack you're a friend of mine."

"Thank you. And when Rose comes down looking for me, will you let her know that I'll be back in time to escort her to the hospital this evening?"

"Aye." As Charles strode toward the door, Patrick added, "Have a care out there. I don't know who's looking for you exactly, but I'd hate to see you—or your lovely fiancée—land in trouble three days before you're bound for America."

"Don't worry, I plan to lay low," Charles said. And he hoped Rose would do the same.

Shortly after waking, Rose dressed and ventured down to the shop to look for Charles. "Good morning, Patrick," she said cheerfully.

He glanced toward a customer browsing at the front of the store, raised a finger to his lips, and bustled over to her. "You shouldn't be down here."

"I know," she whispered back, feeling ridiculous. "But Charles isn't upstairs."

"He had to go out for a bit but said he'll be back tonight to take you to the hospital."

Rose tried to hide her dismay. She'd thought they'd spend the day together, talking, shopping...planning their future. But Charles was probably preparing for their trip. "Well then," she said, "why don't I assist you down here?"

"It's too risky. Someone might recognize you. Better if you wait for him upstairs."

"I could stay in the back," she suggested. "I noticed most of the items that you've stored are in need of a bit of dusting or polishing." It was a gross understatement. She could spend a week dusting and polishing items in the back room and not finish the half of them.

"The dust is part of the ambiance," Patrick said, as though mildly offended. "And I'd feel better if you were in your room." The bell on the shop door rang as another man entered and walked to the counter. "I must go, but promise me you'll stay upstairs until Charles returns."

"Very well." She disliked the thought of being cooped up all day but told herself it would be good practice for their long journey across the Atlantic. She spent most of the morning pacing the length of the small room and searching for something productive to do.

She considered writing letters to Owen and Olivia. She could seal and address them and give them to Patrick with instructions to deliver them a week after she and Charles had set sail. But she didn't want to traipse downstairs and ask Patrick for writing supplies—he'd been quite adamant about her remaining in the room.

Besides, just the thought of writing good-bye notes filled her with sadness. What would she say? *"I'm sorry to have left you without so much as a hug, but I'm fleeing from the law. If you're ever in America, do stop in for a visit."* How could she possibly convey the depths of her sorrow at having to leave them? The pain was unbearable, and yet necessary.

No, she would not write the letters today.

Instead, she walked to the room's one window, which overlooked Cannon Street, and peeked through the curtains. In the daylight, she had an excellent view of the shops across the road. The haberdasher's, the milliner's, and . . . Sophia's bookshop.

Colorful stacks of books made an enticing window display, and a sunny yellow door invited passersby to come in and browse. But it wasn't the books that called out to Rose.

Sophia could be in the shop at that very moment. It had been an age since she'd seen her—seen anyone from her family, for that matter. What Rose would give to spend an hour with her talking, laughing, and crying.

It wasn't possible. Not because she didn't trust Sophia—she did. Rose and her half sister were alike in many ways, not the least of which was that they always seemed to be on the outside, just a bit apart from the rest. And she knew that Sophia would understand why she had broken Charles out of prison, and why they'd fled, and why she must now go to America. She would be able to explain it all to Owen and Olivia, and console them when they learned that their sister was gone. She'd make them realize that none of it was their fault and that there was absolutely nothing they could have done to fix the situation.

But Rose couldn't implicate Sophia, couldn't ask her to lie to constables who might come asking questions or to keep a secret from Owen, who was probably desperately searching for Rose at that very moment.

She swallowed and swiped at her eyes. At least she was physically close to Sophia. That would have to be enough.

Without looking away from the window, she pulled the chair closer and sat before it, careful to keep her face mostly hidden behind the curtain. She remained there for a long time, imagining Sophia working in the shop—her efficient movements, her shrewd gaze, her encouraging smile.

And if it made Rose a little lonelier, at least it helped to pass the hours.

People came and went, but Rose especially liked observing the customers as they left with neatly wrapped brown parcels clutched to their chests, wide smiles splitting their faces.

One such gentleman was leaving the shop now. He ducked out, a large package tucked under his arm as he strolled down the street. He had a kindly look about him, and she was wondering if he'd purchased a book for a child or for his wife when suddenly he stopped and turned to look behind him at—

Sophia.

She stood on the sidewalk behind him, without her coat, smiling and waving a man's hat. Slender and impossibly graceful, she laughed and handed it to him.

He took it and bowed gratefully, his cheeks flushing.

Sophia waved away his embarrassment good-naturedly and turned to head back to her shop.

Rose watched as Sophia walked briskly, rubbing her arms, until her simple but pretty light blue gown disappeared through the door.

Perched on the edge of her chair, Rose held her breath as she waited to see if Sophia might reappear.

When she didn't, Rose rested her forehead on the windowsill and ignored the painful lump in her throat. She would not cry.

In a few days, she'd embark on an adventure with the man she loved, and while nothing could make her happier, she had to admit—a part of her mourned the people she'd leave behind.

Chapter Twenty-Eight

$\mathcal{I}$'m glad you're back," Patrick said. "I bought an interesting piece from an old man today. Come see."

Charles had spent most of the day—and the previous two—at the docks loading sacks of grain onto a ship. His back, shoulders, and arms ached like the devil, but the soreness would be well worth it if he could give Rose a ring that told her how much she meant to him.

Something that was oddly difficult for him to express.

He doffed his cap, shoved it under his arm, and rested his elbows on the counter to look at Patrick's latest acquisition. There, on a scrap of black velvet, was a delicate antique ring with a square, light pink stone.

"It's a rose-colored diamond," his friend said proudly.

Charles liked it, and more important, he instinctively knew Rose would. "It's perfect."

"Aren't you curious to know who it belonged to?" Patrick asked.

"Not really." He'd had quite enough stories about jaded courtesans and dissolute rakes.

Ignoring Charles's response, Patrick launched into his tale. "A charming gentleman, frail and bent over a cane, entered the shop this morning. He said that the ring had belonged to his wife, Lord rest her soul, to whom he'd been married for thirty years. She died ten years ago, but last night she spoke to him in a dream and told him that he should sell the ring and use the money to take a little trip to the ocean, to visit the cottage where they spent their honeymoon."

Charles raised a brow. "Don't be a bloody bastard."

Patrick held up his hands, all innocence and sincerity. "What do you mean? It's the truth."

"That's a far-fetched tale if I ever heard one."

"It's what he told me. I swear it on my life." He placed a hand on his chest. "And that's not all. The gentleman said that nothing would make him happier than if the ring went to a young couple who were madly in love, just as he and his Beatrice had been."

Charles pinched the bridge of his nose. "How much did you give him for it?"

"A bit more than it was worth. But I wanted him to have enough to visit the cottage by the ocean."

"Right, the place of their honeymoon."

"What?" Patrick cried. "It could be true."

Charles waited, giving his friend a few moments to absorb the facts.

At last, Patrick slammed his fist on the counter. "Damn it to hell. I'll bet he didn't even need the blasted cane."

"I'll buy the ring from you," Charles said. "For whatever you paid him. I don't want you taking a loss on it, especially after you've given us a place to stay."

The price Patrick quoted was a little more than he had, but Charles could make up the difference if he worked a few hours tomorrow morning before they left. "Keep it in the safe for me, and I'll have the money for you tomorrow."

"It *was* a romantic story," Patrick said. "You should tell Rose. It would likely melt her heart."

Charles snorted as he headed toward the stairs at the back of the shop. "She's not half as gullible as you."

"Our last evening in London," Rose mused. She walked beside Charles on their way to the hospital for what would be her final visit with Mama. They kept their heads covered and looked at the ground, careful to avoid the direct gazes of passersby.

"Are you having second thoughts about leaving? I wouldn't blame you if you did."

"No," she said firmly. "But transitions are difficult. For me, anyhow. I will feel better once we're on our way. It's like we're existing between two worlds, leaving one and going to another. We don't really *belong* anywhere."

"We belong together." He squeezed her hand and her stomach flipped in response.

They walked in silence the rest of the way, and all the while Rose contemplated how much to tell Mama and how to best say good-bye. She had hinted that she would not be in London for long, avoiding most of Mama's questions and keeping her answers intentionally vague. But Rose couldn't delay the unpleasant task any longer.

They entered the large front door of the hospital, braced for the smells of sickness that assaulted them. Charles escorted her upstairs to the room where Mama's bed was, and they paused outside. "Shall I come with you this time? It might be easier."

"No, thank you." Mama was self-conscious even without an impossibly handsome man at her bedside. "Would you give us an hour? That should be plenty of time." And yet Rose already knew it would not be nearly enough.

"As you wish." He glanced around, confirmed no one was looking, and stole a brief but searing kiss on the lips. "Courage, love."

She smiled and sighed as he left. If that was courage, she wanted more.

Feeling lighter, she walked into the large room and made her way toward Mama's bed, only—

She wasn't in it.

Her mouth suddenly dry, Rose picked up her skirts and ran to the nearest nurse. "Where is the duchess?"

"Who?" The young woman looked both bewildered and exhausted.

"My...my mother. The patient who was in that bed, right there." Rose pointed at the bed, chillingly empty and stripped of all its linens. "She was there yesterday." Her voice cracked on the last word.

"Ah, Mrs. Sherbourne. She had a rough night last night, and we moved her to the corner back here so we could keep a closer watch over her."

The nurse motioned for Rose to follow and led the way to a darker, quieter section of the floor. In a whisper, she said, "There she is, resting peacefully. We gave her laudanum a few hours ago. She'll likely sleep for a while."

Rose rushed to Mama's side, looking for the subtle rise and fall of her chest and listening for the raspy sound of her breathing. A faint wheeze came from her throat.

Thank God. Relief washed over her like a torrent of rain, then quickly fled.

As the nurse turned to go, Rose placed a hand on her arm. "Wait. How long will the effects of the medicine last? I must speak with her."

"I don't think so," the nurse replied, not unkindly, but firmly. "She needs to rest. Tomorrow perhaps."

"That's just it. I can't... I won't be able to come back."

"You're her daughter?" Heretofore, Rose had been careful to keep their relationship a secret. Given that she and Charles were running from the law, the fewer people who knew her identity, the better. But none of the nurses here addressed Mama as "Your Grace" or even "Madam." Perhaps Mama hadn't revealed that she was a duchess. Or maybe she had and the nurses assumed she'd begun a descent into madness. Or maybe they believed her, but just didn't give a fig.

"I am her daughter. And I'm leaving London tomorrow. I haven't had a chance to tell her—"

"Rose." Mama called out from her bed, her head tossing on her pillow. "You're leaving?"

"It would appear you're in luck," the nurse said. "But your mother's likely to be groggy. Try to keep your visit short."

"Thank you." As the nurse strode off, Rose reached for the glass of water on the table beside Mama's bed, lifted her shoulders, and pressed the rim of the glass to her mother's lips. "Oh dear. I'm sorry to hear you've been feeling worse."

Mama swallowed a sip and let her head drop to her pillow. "It's to be expected. Where are you going?"

Though Rose doubted she'd remember much of the

conversation, she answered honestly. "To America, with Charles. I'm afraid we won't be coming back."

"That's good. A fresh start." Mama coughed into her blood-stained handkerchief, a raspy, heartbreaking sound. "No one there will know of my misdeeds or the ensuing scandal."

Rose's heart broke for her. "That's not the reason I'm going, you know."

"Why then?" Mama's eyelids fluttered as though she were struggling to keep them open.

"It's complicated, but a woman"—Rose thought it best not to mention Lady Yardley by name—"accused Charles of a heinous crime—a crime he did not commit. He cannot stay here, and since I love him, neither can I." Now that she'd spoken the words aloud, it didn't seem so complicated after all.

"That's awful," Mama said.

"Yes. Awful and unfair."

"Charles is a good and decent man. Why, Diana even hired him as—" She paused and strained to lift her head. "Wait. Is Diana the one who accused him?"

Rose blinked. Mama was far more lucid than the nurse had given her credit for. "Yes, Lady Yardley."

"I once considered her a friend, but she proved to be . . . disloyal."

"I know. I'm sorry, Mama."

"Has Charles denied her accusations?"

"Yes, of course. But what magistrate would take his word over Lady Yardley's?"

"Make her drop the charges," Mama urged.

"Lady Bonneville tried to convince her, but she would not be swayed."

"*I* could sway her."

"What?" A chill skittered down Rose's spine. "How?"

"I know things—things she's done. She would not want them to be revealed."

"No, Mama. I dislike the idea of blackmail, even if Lady Yardley *is* a horrid person."

"Neither Charles's future nor yours should be determined by the likes of her. His name should not be blackened because of her pride and vindictiveness."

"True. But the damage has already been done, I'm afraid."

"She could retract her statement, and she would—to prevent her own name from being sullied."

Perhaps Mama was right. But it was too late. They would be on the ship tomorrow.

"Please," Mama pleaded. "Let me do this for you. I cannot give you much else, but I would give you this—a bit of hope."

Hope. The one thing left in Pandora's box.

Rose swallowed. "Very well. Tell me, and I will pray that your words don't haunt me for the rest of my days."

Mama smiled affectionately. "That's my Rose. Too good for this world, by half. If you would prefer not to know of Diana's wicked deeds, there is another way." Mama licked her cracked lips and continued. "Bring me a paper, an envelope, and a pen."

Rose nodded. "I'll return in just a moment."

"Hurry, my dear girl," she said weakly. "I haven't much time."

On their way home from the hospital that evening, Rose soaked up the chilly night, grateful for the relative freedom that the cover of darkness granted them.

Charles kept looking at her, as though trying to read her emotions—emotions she was still trying to sort through. "How did your mother take the news that you're leaving?"

Rose blinked away tears. "With unexpected grace. She truly wants us to be happy. Oh, and she gave me a present, too. Look." She paused on the sidewalk, reached for the simple chain around her neck, and held the silver locket out for Charles to see. "Inside there are two tiny portraits, sketched long ago. One of Owen and Papa, the other of me and Olivia."

"It's beautiful," he said.

She squeezed the silver locket in her fist. "I shouldn't have accepted it, but knowing I'd never see Olivia and Owen again . . . I simply couldn't refuse. Just wearing it makes me feel closer to them—and to her."

"I'm sorry."

"About what?"

"That you have to leave behind all the people you love."

"Not *all* the people I love." She smiled, but sadness clung to her, casting a pall over the night. They continued walking, her hand in the crook of his arm.

"What will become of her?"

"I'm not certain, but I know that no one should live out their last days all alone. I encouraged her to contact Olivia and Owen after we're gone. Given the chance, I know that they would forgive her, and then maybe she'd be able to forgive herself. However, she was adamant about not wanting to intrude in their lives."

"Your visits brought her a measure of peace," Charles said. "Probably more than you know."

"I hope so. She gave me more than she took." And

Rose wasn't just talking about the locket or the answers she'd once sought. Mama had given her a choice.

She'd used every ounce of strength she possessed to prepare the letter that Rose now carried deep in the pocket of her cloak. Across the front of the envelope she'd written three lines:

Information regarding Lady Diana Yardley.
  To be opened at the sole discretion of my daughter, Lady Rose Sherbourne.
  Signed, Lily Sherbourne, Dowager Duchess of Huntford."

Rose didn't know precisely what was inside, but Mama had assured her that a glimpse of her handwriting on the envelope and the mere threat of dissemination of the deeds recounted therein would be sufficient to make Lady Yardley drop the charges against Charles.

And if the charges were dropped, his name and Rose's would be cleared, and they wouldn't have to leave England—at least not immediately. She could spend a little time with her family and collect some mementos to take with her on the journey.

She felt empowered, knowing that she had a choice in the matter and that she didn't have to run if she didn't want to.

Why, then, hadn't she told Charles about the envelope? He deserved to know about it, for it impacted him most directly. She wanted to share the news with him…but something held her back.

Going to America was his dream, and if he knew Rose had the option not to go, he might try to sacrifice that dream for her sake. Or he might decree that she was better off staying here while he left to pursue a new life.

And she simply couldn't take that chance.

He wanted to be in America, and she wanted to be with him.

"I'm going out again early tomorrow morning, just for a few hours," he said, jolting her from her thoughts.

"To work?"

"Yes. But I promise I'll be back in time for us to gather our things, say good-bye to Patrick, and board the ship."

Rose nodded thoughtfully. She'd never known anyone who worked as hard as he. And though she selfishly would have liked to claim more of his time herself, she respected his dedication.

If he'd seemed distant or a bit preoccupied this week, she supposed she couldn't blame him. After all, he was trying to keep her safe and to prepare for their voyage. They'd spent a part of the afternoon yesterday shopping for a few essentials for her. Undergarments, stockings, and a serviceable dress. And he'd insisted on purchasing a smart new hat that she'd been admiring.

He was unfailingly thoughtful, spoiling her with little treats from the bakery, wrapping her in blankets when she was cold, and borrowing books for her to read. But what she really wanted was for him to take her in his arms and kiss her until she was dizzy with desire, to love her until they were completely lost in each other.

But Charles had been hesitant. He assured her it wasn't for lack of wanting her, but he didn't want to risk getting her with child before the voyage, which he said would be difficult enough without morning sickness.

So at night they'd held each other and kissed without

surrendering to passion. Somehow, she'd resisted the temptation to strip off his clothes and run her hands down his chest, abdomen, and lower. She'd resisted the urge to writhe against him and feel the smooth warmth of his skin next to hers.

"I wonder if Boston has streets like this." Charles interrupted her wanton thoughts, making her flush.

"I doubt it. I don't think there's any place in the world quite like London," she said wistfully.

The pawnshop was only a block away. They walked on the opposite side of the street this time, quickly approaching Sophia's bookshop.

Rose had never passed so close to it, and she knew she should keep her head down, her hood drawn forward.

But she couldn't resist a quick peek inside.

It was dark, after all, and quite late. Chances were, Sophia had long since locked the door and retired for the evening.

So as they passed, Rose looked inside the large bay window past the colorful display of books. There, in the dimly lit shop, in front of a wall of shelves overflowing with books, a woman stood perched on the first rung of a ladder, her back toward them, running her fingers along a row of spines.

Sophia.

Rose stumbled a little, and Charles paused momentarily to steady her.

"How clumsy of me," she said. "I tripped over my own foot."

"Are you all right? You look like you've seen a ghost."

Not a ghost. Just her sister. "I'm fine."

"You must be tired," Charles said. "We're almost there. Come, let's cross the street."

She took his hand to follow, but, unable to resist one last glimpse of Sophia, looked over her shoulder toward the bookshop.

Her sister, still on the ladder, had turned toward the street. She frowned slightly, then gazed directly into Rose's eyes.

Dear Jesus. Gasping, Rose looked away, huddled toward Charles, and scurried across the street toward the pawnshop.

Sophia couldn't possibly have recognized her. Even with the lanterns hanging outside the shops, it was too dark. Besides, it had been only the briefest of glances. There was nothing to fear.

And yet, as Rose and Charles hurried into the front door of their hideout, she had the distinct and chilling sensation that she was being watched.

Worse, the tingling feeling in her shoulder blades told her Sophia wasn't the only one watching them.

Chapter Twenty-Nine

Flank: (1) The side of a horse. (2) To occupy a position at the side, as in The viscountess entered the drawing room flanked by her maid and a frisky, gray cat.

At last the day of their departure arrived. Sleet tapped against the window of the room above the pawnshop, blurring Rose's view of the street below. She'd woken at dawn, dismayed to find the mattress beside her already cold and empty.

She had managed to busy herself for a while, dressing in her new, serviceable gown, twisting her hair into a knot on top of her head, and packing up her belongings.

Those tasks had taken her all of a quarter of an hour, which meant she'd had the rest of the morning to fret.

She glanced at an old clock on the mantel. Where was Charles? He'd said he'd be working, but a few more coins in his pocket wouldn't be much consolation if the ship sailed without them.

She fingered the locket around her neck and checked

that the clasp was secure. The envelope from Mama was tucked carefully in her pocket. They would have no need for it once they arrived in America, but Rose was not quite ready to destroy it. Mama had been rather adamant about providing it, after all, and it had been her gift to Rose. She would keep it safe, if only for that reason.

Patrick had delivered some warm rolls earlier that morning, but Rose was far too anxious to eat, so she'd wrapped them and put them in her bag as well. She and Charles could share them later, after they'd sailed out of the harbor, as they watched the London skyline fade into the clouds and sea.

A pounding on the steps outside their room brought Rose to her feet, and she held her breath as she waited to see who might be approaching. Ever since last night, she'd had the eerie feeling that someone was following her and Charles, close on their heels.

The door burst open and Charles stood in the doorway, smiling and slightly breathless. "Are you ready?"

Heavens. She exhaled slowly, willing her pulse to stop racing. "Yes."

She was ready. Eager to be on her way so that she could stop hiding . . . and begin her life with Charles.

He helped her into her cloak and picked up their bags. "Let's go."

Downstairs, in the pawnshop, Rose gave Patrick a quick, fierce hug. "Thank you," she said. "For being a friend to both Charles and me."

"Come." Charles tugged on her hand. "We haven't time for prolonged good-byes."

"Don't mind him." Patrick's eyes twinkled. "He's jealous, and cranky from waking so early." Turning more somber, he added, "But I know he'll take excellent care of you. And vice-versa."

Too overcome to speak, Rose nodded and waved as they exited the shop...and officially began their journey.

Charles felt the small lump in his pocket. Patrick had insisted he take the elegant ring box, inlaid with ivory. He'd said it was his gift to Rose. If he'd had more time, Charles might have argued, but he didn't. Besides, he knew Rose would like it.

He couldn't wait to see her face when he gave her the ring. And he was eager to marry her too, even if she did descrve a hell of a lot better than him.

Outside, icy pellets assaulted them, and Rose shielded her cheeks.

"I'll hire a hackney," he offered.

"Don't bother on my account," she said. "It's probably just as quick to walk."

"If you're sure." He knew that Rose wasn't nearly as delicate as she looked, but she was accustomed to fancy carriages with plush interiors. She usually traveled with a coachman and footman and a warm brick beneath her feet.

He'd give her those same sorts of luxuries again. One day.

Today, however, the weather served their purposes perfectly, as few people were inclined to stroll in the freezing drizzle. Those who had braved the elements walked briskly, protecting their faces with hats and scarves.

When at last they approached the docks, Charles tapped Rose's arm and nodded his head toward the packet ship. "There it is."

"It looks like a seaworthy vessel," Rose said. "Though that may simply be wishful thinking on my part."

"Maybe by the time we get settled in our cabin, the sleet will have stopped and we can take a quick stroll around the deck."

"That sounds nice," she said, with forced cheerfulness.

"There's nothing wrong with being sad, you know. I am, too."

"You are? Why?"

He sighed. "I'm sad that I had to say good-bye to Patrick and that I didn't have the chance to see my father one last time. I'm sad that I didn't leave London on my own terms and that my name was blackened by Lady Yardley." *I'm sad that you're sad.*

She glanced away and frowned, as though there were something she wanted to say but couldn't.

He understood all too well, for there were things he couldn't say either.

"Here we are." They stood at the bottom of a long gangplank. Rose spied it with trepidation, then eyed the cold gray water lapping at the ship's hull, below. Sailors hustled up and down the narrow walkway, nimbly navigating their way around each other while balancing crates on their shoulders. A uniformed man with a long but neat beard stood nearby, orchestrating the sailors' comings and goings, inspecting boxes, and checking papers.

He waved them over. "Passengers?"

At Charles's nod, he added, "I'll need to see your tickets."

"Right." He set down the bags in order to dig the tickets out of his pocket, then handed them over.

The uniformed man checked them and nodded. "You're free to board. I suggest that you do so quickly. We'll push off soon."

Charles picked up the bags with one hand and offered his

free arm to Rose. He stepped onto the walkway, slick with frozen pellets, and gently tugged her along. "You'll be fine. Slow and steady." He could feel her trembling, probably a combination of fear and the cold. Halfway up the gangplank, he heard a voice shouting from several yards away.

"Halt!"

Rose's fingers dug into his elbow. "Charles?"

His heart pounded, but he kept his tone calm as he spoke into her ear. "He could be calling to anyone. Let's keep walking." He had a sick, sinking feeling in his gut though, and his instincts were practically screaming at him to pick up Rose, dash up the gangplank, and find a spot for them to hide.

But before they could take another step, the voice called out again. "Mr. Charles Holland and Lady Rose Sherbourne. Stop at once, or we'll shoot."

"Oh, God," Rose gasped.

"Move behind me." If there was a gun, he intended to be between it and Rose.

"No! They won't shoot a lady."

"I'm not taking a chance," he said, carefully maneuvering on the slippery gangplank so that he shielded her from the two men brandishing pistols who charged toward them. They stopped on the dock, their guns aimed directly at Charles.

"I'll come with you, peacefully." He slowly set down the bags and held up his hands. "Just let Lady Rose return to her family."

The taller man snorted. "She shot at a prison guard and helped you escape. She's in as much trouble as you are. I'll need to see her hands as well." She released his arm and held up her palms.

"I forced her to help me," Charles called to the men, "and brought her here against her will."

"That's not true!" Rose shouted.

Hoping to drown out her denial, he kept talking. "Look at her. She couldn't hurt a soul. I was the one who assaulted the guard."

"It's over, Holland. For both of you. Leave your bags there and walk down the gangplank, nice and slow."

By now, a crowd had gathered on the docks, eager to witness the spectacle.

"We don't have any choice, Rose. I'm sorry that I let you down, but I'll sort it out. I need you to deny all wrong-doing, do you understand?"

"And let you take all the blame? I think not."

"Please, for me."

"I think I have another solution," she said. "I just need to speak with Lady Yardley."

On the dock below, the taller man glowered and waved the barrel of his gun. "Stop talking. Start walking. Now."

Charles began inching down the plank, with her following close behind. In spite of Rose's optimism, he knew with a certainty that his life was over. The worst part was that after they took him away he'd never see her again.

And he'd never told her that he loved her. He'd wanted to wait, just in case she changed her mind at the last minute and decided to stay in London. He'd thought it would be easier for her that way.

And now he might never have the chance.

"If you care at all for me, do as I say. Go along with my story," Charles instructed. "Seek help from your brother, and forget about me."

He wanted her promise, damn it, but she moved silently behind him, refusing to give it.

Only a few yards of gangplank separated them from

the armed men when a sudden gust whipped his hat off and into the icy water below.

"Oh no," Rose cried. He turned to make sure she was steady and offer her his arm. The wind had blown her hood off as well, and red curls waved wildly about her face.

"Raise your hands!" shouted the man with the gun.

"Rose!" Someone else called out her name from a different part of the dock.

"Owen?" She spun half-way around, gave a little cry——and then she was falling.

As her feet flew out from beneath her and her body leaned to the right, Charles reached for her arm and held tight. But it was too late. Her head clipped the side of the gangplank a second before she plunged into the gray, churning water. Heart in his throat, he followed.

The cold stunned him, making it almost impossible to breathe, but he didn't let go of her. He wrapped an arm around her waist and kicked to the surface, battling the drag of his jacket and her skirts. It seemed he inched upward only to sink again.

Rose felt limp and lifeless in his arms. He needed to get her help. Quickly.

He followed the sound of muffled shouts from the dock and told himself they couldn't be very far away.

Using every ounce of strength he possessed, he kicked his way to the surface and hauled Rose's head above the water. A crowd leaned over the side of the dock, yelling and waving. Someone tossed a thick rope. Charles grasped at it, missed.

His head bobbed below the water, and he pushed Rose up, praying that someone would pull her to safety or that she'd at least take a gulp of air. He prayed that she would be all right.

And then she was slipping through his arm, sliding up and out of the water, and he let her go.

He surfaced, coughing and gasping for air. But he could see Rose on the dock, and she was sitting beside her brother, choking and sputtering, which was a good sign.

Someone on the dock gathered the rope and threw it to Charles once more. This time he caught it and managed to haul himself out of the river with a little help from some onlookers. He collapsed on the ground several yards from Rose and expelled the remaining water from his lungs.

The constables were upon him in no time. One aimed his gun at Charles, the other at Rose—and Huntford was none too pleased.

"What the hell do you think you're doing?"

"She needs to come with us," said the taller one.

The duke snorted as he pulled off his greatcoat and slipped it around her shoulders. Charles felt overwhelming relief. If anyone could protect Rose, her brother could. "I am the Duke of Huntford, and this is my sister, Lady Rose Sherbourne. She's not going with anyone but me, and she's not going anywhere but home. Is that clear?"

"She shot at a prison guard."

"No, she didn't," Charles interjected.

"I'll handle this, Holland," snapped Huntford. To the constable, he said, "Do you realize how ridiculous that accusation is? My sister is a gently bred lady. The very idea is absurd."

"I didn't shoot him." Rose's teeth chattered and her voice rasped. "But I did help Charles escape, and I'd do it again. He's innocent."

"Rose, please," Huntford said. "You've hit your head and are clearly disoriented. You're in need of a doctor's care. I doubt you even know what you're saying."

The taller constable grabbed Charles under one arm and hauled him to his feet. "Put your hands behind your back."

Charles did as he was asked, and spun to face Rose. "Heed your brother's advice."

"Wait," Rose called. "I can prove that the charges against you are false. I have a letter. We can clear your name." She reached into the pocket of her cloak and withdrew a handful of sopping wet pulp. Soggy pieces of paper slipped through her fingers and plopped onto the ground. "No," she sobbed. "Please, no."

"Step aside," said the stockier man, his gun aimed at Huntford. "Your sister is coming with us."

The duke rose to his full, considerable height and stared down his nose at the constable. "Over my dead body."

"Neither your title nor your money grants you immunity from the laws of this fair land, *your grace*. Out of my way."

The constable started to step around the duke, but Huntford shoved him in the shoulder, hard, sending him staggering backward several paces.

"You bloody bastard!" the constable yelled, raising the gun once more.

"Owen," Rose cried out. "Stop this before you get yourself killed. I'll go with them, and you can come for me later."

Huntford glanced over his shoulder at her. "You're not going anywhere."

The crowd had formed a circle around the action and watched the scene unfold with unabashed curiosity. Half of the onlookers seemed to sympathize with the constable, and half with the duke—or perhaps, more specifically, Rose.

"Move," the constable ordered the duke. "Now."

Huntford planted his boots in front of his sister and crossed his arms.

The hairs of the back of Charles's neck stood on end—and not just from the cold.

He didn't like this public standoff. It was not going to end well for someone. If the duke was injured or, heaven forbid, killed, Rose might never recover from her grief.

"Put away your gun," Huntford said, "and I'll forget about this entire incident. I'll ensure that your superiors know your excellent decision may have saved the life of an innocent woman."

Another gentleman pushed his way through the spectators and strode over, limping slightly. He took in the scene and scowled. "What the hell is going on here?"

"Jesus, Foxburn," said the duke. "What took you so long?" Without waiting for a response, he jerked his chin toward Rose. "Escort her home and call for the doctor at once."

Yes. Charles released a breath. Foxburn was the duke's friend, and an earl, if he remembered correctly. If the gentleman could extricate Rose from the current drama, Charles would be forever in his debt.

The stocky constable still had his pistol trained on Huntford, and his jowls shook with anger. "If your friend takes the girl, I shoot you."

The duke snorted, and called over his shoulder to Foxburn. "Do it. Get her out of here."

Rose lifted her head and pushed aside the wet tendrils

that hid her face. "No! Owen, this is madness. Surely we can sort through—"

"Now," yelled Huntford.

Foxburn hurried toward Rose, shielding her with his body. But Charles could see the horror in her eyes as she watched the constable begin to squeeze the trigger.

"Owen!" she cried.

And Charles knew what he had to do.

He kicked the man holding his elbow, twisted free, and dove in front of the duke just as the constable fired his gun.

The bang filled his head, drowning out the sound of Rose's screams and the crowd's shouts. He sailed through the air and slammed into the duke's side.

They both went down.

Charles slid face first over the rough ground, losing a few layers of skin to the pavement. Huntford moaned and struggled to sit.

Charles rolled off onto his side, unable to hear a thing. Chaos erupted around him. People were running, fists were flying.

Where was Rose? He couldn't see her, but he hoped she was far away from the crush. Somewhere safe and warm.

As for him, he was grateful for the numbing cold.

He could barely feel the gunshot in his shoulder. He might not have noticed it at all, if it hadn't been for the warm blood seeping through his shirt and jacket.

And after a few moments of lying there on his side, watching ships bob in the harbor, Charles felt nothing.

Nothing at all.

Chapter Thirty

"Put me down!" Rose kicked her feet, but Ben, Lord Foxburn, continued walking toward his coach, with her slung over his shoulder like a sack of grain.

"How can you leave them there? Owen is your friend. You should be helping him."

Ben sighed. "Believe me, I wish I was back there, fighting alongside him."

"Then why *aren't* you?" Exasperation oozed out of her.

"Because I know that if I were in his position and I had a sister, I'd want him to take her home." He strode up to the coach and set her on her feet, but held tightly to her arm. As he opened the cab door he said, "Think about it for a moment. Getting away from that scene was the best thing you could do for your brother. As long as you were there, he could only think about you. Now he can take care of himself."

Rose swallowed. "A gun fired. What if he was shot? Or what if Charles, er, Mr. Holland, was? Maybe they both were. We must do something."

Ben frowned, and she sensed he was as frustrated as she. "If you promise to go directly home and have the duchess call for a doctor, I'll go back to the docks and lend my assistance."

"I promise," she said quickly. "Thank you."

He hesitated, then said, "One question. Did Holland force you to help him? Or to do *anything* that you didn't wish to do?"

"Never. He is innocent." She raised her chin. "And he is my fiancée."

Ben's eyebrows shot up. "Jesus." He helped her into the coach and spoke to the driver before addressing her once more. "Don't forget your promise, Rose. Home, doctor, rest. I'll return Owen as soon as I can."

"And Charles too?"

The earl shook his head. "I'm not sure there's anything I can do for him."

"But you'll try?" she pleaded. Desperate, she added the one thing that might sway him. "You know it's what Daphne would want."

At the mention of his wife, his blue eyes softened. "Very well. For her—and for you—I will try to help Holland. I hope he knows how fortunate he is." He pulled a blanket out from under the seat, handed it to her with a smile, and closed the coach door. Almost immediately, the vehicle lurched forward, and Rose stared out of the window, watching Ben jog back toward the dock, favoring his right leg.

He *would* do his best. But what if it wasn't enough? She unfolded the blanket and wrapped it around her shoulders but couldn't stop her hands from shaking or her teeth from chattering. A dozen blankets couldn't ease the icy dread she felt deep in her bones.

Anne Barton

A mere quarter of an hour later, the coach pulled up in front of the townhouse—her home. In spite of everything, she took some comfort in seeing the familiar paneled front door, the pretty fanlight above, and the columns on either side. This place was a part of her, and yet she would have gladly left it behind for Charles.

The moment the coach rolled to a stop, the footman bounded into the house. Though Rose would have dearly loved to enter quietly and retreat to her room, it was not to be. Almost immediately, the housekeeper, Mrs. Pottsbury, rushed out the front door followed by Anabelle. Rose's heart squeezed at the sight of her sister-in-law dashing down the walk.

The coachman opened the cab door, and before he could help Rose alight, Anabelle was reaching for her and pulling her into a tearful hug. "Thank heaven above," she choked out, nearly strangling Rose with the force of her embrace. "You've no idea how worried we've been about you. Owen's barely slept, and I—"

Abruptly, she took a step back and held Rose at arm's length. "What's this? You're soaked, and half frozen as well. Are you hurt?"

Rose shook her head. "No, but I went for a swim in the Thames."

A look of horror crossed Anabelle's face. "Dear Lord. Let's get you inside." She pulled the blanket hanging from Rose's shoulders more tightly around her and bustled her toward the front door.

"I'll have a hot bath prepared," Mrs. Pottsbury announced. "And tea as well."

"Thank you," Anabelle said to the housekeeper. "And please send for Doctor Loxton at once." Rose opened her

mouth to object, but then remembered her promise to
Ben. "Also, please send word to Lady Daphne and Lady
Olivia—they'll be so relieved and happy to know Rose is
home."

"Olivia's home from Egypt?"

"She and James returned two days ago. Isn't it wonderful that you're both home?"

Yes, but Rose didn't want a homecoming celebration—
not while Charles and Owen could be fighting for their
lives. She halted in the doorway, and from behind her
spectacles, Anabelle gave her a puzzled look. "Owen
and Ben are at the docks," Rose said. "Owen was trying
to persuade the constables to release me and when they
refused, he became irate."

"Oh dear." Anabelle's forehead creased in concern as
she pulled Rose into the warm foyer and closed the door
behind them. "That can't have gone well."

"There was a skirmish, and just as one of the constables fired his pistol, Charles dove in front of Owen."

Belle paled. "Were they shot?"

"I don't know. Chaos broke out, and before I could get
to them, Ben whisked me away and put me in the coach.
Then he returned to the docks." She clenched her fists. "I
should never have agreed to leave."

"No, you did the right thing in coming here." But
worry clouded Belle's eyes.

Rose clasped her hands. "We could return there now.
Let's go, before the coach leaves."

"It's tempting," Belle conceded, "but that would only
complicate the situation." She shook her head. "Besides,
chances are the outcome has already been decided by
now. The best course of action is for us to remain here

and await news from the men. And in the meantime, I intend to see that you're warm, dry, and well. You've been through a harrowing ordeal."

Rose's legs suddenly felt weak and wobbly. "I've made such a mess of things, Belle. I'm sorry I caused you so much worry."

"Shh, don't be silly." She cast a sideways glance at Rose. "You love him, don't you?"

Choking back a sob, she nodded. "So much so that I almost left all of you. Seeing you now makes me realize how devastating that would have been . . . but I'd make the same choice again if it meant I could be with him."

Belle sighed. "No one should have to choose between family and love." She wrapped an arm around Rose's waist and slowly guided her up the stairs. "Now that you're home, everything is going to be all right—you'll see."

It was difficult to discern who Belle was trying to convince—Rose, or herself.

Because they both knew that if Owen and Charles didn't return to them, nothing would ever be right again.

By the time they reached Rose's room, a fire had already been lit. A maid waited at the end of the bed, a thick dressing gown at the ready. Both the maid and Belle fussed over Rose as they peeled off her wet gown, chemise, and stockings. She slid her arms into the soft warmth of her dressing gown and sank into a chair before the fire while Belle draped a heavy quilt over her lap.

Tea arrived, and Anabelle poured a cup for Rose and placed it in her hands. "Drink and have a bite to eat as well. There's much I wish to ask you, but I suspect Olivia and Daphne will be here any moment, and you'd only have to repeat the story for them. Let us hope that Daphne arrives first, because we both know Olivia will not be content to wait for answers."

Rose's heart ached at the mention of her sister. She'd missed Olivia most of all. And now she'd have to tell her that she'd found Mama—only to discover that she was not at all well. For Belle's sake, Rose smiled and pretended to nibble on a roll, but her stomach rebelled at the thought of eating. Just swallowing her tea proved difficult, and her head was in something of a fog.

Belle's shrewd gaze raked over her face. "You're still shivering. I'll have Maggie fetch another quilt."

It didn't help. Rose was still shaking when the doctor arrived, and he wasted no time examining her. "I felt perfectly fine this morning," she said.

"Prior to hitting your head and falling into the river?" He tenderly probed the knot along her hairline and frowned when she winced. "A nasty bump. You need rest," he said sternly, "and plenty of it. If you don't already have the devil of a headache, you will soon. And you have the beginnings of a fever as well. Little wonder." He shot her a kindly smile. "Nothing a few days in bed won't cure."

He went to put his stethoscope into his bag, when shouts sounded from the floor below. Owen's commanding voice stood out among the rest. "We'll take him to the guest room."

Rose swallowed. She suspected Owen was talking about Charles, and though her heart rejoiced at the possibility he was downstairs, if he couldn't walk himself to the guest room, that was very bad news indeed. She flipped back the coverlet and stepped into her slippers. At the doctor's incredulous look, she lifted her chin. "Come with me, please. I have a feeling your services are needed by someone in worse condition than I."

She swept past him, rushed to the second floor landing, and gasped. Charles was there. And he looked...horrid.

Owen, Ben, and a couple of footmen struggled to carry him up the stairs. His eyes were closed, his face scraped raw, and his mouth pressed into a thin, grim line. He must have abandoned his greatcoat and jacket somewhere, for his torso was clad in nothing but a blood-stained shirt, confirming Rose's worst fears.

Her head throbbed, and she gripped the banister to keep from falling. "Charles," she called out. Owen and Ben looked up at her, but Charles's head only lolled from side to side.

"He's been shot," she said to the doctor. "Tell me what you need, and I'll fetch it at once."

"What I need is for you to return to your bedchamber and try to rest. Trust me to care for him."

But she couldn't leave Charles. Not now. "I promise to stay out of your way," she said. "I just want to be at his bedside in case he wakes."

Doctor Loxton ignored her pleas and frowned at the men on the stairs. "Try not to jostle him so. With each step you take, he's losing blood."

Ben, who had his arms hooked beneath Charles's shoulders, scowled at the doctor. "Consider it lucky if we don't drop him. He's bloody heavy."

The doctor turned to Rose. "Which room?"

"The second door on the right," she said, relieved when he scurried down the hall, presumably to prepare for Charles's arrival.

On the stairs, Owen shot Ben a sharp look. "Easy on the last few steps, Foxburn. It's the least we can do after he took a bullet for me."

Tears burned at the back of Rose's eyes. So Charles *had* saved Owen's life. She prayed it wouldn't cost him his.

She stood on the landing, determined to see the extent of his injuries for herself.

When at last the men reached the top, they paused to catch their breath. She reached for one of Charles's hands and pressed it between hers, wishing he didn't feel so cold. So lifeless. He showed no signs of waking, but she spoke to him anyway. "You're safe now. The doctor's going to help you. I'm here too, and I won't leave you."

It might have been her imagination, but she could have sworn that his eyelids twitched at the sound of her voice. Her gaze went to the wound in his shoulder that oozed blood. The hole in his shirt revealed torn flesh and muscle. She swayed on her feet.

"Step back," Owen said. "Let us take him to Loxton."

Rose released Charles's hand and pressed her shoulder blades to the wall, grateful for its solid support as she made room for the men to pass.

In the foyer below, more voices—feminine ones this time—called out. She recognized Olivia's at once. "Rose? Oh dear God, it *is* you!" Her sister bounded up the stairs, a blur of blue silk, and pulled her into a fierce hug. "When Belle sent word you were home safe and sound...well, I don't mind telling you I wept for joy. Are you really well, though? You look rather pale to me."

"I'm fine."

Olivia shot her a skeptical glance and turned to Daphne, who managed to hurry up the stairs all while managing to look the very picture of grace and elegance. "Does she look well to you?"

Daphne cupped Rose's cheeks and smiled. "I'm so glad

you're home, but I'm afraid I share your sister's concern. I know you are worried about Mr. Holland, but he's in capable hands. There's not a thing we can do for him at the moment."

Rose gulped. Being surrounded by all these people who loved and cared about her was both overwhelming and suffocating. They were only trying to help, of course, but how could any of them possibly understand? "Perhaps you're right," she said softly. "Still, I'd like to go to him now."

"What are you doing out of bed?" *Tsk*ing at Rose, Anabelle walked briskly up the stairs and joined them on the landing.

Anabelle's knowing gaze seemed to peer deep into Rose's soul. Olivia, her usually fearless sister, swallowed, looking frightfully worried and, at the same time, slightly betrayed, as though the secrets Rose had kept wounded her. And Daphne, with her gift for nursing, watched her with an assessing eye, seeming to realize that Rose was not, in fact, well.

And all of the sudden, it was too much. She closed her eyes to shut them out. To shut the world out. That's what she did, after all. When things became difficult, she retreated and hid.

Ghastly images filled her mind, playing themselves out, over and over. Lady Yardley's arms tangled about Charles's neck as they lay on the settee in the library. Charles trudging through the snow, leaving behind a lonely trail of footprints—and her. The deafening sound of the pistol firing in the prison and the bitter hatred in the guard's eyes as she and Charles ran through the dark and putrid prison. Her mother's hospital bed, eerily empty.

The shockingly cold rush of water covering her head as she plunged into the Thames. Worst of all, the sight of Charles being carried up the stairs looking more corpse than human.

She thought she'd grown stronger, that she could face any heartbreak she was forced to bear without hiding from the world again.

But darkness pulled at her, seductive and silent.

She would not succumb to it. She couldn't do that to her family or Charles, in the unlikely event he survived. She couldn't do that to herself.

Her sister and dear friends were right here. Even now, she heard them calling out to her. "Rose, darling?" Through the dizzying parade of scenes in her head, Daphne's voice rang clear. "Look at me."

Rose forced her eyes open. She had to tell her—tell them all—that she wasn't going to run from the pain and hurt again. "Forgive me, I—"

The words died on her lips, and her world went black.

Chapter Thirty-One

Groom: (1) A person who works with horses in a stable.
(2) The man one is about to marry and live with,
happily ever after...

Through the fog, Rose stirred at a raucous noise. It was like thunder but less random. More like...snoring. Of the excessively loud variety—and definitely not hers.

She opened her eyes and gazed around her sweetly familiar bedchamber. Olivia dozed in a chair beside her bed, her neck bent at an awkward angle. The snoring wasn't coming from her, however, but rather from Owen, who was sprawled on the settee in front of the fire, his legs hanging off the end as though he were Gulliver in Lilliput.

Rose pushed herself to sitting, surprised to find that while her head was still oddly heavy, she felt much improved, physically, at least.

Well enough to check on Charles. She swallowed, praying to God that she wasn't too late.

Silently, she slipped from the bed, tiptoed past Olivia, and glided around Owen. Barefoot, she padded down the hall and swung open the door of the guest room. Daphne sat in a chair by the window reading, which Rose wanted to believe was a good sign. It must mean that he was resting comfortably for the moment . . . or that there was nothing else to be done for him.

As she rushed to his bedside, Daphne arched a brow at her. "You know you should not be up."

"Yes," Rose said. "And you know that nothing would keep me away from him."

"You love him." Daphne smiled radiantly. "That changes everything."

"Indeed." Rose swept her fingertips across his brow, then leaned over him and pressed her lips to his cheek. His shoulder had been expertly bandaged, and only a little spot of red had seeped through.

"He looks better," she whispered hopefully, "but you must tell me the truth. How is he? Will he recover?"

"I'm almost sure of it."

"Almost?"

"One always has to watch out for fever, but your Mr. Holland is strong, and his color is much improved. The bullet went straight through his shoulder without damaging the bone. He is very fortunate."

Rose nearly snorted. "You would not say that if you knew what we've been through."

"Perhaps not." Daphne linked an arm through Rose's, put a finger to her lips, and led her to the door. "Sleep is the best thing for him right now. Just as it is for you."

Rose didn't feel tired but knew better than to argue with Daph when she was in no-nonsense nursing mode. "Will you promise to tell me the moment he wakes? And let me know if there's any change in his condition?"

"Of course I will," Daphne said soberly. "I promise."

Mollified, Rose let Daphne escort her back to her room. "There's no one else I'd rather have tending to Charles than you," Rose admitted. "Not even Dr. Loxton has a knack for healing people like you do."

"Why, that may be the nicest compliment I've ever received. But the thing that will truly heal Charles is love. The love you have for each other is stronger than any medicine."

Rose sighed. "I hope so."

When they entered her bedchamber, Daphne smirked at the sight of Olivia and Owen sleeping. "With nurse-maids like these, it's a wonder you survived the night."

Olivia bolted upright in her chair and gaped at the empty bed. "Where's Rose?"

"What?" Owen tumbled off the settee. "Good God. She's missing again?"

"I'm right here." She waved from the doorway. "And I don't intend to run off anytime soon—unless you deem it necessary."

Before she knew what was happening, Olivia and Owen had sandwiched her in a hug so tight she could scarcely breathe.

"I'm off to keep an eye on our other patient." Eyes twinkling, Daphne added, "Olivia and Owen, you might strive to do a better job caring for yours."

"Heavens, yes," Olivia exclaimed. "Back into bed with you. I'll ring for some breakfast, and—"

"While I have you both here," Rose interjected, "could we have a little sibling chat?"

"Does this concern Holland?" Owen moaned. "If so, I'm going to need a drink of brandy."

"No, actually," Rose explained. "I have some news."

Olivia gulped. "Are you with child? Because if you are, I shall need some brandy as well." This earned a scowl from Owen, and Rose was suddenly exceedingly glad that she was *not* in fact, pregnant.

"It's news about Mama." Rose could tell that she'd startled them. Olivia's hands flew to her cheeks, and Owen raked a hand through his hair. "She's here in London, but quite ill, in a hospital."

"What does she want from us?" Owen snapped. "Sympathy? Money?"

"Neither. She didn't want us to find out about her illness—consumption—at all. But I went in search of her, and I'm glad I did."

"I don't understand," Olivia said. "I thought you were in Bath."

"I was, and much has happened. I'll explain it all, but I wanted you to know about Mama. I don't think she has much time left, and though she doesn't feel she deserves your forgiveness, I think it would give her some peace in her final days. It might give you peace as well."

"Jesus," Owen muttered. "After all these years. Is she still the same?"

"In some ways, but also different. She tried to help prove Charles's innocence by writing a note containing information we could use to persuade Lady Yardley to drop the false charges she made against him. Only, the note was destroyed when I fell into the Thames."

Olivia paced. "Then we must go to her, and have her write out the statement again."

"No, do not let that be the reason for your visit," Rose said. "Besides, Mama is weak. Just writing a note may require more strength than she has."

"Why can't she just tell us the information about Lady Yardley?"

"I think she would, but I preferred not to know the sordid details."

"That is the difference between you and me," Olivia said with a sigh. "I prefer to know *all* the sordid details."

Rose smiled and turned to Owen. "I know you're still angry with Mama, and I would never blame you for that. I doubt she would either."

"I simply can't understand how she could abandon her two young daughters." Owen shook his head.

"You don't have to be angry on my behalf—or Olivia's—any longer. Thanks to you, we're grown and happy. Well, I'm still working on the happy part, but our little family has done rather well in spite of all the tragedy we endured."

"Yes, I suppose you're right," Owen said. "You usually are. Or you *were* rather, before you started breaking people out of prisons and stealing away on ships."

"To be fair, I had a ticket."

"Oh, I confess I cannot wait to hear all about your adventures, Rose," Olivia proclaimed. "You make mine look positively tame by comparison."

"No one could accuse you of being tame. I cannot wait to hear your adventures in Egypt."

Owen growled, signaling it was too soon to jest about the events of the past few weeks. "There's much left for us to discuss," he said to Rose, "and for you to decide. But I think our first priority must be clearing Charles's name."

Rose flung her arms around his neck. "Thank you, Owen."

He grunted softly. "Only because I don't want to be accused of harboring a fugitive."

"Of course," she said quickly.

"He may have saved my life, but that's not what changed my opinion of him."

"No? What did then?"

"The fact that he did it for you. He was willing to risk his life in order to save somebody *you* loved. That's the kind of devotion that you, my dear sister, deserve."

"I would be fortunate to have him."

"Several issues must still be sorted out. Even if we're able to persuade Lady Yardley to drop the charges against Charles, your reputation . . . well, I'm afraid it's destroyed."

Olivia piped up. "Having an impeccable reputation is overrated."

Owen arched a brow. "How would you know?"

Ignoring him, Olivia seized Rose's hand and squeezed it. "Follow your heart, the ton be damned."

"I tried that tack," Rose said, "and as a result, Charles was imprisoned and nearly killed. The worst part is that his dream of owning land seems farther away than ever."

Owen rubbed his chin. "That's why he was going to America?"

Rose nodded. "He was determined to make something of himself. For us."

"I can't believe you almost sailed across the Atlantic and left us—without saying good-bye." The bewildered hurt on her brother's face made Rose want to cry.

"I'm sorry. I didn't see any other way, and I was afraid you wouldn't let me go."

"Selfishly, I would have done everything in my power to stop you."

"And now?"

He heaved a sigh that nearly broke her heart. "I will leave decisions about your future to you."

Olivia threw up her hands dramatically. "What I would have given to hear those words not so long ago. Why do the youngest siblings always have it the easiest?"

"Because brave sisters like you blaze trails before us."

"For the love of all that's holy," moaned Owen, "please let us be finished with the trail blazing."

Olivia smiled saucily. "Never."

And Rose began to believe that things just might work out for her and Charles.

If she didn't know better, she'd think that all their trials had been the work of a sadistic, if ultimately benevolent, fairy godmother.

"I've just received a note from Lady Bonneville." From the doorway, Anabelle shot an apologetic smile at Rose, who sat beside Charles's bed, where he slept peacefully.

It seemed to Rose that he should have awoken by now, but Daphne said he was doing well. He certainly *looked* well.

Rose sighed at the sight of his wavy hair, slightly parted lips, and dangerously handsome face. In spite of a few gashes, he might have been an archangel resting after battle.

"The viscountess is no doubt livid with me," Rose whispered. "And I don't blame her. I must qualify as the worst companion in the history of companions."

Belle shrugged. "I doubt it, at least where Lady Bonneville is concerned. The only offense she can't forgive is being boring—and no one may accuse you of that."

"That is true," Rose conceded.

"In any case, it was a brief note. The viscountess is on her way to London and will call on you here, tomorrow afternoon. Forewarned is forearmed."

"Who's armed?" Charles blinked, lifted his head from the pillow, and smiled when he saw her. "Not you, I hope."

Rose's heart turned a cartwheel. "Charles," she breathed, pressing her lips to his forehead. "You're awake at last."

"Sorry to keep you waiting, love." He reached out his left hand and cupped her cheek. "I'm sorry about your fall from the gangplank. Are you well?"

"Now, at last, I believe I am."

Rose had never looked more beautiful—and that was truly saying something. Charles knew that the softness in her eyes was just for him, and he was somehow both humbled and aroused.

Only two things prevented him from hauling Rose into his arms and kissing her silly. The first was his blasted shoulder, which hurt like the devil each time he moved. Still, he would have endured a bit of pain for a kiss if the duchess had not been standing behind Rose, her eyes suspiciously shiny behind her spectacles.

He nodded at his hostess. "I assume I'm in your home. Thank you for the hospitality."

"You are, and it is I who must thank you, Mr. Holland, for saving my husband's life."

"Please, call me Charles."

"And you must call me Belle. Rose has explained some of the trials you've faced during the past few weeks," she said. "I hope you'll allow us to assist you—for Rose's sake as well as yours."

Charles stiffened. The duchess's offer sounded an awful lot like charity. But even if he wished to deny it, he would not be rude—not when Rose stood beside him looking so hopeful. "You're very kind," he said.

"Olivia and Owen are visiting Mama at the hospital," Rose said. "I wanted to go too, but Daphne forbid it."

"I'm glad you're here," he confessed.

"Did I hear Mr. Holland?" A golden-haired woman glided into the room. Charles vaguely remembered the duchess's sister, who hurried to his side.

"This is Daphne," Rose explained. "She's an excellent nurse."

Daphne's kind gaze flicked over his face. "You're looking very well." She took a glass of water from the bedside table and held it to his lips.

He swallowed several gulps. "Thank you."

With brisk, efficient movements, she checked the bandage on his shoulder, peeked underneath, and nodded approvingly. "How do you feel?"

"Not bad, considering."

"You're going to be fine," she announced, "but the wound will take some time to heal. It'll be very sore for a few days, so you must let us know if there's anything we can do for you."

What he craved more than anything was a few moments alone with Rose, but he knew better than to ask for that. "Thank you."

Stepping back, Daphne wrapped an arm around Rose and hugged her.

Belle joined in the embrace too, pressing her cheek to Rose's. "Isn't it wonderful to have her home, Daph?"

"Indeed." To Rose, she said, "I know you were only gone for a month or so, but everything was out of balance while you were away. And when we thought that some evil or misfortune had befallen you . . . well, we were all devastated."

"Especially your brother," Belle chimed in. "Last night was the first night in weeks that he's slept soundly, and I'm certain it's because he knew you were safe and under our roof."

Charles swallowed, moved by the scene.

This was where Rose belonged. With her family, surrounded by the people she loved and who loved her.

But she belonged with him, too.

Somehow, he had to find a way for her to remain a part of all this—while staying true to who he was.

The first step was meeting with the duke.

Later that evening, Huntford strode through the bedroom door and stopped at the end of Charles's bed, looming over him, dark and silent. It was a good thing that he wasn't feverish, or he might have mistaken the duke for an angel of death.

"You're awake," Huntford noted.

"I am."

"Belle said you wished to see me."

"I haven't had a chance to thank you—for bringing me here. If you hadn't intervened, I'd be rotting in prison."

"True. But you wouldn't have been shot either. The least I could do was give you a place to convalesce." Huntford's manner was stiff and formal. He might not be throwing punches, but Charles had the feeling he'd like to be.

He sat up straighter in the bed, wishing he could have managed to put on his trousers, jacket, and boots and met the duke in his study. Daphne, however, in an admirably devious move, had hidden all his clothes to ensure that he stayed in bed.

"I want to apologize," Charles said to Huntford, "for putting your sister in danger and for the damage that I've caused to her reputation. You have every right to be furious with me."

The duke snorted and clenched his fists. "There are two reasons you're still breathing. One, you saved my godforsaken life, and two, Rose seems rather attached to you. But if you have anything to say in your defense, now would be an ideal time to share."

"I love her. And I know she loves you. Which means that in order to make her happy, you and I need to reach some sort of understanding."

Huntford was silent for several seconds. "I'm listening."

"I intend to marry her, and I'd like your blessing. I swear to you that I'll do everything in my power to protect her and provide for her."

"I can believe that you'll protect her. But how, pray tell, do you plan to provide for her?" He swept an arm around the sumptuously decorated room. "You can see the elegance to which she's accustomed."

Charles's heart pounded. Not because he took issue with what Huntford had said—but because he agreed with it. This next part of the conversation would be the most difficult. And humbling.

"I'd like to work for you."

The duke crossed his arms. "As a steward?"

"Yes. I have a knack for making businesses—and estates—profitable. If you have a property that is losing money, give me the opportunity to turn it around. No one would work harder for you than I."

The duke rubbed his chin thoughtfully, clearly intrigued by the idea. "There is a small estate next to Huntford Manor.

I recently acquired the neighboring property from a baron who'd let it fall into disrepair—and I've been pouring money into it ever since. I haven't had much time to devote to it since Lizzy was born."

"I can manage it for you. By this time next year, it will be a source of income—a thriving estate with abundant crops and happy tenants."

"And you would support my sister on your steward's salary? I don't think so." The duke began to pace at the foot of Charles's bed. "Rose tells me that your goal is to become a landowner yourself. If she agrees to marry you, I could make the land a wedding gift to the both of you."

Charles shook his head. "I'd like to propose a different arrangement."

Huntford arched a brow. "Go on."

"Let my salary be half of the income that the estate earns. And allow me to put it toward the purchase of the land."

The duke looked incredulous. "You'd rather buy the land from me than accept it as a gift?"

"Yes."

"I hope to God you have more business sense than you're letting on right now." But the duke leveled him a look of respect as he extended his hand. "You have a deal, Holland. And if Rose will have you . . . welcome to the family."

"Brace yourselves," Olivia announced to everyone in the drawing room the next afternoon. "Here she comes."

The *she* was Lady Bonneville. The viscountess shuffled into the drawing room, paused, and shook her skirts. "Shoo, beast." She scowled at the cat circling her ankles, then shot Rose a similarly withering look. "I brought your little friend from Bath."

Rose leaped from her chair, greeted the viscountess, then knelt to pet Ash. "He seems quite fond of you, Lady Bonneville."

"Nonsense. We barely tolerate each other. However, it kept lingering about as our coach was being loaded. I took pity on the wretched thing and decided to deliver it to you. One minute into the coach ride it started shedding fur all over the velvet squabs, and I knew I'd live to regret this act of charity." She glanced at her maid, who'd entered the room laboring under the weight of the viscountess's infamous red footstool. "Over there, in front of the fire, Audrey."

The maid positioned the ottoman at Lady Bonneville's preferred angle while the viscountess exchanged greetings with Belle, Daphne, their mother, Mrs. Honeycote, and Olivia. When she seated herself and propped up her feet, all the women sat as well, forming a circle. The drawing room suddenly took on the formality and seriousness of a meeting of Parliament. Rose suppressed a shiver.

"I am sure you are all aware that this visit is not purely a social call," Lady Bonneville began. "Rose and I have some unfinished matters to discuss."

Before Rose could respond, Belle raised her chin and addressed the viscountess. "Rose has been through much in the past several weeks, and if you have any business which is unpleasant or distressing, I must ask that you—"

"It's all right, Belle." Rose shot her a grateful smile. "I'm through with avoiding unpleasant and distressing matters. Lady Bonneville is correct. I owe her an apology and an explanation."

The viscountess snorted indelicately. "I didn't ride all the way from Bath to hear you grovel, gel. You did what you did, and there's no undoing it. People are talking about the scandal, of course. On the bright side, you've officially shed your reputation as a quiet wallflower."

"An unexpected benefit," Rose agreed. "But if you're not here to reprimand my behavior, then why did you come?"

Lady Bonneville smiled smugly. "To help you repair the damage to your reputation and provide you with . . . an option."

"Would you like us to give the two of you some privacy?" Belle asked.

"I have no objection to an audience," the viscountess announced.

"Nor do I. We're all family."

"Thank Heaven," Olivia exclaimed. "If you'd sent me out, I'd have been forced to press my ear to the door."

Lady Bonneville rapped her lorgnette on the arm of her chair to draw attention back to herself. Ash hopped onto her footstool and curled up beside her slippers. She glared at the cat but did not shoo it away. "As I was saying. After you abruptly left Bath and the scandalous rumors about prison escapes and such began to spread, I knew that repairing your good name would be nearly impossible. But all is not lost. I have been corresponding with your admirer, Lord Stanton."

Rose blinked. "About me?"

"Indeed. He is quite taken with you and assured me that if you were amenable to a marriage proposal, he would overlook your sullied reputation and—"

"Overlook her sullied reputation?" cried Olivia. "Who does he think he is? The bloody King of England?"

Lady Bonneville sucked in her cheeks. "While your sisterly devotion is to be commended, let us not forget the facts. Rose has been thoroughly compromised. Stanton does not think this is an insurmountable problem, however, as we can simply say that she was coerced. A victim of kidnapping, if you will."

"I was in no way forced," Rose ground out. "And I would never falsely accuse Charles—or anyone—to save my own skin."

Belle narrowed her eyes at the viscountess. "What, precisely, does Lord Stanton hope to gain, besides a wife? *We* know Rose is a prize, but he never struck me as the sort of man who'd be drawn to a woman with her kind and gentle nature."

"To put it bluntly," Lady Bonneville replied, "he is drawn to her dowry. But I think you are all missing the point. Rose now has an option. If she wishes to get back in the good graces of the ton, there is a way."

"I appreciate you coming all this way, Lady Bonneville," said Rose. "But I will never marry anyone but Charles."

"Am I to assume that he's proposed? And that you have set a date?"

Rose opened her mouth, then shut it. "Not yet." They'd discussed it before, of course, before they bought passage on *Perseverance*. The ship that had literally sailed without them.

And in all the commotion of the last two days, she and Charles hadn't had a moment alone. When she looked into his eyes, she saw nothing but love. But would that be enough?

"Well then," said Lady Bonneville, "I suggest that you

keep your options open for the time being. Stanton can give you respectability and a comfortable future."

Rose took a deep breath and stood. "I don't give a fig about respectability and comfort. I want the type of love that takes my breath away and fills my heart with happiness and hope. I want passion and a partner who challenges me to be more than I thought I could be. I want Charles. And if I can't have him, I want no one."

A slow, wide smile spread across the viscountess's face. "Very well. I'll inform Lord Stanton that his attentions are unwelcome."

"Thank you."

"He would have been the safe choice." Lady Bonneville eased her feet off her stool and slowly stood. "And, incidentally, the wrong one. But I think it's important that we women *have* choices, don't you?"

Not trusting herself to speak, Rose nodded, walked up to the viscountess, and embraced her.

Lady Bonneville held her tightly for several moments, sniffled, and pulled away. "Gads. That's enough sentimentality for one day. Audrey, let's take our leave before someone starts playing sad ballads on the pianoforte."

She shot a pointed look at Olivia. "I believe you and I have some additional business to attend to. Fetch your cloak so we can be off." After a whirl of good-byes, she and her small entourage—including her furry friend— left the drawing room, their exit punctuated by the salute of Ash's tail.

Snow fell softly outside Rose's window, but a low-burning fire kept her bedchamber warm and cozy. Everyone had retired for the evening, leaving the house quiet and still—almost magical. She watched the fat flakes stick to her windowpane and slowly melt, then padded across the floor to her bed, wistfully thinking of Charles, just down the hallway.

It had taken a lot of persuading on his part, but Daphne had agreed to give him his clothes back tomorrow, which meant he could go downstairs and they might finally have a few moments alone.

After turning down the lantern, she climbed into bed, slipped under the covers, and laid her head on the pillow.

And something crinkled. Odd, that.

She reached beneath her pillow and felt a small, folded piece of paper.

Intrigued, she sat up, quickly lit the lantern, and opened up the note.

> *Rose,*
>
> *You've waited a long time to receive a letter from me, and I fear that you are destined to be disappointed, for this will be brief.*
>
> *Knowing you are only a few doors down the hall is driving me mad.*
>
> *I need to see you, hold you, kiss you . . . and more.*
>
> *If you're able, visit me tonight.*
>
> *Charles*

He'd written her a *note*. It may not have been poetic, but it was heartfelt and so . . . him.

She tucked it back under her pillow, knowing she would forever treasure it, then glided down the hall to his room. She didn't knock at the door, but tried the handle, found that it turned, and tiptoed into the dimly lit room.

Charles was out of bed, pacing in a pair of trousers. And nothing else, save for the sling that kept his shoulder immobile.

Rose closed the door behind her and leaned back against it. "Where'd you find your trousers?"

He grinned. "In the pianoforte bench. But not until after I'd searched the library and most of the drawing room." He sauntered close and wrapped his good arm around her waist, his nearness leaving her slightly breathless.

"You snuck out of your room?" She slipped her hands behind his back and splayed her palms over his warm skin.

"Earlier this evening. I couldn't stand wearing a dressing gown any longer."

She shrugged. "You wore it well. And there are certain advantages to a dressing gown."

He reached up and tugged the tie at her neck of her nightrail. "So I see."

"You've no idea," she whispered, "how desperately I've missed you."

"I have some idea," he growled. Then he captured her mouth in a kiss that made her knees wobble and her heart pound.

He pulled back an inch, his eyes searching her face. "There's so much I need to say to you, and it really shouldn't wait."

"I don't think a few more minutes will make a huge difference in the larger scheme of things. The talking can wait."

With a knee-weakening grin, he locked the door. "Fair warning. The things I intend to do to you are going to take more than a few minutes."

"God, I hope so."

He wrapped his good arm around her waist, lifted her off the ground, and gently laid her on the bed. "I love you, Rose."

"And I love you."

She held out her arms to him, frustrated by the short distance that separated them. It seemed *something* had always separated them. The difference in their stations. His challenges with writing. False accusations. Imprisonment *and* gunshot wounds.

But now, at last, they were together, and all the barriers were gone. Her heart felt light and full at the same time.

With a growl, he stretched out beside her, propping himself on an elbow. "I'm going to spend the rest of my life trying to make you happy."

"You already have." She kissed his cheek, careful to avoid the scrape, then glimpsed at the bandage beneath his sling. "I don't want to do anything that might hurt your shoulder. Perhaps we should wait."

"That's very funny," he murmured. "No more waiting."

True to his word, he lowered his lips to hers and kissed her until her head spun with desire. The taste of him intoxicated her and left her breathless, aching with need. Encumbered by the sling, he was forced to be creative. He used his teeth to remove her nightrail and teased her nipples with his tongue. He caressed her belly with his cheek, abrading her skin with his light beard.

It all worked out extremely well.

She helped him out of his trousers—not exactly a hardship—and sighed at the sight of his naked body. Lean and muscular, hard and smooth, he looked impossibly handsome and eminently male.

He sat up on the mattress, leaning against the head-board. "Come here."

She crawled closer, nuzzling his shoulder and wantonly brushing her breast against his arm. Circling his arm about her waist, he easily pulled her onto his lap so that she faced him, straddling his legs.

With the pad of his thumb, he drew tantalizing little circles on the inside of her thigh. Her head fell back, and he kissed the length of her neck and the curves of her breasts till she whimpered with need. When his fingers found her entrance, she cried out from the jolt of pleasure.

"Oh, Charles." She reached between them and stroked the length of him, reveling in the way he moaned in response to her touch.

"I don't think I can't wait any longer," he panted.

Relieved, she guided him inside her. "Neither can I."

Her hair fell around them like a curtain, creating a world where only the two of them existed. He gripped her hip with his good hand as he thrust, slowly at first, then faster, setting up a rhythm that stoked their desire till it nearly engulfed them both.

As the pulsing in her core grew more intense and her body raced toward release, she cried out.

"Shh," he soothed, his breathing ragged. "We don't want to wake anyone."

Her head fell back, and she whimpered again. "But it feels so . . . good."

"Bite my shoulder instead."

She blinked, still dazed. But in the end she had little choice really, because when the blaze of pleasure over-took her, she simply had to hold on and let it carry her to its sweet, earth-shattering conclusion.

Charles's own release followed on the heels of hers, so powerful that it shook them both.

She collapsed on him, sated and inordinately pleased that they had managed to make love in spite of his sling.

They snuggled under the covers and listened to icy pellets tap the window as their breathing slowly returned to normal. Shyly, she kissed the pink bite marks on his shoulder. "Sorry about that. You only had one good shoulder, and now..."

"*That*," he said with a heart-stopping smile, "is nothing to apologize for. I like your wild side."

"I always suspected I had one," she admitted with a yawn.

"Wait, before you drift off to sleep, there's something I must give you."

"Right now?"

"Yes. There was another reason I went searching for my clothes."

"I never knew you were so modest."

He grinned. "Hardly." He reached into the drawer of the bedside table and withdrew a small box. "This was in my coat the day I was shot. I was afraid it might have been lost in the river, but when I dug my clothes out of the pianoforte bench, it was still safe in the breast pocket. It's for you."

Her chest squeezed as she took it from him and opened the lid. There, on a tiny silk pillow, was the loveliest antique ring she'd ever seen. She swallowed. "It's beautiful."

"It reminded me of you. Beautiful, yes. But also timeless, elegant, and resilient. When I look at you, I see my past, present, and future." He slipped it onto her finger. "Will you marry me?"

"Yes." He'd barely finished the question before the word tumbled out. But it wasn't as though she had to think about it. "I'll go anywhere with you, Charles. I want you to achieve your goals, and I know that you will. Once you're well, we can go to America if you like. As long as I'm with you, I'm home."

"Oh Rose." He hauled her close and speared his fingers through her hair. "I'm humbled that you would do that for me, for us. But this is your home. After I saw you with your brother and sister, I knew that I could never take you away from them. And I've found a way that we can stay in England...if you wouldn't mind spending most of the year near Huntford Manor."

"Mind? That would be wonderful! But how?"

"I made a deal with your brother. If I can turn the small neighboring estate around, I can buy it from him."

"That's...that's perfect. But what of your dream—to make a life in America? I can't let you forsake it."

"My dream was never to leave England. It was to own land and manage an estate—with you. *For* you."

Her eyes welled. "Really?"

He nodded and cradled her cheek in his palm. "You'll never want for anything, I promise you...except, perhaps, ball invitations."

"If that is true, I shall consider myself fortunate. I have some good news for you as well."

"I refuse to believe this night could get better," he murmured, raining kisses over her forehead, nose, and cheeks.

"Olivia and Lady Bonneville visited Lady Yardley in her London townhouse today. She's agreed to drop the charges if Olivia keeps the salacious gossip she knows about Lady Yardley to herself."

He chuckled. "How is Olivia at keeping secrets?"

"Horrid. But it doesn't matter. Lady Yardley has already told the authorities that she was mistaken about your identity. You're officially a free man."

"I take back what I said before."

"Which part?"

"About not believing this night could get better." He ran a hand up the inside of her thigh, sending delectable chills through her body. "It's about to get much, much better."

She melted into him, pressing her lips against his neck. "Are you certain your shoulder can withstand another round?"

"Try me."

Rose sighed happily. For it seemed that once in a while, nice girls *didn't* finish last.

Discover how the scandalously sexy
Honeycote series all began...

Please see the next page for
an excerpt from

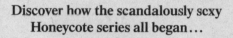

Chapter One

*Alteration: (1) A change made to a garment in order
to improve the fit or style. (2) A change in plans, often
necessitated by misfortune, as when one is unexpectedly
apprehended during the commission of a crime.*

London, 1815

*E*xtortion" was an ugly word. It put one in mind of a villain who fleeced the pockets and slandered the names of hapless victims.

What Miss Anabelle Honeycote did to support her family was most certainly not *that*.

Perhaps her actions met the crudest definition of the word, but she preferred "accepting coin in exchange for the solemn promise to safeguard secrets." Much less nefarious, and a girl had to sleep at night.

The primary location in which Anabelle harvested secrets was not a seedy alley or gaming hell, but a small reputable dress shop situated on Bond Street where she worked as a seamstress. Mama would be appalled if she knew about the money-making scheme, but, truth be told, Anabelle would have extorted money from the Archbishop himself to pay for Dr. Conwell's visits. He was Mama's only glimmer of hope—and he wasn't cheap.

Someone in their household had to be practical. That someone was Anabelle.

She wiped her sleeve across her damp brow and swept aside the muslin curtain that led to the workroom in the back of Mrs. Smallwood's dress shop. Bolts of fabric stacked neatly upon shelves lining one long wall created a colorful patchwork that never failed to tickle Anabelle's imagination. While some material would become serviceable underclothes for a spinster aunt, some might be destined for the train of a duchess's gown, lovely enough to grace the Queen's Presentation Chamber. Anabelle liked thinking such a leap in social standing—from modest workroom to St. James's Palace—was possible. Not that she had grand ambitions, but being pinned to her current station in life like a butterfly to an entomologist's collection rankled.

She glided past a large table laden with dress parts set out like the interlocking pieces of a puzzle. The disembodied sleeves, collars, and skirt panels lay lifeless, waiting for her to transform them into something vibrant—something more than the sum of its parts. After all, anyone could make a functional dress. The challenge was to create a garment that felt magical—the fabric texture, the gown's lines, and the embellishments blending in perfect harmony.

Though occasionally, she mused—plucking a simple yet elegant white silk ball gown from the rack of her current projects—a dress required *less* rather than *more*.

The creation she held, Miss Starling's newest ball gown, was a fine example. Anabelle twirled it in front of her, checking for loose threads and lint. Satisfied, she walked briskly through the workroom and into the shop's sitting area with the gown draped over her arm. When she held it up for Miss Starling to see, the young woman's face lit with pleasure.

"Why, Miss...Honeycut, is it?"

"Honeycote."

Miss Starling gave a smile that didn't reach her deep blue eyes. "How talented you are. This gown is magnificent. I must try it on."

Anabelle nodded demurely and led the beautiful woman toward the dressing room located at the end of the shop away from the front door. Miss Starling's mother hopped up from the chair where she'd been sipping tea and toddled behind, calling out over her daughter's shoulder, "Is that the dress for the Hopewell ball? Gads. It looks awfully *plain*, darling. Money is no object. Have the girl add a few bows or some trim, for goodness' sake."

Anabelle opened her mouth to object but caught herself. If her clients wanted frippery, who was she to deny their wish? Mrs. Smallwood had taught her the importance of pleasing her clients, no matter how garish the outcome. At least she knew her employer valued her skill and dedication.

The problem was that even though Anabelle toiled at the shop day after day, she earned a meager ten shillings a week. If she only needed to pay for her own food and lodging at a boardinghouse, her salary would be enough. But Mama was too ill to move from the small rooms they let, and her medicine was dear.

It had been three months since Anabelle had last written an anonymous note demanding money in exchange for her silence. On that occasion, Lady Bonneville had paid thirty pounds to prevent the details of her torrid affair with her handsome butler—who was half her age—from appearing on the pages of London's most widely circulated gossip rag.

The outspoken viscountess was one of her favorite customers, and Anabelle disliked having to threaten the woman; however, the money she'd paid had seen Anabelle's family through the spring months. Mama's cough even seemed a little less violent after she inhaled the medicated vapor Dr. Conwell prescribed. But their money had run out, and a stack of bills sat upon the table in their tiny parlor.

Yes, it was time to act again. Papa, God rest his soul, had been a gentleman, and her parents had raised her properly. Though her scheme was legally and morally wrong, she wasn't entirely without scruples. She adhered to a code of conduct, embodied by her List of Nevers. She'd written the list before issuing her first demand note nearly three years ago:

1. Never request payment from someone who cannot afford it.
2. Never request an exorbitant amount—only what is necessary.
3. Never request payment from the same person on more than one occasion.
4. Never reveal the secrets of a paying customer.

And finally, most importantly:

5. Never enter into any form of social interaction
    with a former customer.

This last rule was prudent in order to avoid detection but was also designed to prevent her from having to
engage in hypocrisy, which she found unpalatable in the
extreme.

Just running through the List in her mind calmed her.
As usual, she'd listen intently this morning for any gossip
that might be useful.

The most fertile ground in the shop was the dressing
room, which was really just a large section of the shop's
front room partitioned off by folding screens draped with
fabric, providing clients ample privacy. The centerpiece
of the dressing area was a round dais which had been
cleverly painted to resemble a cake with pink icing. Anabelle's mouth always watered at the sight of the wretched
thing, and since she'd had nothing more than a piece
of toast for breakfast, today was no exception. A large,
rectangular ottoman in one corner provided a perch for
mothers, sisters, friends, companions, and the like. Miss
Starling's mother made a beeline for it, and Anabelle
helped the younger woman remove her fashionable walking gown and wriggle into the new dress.

The small puffs of sleeves barely skimmed the debutante's shoulders, showing the lovely line of her neck to
advantage, just as Anabelle had hoped. Some adjustments
to the hem were necessary, but she could manage them in
an hour or so. Miss Starling stepped onto the platform and
smoothed the skirt down her waist and over her hips.

The rapturous expression on Mrs. Starling's face told
Anabelle she'd changed her mind about the need for

embellishments. The matron slapped a gloved hand to her chest and gave a little cry. "Huntford will find you irresistible."

Miss Starling huffed as though vexed by the utter obviousness of the statement.

Anabelle's face heated at the mention of the Duke of Huntford. He'd been in the shop once, last year, with his mistress. His dark hair, heavy-lidded green eyes, and athletic physique had flustered the unflappable Mrs. Smallwood, causing her to make an error when tallying his bill.

He was the sort of man who could make a girl forget to carry her tens.

"The duke will be mine before the end of the Season, Mama."

Anabelle knelt behind Miss Starling, reached for her basket, and began pinning up the hem. As she glanced at her client's reflection in the dressing room mirror, she avoided her own, knowing her appearance wouldn't hold up well in comparison.

Miss Starling's blond locks had been coaxed into a fetching Grecian knot at the nape of her neck, and her eyes sparkled with satisfaction. The white gown was beautiful enough for Aphrodite.

Anabelle pushed her spectacles, which were forever sliding down her nose, back into position. Kneeling in the shadow of the Season's incomparable beauty, Anabelle was all but invisible—highly depressing, but for the best.

Mrs. Starling was nodding vigorously. "When we passed Huntford earlier, he couldn't take his eyes off of you. There is not a miss on the marriage mart who rivals your beauty or grace, two virtues sorely lacking in his household, I might add. It was very charitable of you to befriend his sisters—and clever, too. An excellent excuse to visit and show him what a fine influence you'd be as a sister-in-law." Mrs. Starling fanned herself and rambled on. "The sisters are quite homely, are they not? Gads, the one with the freakishly enormous forehead—"

"Lady Olivia," Miss Starling offered helpfully.

"—bounded out of the bookstore like a disobedient puppy. And the younger girl with the wild, orange hair—"

"Lady Rose."

"—is so meek I don't believe I've ever heard her string two words together. Don't ask that one about the weather unless you've a pair of forceps to pull a reply out of her. What a shame! Especially since the duke is the model of graciousness and propriety."

The last comment made Anabelle stab her index finger with a pin. The devilishly attractive duke a paragon of good behavior? She'd seen the lacy undergarments he'd purchased for his mistress. They weren't the sort of things one wore beneath church clothes.

Anabelle sat back on her heels to better gauge the evenness of the silk flounced hem. It was perfect. Since the conversation was growing interesting, however, she clucked her tongue and fiddled with the flounce a bit more.

Miss Starling smiled smugly. "Huntford needs a wife who will help him ease his awkward sisters into polite society, and he shouldn't dither. When I went riding with Lady Olivia last week, she all but confided that she's developed a tendre for the duke's stable master."

"No!" Mrs. Starling sucked in a breath, and her ample bosom rose to within inches of her chin. "What did she say?"

Miss Starling pressed her lips together as though she

meant to barricade the secret. Anabelle tried to make herself smaller, more insignificant, if that were possible. Finally, Miss Starling's words whooshed out. "Well, Olivia said she'd met with him on several occasions... *unchaperoned*."

"The devil you say!"

"And she said she finds him quite handsome—"

"But, but... he's a servant." Mrs. Starling's face was screwed up like she'd sucked a lemon wedge.

"*And* Olivia said she thought it a terrible shame that the sister of a duke shouldn't be able to marry someone like him."

The matron's mouth opened and closed like a trout's before she actually spoke. "That is *beyond* scandalous."

Scandalous, indeed. And just what Anabelle needed. She sent up a silent prayer of gratitude, even though the irony of thanking God for providing fodder for her extortion scheme was not entirely lost on her.

The duke was an excellent candidate. He had plenty in his coffers and probably spent more in one night at the gaming tables than Anabelle had spent on rent all of last year. She wouldn't demand more than she needed to pay Mama's medical bills and their basic living expenses for a couple of months, of course. Considering how damaging the information about Lady Olivia could be, the duke really was getting an excellent bargain. Better that he learn about the indiscretion now, *before* Miss Starling managed to disseminate it to every county.

Keeping her face impassive, Anabelle stood and loosened the discreet laces at the side of the ball gown. After Miss Starling stepped out of it, Anabelle gathered it in her arms, taking extra care with the delicate sleeves. As she helped her client slip back into her walking dress, she asked, "Will there be anything else today, ma'am?"

"Hmm? No, that's all. I'll just linger for a moment and freshen up. I'll need the gown by tomorrow."

Anabelle inclined her head. "It will be delivered this afternoon." She was whisking the gown into the workroom, thinking how fortunate it was that the shop was not very busy that morning, when a bell on the front door jangled, signaling the arrival of a customer.

Three, actually.

Mrs. Smallwood's shrill voice carried throughout the shop. "Good morning, Your Grace! What a pleasure to see you and your lovely sisters."

Anabelle's fingers went numb, just like the time Papa had caught her in his study taking an experimental puff on his pipe. There was no way the duke could know what she planned. Swallowing hard, she tried to remember what she'd been doing before he arrived. It suddenly seemed important that she appear very busy, even though she was out of sight.

The duke's voice, smooth and rich, seeped under her skin. She couldn't make out what he was saying, but the deep tone warmed her, so much so, she felt the need to fan herself with her apron. Perhaps Mrs. Smallwood would realize she was working on a pressing project and spare her from having to—

"Miss Honeycote!"

Or, perhaps not.

With the same eagerness that one might walk the plank, Anabelle hung the ball gown on a vacant hook and pushed her spectacles up her nose before returning to the front room. It seemed to have shrunk now that the Duke of Huntford occupied it.

Before, the two elegant wingback chairs and piecrust table had seemed to be the correct scale; now, they looked like children's furniture. The duke's broad shoulders blocked much of the morning light that streamed through the shop's window, casting a shadow that reached all the way from his Hessians to Anabelle's half boots. His thick head of black hair and green eyes made him appear more gypsy than aristocrat, and he had the wiry strength of a boxer. He wore buckskin breeches and an expertly tailored moss-green jacket, which she could fully appreciate, as a seamstress *and* a woman.

Belatedly, she remembered to curtsey.

Mrs. Smallwood shot Anabelle a curious look. "Lady Olivia and Lady Rose each require a new dress. I assured His Grace that you would work with them to design gowns that are tasteful and befitting their station."

"Of course." The sister whom Anabelle deduced must be Olivia had wandered to the far side of the shop and was fingering samples of fabric and lace. She appeared to be a couple of years younger than Anabelle, perhaps nineteen. Rose was obviously the younger sister; she played with the button on the wrist of her glove, eyes downcast.

The duke's intense gaze, however, was fixed on Anabelle. For three long seconds, he seemed to scrutinize her wretched brown dress, ill-fitting spectacles, and oversized cap. If the dubious expression on his ruggedly handsome face was any indication, he found the whole ensemble rather lacking. She raised her chin a notch.

Even Mrs. Smallwood must have sensed the duke's displeasure. "Er, Miss Honeycote is extremely skilled with a needle, Your Grace. She has a particular talent for creating gowns that complement our clients' best features. Why,

Miss Starling was delighted with her latest creation. Your sisters will be pleased with the results, I assure you."

The duke was silent for the space of several heartbeats, during which Anabelle was sure he was cataloguing the deficiencies in her physical appearance. Or perhaps he was merely debating whether a mousy seamstress without a French accent was qualified to design his sisters' gowns.

"Miss Honeycote, was it?"

He was more astute than the average duke. "Yes, Your Grace."

"The gowns must be modest."

As if she would design something indecent. "I understand," she said. "Are there any other requirements?"

More silence. More glaring. "Pretty."

"Pretty?"

He frowned and adjusted his cravat as though he couldn't quite believe he'd uttered the word. "Pretty," he repeated, "to suit my sisters."

Rose lifted her head to look at him, her skepticism obvious. In response, the duke wrapped his arm around her frail shoulders and smiled at her with a combination of pride, protectiveness, and love. It was powerful enough to coax a smile out of Rose, and in that instant, Anabelle could see Rose *was* pretty. Stunning, even.

The whole exchange left Anabelle slightly breathless. Devotion to one's family was something she understood—and respected. The duke's interest in his sisters went beyond duty, and that bit of knowledge made him seem more...human.

Oh, she still planned to extort money from him; there was no help for that. But now, she found herself anxious to design dresses that would delight the young ladies *and* simultaneously prove her skill to their brother. Perhaps, in some small way, it would make up for her bad behavior.

Miss Starling swept out of the dressing room, her mother in tow. Every head in the room swiveled toward the debutante, her beauty as irresistible as gravity. Olivia dropped a length of ribbon and rushed across the shop to join her sister. Rose moved closer to the duke.

"Good morning, once again, Your Grace," Miss Starling said, all tooth-aching sweetness. "How delighted I am to see my dear friends Lady Olivia and Lady Rose twice in the same day. *And* how fortunate that I am here to offer my assistance with their gown selections. Gentlemen don't realize the numerous pitfalls one must avoid when choosing a ball gown, do they, ladies?"

Olivia replied with an equal measure of drama. "Alas, they do not."

"Never fear. I have plenty of experience in this sort of thing and am happy to lend my expertise...that is, if you have no objection, Your Grace." Miss Starling unleashed a dazzling smile on the duke.

His intelligent eyes flicked to Anabelle, ever so briefly, and the subtle acknowledgement made her shiver deliciously. Then he returned his attention to Miss Starling. "That is generous of you."

Preening like a peacock in the Queen's garden, Miss Starling said, "You may rely on me, Huntford. A fashionable gown can do wonders for a woman's appearance. You won't even recognize your sisters in their new finery. Why don't you leave us to our own devices for an hour or so?"

The duke searched his sisters' faces. "Olivia? Rose?" Olivia nodded happily, but Rose cowered into his shoulder. He gave her a stiff pat on the back and looked imploringly at Miss Starling, who had managed to find a small mirror on the counter and was scowling at the reflection of a loose tendril above her ear. No help from that quarter was forthcoming, and Rose's cheek was still glued to his jacket. The more he tried to gently pry her off him, the tighter she clung. He turned to Anabelle and held out his palms in a silent plea.

Startled, she quickly considered how best to put the young woman at ease and cleared her throat. "If you'd like, Lady Rose, I could start by showing you a few sketches and gowns. You may show me what you like or don't like about each. Once I have a feel for your tastes, I shall design something that suits you perfectly." Noting Rose's shy yet graceful manner, Anabelle hazarded a guess. "Something elegant and simple?"

Rose slowly peeled herself off of her brother, who looked relieved beyond words.

"Why don't you and your sister make yourselves comfortable?" Anabelle waved them into the chairs beside her and winked. "I promise to make this as painless as possible."

The duke leaned forward and gave Rose an affectionate squeeze. "Very well." Anabelle endeavored not to stare at his shoulders and arms as they flexed beneath his jacket.

Miss Starling snapped her out of her reverie. "We'll need to see bolts of French pink muslin, green silk, blue satin, and peach sarsenet, as well as swansdown and scalloped lace." Anabelle had started for the back room, rather hoping all the items were not intended for the same dress, when Miss Starling added, "And bring us a fresh pot of tea, Miss Honeycut."

"Honey*cote*." In a shop teeming with women, there was no mistaking the duke's commanding voice.

Anabelle halted. She imagined that Miss Starling's glorious peacock tail had lost a feather or two.

"I beg your pardon?" the debutante asked.

"Her name," said the duke. "It's Miss Honeycote."

With that, he jammed his hat on his head, turned on his heel, and quit the shop.

A few hours later, Anabelle tiptoed into the foyer of the townhouse where she lived and gently shut the front door behind her. Their landlady's quarters were beyond the door to the right, which, fortunately, was closed. The tantalizing aroma of baking bread wafted from the shared kitchen to her left, but Anabelle didn't linger. She quickly started up the long narrow staircase leading to the small suite of rooms that she, Daphne, and Mama rented, treading lightly on the second step, which had an unfortunate tendency to creak. She'd made it halfway up the staircase when Mrs. Bowman's door sprang open.

"Miss Honeycote!" Their landlady was a kindly, stoop-shouldered widow with gray hair so thin her scalp peeked through. She craned her neck around the doorway and smiled. "Ah, I'm glad to see you have an afternoon off. How is your mother?"

Anabelle slowly turned and descended the stairs, full of dread. "About the same, I'm afraid." But then, persons with consumption did not usually improve. She swallowed past the knot in her throat. "Breathless all the time, and a fever in the evenings, but Daphne and I are hopeful that the medicine Dr. Conwell prescribed will help."

Mrs. Bowman nodded soberly, waved for Anabelle to

follow her, and shuffled to the kitchen. "Take some bread and stew for her—and for you and your sister, too." Her gaze flicked to Anabelle's waist, and she frowned. "You won't be able to properly care for your mother if you don't eat."

"You're very kind, Mrs. Bowman. Thank you."

The elderly woman sighed heavily. "I'm fond of you and your sister and mother…but luv, your rent was due three days ago."

Anabelle had known this was coming, but heat crept up her neck anyway. Her landlady needed the money as desperately as they did. "I'm sorry I don't have it just yet." She'd stopped during the walk home and spent her last shilling on paper for the demand note she planned to write to the Duke of Huntford. "I can pay you…" She quickly worked through the plan in her head. "…on Saturday evening after I return from the shop."

Mrs. Bowman patted Anabelle's shoulder in the same reassuring way Mama once had, before illness had plunged her into her frightening torpor. "You'll pay me when you can." She pressed her thin lips together and handed Anabelle a pot and a loaf of bread wrapped in a cloth.

The smells of garlic, gravy, and yeast made her suddenly light-headed, as though her body had just now remembered that it had missed a few meals. "Someday I shall repay you for all you've done for us."

The old woman smiled, but disbelief clouded her eyes. "Give your mother and sister my best," she said and retreated into her rooms.

Anabelle shook off her melancholy and ascended the stairs, buoyed at the thought of presenting Mama and Daphne with a tasty dinner. Even Mama, who'd mostly picked at her food of late, wouldn't be able to resist the hearty stew.

She pushed open the door but didn't call out, in case Mama was sleeping. After unloading the items she carried onto the table beneath the room's only window, she looked around the small parlor. As usual, Daphne had tidied and arranged things to make the room look as cheerful as possible. She'd folded the blanket on the settee where she and Anabelle took turns sleeping. One of them always stayed with Mama in her bedroom at night. Her sister had fluffed the cushions on the ancient armchair and placed a colorful scrap of cloth on a side table, upon which sat a miniature portrait of their parents. Daphne must have pulled it out of Mama's old trunk; Anabelle hadn't seen it in years. The food forgotten, she drifted to the picture and picked it up.

Mama's eyes were bright, and pink tinged her cheeks; Papa stood behind her, his love for his new bride palpable. Papa, the youngest son of a viscount, had sacrificed everything to be with her: wealth, family, and social status. As far as Anabelle knew, he'd never regretted it. Until he'd been dying. He'd reached out to his parents then and begged them to provide for his wife and daughters.

They'd never responded to his plea.

And Anabelle would never forgive them.

"You're home! How was the shop?" Daphne glided into the parlor, her bright smile at odds with the smudges beneath her eyes. She wore a yellow dress that reminded Anabelle of the buttercups that grew behind their old cottage.

She hastily returned the portrait to the table. "Wonderful. How's Mama?"

"Uncomfortable for much of the day, but she's resting

now." Daphne inhaled deeply. "What's that delicious smell?"

"Mrs. Bowman sent up dinner. You should eat up and then go enjoy a walk in the park. Get some fresh air."

"A walk would be lovely, and I do need to make a trip to the apothecary."

Anabelle worried her bottom lip. "Daph, there's no money."

"I know. I believe I can get Mr. Vanders to extend me credit."

Daphne probably could. Her cheerful disposition could melt the hardest of hearts. If she weren't chained to the apartment, caring for Mama, she'd have a slew of suitors. She retrieved a couple of chipped bowls and some spoons from the shelf above the table and peeked under the lid of the pot. "Oh," she said, closing her eyes as she breathed in, "this is heavenly. Come sit and eat."

Anabelle held up a hand. "I couldn't possibly. Mrs. Smallwood stuffed me with sandwiches and cakes before I left the shop today."

Daphne arched a blond brow. "There's plenty here, Belle."

"Maybe after Mama eats." Anabelle retrieved the paper she'd purchased, pulled out a chair, and sat next to her sister. "I'm going to write a letter this evening." There was no need to explain what sort of letter. "I'll deliver it shortly after dark."

Her sister set down her spoon and placed a hand over Anabelle's. "I wish you'd let me help you."

"You're doing more than enough, caring for Mama. I only mentioned it so you'd know I need to go out tonight. We'll have a little money soon."

Later that night, after Daphne had returned with a vial of medication as promised, Anabelle kissed her mother, said good night to her sister, and retired to the parlor.

She slipped behind the folding screen in the corner that served as their dressing area and removed her spectacles, slippers, dress, shift, corset, and stockings. From the bottom corner of her old trunk, she pulled a long strip of linen that had been wadded into a ball. After locating an end, she tucked it under her arm, placed the strip over her bare breasts, and wound the linen around and around, securing it so tightly that she could only manage the shallowest of breaths, through her nose. She tucked the loose end of the strip underneath, against her skin, and skimmed her palms over her flattened breasts. Satisfied, she pulled out the other items she'd need: a shirt, breeches, a waistcoat, and a jacket.

She donned each garment, relieved to find that the breeches weren't quite as snug across the hips as they'd been the last time. Finally, she pinned her hair up higher on her head, stuffed it under a boy's cap, and pulled the brim down low. It had been a few months since she'd worn the disguise, so she practiced walking in the breeches— long strides, square shoulders, swinging arms. The rough wool brushed her thighs and cupped her bottom intimately, but the breeches were quite comfortable once she became accustomed to them.

Her heart pounded and her breathing quickened, not unpleasantly, as she tucked the letter she'd written to the Duke of Huntford—left-handed to disguise her handwriting—into the pocket of her shabby jacket. A few subtle inquiries had yielded his address, which was, predictably, in fashionable Mayfair, several blocks away.

A woman couldn't walk the streets of London alone at night, but a lad could. Her mission was dangerous but simple: deliver the note to the duke's butler and slip away before anyone could question her. She should be quaking in her secondhand boys' boots, but a decidedly wicked side of her craved this excitement, relished the chance for adventure.

She sent up a quick prayer asking for both safety and forgiveness, then skulked down the stairs and out into the misty night.

Fall in Love with Forever Romance

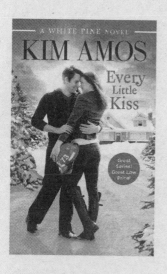

EVERY LITTLE KISS
by Kim Amos

Casey Tanner, eternal good girl, is finally ready to have some fun. Step one: a fling with sexy firefighter Abe Cameron. But can Abe convince her that this fling is forever? Fans of Kristan Higgins, Jill Shalvis, and Lori Wilde will fall for Kim Amos's White Pine series!

HOPE SPRINGS
ON MAIN STREET
by Olivia Miles

Now that her cheating ex-husband has proposed to "the other woman," Jane Madison has moved on—to dinners of wine and candy, and to single motherhood. When her ex's sexy best friend Henry Birch comes back to town, their chemistry is undeniable. Can Henry convince Jane to love again? Find out in the latest in Olivia Miles's Briar Creek series!

Fall in Love with Forever Romance

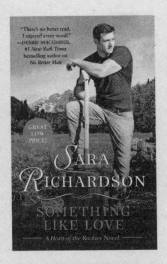

SOMETHING LIKE LOVE
by Sara Richardson

Ben Noble needs to do some damage control. His heart has always been in ranching, but there's no escaping the spotlight on his high-powered political family. The only thing that can restore his reputation is a getaway to the fresh air of Aspen, Colorado. Not to mention that the trip gives Ben a second chance to impress a certain gorgeous mountain guide. But Paige Harper is nothing like the shy girl he remembers...she's so much more.

WALK THROUGH FIRE
by Kristen Ashley

Millie Cross knows what it's like to burn for someone. She was young and wild, and he was fierce and wilder—a Chaos biker who made her heart pound. Twenty years later, Millie's chance run-in with her old flame sparks a desire she just can't ignore...Fans of Lori Foster will love the latest Chaos novel from *New York Times* bestselling author Kristen Ashley!

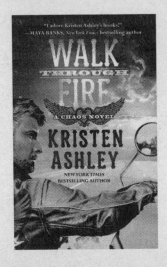

Fall in Love with Forever Romance

ONE WILD WINTER'S EVE
by Anne Barton

Lady Rose Sherbourne never engages in unseemly behavior—except for
the summer she spent in the arms of the handsome stable master Charles
Holland years ago. So what's a proper lady to do when Charles, as devoted
as ever, walks back into her life? Fans of Elizabeth Hoyt and Sarah
MacLean will love this Regency-era romance by Anne Barton.